MW00944794

Sullivan's Stand

Hegemony, Volume 2

Andrew Vaillencourt

Published by Andrew Vaillencourt, 2019.

SULLIVAN'S STAND

First edition. November 22, 2019.

Written by Andrew Vaillencourt.

Also by Andrew Vaillencourt

Hegemony
Sullivan's Run
Sullivan's Stand

The Fixer
Ordnance
Hell Follows
Hammers and Nails
Aphrodite's Tears
Dead Man Dreaming
Head Space
Escalante

Standalone
Thor's Day

Watch for more at www.AndrewVaillencourt.com.

CHAPTER ONE

E very creeping shadow stretching from the alleys clutched at Sullivan's heels with naked malice. He met them with the tight smile of a man intent upon acts of great violence unencumbered by prejudice. Danger recognized danger, and hell itself showed respect where it was due. The hungry black claws of a night-dark city dissolved to translucent gray wisps long before touching the big man with the twisted grimace.

Both the pedestrian lanes and the streets lay clear of people. This was as expected, because the man in the low hood and long coat stalked an area of the Boston Metro populated mostly by offices. With no late-shift workers behind their Lexan panes, the windows sat black and cold to both eye and touch. Sullivan walked past them without looking in. He preferred to keep his attention where it could do the most good. Blue eyes darted left and right under the low edge of his hood, seeking all the imagined dangers lurking in every dim crevice. To his eyes, the gray plane of concrete glowed a garish blue-white under the streetlights. Sullivan found the color ugly, but he knew that particular frequency maximized the benefits of human night vision. Thus, the light fought back against every shadow without employing blinding intensity. The streets were safer for it, yet this did not stop him from hating the awful sheen that desaturated all the color from the world around him. Sullivan's eyes were far more sensitive to the color than most, and he supposed the discomfort was an artifact of his birth. Yet another perk of his unique circumstances. Lucky him.

Passing under a street lamp became an ordeal. To him, every surface took on a washed-out featureless glow as if illuminated from within. It forced his eyes into a deep squint whenever he strayed too close to a puddle of that horrible light. He tried in vain to stay in the shadows. Not just for the sake of his poor eyes, but to hide his face from the all-seeing vigil of the municipal traffic grid as well. Such efforts were wasted this close to downtown. The modern city tolerated no blind spots, and the grid saw all. He made do with the hood pulled low over his eyes and the scruffy beard he had allowed to grow. He hoped this would be enough to confuse the facial-recognition software searching for known fugitives among the passengers and pedestrians foolish enough to amble through their scanning cones.

He passed the block of offices and the storefronts and kept walking. Gradually, the buildings shrank as he moved away from downtown. Tall gleaming glass towers shriveled into squat warehouses and brown tenements. With every step he took, each block he put behind his broad back sat darker and more grim than the previous. The awful lights grew further apart and the traffic scanners surrendered their overlapping fields of view, leaving wide blind spots. He moved more quickly for it.

Before long, his faster pace took him through angry and squalid neighborhoods with fewer lights and even more prying eyes. This did not bother Sullivan. The type of eyes that were awake and on the streets at this hour did not bother him. He understood these eyes. They were greedy, scared, belligerent eyes. Worst of all, they were desperate eyes. These were the kinds of eyes that saw opportunities in places more civilized folk knew to steer well clear of. Still, he did not mind their stares. The dangers of a bad neighborhood at night ignited little more than the barest hint of tactical wariness in his thoughts. The awkward weight of the pistol strapped to his hip reminded him with every step that he was more than prepared for any s petty harassment the locals might try. His body language must have conveyed as much, because the eyes merely watched as he passed.

He found he preferred the crawling darkness of this section of town to the luminous gray silence in his wake. Out here, the inhabitants valued the anonymity of their businesses enough to routinely vandalize traffic scanners. Because taxable income was scarce this far from downtown, maintenance on the street lights had been permitted to lapse as well. In another time, this might have been a slum or a ghetto. The Boston Metro public works department would of course countenance no such thing, so even as the people in it betrayed the stark reality of their circumstances, the neighborhood itself still wore the thin veneer of simple urban cleanliness. A few times per year, a swarm of municipal employees would come out here, pick up the trash, repaint the buildings, and fix all the broken infrastructure. Sullivan curled a lip at the irony of it all. Boston had not solved the problems of crime, poverty, addiction, and hunger. It slapped a nice coat of paint over the issues twice a year and promptly left them there to fester.

He stopped in front of a low-income housing complex. The door glowed in that icy blue-white aura that hurt his eyes, beckoning in digital lettering for him to present his ID card. His hand fumbled in the pocket of his coat and emerged with a small plastic rectangle. He placed it against the reader and waited. The panel's red lettering blinked to green and the door slid open with a squeal. He moved inside and pushed through the bright vestibule to find himself in a narrow hallway. The corridor transitioned back to near darkness once the door closed behind him, and Sullivan began the last part of his journey with increased caution.

The hardest part was keeping silent.

Every floorboard and every stair seemed hellbent on announcing his presence with a creak or a groan far louder than Sullivan thought necessary. He had never stopped to consider how his weight might make sneaking around more difficult. Stealth fell into a category of skills the big man had never seen the need to develop, and the audible intensity of his approach mocked this oversight with every noisy step.

Still, he tried. In truth, the probability of anyone being close enough to hear him was remote. The location had been selected for privacy and it appeared that the choice was sound. Appearances could be deceiving, so he continued his lame attempt at caution out of stubborn habit. He was a predator by nature, and he understood that the best possible place to stage an ambush would be inside this building.

He found the stairwell at the back of the hallway unlocked. This was per the plan and it reassured him a little. This area was as dark as the hall, with only the anemic glow from one or two emergency lights giving shape to the stairs and railings. Sullivan's eyes preferred this, and he ascended with slow, wary steps until he found a door marking the third floor. He pushed through it, wincing at the shriek of un-oiled hinges and cursing the low-tech slum for not having sliding doors. The hallway before him was dotted with doors. On opposite sides, plain gray rectangles with illuminated numbers stared outward. The soft blinking of tiny red lights at each handle indicated that the doors were locked.

Light spilled onto the stained carpet from beneath one of these doors in a blunt wedge that slashed across the darkness. Sullivan smiled. To keep the noise to a minimum, Sullivan moved along the wall as he approached. He hoped that the edges of the floor would be less inclined to complain about his two-hundred and sixty pounds than the middle. For whatever reason, the floor decided not to protest in any manner audible to the human ear, and Sullivan soon stood before the lit door unnoticed.

A group of people talked in hushed tones on the other side. His hearing was not up to the task of deciphering their conversation. He caught bits and pieces of disjointed talk when someone raised their voice, but nothing he could use. It did not matter. They would all be talking soon enough. His hand brushed the handle of the Hudson H10 on his right hip and his face twitched. Gunplay never sat well with him. Only recently had he discovered the reason for this and in hindsight it should have been obvious. He was not stupid, though. He carefully considered drawing the weapon. It was powerful. Thirty rounds of ten-millimeter caseless hollow-points sat ready to go within the magazine. A low bore axis and dynamic counterweight kept recoil to a minimum, and in his powerful hands the large weapon would dance like a fire-spewing ballerina. Sullivan could say without bragging that his skills coupled with this gun would have no trouble at all clearing the room beyond of all hostile life before anyone in it knew what was happening.

If killing everyone inside was his goal, then he supposed a wise man would use the gun. But he was here for information, and that meant live people and privacy. The gun precluded either of those things, so his hand merely brushed along the stippled grip and ensured the dangerous thing was securely seated in its holster.

He would do this the old-fashioned way. The fun way. This was the way he liked best, because it was what he had been made to do. His hand came up and rapped sharply on the door three times. All noise from inside stopped. Sullivan could feel the surprise and tension from the people on the other side of that door. He waited three full seconds for that tension to melt into fear, and then he knocked again.

"Who's there?" said a man's voice. The speaker was trying to sound bold and commanding. He failed miserably.

"Santa Claus," Sullivan growled. "Open up if you want your presents."

Sullivan's smile widened at the sounds of weapons being readied. The familiar rush of stress hormones set his senses on edge, and he welcomed the cold prickling of his skin like an old friend. Until recently, he might have chased these feelings looking for the boiling center of his unending anger. Now he knew there was no boiling center. He was angry all the time because his brain was built for aggression. The anger was his fuel, the source of the strength and focus that made him the best at what he did. Time seemed to slow, and it took what felt like an eternity for the door to open. When it did, an old-fashioned hook and bar prevented the door from exposing more than a few inches of the aperture. The right side of a man's face peeked through the gap, a bloodshot eye flicking up and down to assess the unexpected caller.

Sullivan did not wait to be recognized. A booted foot struck the door with a crack, and the flimsy privacy bar tore free of its moorings. The door struck the man in the nose, sending him staggering backward into the room beyond. Sullivan followed. The door opened into a narrow space with a small kitchen to his right and a living area directly in front. The man with the bloody nose lurched back into the open space, conveniently blocking Sullivan from anyone with the wherewithal to open fire upon him. Two others, a man and a woman, burst upright from worn couches with gaping mouths. The bleeding man found his footing and brought a hand up to take aim with a small pistol. Sullivan snatched the weapon from his grasp and drove a fist into his chin hard enough to break teeth. He did not have time to follow up if he wanted to end the fight without gunfire, so he turned and threw the captured pistol into the face of the other man.

The gun bounced off his forehead, opening a long cut and eliciting a screech of pain. The man instinctively brought his hands to the wound, having forgotten one of them held a gun. Sullivan grabbed the ancient pistol from his sputtering victim and turned to the woman. She stood four paces away, gun aloft and wide eyes burning into Sullivan's face. He could see she was less than a half-second from pulling the trigger, and her shaking hands would not be much of a handicap at the extremely short range. He ducked and lunged. When her target suddenly dropped, the woman hesitated, and this bought more time than Sullivan needed to close the distance. He slugged her in the gut with enough force to bring her feet off the floor and send her retching to the grimy carpet.

The first man, still leaking blood from his broken nose and busted lips, dove for his legs and Sullivan put him to sleep with a rising knee that ruined his jawbone. The man with the cut forehead made his last stand with a hurled plastic chair. The flimsy missile bounced off Sullivan's torso with all the effect of a light breeze, and the sadistic smirk twisting his features was all the warning the enemy received before the big man responded to the insult. Sullivan punished the hapless hood with a series of crisp rights and lefts that shattered his meager defenses along with most of the bones in his face. He slumped against the wall and slid to his rump with a dazed and unfocused expression, oozing blood and mucus from the ruined holes in his face.

With no more foes in the fight, Sullivan found himself alone with a cocktail of stress hormones and endorphins soaking his brain. He was angry, elated, focused, and frantic all at once. With no targets to engage and no fight to win, the combined effect left him uncomfortable and aggravated. Understanding the underlying causes behind his current mental state did nothing to prevent the inevitable surge of malevolent irritation to follow. He tried to control it. As expected, success proved elusive. His eyes went to the crumpled bodies of his foes, and he evaluated each for potential usefulness.

The first man would be no help. Sullivan had broken his jaw so badly he would not be able to speak for months. One look at the second man's destroyed face told Sullivan that this one would not wake for a long time, if at all. His anger swelled, this time at himself for hitting too hard. He was supposed to have better control than this. The truth was easy to see and it frightened him. He could have restrained himself. The reality was that he had struck these men exactly as hard as he *wanted* to. As if to drive the point home, the woman coughed behind him. Teeth locked together in a poorly concealed snarl, he turned to face her.

She writhed on the floor by a rickety wooden shelf. Her mousy brown hair was past her shoulders and might have been pretty were it not so tangled and unkempt. She wore tight black pants and an iridescent pink tee shirt liberally dotted with tears and holes. These looked intentional, as if removing material from an otherwise perfectly good shirt was some sort of fashion statement. Sullivan did not understand women's fashion, so he did not try to sort it out. He watched her struggle to breathe for a few more seconds before stepping over to her prone body.

"You gonna puke?" he asked. Not because he cared about her health, but because these were new boots and he did not want them covered in vomit.

Her reply came as another protracted bout of hacking. After several seconds she managed to look up. Tears streamed from her bloodshot eyes, and the disconnected twitching of dilated pupils began to tell Sullivan all he needed to know about her condition. She did not speak, so Sullivan prodded her with a boot. "You on a nod? What'd you take? You gonna be useful or do I need to encourage you?"

Her head bobbed a jerky affirmative. When she spoke, her voice was little more than a tortured croak. "Please don't hurt me anymore!"

"Lady, you were gonna shoot me in the back, so let's skip the damsel routine, all right? You're no frail daffodil and I'm no Galahad." Sullivan sat on the worn-out coffee table, upending some bottles and other random items. He looked at the mess and scowled. "Let's see here. Looks like some good old fashioned cocaine," he winked at the woman. "Nothing like the classics, huh?" Then his gaze went back to the table. "What's this? Some kind of new opioid?" He picked up a yellow tablet and held it up. The woman looked at it with undisguised hunger. "Figures. I can't keep up with all the new shit on the streets these days."

"I don't know nothin', okay? Are you a cop?"

Sullivan snorted an ugly laugh. "Hell no. I used to be a warden, though."

This appeared to confuse the woman. "Warden? But we ain't no GiMPs—"

"Careful," the big man said with a raised eyebrow. "That word might offend someone like me. You don't want me to get offended, do you?" She remained silent, so he continued. "I'm not a warden any more. So if I'm not a cop, and I'm not a warden, I guess you're wondering who the hell I am and what I'm doing here, huh?"

She could only nod in response.

"I need to find Rocco. We can skip the part where you claim to not know anyone named Rocco because I already know he's the one who sets you guys up, and I already know you know how to find him."

"He... He..." she stammered. "He... finds us, you know? We don't, like, go to his house or nothin' like that. I can't just take you to him!"

"Honey, I know exactly how Rocco manages things. I'm not after his drugs, and I don't need you to take me to him. I need to send a message up the chain, and Rocco is the guy I trust to do it."

"What do you want me to do?"

"Get out your phone and call him. Right now. When he picks up, you hand it to me."

"That's it?"

"Yes."

The woman frowned. "Why did you hurt Tommy and Punter then? You could have just asked!"

"I needed to make a point, doll."

"What point?"

"If you don't take me seriously, you might get ideas about what you can and can't get away with. Now you know what can happen if you irritate me."

This seemed to mollify the woman, and she reached into her pocket. Her hand emerged holding a small silver device. Sullivan whistled. "Wow. That's a real nice phone for a street dealer. Rocco still takes care of his people, I see."

She declined to reply, but slid her thumb across the screen. Leaving the device in speaker mode, Sullivan heard the line chirp three times before a familiar voice emerged.

"Bridget, it's two in the goddamn morning. I swear to god if you are high on my shit right now I will fucking gut you. What the hell do you want?"

The woman said nothing and extended the phone to Sullivan. He took it and said, "Rocco. It's John. I want to see the old man."

There was silence for a long time. Then the voice from the phone said, "That really you, Johnny? I heard you were a fed."

"I'm not anymore."

"Johnny, I—"

"Call me 'Johnny' one more time and I'm gonna get pissed, Rocco. I need to see the old man."

"It's been a real long time, John. I guess you heard he's getting out early, huh?" The voice sighed. "Come on, kid, you know shit don't work like that. Not even for you. I can't just march you up to the boss and—"

Sullivan's irritation, poorly controlled at the best of times, began to creep into his tone. "Rocco, I am not fucking around here. You get me to see the old man, or I'm going to start taking your operation apart piece by piece. When Mickey asks where the profits are going, maybe then you can tell him that I am looking for him. How's that sound?"

"Bridget still alive?"

"Yes. Her two pet dipshits are in bad shape, though. One of them may not make it."

"Christ, John. Just don't kill anyone yet, all right? I'll send it up the chain, but I gotta warn you. This is some bad juju you wanna fuck around with. Why can't you just stay clear of the boss? I don't want nothing bad to happen to you."

"Not my style, Rocco."

"I suppose not. I heard you killed Vincent Coll. That true?"

"What do you think?"

"I think if anybody could drop that sick bastard, it'd be you."

"There you go, then."

"How do I find you when I hear from Mickey?"

"I'll check in with your people periodically." The tinge of sadistic glee coloring this statement made it very clear what 'checking in' was going to look like.

Rocco received the message. "John, come on man! Don't be busting up my operation! Please!"

"Work fast, Rocco. I'd hate for you to run out of dealers before you get the message to my old man."

CHAPTER TWO

Sullivan clomped away from the drug den with his head down and his hands stuffed into his pockets. His right hand hurt, throbbing with a dull rebuke for his lapse in judgment. He had hit those men harder than necessary, and the why of it soured his stomach like too much cheap take-out.

In the past, regulating his offensive output had been the sort of thing warranting only the tiniest bit of thought. If a person found themselves coming to blows with John Sullivan, then John Sullivan took it for granted that the risks had been accepted by all parties. If such a person found himself killed or permanently maimed due to a choice of opponent, such was life. This had always been a habit born of pure pragmatism. Sullivan's intentions rarely went much further than putting a threat down, though this pragmatic bias often engendered a proclivity toward excessive force. The geneticists responsible for his bone and muscle density had ensured that such force was always available, and his father's attention toward world-class instruction ensured that the requisite timing, technique, and skill were present as well.

It was simply a good strategy, and Sullivan had never seen a reason to question this or apologize for it. Some men were born fighters, but John Sullivan was something else entirely. Cell by cell, from the ground up, he had been built with combat in mind. Every part of his body had been tweaked to make him better at violent conflict with no thought spared for his quality of life otherwise. Even his mind betrayed his provenance. At any given moment his brain swirled with neurotransmitters especially concocted to make him mean and aggressive. Whenever his stress load increased, a devious feedback loop would calm him down and enhance all his abilities by several degrees. It was never a good idea to push Sullivan, because the more you hurt him, the tougher he got.

And therein lay the problem. A ninety-pound junkie with a pistol was never going to be his match. No one in that apartment had a prayer in the world of taking him down, and Sullivan had bashed them mostly to death, anyway. Guilt was one of several emotions that had been nearly eradicated by his creators, but something about his behavior felt... wrong. He did not feel guilty over what had happened, nor was he plagued by shame. After several long moments of quiet stalking, a word came to mind that seemed to fit the bill.

Disappointment.

Sullivan was disappointed in himself. There were plenty of ways he could have handled that interaction, and he had chosen the one that allowed him to hurt people. He had chosen it because he wanted to hurt those people and that was the sort of thing psychopaths did. Sullivan did not think he was a psychopath, though every once in a while he caught himself doing something that caused him to re-examine the question.

Shaking his head, Sullivan swung around a handrail and into a subterranean tram tunnel. He boarded the first car that stopped, not caring where it was going, and sat down inside. When it stopped, he left and crossed the platform to catch another car. He repeated this process four times just to completely randomize his route. Satisfied, he exited the Sub-Transit station and began the long walk across the ugly parts of town. He avoided moving walkways and busy intersections where the highest concentrations of traffic cameras were located. His allies had ways of fooling facial recognition, but a wise man did not tempt fate any more than necessary.

While still a quiet walk, keeping near the tram lines meant there were enough people out on the streets to jar Sullivan out of his self-reproach session. The occasional pedestrian leaving a third-shift job or just leaving for a pre-dawn punch-in forced Sullivan into a state of tactical semi-wariness. Most of these folks ignored him, as nobody out on the streets at this time of night wanted anybody in their business any more than Sullivan did. A few women of the night beckoned him with shallow smiles and promises they could not keep. Sullivan afforded these no more than an appraising glance. The distraction they presented might be welcome, though the company suggested little more than hasty release and the practiced performance of a reluctant professional. He walked on.

His motel leaned into view after an hour of walking. Brown, ugly, old, and uninviting, the large screen on its dreary facade blinked and flickered as it advertised rooms and rates. A few rough-looking men loitered near the entrance, and a few more disheveled street people hunched in the adjacent alleys. None made eye contact with the big man as he clumped through the hotel entrance and into what amounted to its lobby.

The desk attendant looked up when Sullivan's shadow crossed the counter.

"Hey, Mister Sully," he called out.

Sullivan turned and fixed him with a baleful stare.

"There's a, uh... somebody up in your room. Says you know him?"

"And on those unimpeachable credentials you let this mysterious person into my room?"

"He, uh, he was very convincing, okay? Don't get mad at me. I got a business to run, all right?"

Sullivan did not appear mollified. "Fine. Don't get mad at me if I have to kill him, then."

The attendant's eyes bulged. "What?"

Sullivan pulled his coat back and rested a hand on the butt of a large pistol. "Coin flip, really. I'll try to be clean about it."

"Wait!" The attendant started to stand. "You can't just—"

The muzzle of Sullivan's Hudson snapped into place right between the attendant's eyes. "Sit," he commanded.

The attendant sat.

"Good boy," mumbled the big man. "Now stay." He replaced the gun in its holster. "I'm going to go deal with this. If there is some kind of assassin or murderer in my room, I'm going to kill it. Then I am going to come down here and beat you within an inch of your sorry life. Did this guy look like an assassin?"

"I don't know what an assassin looks like! He was a big guy. Real big."

"And this real big guy managed to get you to open up my room, huh? What'd he do, offer you cookies?"

Now the attendant seemed to shrink even more. His mouth worked without words while his brain searched fervently for a plausible lie.

Sullivan sighed and held out his hand. "Give it to me."

"Give what to you?"

"All the money he paid you to get into my room. Give it to me."

"He didn't pay—"

Sullivan's hand snaked out and grabbed the attendant by the back of his collar. Without so much as a grunt of effort, he dragged the man over the counter and held him a foot off the ground. "Buddy, if this big guy wanted the key to my room, all he needed to do was beat the code out of you. You aren't beat up, so I have to assume you were paid."

The attendant's limbs flailed in useless protest against his predicament. "He said you were old friends! Promised me there wouldn't be no trouble!"

Sullivan put his nose an inch from his prisoner's. "Give me the money back and maybe there won't be."

Defeated, the desk clerk dug a hand into his pocket. He extracted a handful of small plastic cards and held them out to Sullivan. "That's all of it, okay? Put me down!"

Sullivan dropped him. With a pathetic yelp, the attendant collapsed to the floor in a heap. After untangling his limbs the scrawny man stood with a sour look for Sullivan. "I hope he kills you, asshole!"

"Maybe he will," Sullivan replied. "Everybody has to go sometime." He began to walk to the elevator, adding a final instruction over his shoulder. "Don't be letting any more people into my room if you expect to enjoy a long life with working limbs."

Sullivan did not pause to assess the impact of his threat. He did not have to because it was not a threat. Again, a swell of disappointed self-recrimination made him shake his head. He made a mental note to look into his new emotional state with more care going forward. Things had been changing in his head of late and he could not say if he liked it or not.

As was so often the case these days, Sullivan did not have the time to explore his issues. For now, he would have to focus on the mysterious stranger waiting in his room. Though in truth Sullivan did not think it was a problem. If his suspicions about the occupant were accurate, then he was in no danger. If they were not, then the unwelcome guest could deal with a John Sullivan deeply ambivalent about the survival rate of uninvited callers.

In front of his door, Sullivan paused to brush the grip of his Hudson. Like earlier, the movement was reflexive, his hand just touching the stippled backstrap in a nervous, unconscious gesture. Sullivan's relationship with guns was complicated. He found their usage to be deeply unsatisfying in a manner hard to articulate. Connecting to his emotions in a fight had always been difficult and frustrating. The distance and detachment of gunplay made the divide between his actions and feelings so much harder to cross. These days he understood where the disconnect was born and why it existed. He liked to think that he was coming to terms with the things done to his brain and growing beyond the near-insanity of his horrible upbringing. Then again, the thought of killing a man with the tiniest twitch of a finger still felt like trying to get a satisfying meal out of a bowl of fog. Perhaps he still had some work to do on that front.

Sullivan keyed the door code and listened for the click of the lock disengaging. He pushed the door open with a rough shove and stood to the side of the opening. Peering around the door jamb he saw nothing but the brightly lit interior of his motel room. The foyer led into a bedroom, though Sullivan could not see around the corner to the desk and chair he knew was on the other side.

The door to the bathroom was closed and Sullivan could see the light was on inside. He squinted and listened. The sound of the toilet flushing told him that whoever was inside was either the worst assassin in recorded history or just a guy taking a piss. He assumed the latter. Sullivan stepped inside and drew the pistol. When the bathroom door opened, he leveled the weapon at the specter exiting.

What came through the door did not notice at first, because the man had to stoop to navigate the opening. When an enormous bearded face poked out, the eyes caught sight of the man and the gun before him and scowled.

"You shoot me with that and I'm gonna get real irate, runt."

Sullivan holstered his pistol and stepped out of the way. "You could have called first."

The rest of the giant sidled through the bathroom door with some difficulty. Uncoiling to his full height, Patrick Fagan grimaced at the low ceilings. At a mere eight feet, the water-stained panels hovered six inches from the top of his head, and the four-foot-wide entrance foyer rubbed his shoulders when he stood square.

"It's good to see you, too," Fagan said. "And no one trusts standard communications channels anymore." The giant pushed past Sullivan into the sleeping area and sat on the bed, which groaned in abrupt protest at the sudden addition of a quarter-ton of load.

"No one should," Sullivan said, joining Fagan in the bedroom. "How are you, by the way?"

"Eight weeks in the hospital, another ten weeks on light duty. Best vacation I've ever had," he said. "I used the time to get back in shape and sort myself out."

"I'm sorry I never visited," Sullivan said. He realized he actually meant that, surprising himself. "I killed Coll, by the way."

"I heard. I'm two minds about that."

"You wanted a rematch?"

"First fight I've ever lost, Sully." Something in Fagan's voice put Sullivan on edge. He lacked the emotional range to figure it out on his own. Fagan filled in the blanks. "But I can't lie. Part of me is glad it will never happen. He wasn't human, Sully. I almost died and it fucked me up in the head. Coll was..." he trailed off, unable to elaborate.

"He was like me, Fagan," Sullivan supplied the answer. "Coll and I are a different breed. Custom-made chimeras, top of the line designer products. That kind of thing. You weren't fighting another GMP. You were fighting a machine designed by experts for the specific purpose of killing. He could do things, Fagan. His mind connected his muscles in ways that are hard to understand."

"Like yours?"

"Similar, but not exactly the same. I barely understand it myself. I can tell you he was faster than me, and more driven to boot." Sullivan shook his head, remembering his own bout with the infamous Vincent Coll. "He almost killed me, too, if it makes you feel better. He was like nothing I'd ever seen before. They built a super-killer and ran him on the ragged edge of insanity."

"Yeah." Fagan's reply was a hoarse whisper. "That really puts your situation in perspective. For what it's worth I'm glad you're not a psycho."

"I might be worse," Sullivan answered. "We know they designed my brain to dump dopamine when I start to get too angry or scared, but Doctor Platt thinks that might cause its own problems. I can't feel anything very strongly, and empathy is shot."

"It's why you're such a grouchy asshole."

"Yeah, but something's changing. Recently I have been feeling... things. Empathy is still not there, but I'm starting to get flashes of sympathy. I get mad about the bad things happening, even though I can't relate to the suffering of others. I don't get it and I don't know what to do about it."

"Should we be nervous?"

Sullivan shrugged. "Who knows? Platt still thinks I'm a psycho, but Maris thinks I might be maturing. My brain may be looking for ways to override the modifications. Whatever the reason, I'm changing and it kind of scares me."

"I can tell."

Sullivan locked eyes with Fagan. He looked annoyed. "How's that?"

"Sully, in the last thirty seconds you just spoke more about your emotions to me than you have in the previous three years."

"Shit."

"Relax. It's probably a good thing."

Sullivan raised an eyebrow. "Probably?"

"Look on the bright side. It wasn't enough sympathy to get you to visit me, right? So you are still at least eighty percent asshole."

"I really am sorry about that—"

Fagan waved a hand. "I get it. Things are really fucked up at GEED these days. You need to stay very far away."

Sullivan was happy for the change of subject. "How bad?"

"Officially, you are considered 'on assignment' still. But everyone who matters knows you're off the reservation. All the first-class wardens have orders to bring you in if they find you, but no one wants the press to start blabbing about the most famous GMP warden in the world going rogue. Horowitz is handling the other wardens and running as much interference with the director as she can."

"You know about it all?"

Fagan nodded. "Horowitz read me in on the director. It's bad, Sully. The corruption goes all the way to the top. GEED leadership has been working for the other side for more than a decade now."

"Man, it's so much worse than that, Fagan," Sullivan said. "This conspiracy has been using GEED to funnel GMPs into jobs and services that will benefit their revolution. They're deliberately cultivating resentment and anger in the GMP population as they do it. When the time comes, they are going to have an army of super-soldiers already manning key government roles."

"Horowitz worked that out on her own. Which brings me to my little visit tonight." Fagan pointed to a locked canvas bag on the desk. "The haul from Chicago. Decrypted, cataloged, and indexed. I haven't had time to look through it much, but what I've seen is fucking terrifying, Sully."

Sullivan gave the bag an appreciative look. "She really did it, huh? That could not have been easy."

"Captain Horowitz is a lot smarter than you ever gave her credit for, Sully."

"Yeah," Sullivan said, wiping his eyes with a thumb and forefinger. "I never knew how much bullshit she was managing behind the scenes. It's a miracle she's still alive."

"She protected us all," Fagan agreed. "Without any of us ever knowing what it cost her."

"What about you?" Sullivan asked. "Where do you stand?"

Fagan's scowl was expressive. "It's real easy to forget how amoral they made you. Where do I stand? Sully, there is a huge organization of criminals and corporations trying to convert our entire global republic into a medieval mess. They want to control the world's population, use GMPs to subjugate norms, and create an untouchable hegemony of elites. Where the fuck do you think I stand?"

"I had to ask—"

"I know wrong from right, Sully. These bastards have to be stopped. Period. Mama Fagan didn't raise a coward."

"It's just a lot to ask, man. You have parents, family to think about. You go down this road with me, and there is no coming back. We win, or we die."

"Wouldn't have it any other way. My parents will understand."

Sullivan's shoulders rose and fell. "All right then." He tried to smile. "And I have to admit I'm really glad to have you on board, partner. I don't know what I'm doing out here."

Fagan nodded. "You never know what you are doing. That's why you need me. Somebody has to remind you to think first and punch later. " He gestured to the dingy room around them. "We running ops out of motels or the KC Complex?"

"The Complex for now. I'm hooked up with the Railroad. The short version is that I killed, Coll, recovered Platt and the girl, and now the Railroad is backing my plays to shut down this conspiracy. Their network is incredible, and it's keeping me off the grid for now. It lets me move around without looking over my shoulder all the time."

"Well, I am officially on leave of absence from GEED, due to my injuries and the psychological trauma of getting beaten and stabbed with a piece of re-bar." Fagan tried to make the remark sound causal, though a tiny twitch of his cheek told Sullivan that the big man had not yet defeated all his demons over his encounter. "My clearances should all still work until they catch on to me. We will need to think about extracting Horowitz soon, too. She's on the knife's edge every day and she is going to slip, eventually. I think we owe it to her to have a plan for when it happens. Other than that, this is your operation, Sully. What's the next step?"

"Mickey Sullivan is the key to this, Fagan. He'll be out any day now. I'm working on getting a face-to-face with dear old dad. But it's not easy. Even for me."

"You're busting heads, aren't you?"

Sullivan had no answer. Fagan grunted. "You really are a one-trick pony, man."

"I'm hitting him in the wallet. It's the best way to get him to notice you."

"I suppose you'd know best," said Fagan. "But you know he's probably got a plan for you, right?"

"Mickey always has a plan for everything," Sullivan said. "He's got the whole world dancing to his tune and always has. But he has tunnel vision where I'm concerned. It's the only weakness I can find."

"Let's hope it's enough," Said Fagan with a sad smile. "Because he's way ahead of us and picking up speed."

CHAPTER THREE

The release of Michael Sullivan was nothing less than a media circus.

The Great Oaks Minimum Security Correctional Facility needed federal marshals and a full contingent of GEED wardens just to hold the perimeter. Every wannabe InfoNet celebrity, every twenty-four-hour news provider, every pundit, commentator, and political hack in North America swarmed the modest campus like angry locusts. They scuttled across every unsecured surface, hungry to be the first to see the world's most notorious criminal walk out a free man.

The Sons of Adam sent their agitators to incite a riot. The hooligans, clad in red and black, waved signs calling for the death of Sullivan and the eradication of all genetically modified people. They hinted at violence without causing any. They goaded and harassed. They begged for someone to start a fight so they might finish it without blame.

The Human Condition sent their own people to counter-protest. Their signs demanded equality and reparations for the oppressed GMP population. Their voices chanted for the repeal of the Genetic Equity Act and the disbanding of the Genetic Equity Enforcement Department. They lobbed accusations of fascism at both the government and the SoA, but they restrained themselves from physical violence.

The local Municipal Law Enforcement Office had sent a veritable army of uniformed officers to dampen the fervor of all players with the promise of tear gas and incarceration for any who stepped out of line. This prevented a full-scale riot, but left tensions among the assembled masses palpable enough to cut with a knife.

A hundred drones buzzed in lazy circles, high-definition cameras scanning constantly for any sign of the famous mobster's emergence from the boring gray front of the prison. None passed the invisible line in the sky where the prison walls separated the courtyard from the parking lot. The inert frames of several drones sat in ungainly heaps on the grass just inside the barrier. No one bothered to pick them up, as their corpses had been left as a reminder to overzealous operators of the consequences of violating prison airspace. Several powerful microwave emitters waved back and forth in menacing arcs, begging another fool to try their luck. None did. The drones hovered and circled near the perimeter like ravenous buzzards waiting for a weakened animal to die.

Near the main gates, a brutally attractive journalist was reporting live. Her bleach-blond hair bobbed in time as she intoned her report into the lens of a floating drone. "Good morning everyone. This is Bonnie St. Claire from News First Information Network reporting live from the Great Oaks Federal Correctional Facility. We appear to be mere moments away from the controversial release of Michael Sullivan. Initially sentenced to more than a hundred years in prison for numerous violations of the Genetic Equity Act, his prison term has been cut short by last month's revisions to sentencing guidelines for GEA violators. With his time already served exceeding the new limits, Michael Sullivan is set to be released today as a free man." She turned to gesture at the prison gates. "Somewhere just beyond those gates is Michael Sullivan and his legal team, presumably completing the final documentation for his release. Sullivan is most notorious for financing the creation of one of the few true chimeroid human beings in existence. His participation in the production of Warden First Class John Sullivan was the catalyst for his eventual arrest and incarceration in one of the most egregious violations of the Genetic

Equity Act ever recorded. News First Information Network attempted to reach both Warden Sullivan and GEED for comment, but both have declined to respond as of this moment."

She turned back to her floating camera and gave the people what they really wanted. "Of course, it is also alleged that Michael Sullivan is the leader of one of the most extensive criminal empires in the world. Sullivan denies this, and has asserted that he merely respects humanity enough to accept that genetic modification is crucial to the future of the species. In a press release received late last night, Sullivan reaffirmed his desire to further the cause of GMP equality, and he offers no apologies for ignoring the law in creating the man he calls his son. He goes on to add that he will henceforth limit himself to employing legal means in pursuit of this end."

A commotion rippled through the crowd, and the reporter touched a hand to her ear for a moment. "Okay, people. It looks like this is it."

The drone rose above the crowd for a better angle. Bonnie's voice stayed with it. "Yes! The prison doors are opening and we can see several people emerging..."

A tense knot of three intimidating men wearing jet-black suits spilled through the prison exit. They fanned out slightly and scanned the courtyard with cool professional intensity. The bodyguards waited a full ten seconds before one of them signaled to someone inside the tinted glass vestibule. The mirrored door panel slid to the side and a disheveled man in a gray suit stepped out. Bonnie St. Cloud identified the new arrival for her subscribers. "We can see Sullivan's people now. That's Malcolm Hargrave, Michael Sullivan's lead attorney in front. It looks like he's preparing to give a statement." She paused. "Yes, we've just been given clearance to bring the camera into the courtyard..."

The drone zoomed past the prison gate and zeroed in on the white-haired lawyer. Two dozen similar hovering cameras settled into position, buzzing like dragonflies while millions of eyes watched through the tiny cameras.

Malcolm Hargrave's jowly face looked straight ahead, his eyes fixated on no specific point. He spoke with a strong, if slightly breathy, voice. "Thank you all for meeting us on this historic day. Michael Sullivan has been a political prisoner of the corrupt and my-opic system that subjugates innocent men and women in the name of 'fairness.' His release marks the beginning of several new initiatives that he hopes will be the catalyst for a newer, braver, and more fruit-ful world for everyone."

Hargrave stepped to the side and gestured to the open door of the vestibule. "At this time I'd like to give Mister Sullivan the floor to speak for himself."

Michael Sullivan stepped from the shadows and into the light of freedom for the first time in two decades. He was tall and lean. His team had spent several hours getting him cleaned up and presentable, and their care was apparent in the perfect lines of his suit and the crafted perfection of his hair and make-up. Sullivan did not look like a man who had spent twenty years in prison; he looked like he had just stepped from a luxury penthouse in Paris. His skin was tan, his hair spun silver. He smiled with bright white teeth and sparkling blue eyes. His voice was smooth as butter and twisted sharply in a thick Boston accent.

"Thank you everybody for seeing me off, eh?" He paused so peo-ple around the world could have a chuckle. "I apologize for having to do this via InfoNet, but not everybody in the crowd is happy to see me excused from the most excellent hospitality of our prestigious penitentiary system. First and foremost, I want the world to know that I bear no ill will toward the administrators and exemplary staff of this fine institution. At no point during my incarceration did I ex-perience anything but respectful and professional treatment. I was totally guilty of the crime that sent me here, and I can't blame those guys and gals for doing their jobs. Secondly, I came to some realizations during my time inside, and it has become obvious to me that the system that enslaves and marginalizes genetically modified people will not be changed by breaking the law. I can see now that I went about making the world a better place the wrong way." He cocked an eyebrow and flashed a charming smile. "I figured I knew what I was doing, right? Sue me for being young and impulsive." He paused again for anticipated laughs. Hargrave patted him on the shoulder. "The change will have to come from within, and that means we have to become the change we want to see in our world. Politicians made this mess. Politicians are the ones who took my boy from me and forced him to hunt down his own. We aren't going to fix nothing until we fix them. That is going to be my mission from here on out, folks. All of my time and effort from this moment forward is going to be spent on fixing the corruption and moral bankruptcy that allows the government to decide who gets to be what they're going to be. Now that's all I've got to say right now, but you can bet your last dollar you'll be hearing from me soon enough. Thanks everybody!" Michael Sullivan beamed a huge grin and waved a friendly hand to all the drones as his team ushered him to a waiting limousine.

The doors slammed shut, hiding the smiling man behind mirrored black windows and thick armored doors. Once inside, his oily politician's smile faded and weariness overtook his expression in the form of deep lines radiating from the corners of his eyes. Hargrave sat across from Sullivan, looking every bit as haggard as his boss. The lawyer offered a banal assessment.

"The InfoNet bubble-heads seemed to eat it up."

Sullivan nodded. "Yeah, but they always do. Here's hoping they run with my political shit and stay away from the other stuff. I never saw myself in the political arena, right? All we need is some video of me from the old days popping up."

"Our people have been scanning the InfoNet and scrubbing anything relating to you for more than two years now, Mickey. It's obviously not a guarantee, but the lack of corroboration will weaken anything that does turn up. We can lean on the jailhouse conversion angle if we must."

"Oh yeah, Mal," Sullivan said with a tired smirk. "I'm all kinds of reformed now." Then he changed subjects. "What's the story with John?"

"No one really knows. He went on assignment to the KC Complex four months ago. He encountered both the Railroad and Vincent Coll—"

"Told those fuckers not to send Coll," Sullivan interrupted.

"Well, they sent him anyway. We know John killed Coll down there, but he disappeared immediately afterward. We have to assume Mortensen played his part and John is now at least somewhat cognizant of what you have been up to."

"Hence the disappearing act," Sullivan said.

"Exactly," Hargrave replied.

"Good," Sullivan said. "Now that he's not hiding under GEED skirts, it ought to be easier to bring him back in line."

"Not everybody shares your enthusiasm for that," Hargrave said, a touch of warning in his tone.

"I'm not stupid Mal, I get that. I just don't fucking care. If those Corpus Mundi fucks had listened to me in the first place, they wouldn't be in this mess at all. Sooner or later they're gonna figure out that I'm smarter than they are and stop pissing me off by trying to make decisions. They've lost Coll already over our little pissing match. You'd think they'd learn. It took way too much time and money to develop John into what he is. They're ready to scrap it all because they can't control him like they did Coll and the others. Fuckers lack creativity. Johnny's been dancing to my tune his whole life and he didn't even know it till I had Mortensen spill just enough to get him to do exactly what I needed him to." His head shook in frustration. "What are they pulling now?"

Hargrave shifted in his seat, his discomfort with the question apparent. "They have tabled the issue of your son for now and are focused on bringing in the girl."

"Have we confirmed any of what they are saying about her?"

"We have. The data we managed to recover corroborates Doctor Platt's suspicions."

Sullivan did not sound convinced. "So she's really immortal, huh?"

"In the sense that she will age very slowly, yes. No other beneficial mutations appear present. Recall and intelligence well above average but not superhuman as of the last set of tests."

Sullivan acknowledged this with a nod and plowed ahead to what was really bothering him. "And the secret to youthful-looking skin is why these fuck-ups jumped the gun on our operation?"

"Come on, Mickey." Hargrave pointed to his boss. "You know damn well it is a very disruptive discovery. This breakthrough will have marketplace implications that go well beyond our current chimera projects."

"You sound like you agree with them."

"I think they are right to prioritize this, yes. If we can duplicate this mutation, we will be able to sell near-immortality to anyone with the means to pay our price. It positions us as the gatekeepers of everlasting life, and that is worth more than money. We won't need to take over politically, because we will be the de facto ruling class in short order either way."

"We still need more political leverage."

"Corpus Mundi does not believe so."

"That's because they underestimate the will of the Global Republic. Those bleeding hearts are going to socialize this shit faster than you can say 'for the good of the people.' That's just what they do. It'll be genetic equity all over again."

Hargrave harrumphed. "For what it's worth, I agree with you on that, Mickey. But they started the ball rolling, anyway. Getting you released is supposed to look like a conciliatory gesture, but my gut says they'll be looking to cut you loose as soon as they think they can. I mean, now that the kid has changed the game they probably think they can do this without you."

"Good." The mobster's face was a brutal sneer. "Let them try. Cut off their line of credit, Mal. Let's force their hand. They can come to the table or they can go to war."

"And if they choose war?"

"I'm not too worried about that," Sullivan said with a smile. "I know what to do with uppity corporate types who forget their obligations. But my guess is that they'll try something more subtle, first. I bet you a thousand bucks they've got another investor lined up. That's the only reason I'm out."

"Really?" Hargrave sounded confused.

"They sprung me to kill me, Mal." Mickey leaned back and curled a lip. "They're gonna take a swing at me, you mark my words."

The lawyer nodded. "Clever. You have a plan?"

"Of course I do." Mickey leaned forward to give Hargrave a friendly swat on the knee. "I'm going to do what I always do. I'm gonna sic Johnny on 'em."

"How do you plan to make that happen... or do I even want to know?" Hargrave wiped his eyes. "We don't even know where John is at the moment."

"First of all, Johnny is going to come to me, Mal. Mortensen and Coll will have him all kinds of fired up. That boy can't walk away from a good scrap, and he'll want his time to reckon with me for sure."

"But I can't imagine he is going to be amenable to whatever your plans are, Mickey. He will be angry, and you remember what that was like, don't you?"

Sullivan brushed this aside with a dismissive wave. "Please. All I gotta do is point him at Corpus Mundi. I won't even have to lie. They're the ones doing most of the bullshit he'll be mad about. I'll give him what he wants, and he'll go do what he does best. It'll be fun to let him knock those academic dipshits around a bit. They'll be begging me to pull him back in no time."

"And you will have once again proved that your methods work best."

Sullivan tipped an imaginary hat. "Exactly. Those idiots think they're making high-tech biological machines to serve mankind. That's a real short game. I want to create the next level of humanity. Fuck service. My boys aren't slaves. They're operatives, soldiers, fucking stakeholders, man. They'll be loyal because they want to be, not because they think they have to be. Johnny is doing what he thinks is right, and that's why he beat Coll. As long as I can keep that going, my boy is gonna be the goddamn prototype for a whole new race."

"You always did dream big, Mickey."

"What can I say?" The mobster leaned back in his seat. "I'm a goddamn visionary."

CHAPTER FOUR

S ullivan could not deny that he was enjoying himself.

He had graciously waited seventy-two hours before venturing out into the crisp New England night air once more in pursuit of Rocco's drug dealers. Now that he was out and hunting, stalking the streets of Boston felt strangely comforting. With his hood low over his eyes and his coat tails swishing around his legs, Sullivan could almost pretend he was a normal person walking down a normal street on some sort of normal-person errand. That was not what felt so right to him, though. The hour was once again well past midnight, and the streets were neither friendly nor welcoming. What seemed so familiar and pleasant to Sullivan was the rare coincidence of his baseline agitation matching the reality of his circumstances.

He was even further outside the Boston Metro than last time. His sojourn had taken him well beyond the traffic grid and into the rough tenements of those who could not afford to live where services were even slightly better. Even the most cursory attention to managing blight rarely made it this far from downtown, and Boston Municipal Law Enforcement almost never ventured so many miles from the safety of the traffic grid and its all-seeing eyes. Out here they relied on drone patrols to keep the peace, and it was mostly the drones that suffered for it. Like a badge of honor, both the people and the buildings in this section wore matching cloaks of misuse and neglect. This felt right. John Sullivan walked through dark and dangerous streets in a dark and dangerous mood. He was always in a dark and dangerous mood, but at least this time it was appropriate. The synergy made him feel like less of a freak.

Sullivan's not-so-fond memories of his father's drug czar were still useful, at least. As expected, Rocco had moved his operators further outside the convenience of the suburbs to hide them from Sullivan. It did not work. Sullivan could spot a drug dealer at a thousand yards and the dangerous slums of unincorporated Boston held no great terrors for one such as he. Sullivan knew exactly where to go to find his prey and it took him less than an hour to do it. He found an old three-level tenement house wedged in between a convenience store and a liquor store. The house itself betrayed nothing, but the man asleep in the alley gave it away as sure as a neon sign. Sullivan stepped right up to the snoring bum and grumbled, "You wanna tell them I'm here, or should I go right up?"

The bum shifted and fixed Sullivan with a bemused glare. An assessment took place while the two men stared at each other. Then, the bum uncoiled from his sleeping spot and rose to look Sullivan in the eye. He was as tall as Sullivan, with matching width and a wary tension in his broad shoulders. He wore a green army jacket and a black wool hat, from under which his brows furrowed like angry caterpillars. The imperious glower from the bum was met by a lopsided grin from Sullivan that managed to look more like an invitation to violence than any kind of mirth.

The man in the army jacket broke the silence. "You need to turn around and walk away, man. Rocco says he's working on it."

Sullivan could have complied. With his message delivered, Sullivan could have left the lookout without incident and made his way back to the lice-infested hostel where he was staying. But then Rocco might get the impression that he had been handled, and this was something Sullivan could not abide.

"Rocco is moving too slow."

"Walk away, man." The lookout's tone carried a clear warning. "Whatever your problem with Rocco is, it ain't worth the pain."

"Pain?" Sullivan said with a snort. "I've known Rocco since I was eight years old. He's good at two things: selling drugs and avoiding work. Pain is not in his wheelhouse."

"Maybe it's in mine." This was meant as a threat, Sullivan knew. In fairness, the low tone and intense scowl that accompanied the words were suitably intimidating. Sullivan saw no false bravado, no counterfeit confidence in his stance or expression. This was a big, mean sonofabitch, and he was probably used to people backing down. Part of him thrilled at the ramifications of someone willing to stand up to him without fear.

"Maybe," Sullivan said. "Maybe it just looks that way to folks without your advantages." It was a stab in the dark, but the twitch in the lookout's jaw told Sullivan his hunch was good. "Knocking around regular folk tends to give juiced up bastards like us a weird sense of perspective. Before you go ahead and do something you're going to regret later, maybe you should ask yourself why Rocco is paying for GiMP muscle in this part of town. What exactly does Rocco know that you don't?"

The man in the army jacket shifted slightly, his discomfort with the question writ large in his body language. "Doesn't matter. I got paid to keep you out of that house. So I'm gonna do exactly that. How you wanna play it, man?"

Sullivan punched him in the face. Not wanting to telegraph the blow, he didn't get to shift his footing for a proper overhand right. This kept the hit from breaking the bones of his hapless foe's face. The surprised lookout took the hit across his nose and blood erupted from his nostrils in two vermilion streams. He lurched backward until his back struck the wall of the alley. Rebounding from the dirty gray bricks he lunged for Sullivan like an enraged elephant.

Sullivan's suspicions about the man's GMP status were strengthened by the speed of the bull rush. Even with his own gifts, the alley was too narrow to dodge the attack and Sullivan was forced to meet the charge head on. The lookout's strength matched his speed, and arms like steel cables wrapped around Sullivan. The lookout drove against Sullivan's chest and tried to hurl him to the ground with a twisting, wrenching action. A brawler by nature, the man in the army jacket had made a mistake very common to people who enjoyed genetic modifications granting advantages: he had never learned to fight someone as strong and fast as he was.

The people responsible for John Sullivan's training had allowed for no such oversights. Most of his childhood had been spent getting beaten up and tossed around by world champion fighters with precious little patience for sloppy technique and lazy strategy. Sullivan shifted his grip under the lookout's arms and cinched him tight. The man's feet left the ground when Sullivan spun, and all the impressive force of his headlong charge morphed from advantage to liability with one subtle twist of Sullivan's hips. He struck the far wall with a dull thump and dropped to the ground. He bounced up with a snarl, but found only Sullivan's booted foot to greet his renewed assault. A brutal front kick to his guts sent the lookout back against the unforgiving bricks of the liquor store wall.

"Stop me if you've heard this one," quipped Sullivan.

The lookout roared in wordless fury and lunged again.

Sullivan rotated on one heel and kicked the man's legs out from underneath him. The sound of air escaping lungs punctuated his return to the cold concrete of the alley floor. "A clever man knows that you don't need a parachute to go skydiving..." Sullivan said, voice dripping with sarcasm.

The lookout rose again and surged at Sullivan with a looping haymaker right. Sullivan dodged easily and punished his foe with a kick that brought the man to his knees. Before the man could recover, Sullivan grabbed a handful of his drab army-surplus jacket and hauled him upright. Lifting the man to his tiptoes, Sullivan grinned into the bleeding face. "...but a wise man knows that you need a parachute if you want to go skydiving *twice*." Sullivan turned and threw the lookout over his hip. The man landed flat on his back with a grunt. Sullivan dropped a knee onto his solar plexus and held his opponent down, pinned to the ground like a butterfly by Sullivan's weight and strength. He flashed a toothy, sadistic smile down to the beaten man. "Brother, you ain't wearing a goddamn parachute right now. I suggest you stop jumping out of metaphorical airplanes before my mood gets any more uncharitable."

The lookout was not a smart man by any objective measure. It took several seconds for Sullivan's oblique threat to make any sense in his battered mind. He did understand how outclassed he was, and dignity notwithstanding, discretion now appeared to be the better part of valor. He held out his hands in surrender. "You win, man. I'm done."

"I know," Sullivan said. "I'm just glad you figured it out before I killed you. Any more like you inside?"

"Three," the man said. "Two MINKs and an APE."

"GMOD scores?"

"How the hell would I know? Knowing Rocco? Threes and fours at best."

"Good," Sullivan said with a curt nod. "You can tell them I'm coming up, if you want. I don't care."

"You're really him, aren't you?"

"If you knew that, why'd you take the job?"

The man sat up and pinched his bleeding nose. "We didn't know. But the street has eyes and ears. I didn't believe the rumors, so I took the job. Rocco's money is always good and it was a chance to move up the ranks." He shrugged. "So much for that. You gonna take Rocco down?"

"We'll see."

"Mickey won't like that."

Sullivan let his eyes add the emphasis his voice did not. "I don't give a fuck what Mickey likes."

This drew a snort from the bleeding lookout. "Your funeral, man."

"Get out of here," Sullivan snarled, his charitable nature evaporating at the thought of dealing with Mickey Sullivan. "I see you again and your career is over. Get me?"

The lookout stood up. "Loud and clear, man. Nice knowing you." He turned and shuffled out of the alley on wobbly legs.

Sullivan exhaled a cleansing breath and tried to recollect his thoughts. He had been doing so well. He had managed his emotional intensity during the fight better than the last one. He had not hit too hard or injured the man any more than necessary, and that was an improvement. He never lost his temper, though the cocktail of neurotransmitters and endorphins that soaked his brain under stress made it hard to judge whether he was going too far or not far enough. He simply felt nothing at all one way or the other. The feedback loop between situational awareness and emotional intensity had been severed by his creators to make him effective under stress. He could observe, make decisions, and execute strategies completely unencumbered by normal human stress responses. He was built for that sort of thing. However it also made value judgments about tactics very difficult. His inability to get very angry, and the corresponding lack of empathy left an emotional void that used to frustrate him. In the past his desire to feel normal manifested as excessive risk-taking. Now, with a better understanding of what was going on in his brain, he discovered a whole new crop of problems.

With neither the time nor the inclination to deal with his neurochemical evolution, Sullivan proceeded to the front door of the tenement house. He soothed his frustration with the knowledge that he was about to get more practice. Two MINKs would be enough of a challenge, and an APE on top of it definitely piqued his apprehension. Often mistaken for a MINK himself, Sullivan knew very well how myostatin inhibition and neuro-kinetic augmentation could turn a good fighter into a monster. The APE, with his agility and proprioception enhancements would be an interesting opponent as well. The big issue would be guns. MINKS made for good marksmen because their nervous systems handled sensory feedback much faster than normal. APEs, on the other hand, were practically magic with a firearm. Sullivan enjoyed quite a few proprioception tweaks himself, and the thought of level four APE slinging pistols at him inside an enclosed space was more than a little daunting.

The door stood before him. Brown, paint peeling, and ugly, it beckoned with a bored sort of foreboding. The door did not care if Sullivan opened it or not. Nor did it care if several genetically-enhanced killers waited just beyond to gun him down. He considered betting his own speed and reflexes against those of a possible APE shooter by bursting through the decrepit portal with his own gun blazing. Figuring his odds of success to be roughly equal to the odds of getting shot in the attempt, he stepped back to look for an alternative.

By this point he knew that the lookout would have warned the people inside, so a decision needed to be made. Sullivan opted to skip the front door entirely. He backed up for a running start, then ran at the wall. Planting a foot onto a lighted bollard he launched his body as high as he could and stretched out for the ledge of a second-floor window. His fingers closed over the rough masonry and clamped down like vises. His body slapped against the facade with a soft 'thump' and Sullivan's feet scrambled for purchase. Finding the ledge of the door with the sole of his boot, Sullivan pulled himself to the window and drove an elbow against the clear panel as hard as he could. The Lexan cracked and buckled, dragging the flimsy frame away from the wall. A second elbow smashed the whole assembly inward and Sullivan was through the hole less than a second later.

He rolled to his feet in a dark corridor with his gun in hand. No targets presented themselves, though he could hear the muffled curses of people below scrambling toward the stairs. Based upon the direction of the shuffling and cursing, he surmised that the stairwell had to be at the end of the corridor. He sprinted in that direction. The door at the end of his hallway was just starting to open when he got there. Sullivan hit it with a shoulder like a freight train, sending the man behind it flying backward.

Sullivan leaped back instantly, and his caution proved warranted. Four gunshots split the dark of the stairwell just as he reversed direction and sent chips of cinderblock flying from the wall. Sullivan was already back into the second-floor corridor and returning fire. He had no visible targets, but he knew where the enemy was going to be so the H10 roared to life anyway. A string of ten-millimeter bullets lanced outward and filled the gap with lethal projectiles.

A figure lurched from the darkness. The lean man held a gun aloft but Sullivan could see that the light of life had left his eyes. Three steps into the hall and the outstretched weapon slipped from slack fingers. The gunman's knees went limp he fell face-first to the faux-wood floor.

"Amateur," Sullivan grunted.

He entered the stairwell gun-first, sweeping left and right until he was confident no others awaited him inside. Then he ran up the stairs to the top floor. He paused at the top to listen through the door. He heard some whispering from the corridor beyond coupled with the sounds of surreptitious movement.

Fully engaged in combat, Sullivan's mind crackled with latent electrical energy. Cortisol, norepinephrine, acetylcholine, and a host of other stress and aggression chemicals soaked his gray matter in a neurochemical soup that would drive any normal man into an insane berserker fury. But a thick blanket of dopamine kept his thoughts calm and focused. Instead of a psychotic break, Sullivan settled into a terrifying icy resolve. A frigid calm overtook his features, accelerating his reflexes, galvanizing his will, and flooding his muscles with extra energy.

There was a genetically modified thug on the other side of the door. A powerful man whose muscles and bones grew stronger every day of his life because his body had been bred to resist myostatin. He would be big, strong, fast, and tough.

Sullivan figured he was going to enjoy this.

At least as much as he could enjoy anything when his cortisol levels ascended to these levels. Suitably abashed by his moment of sadistic hope, he threw his shoulder into the door and dove for the floor. The MINK waiting for him had excellent reflexes, but he was not superhuman. The supersonic crack of a bullet speeding past his ear told Sullivan that the enemy had jerked the trigger instead of squeezing it. The thickly muscled silhouette obstructing the hallway was barely eight feet away so Sullivan elected not to shoot the man where he stood. One press of his foot against the floor sent Sullivan forward in horizontal flight, smashing his heavy shoulder into the shooter's gut. The impact stunned the man, and the pistol bounced off Sullivan's back when the shock spoiled his grip on the weapon. Sullivan kept driving forward, kept pumping his legs. His speed and strength lifted the shooter from the floor and for a second both men were airborne.

When they came down Sullivan was on top. The crash of more than five-hundred pounds of genetically engineered brawlers hitting the floor at speed made the doors jump in their frames. The gunman cried out. A guttural, pained bark of frustration blasted from his lungs. Sullivan ignored it and leaped astride the man. Four jackhammer punches followed and the gunman lay still, blood pouring from his ruined lips and nose.

One APE. One MINK. That left one more MINK to go. Sullivan figured that the final guardian would be protecting whatever dealer Rocco had stationed here, possibly Rocco himself. A thin shaft of light bled from under the last door at the end of the hall.

Sullivan smiled and charged.

The door crumpled like wet tissue and Sullivan saw the widening eyes of a burly man flash just as his fist made contact with the slab jaw beneath them. Two more punches dispatched the final guardian with a speed and brutality that demonstrated a marked decline in his patience with Rocco's ambush. The heavily muscled thug fought gamely for the entire four seconds he lasted. Then, like the rest, he ended up a broken mess leaking fluids onto the floor. Sullivan looked down on the mangled body to check for signs of renewed aggression, and satisfied, he wiped blood from his knuckles onto the unconscious man's jacket.

The voice from the corner surprised him. It did not sound like a drug dealer to him. The buttery Bostonian drawl filled the pit of his stomach with an arctic malevolence and twisted his face into a dark scowl.

"Well, Johnny, you sure have grown, huh?"

CHAPTER FIVE

While John Sullivan's face smoldered with an altogether different sort of heat, Michael Sullivan's toothy countenance beamed legitimate warmth from across the dim room. The two men stared at each other for a long moment, both pretending that the broken man quietly writhing on the carpet was not there.

Finally, the younger Sullivan broke the silence. "I should have figured you'd show up, eventually. I have questions."

"Everybody has questions, Johnny."

"You want to talk in front of the help?" The younger Sullivan gestured to the downed man.

"Clear out, Ronnie," said Mickey. "And tell Rocco he is up shit's creek with me for hiring you useless pricks."

The goon dragged himself to the door on legs still not ready to bear his weight. He gave the big man a wide berth. When the thug had lumbered into the hall, the door closed behind him as if of its own volition. This left the two Sullivan men alone in the office. John spat his disapproval. "Typical Mickey Sullivan bullshit."

"What?"

"Those guys never had a chance. You knew that before I ever showed up. But you're still gonna give Rocco hell because they couldn't take me."

Mickey bobbed his head in an enthusiastic affirmative. "Rocco told me you were coming for me, and I told him to handle you."

"Rocco couldn't handle me when I was fifteen. What made you think he could now?"

"That's not the point, Johnny. I give people impossible tasks all the time. How they handle them is what tells me what kind of guy they are. Rocco will never be cut out for anything other than middle-management and shit like this is why. He let you tear through his distributors, and when he had the chance to put a stop to it, he sends four goons to jump you. Fucking uninspired, unimaginative, and plain damn ineffective. If he had figured out how to bring you to me on a platter, then I'd have been impressed. You're tough, but you ain't unbeatable, Johnny."

"Still undefeated."

"Bullshit, kid."

That stung the younger man. Mostly because his father's meaning was clear. He was not talking about John's ability to win a fistfight. In the greater conflict between the two men, the older Sullivan was well ahead of the younger. Both men knew it.

"Fine," John admitted with a wave. "You definitely have had it over on me for a long time. But not anymore."

"Don't I know it!" Mickey's broad smile stretched his face. "You fuckin' showed 'em all, Johnny! Nobody had you pegged for icing Coll." The smile grew even wider. "Except me, of course. When I heard they were sending Vinny after you, I knew those fucks thought they were teaching me a lesson. They were gonna get you killed so I would learn to do things their way." He shook his head with a laugh. "Those guys do a great job building badass GiMPs, but they don't know shit about cultivating talent. So yeah, I made sure Coll knew there was money in it for him if he brought you back in. I wanted you to have a fair chance at the bastard. They knew what I was up to, of course. But it was like a bet, y'know? I was betting you could take him, and they were betting you couldn't. I won."

"Who's 'they?'"

"C'mon, Johnny. That'd be telling! Didn't Mortensen blab enough for you to figure it all out?" Mickey wagged a finger. "Big players all around, Johnny."

"What do you want from me?"

"You're the one busting up smack peddlers, kid. I should be asking you that."

"I don't want shit from you but answers. Which corporations are behind this? Which mobs are in your little play group? Which politicians are already on board?"

"You walked a hell of a long way to ask a bunch of questions I sure as shit ain't gonna answer, Johnny. You're smarter than that."

The big man lunged, gathering the lapels of Mickey's suit in a grip of iron. Without visible effort the snarling man hoisted Mickey from the floor and held him aloft, leaving the soles of expensive Italian oxfords hovering a full ten inches above the dirty carpet. His voice a throaty whisper, the younger Sullivan growled into the blank face of the only family he had ever known. "This isn't like before, old man. I'm not a fucked up sixteen-year-old kid anymore. You give me answers or I'll start hurting you in ways that don't heal quickly."

Mickey, for his part, did not appear the least bit intimidated. "No, you won't. I own this fucking town. I own the streets, I own the cops, I own the feds. I own every pair of eyes and ears from here to New York City. You are alive because I haven't decided to have you killed yet. I've gone to great lengths to keep you up and running, boy. You ain't no GEED warden anymore. You ain't nothing but another rogue GiMP these days. You wanna deal with me? You do it like everyone else. With fucking respect, like a goddamn professional. Just like I taught you all those years ago. Now put me the fuck down before I make an example of you."

"I'm not afraid of you, old man. Bring it all on. I don't care."

"Yeah, but does your old captain care? What about your ex-partner?"

The fists clenched tighter, and Mickey laughed. "I'm not talking about fighting you Johnny, I ain't that stupid. I'm talking about teaching you some shit. You can't beat me with your fists, so if you really want a crack at being the hero, you gotta learn to toe the line with me."

John's hands shook with frustration. His eyes burned with restrained violence. His mind was clear, though. He knew that his father had the upper hand, as he always did. Mickey twisted the knife with a mean chuckle. "Come on, tough guy. Either put me down or start swinging. Make a fucking choice, boy."

There was no choice to make, and both men knew it.

Mickey dropped to the floor with a thud.

"Good call," the older man chuckled as he rose to his feet. "Let me show you how adults do shit. First of all, you want to know what's up so you can ruin the plan. That's bullshit, and I ain't gonna let that happen. But I do need help managing the other players because they are dipshits who are fucking it all up. That's your negotiating position. Instead of barging in with your balls in a twist, you could have just opened with that."

"You were never good at sharing power."

"I'd argue with you if I thought you were lying, but you aren't. So here's the thing. You can't stop what's coming. Mostly because it's already here. The New Global Republic is pretty much a republic in name only. We got enough of the ranking members sewn up to steer the damn thing, but not enough to completely control it. I need leverage on the holdouts, and I need my partners to stop pushing the timetable up so much."

"They want the girl."

"Of course they do. She's holding the keys to fucking immortality. Folks get weird about that sort of thing."

"And you don't?"

"She's a genetic anomaly of dubious origin. I ain't no triple PhD like Doctor Platt, but I've been around enough to know it'll take decades to sort out that mutation. I ain't got time for that. We gotta lock in the Republic, and right fucking now. To hell with the girl."

"There is no 'we,' old man."

"Sure there is, kid. Because I am going to offer you something you want."

John's eyebrow rose. "I'm listening."

"That'd be a first," mumbled Mickey. Then louder, "I'm gonna let you keep the girl and the doc. I'm serious. Fuck 'em both. I don't care right now. They can walk, and I'll help you walk 'em, too."

John's face went blank. Emotions squirmed beneath the surface like snakes in a bucket, conflicting and tangling strings of feelings and desires writhing against the rigid calm of his expression. His attempt to hide the conflict failed, and Mickey's toothy grin grew wider.

"That's how you fucking negotiate, kid. That's what you gotta learn. I came here already knowing what you wanted, and I figure I can give it to you. The next part is to ask for something in return that ain't that big a deal." He pantomimed balancing things in his hands. "I offer you something big, and then I ask for something small. Bam! That's how I get what I want."

"And what is this small thing?"

"My partners have some interests in genetic engineering that are interfering with their attention to our political aspirations. That little kid being one of them, but there are others. I want you to, ah, *degrade* their ability to pursue those interests so they can get back to the business of securing the Republic."

"So you can take over the world?"

"Don't be a dumbass, Johnny, I'm doing this so *you* can take over the world." When Mickey saw John's sour frown, he sighed. "Look at me, Johnny. I'm a chubby old gangster. I drink too much, I fuck anything in a skirt, and I like food that's high in fat and low in vitamins. I barely graduated high school, for fuck's sake. Yet still I managed to build an empire. How? Because people are goddamn sheep, and not particularly bright sheep, either." His head shook in disgust. "Now look at you. You are twice as strong as any man, smarter, faster, sharper, *better*. You were born to rule, Johnny. Literally. You think I bought into the whole 'urban pacification' thing? I had no intentions of financing another super-grunt for some corporate dipshits to peddle to rogue governments." He spat on the carpet. "Fuck no. That's why I raised you myself. None of that regimented barracks shit. No eggheads with clipboards tracking every time you pissed yourself or grew another inch. Hell no. I put you in *my* house, fed you from *my* table, got you the best of everything. Your training was better, your education was better, your life was better. All so you would learn how to be a man, not a product. That's why you beat Vincent Coll, you know. He was a goddamn product. A pure-bred dog trained to be vicious. I made you into a lion, Johnny. You are the king of the jungle, and the fucking sheep are gonna do what you say, 'cause that's what sheep are for."

"I do not buy that for one second, old man." But he did buy it. John's childhood had been a living hell, and Mickey described it like the idyllic past of a pampered prince. In some ways Mickey was right, of course. He *had* beaten Vincent Coll. The chimera killer had been every bit John's physical match, and only the quality of his training had allowed him to win that fight. That Mickey Sullivan had almost nothing to do with that the old gangster would never admit. In his mind, the mere act of hiring the men and women who had taught John how to live with his genetic predisposition toward anger gave him the credit. This was exactly the sort of arrogance he had come to expect from Mickey Sullivan.

The elder Sullivan continued, unaware of his son's internal conflict. "Why not? I don't need to rule the world. I'm already rich as hell. I can buy anything I want, and I already have all the power I can use. Hell, I just did twenty years in a prison where I owned every employee including the warden. I tell ya, kid, it was like staying at a nice hotel. I ain't in this game because I want to rule the world, Johnny. I'm in this game because I love to play." His expression grew serious. "The GiMPs and chimeras are coming, Johnny. My partners are making sure of it, and even I couldn't stop them if I wanted to. They don't understand what it is they're doing because their hardons for the money and prestige are blinding them to the goddamn consequences. Every kid born in the last twenty years has been modified for immunity, health, and longevity. But that ain't shit. In fifty years, every child born on this planet will have some kind of modification to be better. Nature is fucking competitive, Johnny. Human nature more than any other kind. The GiMPs *will* become the dominant species of human being within a hundred years. Non-fucking-negotiable fact." Mickey's teeth gleamed in the bad light. "The Genetic Equity act is the last dying gasp of bronze-age idiots. It can't work because progress gives no fucks about tiny minds. There are almost a million GiMPS in government service right now. Most of them are pissed off about that, and nobody but me seems to think that's a problem."

John shook his head in violent disapproval. "I know for a fact you've been involved with that. You've been using GEED to build yourself an army of disenfranchised GMPs. You want them mad, and you don't care how they get that way. Don't act like you're worried about the poor oppressed people."

"I'm not, but it doesn't hurt to have the GiMPs seeing me as a savior when they get it in their heads to rise up." The older man bared his teeth, killing the smug grin he had been wearing. "There's a reckoning coming, kid. Maybe it goes smooth and quiet, maybe it goes ugly and loud. But either way, my interests will be taken care of. I want to die old, fat, rich, and watching my boy run roughshod over those arrogant over-educated pricks in the new world order. I'm just taking steps to make sure that's what happens."

Finally John saw a crack in the old man's facade. "You're scared."

"Of course I am, Johnny. The hyenas are circling. But I got me a fucking lion so I'm feeling good about my chances."

"You don't 'got' anything."

"Don't I? You've been dancing to my tune your whole life. You'll dance this time, too."

John could feel it. He could feel the constellation of choices collapsing. Every path he thought had been open closed. Each word the grinning bastard said forced him to consider fewer and fewer options. He could kill his father right now and take his chances on escaping. This felt stupid. If Mickey Sullivan said he had eyes all over the block, then it was probably true. John was fast, strong, resourceful, and tough. He was not bulletproof. A three-foot scar running from his armpit to his hip was proof of that. A running gun battle through Boston meant either death or apprehension by Boston Metropolitan Law Enforcement personnel. Neither option worked for him. He considered taking his father as a hostage, but he could not figure out how to benefit from that. He was trapped and he knew it. As the situation drove him to deeper and deeper levels of seething fury, the icy tendrils of the resulting calm forced him to accept the truth of his situation. Mickey had won again. Like he always did.

His father never doubted his victory. "Come on, Johnny. You don't really got a choice, here. Look on the bright side. Helping me out will mean fucking up the bastards who sent Coll after the girl and the doctor."

John's voice was a dead thing, like the whisper of a ghost from some forgotten dungeon. "What about the girl? What happens if I do this for you?"

"Well, if you are successful, my partners will have to back off of her. If you do this thing for me, then I'll make sure the other players back off too. I have plenty of sway over most of them. These corporate types think they don't gotta listen to anyone who doesn't own stock, though. That's what I need you for. You're gonna send a message about not respecting Mickey Sullivan. Once that message is delivered, the girl and the doctor can go wherever they want."

"How do I trust you?"

Mickey laughed in his son's face. "You don't, kid. You ain't supposed to trust me. I'm a fucking mob boss, and I hear mob bosses are fucking untrustworthy pricks. But if I go back on my promise, you can just hunt me down again. I ain't got no way of stopping you, right? If you go back on your promise, I'll cut the whole goddamn world loose on the kid. You think Coll is all they got kicking around in their labs? You think he's the worst thing to come out of the creche?" Mickey shook his head slowly. "Kid, you got no fucking clue how bad it can get. But that kind of drama is bad for business so I'd rather do it this way. So trust me or don't. Your call."

Resignation dragged on John's reply. He wished he could be more angry. He craved the sort of uncompromising rage that would give him an excuse to kill this man without thinking of the consequences. It was not there. It never had been and it never would be. Mickey had seen to that. "Who am I going after?"

"Little outfit called Corpus Mundi. They are the latest big biotech up-and-comer. They made you, for instance. Coll too. They've gotten uppity because they've figured out how to produce designer chimera templates that actually produce healthy babies once in a while. They stopped paying attention to the plan when the news about that kid broke. All they care about now is producing immortal chimeras. I need them to toe the line again. I've pulled my money out to punish the assholes, but someone else is financing their research still. You can either scare the shit out of Corpus Mundi or you can find that new investor and convince them to withdraw their money. Either way works for me."

"So mob shit, then."

"Mob shit, it is."

That he had been outmaneuvered was not in question. However, John could not help but notice that Mickey was still treating him like the sixteen-year-old he remembered. So much had changed in the intervening years and it looked to John like Mickey failed to see the changes. Normally a shrewd judge of people, Mickey Sullivan appeared to have a blind spot where John was concerned. It might be the only weakness in his plans, so John Sullivan tucked that information away. He let his eyes meet his father's. The younger Sullivan did not know what the elder saw in this thing he called his son, but John's voice brooked no misunderstandings. "You and I are not finished. Do not think for one second that I don't know what you are up to. Using me might seem like a good idea right now, but rest assured old man..." John turned his back on Mickey and stalked out the door. Over his shoulder he growled, "...you are not going to like how this ends."

Mickey chuckled and waved to his son's back. "Maybe not, kid, but I love how it's starting!"

CHAPTER SIX

Mickey Sullivan's appearance at the drug den surprised Fagan as much as it had his partner. His bushy eyebrows pressed together in a scowl as the younger Sullivan briefed him on their conversation. The giant's first question was the most pressing.

"He threatened Horowitz?"

Sullivan answered the giant with a terse nod. "And you."

Fagan scrunched his face in confusion. "How many sides is he playing here? Does he know Horowitz is helping you?"

"I don't think he's figured that out yet. It sounded like he's just leaning on anyone he thinks I'll worry about. Making the point that he can touch anyone he wants to." Sullivan flopped backward to lay on the bed and rubbed his face with the palms of both hands. "Mickey only ever plays for his own side. I know he has a final goal in mind, and I can sort of see what it is. But he has short-term goals too. The most important one appears to involve me dealing with some biotech company called Corpus Mundi."

"I've heard of them. They were a small lab collective that managed to secure a few good patents during the war. They went public after the Genetic Equity Act passed and their stock took off like a rocket. They part of his group?"

"Hard to say. They made Coll and they made me. Mickey funded much of that, but he pulled his money when they got obsessed with Emilie."

"But that didn't stop them?"

"They found other investors. Mickey doesn't know who's footing the bill and I think that's spooking him. As long as he was the bank, he had control. Now that others are ponying up cash, I'm guessing his grip on the conspiracy is slipping."

Fagan smirked under his voluminous black mustache. "Corporations don't understand mobsters real well, do they?"

Sullivan could not hide the scorn in his reply. "Corporations assume lawyers and dollars are the only way to get what you want. It still reeks of stupidity on their part, though. It's not like anybody out there doesn't know that Mickey got where he is by employing more 'hands-on' strategies."

Now Fagan snorted. "You overestimate academic types, and Corpus Mundi was founded by them. They might be brilliant scientists, but most have no comprehension of how things get done when the lights go out."

"Which brings us to Mickey's terms..."

"And those are?"

"I'm supposed to bring Corpus Mundi back in line. Either by taking the mysterious financier off the table or convincing Corpus Mundi to abandon Emilie some other way."

Fagan paused for several moments to consider this. "He's nothing if not clever, isn't he?"

Sullivan declined to respond. Fagan continued. "Going after Corpus Mundi directly is something you'd probably do anyway. Now that we know they are explicitly involved, why not start there? Locating the financier is good for us, too. The more threads we tug, the more likely we are to unravel the whole thing."

"That's just it," Sullivan growled. "He's playing us. He's giving us things we want so we'll do his dirty work. He wouldn't be offering me anything at all if it didn't serve his purposes."

Fagan scratched his head. "And if Mickey wants to hurt Corpus Mundi, then that tells us Corpus Mundi is not the real bad guy. Or at least not the main bad guy."

"Exactly," said Sullivan. "It means they are a resource he wants to reacquire. They have value to him still. He wants to teach them a lesson, obviously. Probably set the example for anyone else who has pissed him off, too."

"Why you, though? Couldn't he just use his normal muscle?"

Sullivan shook his head. "Hell no. I'm one of the four original prototypes. Mickey made a big deal out of raising and training me himself, which pissed off his partners. They wanted Coll to kill me to show Mickey that he was wrong. It was like a fucking game to them all. But what's this? I killed Coll, didn't I? Mickey makes his point. Next, Mickey is going to get me to slap around their main producer of chimeras." Sullivan sat back up. "This is Mickey proving his superiority and sending a message at the same time. He's telling everyone that not only is Mickey Sullivan meaner than they think he is, but smarter too."

"They are going to regret springing him from prison, aren't they?"

Sullivan nodded enthusiastic agreement. "Depending on exactly who 'they' are, I suspect they regret ever partnering with him in the first place."

"Can we exploit that?"

"I aim to."

"You got a plan?"

"Sort of?"

Fagan slumped in the chair. "That's a 'no.' We need a plan, Sully. Not a headlong charge into certain death. Not a loosely defined set of goals, either. A real plan like a grown-up would have."

Sullivan graced the giant with an evocative frown. "I know, okay? First thing is to decide which angle to attack. Do we just start hammering Corpus Mundi? Or do we look for the money trail?"

"Going after Corpus Mundi feels like the easier job. We pick an executive, grab 'em, squeeze 'em, and then see what they do." He smiled. "You know, the usual mobster extortion bit. You ought to be good at it."

"But it will spook the players early," Sullivan mused. "If this whole collaboration gets it in their head that we are on to them, they might go to ground." He paused to consider this and then added, "Or worse. They might get openly hostile."

"What's this? Is John Sullivan actually advocating for subtlety? Are you feeling okay?" Fagan held up his index finger. "How many fingers am I holding up?"

Sullivan replied with a raised middle finger. "This many, asshole. And yeah, I'm wondering if we might want to dig into Corpus Mundi quietly at first. Mickey gave us a lead. It feels silly not to try to at least run it down. We can pretend to be doing his dirty work while managing our own investigations for a little while. Isn't that what Horowitz has been doing?"

"Fair point," Fagan said. "But you and I don't really have the skillset for a deep dive financial audit of a major corporation. Not unless you got a forensic accounting degree while I was in the hospital."

"Yeah. Would you believe I didn't? But they have to file quarterly reports, right? Don't they have stockholder lists, records, stuff like that?"

"Sure."

"Then what we are really looking for are new names and anomalies. When Mickey pulled his money, somebody filled in the gaps."

"You think it'll be that easy?"

"No. But it's a start."

"No, it's not," Fagan sighed. "Think, Sully. Mickey can afford an entire army of investigators and accountants to find this stuff out. If he doesn't know, then it's because he already tried that route and failed."

Sullivan's face fell. "Damn it. You're right. What the hell is his game?"

"You're asking the wrong question, Sully. If you want to know why he's doing something, then all you need to look at is the 'how' of it. If this new financier is so well hidden that all the best investigators in the world can't root it out, why the hell is he sending you? What can you do that all his other people can't?"

"So we're back to mob shit, huh?"

Fagan nodded. "I think so. Mickey wants you to scare somebody. You already said as much." Now it was Fagan's turn to grouse. "But who? We've already figured out that it isn't as basic as pushing out this new partner. I hate not knowing the real target."

Sullivan shared his partner's frustration. "With Mickey it could go either way." Then his eyes fell on the canvas bag. "What are the chances there's something helpful in there?"

"From what the cybercrime folks said, it's mostly about the chimera projects. Nobody has gone through it all in detail. Horowitz pulled it from evidence as soon as the encryption was broken. She told the director it was to keep any prying eyes away from sensitive information." Fagan snorted. "Probably made him look like a hero to good old Mickey."

"You think Mickey knows we have it?"

"You think Horowitz would still be alive if he suspected her?"

"Good point." Sullivan shifted gears. "You know what? We should be talking to Platt about this. You and I don't know shit about how to build a chimera, or what it takes to set up a production facility."

Fagan's face brightened. "But she sure as hell does. Where is she stashed?"

"Deep in the KC Complex. Real deep."

"Probably for the best," the giant said with an appreciative tilt of his shaggy head. "How much of this are we going to tell the Railroad?"

"Good question," Sullivan replied. "I don't have any trust issues with them, but their ranks are full of fanatics. Probably not a good idea to hand it all over just yet."

"So we are going to take a trip to the Midwest, huh?" Fagan's smile was thin and unconvincing. "I do so love those long 'loop rides."

"Not so fast, partner. Corpus Mundi has a big facility outside the Metro. Lots of pre-market product testing. If anyone has been getting illicit funding, it'll be a place like that. I think we should take one swing at them while we're here, just to show Mickey that we are on the job."

"Mobster shit?"

"Maybe something a touch less overt. I'm not really prepared to shake down an executive just yet. I'd like to see if we can't get them to tighten up their ship a bit. Shake the tree just enough to see what makes them nervous."

"Not a bad idea. The best way to find stolen property is to scare the thief and see where he runs to."

"Exactly," Sullivan said. "And the best way to see what a corporation is hiding is to let them think we are close and then catch them moving it."

"What do you have in mind?"

What Sullivan had in mind was for Corpus Mundi's South Shore product testing lab to get a surprise visit from Warden First Class Patrick Fagan. The big man put the plan in action the very next day, storming the unassuming office building with all the bluff and bluster of a federal agent on the warpath. The defenseless receptionist standing guard over the bright lobby found his vehement protestations to be impotent in the face of a first-class warden and his official credentials.

"Warden Fagan!" The middle-aged man in the blue suit huffed and puffed as he tried to keep up with the elongated strides of a man two feet taller than himself. "Warden Fagan! You can't go in there!" With a burst of speed the receptionist overtook Fagan and inserted himself between the giant and the door to the main laboratories. A soft pink hand extended to halt the warden, and Fagan paused to grace the determined guardian with an expression that managed to convey amusement and dire threats in equal proportion. The receptionist stood his ground for three seconds. Arm extended, feet planted, face florid and indignant.

At four seconds, the man's brain began to make the connections between the nature of his behavior and the potential consequences. His facade of righteous affront wilted like lettuce left to age on a countertop. His hand drooped, the fingers relaxing and shoulders sliding into a contrite slouch. His voice lost its edge, and his next words came without the fire of his initial objections.

"Warden Fagan, please. Corpus Mundi is happy to comply with any requests that GEED might make of us, but you simply must understand there are procedures—"

"I know the procedures. My department wrote them. They make us take a class on them."

"Then you can see why I can't just allow you to walk into the testing laboratories without prior notice! There are sensitive operations in there. Not to mention the trade secrets, health risks, and general financial entanglements. Forgive me, but you do not have the legal authority to just barge in."

"I promise you, little man, that I have not yet begun to barge." Fagan let his look of official disdain crack and smiled warmly down on his prey. "Listen man, somebody up at GEED has got a serious bug up their ass about Corpus Mundi all of a sudden, okay? I'm supposed to do a surprise inspection. Me. A first-class warden stuck doing site visits on a test facility. That should tell you something, all right?" The big man heaved a theatrical sigh. "We both know that there is nothing wonky going on here. I get it. You get it. Nobody is fooling anybody here, right?"

"Precisely—"

"But I have to do the inspection, and I have the legal authority to walk any part of this facility not deemed biologically unsafe. Naturally, you went ahead and had anywhere that does anything interesting classified as such to keep us out. I've been doing this dance for a while now. I get it. But here's the thing. Your company obviously pissed somebody off, because they have first-class wardens harassing you. This is the sort of crap we give year-one third-class rookies to do. So do me a favor. Call whatever middle manager runs this place, have him walk me around, sign my report, and we'll all go back to our lives, okay?"

The receptionist's face trembled for several long seconds as indecision raged across his features like warring tribes. Finally, he touched a finger to his ear and spoke to someone Fagan could not see.

"Mister Hanson? Yes. It's the front desk. There is a warden here for a surprise inspection and he is rather insistent. Could you perhaps come speak with him?"

There was a pause, and Fagan imagined the poor gargoyle was receiving a blistering rebuke for bothering his superiors with something as trivial as a GEED walkthrough.

"Well, you see, sir. This is a first-class warden, and he has made it clear that he is not going to be satisfied with my signature."

Another pause, and Fagan suppressed a smile at what he presumed would be the manager's abrupt change in demeanor. The receptionist looked up and intoned dryly, "Mister Hanson is on his way down. He will take care of you."

"Thanks, pal," Fagan said with a friendly nod. "I'll wait right here."

Hanson turned out to be a bald, portly, sweaty, pale-skinned man with a look of deep unease on his pinched features. He wore a suit that someone had told him looked good, though it was obvious to Fagan that the person in question was a liar. The man approached Fagan as the warden stood against the wall.

"Warden Fagan?" Hanson spoke his name as a question, as if somebody other than the looming giant might have been sent by the agency responsible for enforcing the laws regulating genetic modifications.

Fagan had to laugh. "Figured that out, huh?"

Hanson actually shuffled his feet. "Yes, well... uh... you do stand out. My name is Harry Hanson, and I am the Vice President of Product Testing here at South Shore. I understand you need to do some kind of inspection?"

"That seems to be the case. Let's get this over with."

"Certainly. What would you like to see?"

Fagan let his shoulders rise and fall in a big shrug. "I don't want to see anything, really. I haven't done an inspection in like seven years, to be honest. The top brass is obviously sending a message to you guys for some reason. I don't know how you pissed them off, but I'm supposed to lean on your permitting and financials. There anything in your permits or financials I need to know about?"

This was a calculated gambit. The permits themselves were uninteresting to Fagan, yet including them in his request would serve to elevate Hanson's stress. If Hanson seemed nervous about having his permits examined, that would be normal and indicate that things were per the usual for an inspection. If the request for financial records bothered him more than that, then it was a sure bet Hanson's group was up to no good. Fagan had his answer almost immediately.

"What could GEED possibly want with our financial records?" The man's voice positively wobbled with fear.

Fagan twisted the knife. "Brass thinks that with Mickey Sullivan out of prison, you folks might be getting some mob cash. That's the rumor at least."

Hanson's features relaxed. He brushed the lapels of his jacket down with clammy hands. "Well, Warden Fagan, you can rest assured that your superiors are wrong. Come with me and I'll show you what you need."

The rest of the inspection went without incident. Fagan already had everything he needed. Hanson's sudden burst of confidence meant there would be no evidence of mob money. Harry Hanson already knew the money was coming from elsewhere, and now the doughy little man became an interesting target. His lack of fear told Fagan that the illicit source was legitimate enough to avoid legal risk, as well. That meant a corporation or well-heeled donor. With a surreptitious smile, the big warden made a mental note to inform Sullivan that if any executive was worth picking up and squeezing, Harry Hanson was probably going to be a solid candidate.

CHAPTER SEVEN

From behind her own crystal glass, Margaret McLeod watched the bald man in the ill-fitting suit place his drink on the table. A pale hand waved off the waiter who appeared as if by magic to refill it. She could tell the drink had not been to his liking, though this was nobody's fault but his own. It surprised her not at all that he did not care for scotch. His decision to order the most expensive drink the restaurant offered had nearly backfired when the fiery liquid had first burned his throat. Too invested in the facade to back down, the pudgy fool was thus forced to suffer through the pricey beverage with dainty, civilized sips. Like so much of his appearance, the drink was a signal to those around him that he was very, very, rich. It was important that people know he was rich, because how else would he get the respect and deference he deserved?

For her part, Margaret was in no way fooled by the display. She observed his protracted agony and the inadequate attempts to mask his discomfort with an internal smile far more amused than the sly smirk she wore on her face. Much of his pain was for her benefit, she knew. He was trying to impress her, as most men did. As with most men, the harder he tried, the less impressive he became. Nothing made this point clearer than watching a fat executive struggle through a glass of the Glenlivet Nadurra Oloroso. A fan of that particular dram herself, Margaret McLeod had ordered hers with one large ice sphere and a splash of water. The whiskey was cask-strength and more than 120 proof. For her part, Margaret's alcohol tolerance fell nothing short of legendary, so strong spirits never bothered her. Of course, in a fit of macho stupidity the oaf ordered his 'neat,' and thus consigned himself to a burned esophagus and a solid buzz. Any real scotch aficionado would know that adding water to taste was expected, so his discomfort was not only unnecessary, but counter-productive as well. The act was all so boring and affected, and it went well beyond his poor understanding of good liquor. The totality of his appearance betrayed him as a man weak in both confidence and substance.

His suit was in the latest style. Far too flashy for an aging executive to wear, the dark blue jacket did not flatter his rotund shape at all. The terrible fit and fresh creases told her that he had bought the suit that day, which made his folly even more depressing. The man probably had a closet filled with perfectly tailored suits, so the last-minute purchase announced his poor self-esteem with every unsightly seam. She imagined him staring into a closet full of well-fitted suits and storming out crying, "but I have nothing to wear!" 'Pathetic' was the only world she could conjure up to describe him. He looked ridiculous.

Another trick popular with her date was making overtly obvious statements and waiting for others to respond. He probably thought that this hid how poorly he understood the topics and made it appear he was being a leader. He was not, of course. He spoke in banal observations and hoped that someone in the room would pick up the thread for him before anyone found out how scared and clueless he was. She could smell the fear oozing from his very pores.

"Michael Sullivan is going to be a problem."

There it was. The bare assertion of a fact so obvious a toddler could have made it. As expected, nothing followed. He looked at her with his head tilted and a single eyebrow cocked in anticipation of her response. She wanted to slap that stupid look off his face and shout, "Michael Sullivan is always a problem! He's made his whole career out of being a problem! He's a mobster, you idiot! A mobster you've been disrespecting for most of three decades! Of course he's going to be a problem!"

But she did not. She did let him hang with that stupid look on his face for several extra seconds. She waited until her nose detected fresh rivulets of anxious sweat run down his back before letting him off the hook.

"Well, naturally, Harry. Your people have not exactly been team players lately. People like Mickey are very focused and driven. You can't just switch goals mid-stream and expect them to come along." Her voice was like warm honey, her smile like pulling back the curtains at sunrise. Her eyes, which she now leveled at her dinner guest, were the color of cafe mocha and radiated heat like a stone fireplace.

Harry's reaction to her response was to blink and repeat, "Mickey?"

The woman, however, knew so much more was going on with her guest. The smell of fear in the man's sweat shifted and she detected the metallic tang of androstedionone in the sheen collecting on his upper lip. She could see the slight flush at his neck when she spoke. She heard the subtle shifting in his chair. Merely saying Harry's name aloud had sent the man into acute sexual arousal. She picked up her own glass and turned her head to drink. This exposed her long, graceful neck and let Harry have a good look at the expanse of chest exposed by her daring-but-not-trashy neckline. After a long sip, she turned back to Harry and continued her answer.

"Mickey is what he likes to be called. I don't think getting him out of prison was as good an idea as you thought it was."

The fear-smell returned. "It's done. It no longer matters whether we like it or not at his point. We needed him out because the GMPs respect him. With the timetables as they are right now, his influence is going to be crucial."

She reached across the table to give his hand a gentle pat. It was clammy and cold, but the touch seemed to revitalize him. "Relax,

Harry. Mickey can be handled, but it won't be easy. Especially since killing him will have far-reaching implications for all parties."

"For now. We are working on solidifying our control of the GMP population without him. As for his money?" Harry tried to look sly, "We have secured another financier."

"For now," she echoed. "Mickey will take care of that first once he's out."

"How would he do that?"

"Silly Harry," she cooed. "You have to stop thinking of this as a business arrangement. Mickey is a mobster, dear. He might decide to kidnap every board member's family, or kill all their dogs, or perhaps something even more horrible."

"He wouldn't do that." Harry did not sound like he believed his own words, and the woman smiled even wider.

"Maybe not. But don't think he won't be up to something. You sent Vincent Coll after his son, you know. You're lucky he found that amusing and not a personal insult."

"It's not his son."

She batted her eyelashes his way for a second, just to keep him reeling. "Mickey would beg to differ, Harry. I understand you had a visit from GEED earlier. Let's not forget that Mickey owns GEED. Do you believe in coincidence?"

She saw the moment of shock in his face, followed by chagrin that he had not made that connection himself.

Margaret's unvoiced rebuke remained hidden behind her flawless smile. "So Mickey is already leaning on you, and his son is somewhere out there in the wind with your secret project." Her head shook back and forth in a slow arc and she pursed her lips. "It won't do to underestimate either Sullivan moving forward." Harry's sympathetic nervous system turned his sweat into a complex stew of competing information. She could still smell the fear, and his desire for her remained obvious. As she continued to make his emotions dance to her tune, the information grew muddled.

Frustration came next, evident in the elevated pitch of his voice. "Well, they sent me here to talk to you about it. I assume you have a plan?"

"I'm getting there." She let her own voice stay low and calm. It soothed his growing ire while her own pores released a bio-engineered copulin analog in high concentrations. The effect on Harry was instantaneous and predictable. He shifted in his seat again, as a growing pressure in his ill-fitting pants drove him to find a more comfortable position.

The last of her whiskey disappeared down her throat and she graced Harry with a devastating smile. "It's getting stuffy in here and this conversation is about to get delicate. Do you want to come up and discuss this where there are no prying eyes?"

Harry wanted nothing more desperately than he wanted to follow this woman to her apartment. His eagerness was writ large in the increased dilation of his pupils and the florid condition of his neck. He paid the bill with a swipe of his vault and stood up with a jerk. The woman remained seated, fixing him with an expectant gaze for several seconds. Harry realized with a start she was waiting for him and he offered his hand to her. "Milady?" he said with all the charm he could muster. It was not a lot of charm. She took the proffered hand anyway and rose like a ballroom dancer to be led from the table. She pulled Harry in close, hooking his arm as they walked out of the restaurant and toward the exit.

They chatted as they walked. Margaret kept the conversation light as she steered the tottering executive through bright streets and toward a posh hotel. Once safely in her suite, she turned her attention back to the business at hand.

"Do you want a drink?" She asked politely while walking to the bedroom. She swept a hand toward the well-stocked bar in the living room and added, "Fix us something, will you? I need to get out of this dress."

She chose her words carefully, and the unsubtle innuendo had the predicted effect. Harry sputtered and jogged to the bar to fiddle with its contents. Margaret entered the bedroom and let her plastic smile fade. She slipped out of her dress and stood naked in the soft light leaking from the open bathroom door. Catching sight of herself in a full-length mirror put an altogether different smile back on her face. It was easy to be surprised by the stranger looking back at her. Some of the features she found there were familiar ones. She was lean and long-legged while also curvy and statuesque, for instance. Good genetics and a life of exercise had gifted her with the muscle tone of a dancer and the shape of an underwear model. Other parts of the woman staring back from the reflective pane were new and exciting. For this stalk she had opted to set her bustline to that of a well-endowed teenager and adjusted her facial contours to a woman of vaguely Mediterranean origin. Her skin was set to the color of a fresh latte and no quantity of scrutiny would find a single blemish upon it. Though a man might be delighted to keep looking for a good long while, she supposed. So it always went when she took on a role for a client. Some body parts were not as malleable as others, and the various configurations always made her think of a family with hundreds of beautiful daughters. Every one looked alike, though no two were identical. Of course, one aspect never changed through all her myriad incarnations. Her proportions, sculpted by genetic engineers to align with a scientifically determined model of feminine perfection, never failed to draw the eye where she needed it.

Margaret was gorgeous by any measurable standard, and she knew it. Then again, she was supposed to be. She gave herself a wink in the mirror then grabbed a robe and a bottle from the nightstand. She shrugged into the robe and tied the belt into a loose knot. This left the red silk to slide along her shoulders and leave the front artfully askew. The resulting view of her décolletage looked as accidental as it did inviting. It was probably more tradecraft than poor Harry warranted, but Margaret was a professional and with that came professional pride. One more look in the mirror told her she was ready, and she swayed back into the living room with a carefully molded expression on her face.

The pudgy executive nearly dropped the glasses in his hands when he saw her. His eyes bulged from their sockets and his immediate flop sweat swamped her nose with the moist stink of his desire. She managed to hide her revulsion, but only just. She brought a hand to her mouth to buffer the olfactory assault, hiding the true reason for the gesture with a throaty chuckle.

"I told you I wanted out of that dress, Harry," she purred. When the man did not respond, she stepped closer and took one of the glasses from his hand. She sipped at it and suppressed a gag. Harry was no more a mixologist than he was a seducer of women, she noted. Still, the noxious combination of liquors blunted the smell of the various chemical byproducts of his arousal. Most men she encountered had far more poise than this unimpressive specimen. The strength of his response took her aback.

Men were interesting creatures, Margaret noted. She had made only the barest attempt at subtlety up to this point. A confident man would have read all her signals so far and perhaps tried to skip to the finale. A clever man might drag the charade out because they both enjoyed the game. A clueless man might need stronger signals to know a game was even afoot. Then there were men like Harry. Men so weak and ineffective that, even knowing they were being seduced, lacked the very testicular fortitude it would take to seize the opportunity. Harry was a dog who had chased a car, and upon catching it discovered that he had no idea what to do with one. Margaret was not above getting pleasure from her business when the opportunity arose. The one would never interfere with the other, naturally, but she enjoyed a good night of soaring passion as much as the next girl. Poor doomed Harry was going to be all business, that much was clear.

Fortunately, Harry did not pick up on her discomfort. He stared at her with a stupid look on his face and his jaw working in wordless rhythm. Margaret clinked her glass against his, startling him. "There's another robe in the lavatory behind you, Harry. Go get comfortable. We have a lot to discuss and it is going to be a long night. Might as well enjoy ourselves."

The doughy CEO waddled off to the lavatory with a bounce in his step. The not at all alluring sounds of a fat man struggling with his ill-fitting suit reached her ears a moment later and Margaret wondered if it was possible to roll your eyes so hard your optic nerves tore free. While Harry was thus occupied, Margaret dumped the heinous potion he had made for her and mixed herself a gin and tonic. Then, resigned to what came next, she arrayed herself on the couch. A quick check of her reflection in the mirror behind the bar ensured that all the parts of her that might interest Harry were almost-but-not-quite visible. When he emerged, he saw the woman leaning back with her legs crossed and sipping her drink. She watched his Adam's apple bounce as he swallowed and heard his shallow breathing wheeze from between his lips.

"Come sit," she said.

Harry had stuffed his portly belly into a robe identical to hers. His bony legs and ankles flashed pasty-white as he scurried across the carpet to the couch. Margaret took another sip from her drink to fill her nostrils with the aroma of gin, and then said, "You look a fright, Harry. What's wrong?"

"I uh..."

She thought for a moment the idiot might answer truthfully. He must have had some concept of how stupid that would have sounded, so he obfuscated. "This whole situation with Sullivan is just really untenable. I don't normally handle this end of operations, so I'm somewhat out of my comfort zone." He sat down next to her on the couch. "But you came highly recommended. Also, since my company played a big role in getting you where you are today, I was hoping that there would be some uh..." he gulped, "...Professional consideration."

"Why, Harry! How forward of you!"

The man back-pedaled. "Nothing untoward..."

Margaret was certain that all of his intentions for their arrangement were entirely 'untoward,' yet she let him continue. Watching him squirm entertained her.

"...But where Mickey Sullivan is concerned, nothing can be left to chance. That is why we reached out to you, Ms. McLeod. We need your skills and abilities to succeed where other operatives have failed."

"What skills are we talking about, Harry?"

"I think you know what we need, Ms. McLeod."

She laughed. "I suppose I do. Well, Harry, I think I can help you with your little problem. I can even extend some of that professional consideration you asked for." She placed her drink on an end table. "Right now, if you like."

"What...?"

"Don't be coy, Harry. We are all adults here. I can see what you really want." She untied the belt from her robe and opened it with a bold flourish. "It would be my pleasure," she lied.

Harry had lost his ability to speak, though his base instincts appeared in good working order. He leaned toward her with hands grasping like a tipsy teenager in the back of a car. She stopped him with firm but gentle hands. "No no no. No rushing. Turn around."

Confused, Harry turned on the couch so his back faced her. "Good," she cooed. She pulled the robe from his shoulders exposing the flabby expanse of his back. Taking the bottle from her bedroom in one hand she squeezed a clear gel into the other and began to gently massage the exposed flesh. "How's that?" She asked.

"That's very nice," Harry moaned. "You want me to do you next?"

"Oh, we'll get to that. Trust me," she said. Her hands ran over his shoulders, working the gel into his neck, then she pressed her breasts against his back and rubbed all the way down his chest. He shuddered at the contact, breathing faster and faster as her hands worked down his torso. The liquid was slick and smooth, and she worked it into his skin with strong, probing fingers. She felt the racing of his heart under her fingertips, the heat of his skin nearly burning her sensitive nerve endings. A tremble began in the muscles of his stomach and Margaret stifled an annoyed sigh. She had not touched him anywhere all that erotic, and he was already inches from release. For a moment she considered giving him that final gift. What would it cost her, to give the man one last orgasm before he died? Then she decided he had not earned it. She dug the fingernail of her right index finger into the soft flesh of his chest, right over his heart. Her left she pressed into his back, just to the left of his spine.

Harry probably thought this was part of the foreplay. In a way, he was right. An electric current leaped from one fingernail to the other at a little more than a quarter of one ampere. The gel covering his skin prevented this from causing any sort of burn that might make a coroner suspicious, and the shock was weak enough to avoid damaging or scarring any internal organs.

It stopped Harry's heart cold.

She had to hold it there for eight or nine seconds, just to make sure that the organ did not resume a normal rhythm when she finally let him go. Harry lurched, gasped, and thrashed for most of that time. He was larger and heavier than she was, but Margaret McLeod was stronger than she appeared. She held on tight, one arm wrapped around him from behind, the other pressed against his back. When she felt sure his heart was well and truly stopped, she released him. His body slumped to the carpet with open eyes and twitching jaw. He would not die for several more minutes, though he was unconscious in twenty seconds from lack of oxygen to the brain.

She waited. There would be no point in leaving before his death was certain, and she used the time to call her client. When she had secured the line and keyed in the code, a man's voice answered.

"Is it done?"

"Yes. Well, it's doing. Brain death won't occur for another few minutes. I'll stay until the body starts to cool."

"Any issues?"

"Of course not. He died of a heart attack. Nothing short of a full autopsy from a very lucky genius will say differently."

"Perfect. When you are ready, we have another job for you."

"I'm always ready," she said. "I'll call you when I'm clear."

CHAPTER EIGHT

John Sullivan did not believe in coincidence. The universe had always been quite clear in its disdain for his ambitions, and the untimely demise of Harry Hanson was merely the latest setback in a life composed almost entirely of setbacks. He found he could not even get all that angry about it. Whether this was due to the tampering with his brain, or because he was so accustomed to this sort of bad break, he could not say.

Fagan, however, suffered no such emotional limitations. "Holy shit, Sully. That was fast. Like, too damn fast. I talked to that pudgy prick not twenty-four hours ago. He was alive and lying to me yesterday morning, and twelve hours later he's dead in a hooker's apartment from a heart attack?" The great shaggy head shook back and forth in vehement denial. "No fucking way."

"We wanted to shake the tree," Sullivan said with a wry sigh. "Tree is shook, I'd wager."

"You think it was Mickey?"

"Nope. Mickey wants us on the job. Killing our first lead only helps the other side. It has to be them."

"How could they possibly know we are even looking their way yet?" Fagan failed to suppress his frustration. "*We* barely even know we are looking their way!"

The pair were walking to the Boston Hyperloop station. Or to be more precise, they were stomping that direction with grim sneers and irritated eyes. With nothing left to investigate in Boston and the enemy well ahead of them, the pair had decided to return to the safety of the KC Complex. Sullivan chewed on a piece of beef jerky as they walked. "Maybe they don't know anything about us. Maybe they believe GEED is too close, or that Hanson was too weak a link to manage a government investigation. Your showing up might have just been the last straw for him."

The giant remained unconvinced. "They gotta know Mickey owns GEED, though."

Sullivan swallowed a hunk of chewy meat. "That doesn't mean GEED can't run legit operations, still. Mickey can't just wield GEED like a club, man. That'd be too obvious. If the Republic catches on to him they'll purge the whole agency. He has to let them run investigations the way they are meant to at least a little bit. Otherwise he'll blow his whole operation."

"I think you're reaching Sully. They are on to us."

Fagan was probably right, and Sullivan acknowledged this with a shrug. "Then I am forced to agree that they jumped on Hanson way too damn fast. It shows too much of their hand, if you ask me."

"How so?"

"We took a stab in the dark with Hanson. He was a solid lead but no more than that. Killing him tells us in no uncertain terms that we are on the right track."

Fagan huffed. "Leave it to you to find a silver lining in a man's murder."

"Murder? I heard it was a heart attack," Sullivan deadpanned.

"Yeah. And if my grandmother had wheels, she'd be a wagon."

"Wasn't your grandmother a sasquatch?" Sullivan asked, his voice all innocent curiosity.

"Tells you what kind of badass my grandfather was," Fagan replied without missing a beat.

"A man truly worthy of his legend, then."

"That's what Grandma always said."

Anyway," Sullivan returned to the matter at hand. "Hanson must have known some shit. If nothing else, it means that his boss knows some shit. We just need to start climbing up the ladder of people who know some shit until we find someone too important to die mysteriously."

"Gonna be a lot of dead corporate VPs, I suspect."

"The world will be better for it, I'm sure." He fished another piece of jerky from his pocket and started into it. "The real mystery is this: who's doing the killing? Is Corpus Mundi protecting their operation, or is the mystery financier protecting their identity?"

Fagan had a more pressing question. "You gonna share any of that jerky? I'm starving."

The two men shared a side effect of their respective genetic heritages in that their daily caloric needs were astronomical. Fagan's due to his mass, and Sullivan due to his severe myostatin inhibition. Sullivan handed a large piece of jerky to the giant with a grimace. Fagan accepted it with a smile and shoved the whole thing into his maw. He put on a thoughtful frown while he chewed his snack for a few seconds and then added, "If it's the money people, then killing off execs is going to make their relationship with Corpus Mundi real tense.

"Here's hoping," Sullivan replied. He gestured to the 'loop station now looming before them. "I guess we'll just have to see. Ready for a brisk ride to the Midwest?"

"Do, let's," said Fagan. Though his voice held no enthusiasm.

Sullivan decided to use the four-hour hyperloop ride as an opportunity to study the data his former captain had smuggled out to him. He ignored the heavy technical literature, as he lacked the academic background to understand it. However, progress reports, meeting notes, and memos shed a light on his own circumstances that the former warden did not find pleasant. Before an hour had passed, Fagan detected the general deterioration of Sullivan's mood, as the darkening features of his partner precluded the necessity for special training or skills in the science of psychology. All he had to do was watch Sullivan's face grow increasingly pinched and drawn with each swipe of the screen. When Fagan at last saw the white flash of bared tooth, the big man decided to bring Sullivan out of his research.

"No good news in there, huh?"

Sullivan looked up, his expression both annoyed and confused. "What?"

Fagan gestured to the tablet in Sullivan's hand. "I'm guessing the intel from Chicago is pretty grim. Either that or you're constipated. You tell me."

Sullivan dropped the tablet onto the seat next to him. He looked up to the 'loop car ceiling and blew a long cleansing breath. "I don't even understand the scientific stuff, but what I'm piecing together from the administrative chatter is some awful shit, man."

"Like what?"

"Like more than sixteen hundred zygotes in my lot. Of which barely a tenth made it to the creche. From those?" Sullivan held up a single index finger. "Only one viable fetus."

Fagan gave a low whistle. "That's... that's awful, man."

"And expensive at a four-hundred-grand a zygote. There was a lot of cross talk in the meetings about abandoning the project altogether. Vincent Coll was the first of us, and it looks like they got him out with a production lot of less than four-hundred zygotes. Most of the players thought that this was good enough and didn't want to keep wasting money trying to improve on him."

"But they did it anyway?"

"I'm here, aren't I? Something about Coll wasn't good enough for a few of the collaborators, and they were willing to pay for a better model. It looks like the product development teams thought he was too similar to existing products like berserkers and MINKs with high GMOD scores."

"Any names?" Fagan knew better than to hope, but he asked anyway.

"Nope. All code names. But I think we can both guess who was the most insistent on pursuing my creation. Code name was 'Narrowback.'"

Fagan's face scrunched. "What the fuck is a 'narrowback?'"

"Originally it was a slur for anyone who couldn't work a full day in the Irish tradition, which is to say someone who couldn't do sixteen hours of backbreaking manual labor. A weakling or layabout. Later it became a dirty word for the children of Irish immigrants in America."

"Guessing that's our friend, Mickey?"

"Good guess. You must be some kind of detective or something."

Fagan ignored the jab. "He really was hell-bent to get you, huh?"

"According to this, about five percent of my DNA is directly from him. Apparently that was enough personal investment for him to be real damn committed to my birth. There was some chatter that his inferior contributions were what was causing the issues with developing viable fetuses."

"I bet he loved hearing that."

"Old Narrowback was rather specific about his position on that issue."

Fagan pointed a finger at Sullivan. "You know, that kind of explains why he is so invested in you outperforming the other prototypes. If the only real difference between you and the others is a couple tablespoons of his DNA, then..." Fagan held out his hands, letting Sullivan finish the thought.

"Oh god, that does sound like Mickey, doesn't it? His ego is fucking enormous."

Fagan nodded his agreement before changing the subject. "Anything on the other prototypes in there?"

"Not much yet. If I could decipher the biology, I'd know more. As it stands, Platt will have to do that. The admin shit speaks of them in very general terms. The other two came after me, so chronologically, I'm not up to their production notes yet. There are at least two more, which matches what Mortenson told me. Each one is designed to fill a different role in urban pacification. Whatever the hell that means."

Fagan picked up the thread. "Urban pacification is really complex, man. You need the right mix of carrots and sticks to keep the regular folks in line without pushing them to revolt. What they are trying here actually makes a whole lot of sense."

Sullivan failed to follow his partner's train of thought. "What do you mean? Most fascist governments just put the boot to the populace and called it a day."

"And how many of those lasted more than a few decades? How many made it a whole century?" Fagan shifted in his seat, excited to have insight on something important. "The most successful ones like the Chinese or even the Romans were way more subtle than that. They used a bunch of different methods at the same time. Some straight-up boot-to-the-head shit, sure. But also lots of misdirection. That's what these bastards are pulling."

"So you think Coll wasn't compatible with their plans? A bad prototype?"

"Maybe not. Who the hell knows, right? No matter how subtle you want to be, I figure sometimes you just need a guy murdered. So Vincent Coll was a killer, a hitman, really. Say you find yourself with an unruly politician. Maybe you got a community leader not stepping in line? Send Coll." Fagan snapped his fingers. "Troublemaker is killed. Message to the populace sent. It makes sense to build him strong, tough, devious, and merciless. It fits, you know?"

"I'm all of those things, too."

Fagan shook his head. "Nah. You're different. They gave Coll psychotic tendencies. You are several varieties of asshole, Sully. But you are no psycho."

"It was touch and go for the first fourteen years of my life, partner," Sullivan reminded him. "In the records, it looks like I was really just a variation on Coll, though. There is a lot of overlap in our genotypes." Sullivan thought about this for a moment then huffed. "But you might just be on to something here. For me they added rate-limiting steps to prevent psychotic breaks and extreme mood swings, so I think they spotted the problems with Coll early on."

"You're still stuck on Coll being a bad prototype," Fagan said with a wag of his finger. "During the war the Chinese proved that a touch of legit psychosis made for better killers. I don't think Coll was an accident or a mistake."

"You figure he was what he was supposed to be? A super-killer?"

Fagan's tone grew serious. "I'd say so. He almost killed me, Sully. Nobody has ever beaten me like that."

"Or me," Sullivan agreed. "But I still won. What does that make me?"

"Don't go down that road. Everything I've heard from you and Horowitz says that you were never supposed to be a killer. You're less violent than Coll, even on a bad day. But you are also more physical, right? Coll was expedient. Get in, kill the problem, get out. You, on the other hand, were deliberately designed to be more hands-on. It seems to me like they wanted you dangerous but not unreasonable. I assume the John Sullivan model would be called up for street-level problem solving. The type of stuff where wholesale slaughter is counterproductive."

"You've been doing some research, I see."

"Eight weeks in the hospital, ten weeks of recovery. Had a lot of time on my hands. Thanks to Horowitz I've read a shit ton on urban pacification. Every big regime from ancient Greece to Soviet Russia and the Pan-Asian alliance had systems designed to keep a heavily subjugated population stable and producing for the ruling class.

Because that's what's actually important. Political power is useless if there is no wealth to exploit."

"Revolutions are notoriously bad for business," Sullivan agreed.

Fagan chuckled. "Exactly. The more successful ones, ones that lasted for more than a decade or two? Those fuckers didn't use wholesale slaughter. They used low-level intimidation and a steady supply of instant gratification. Just killing everyone doesn't work because there is only so much bullshit even a weak man will put up with before he feels like there is nothing to gain or lose anymore. It's like I said. You need the folks afraid enough to behave, but not so angry they revolt."

"So to keep the folks calm you bring in a guy like me. I'm less scary than a psycho like Coll?"

"Think about it, Sully. You can be reasoned with. You can assess and make a value judgment. Coll could barely order a peanut butter sandwich without killing a dozen people."

Sullivan had to admit this was true. "Platt said that they deliberately put barriers between my emotions and decision-making ability. When I fought Coll, I was actually jealous of how easily he was able to use anger to fuel his fighting."

"Because you can't?"

"Yeah. The more stress I'm under, the calmer I get. Colder, too."

"Now imagine dealing with a disgruntled shopkeeper in some dirty sub-metro enclave. Coll would simply kill the poor bastard if he didn't fall into step right away. You, on the other hand, will assess, evaluate, decide, and act in a measured manner."

"I dunno about 'measured,' partner. They made me all kinds of mean and angry, too. You know me too well to think that I'm some kind of level-headed negotiator."

Fagan snorted. "I meant measured in a relative sense. You won't kill that guy, but you'll convince him to see things your way in the end. And he'd regret the conversation enough to stay out of trouble afterward."

"I guess that makes sense," said Sullivan. "Makes me wonder what the other two prototypes are, though. Your reading give you any ideas on that?"

"Offhand I'd guess soldiers, spies, administrators, or entertainers."

The last one drew a scowl from Sullivan. "Entertainers? Really?"

"Bread and circuses, runt."

Sullivan shook his head. "Here's hoping that we only have to deal with genetically engineered jugglers, then."

"Could be gladiators, too."

Sullivan finally had a riposte. "They'd use SOAPs for that. These other two definitely aren't like you. The program is aggressively anti-acromegaly in all the notes."

"Well that's just plain unfair." The big man's lament arrived with a generous helping of feigned indignation. "I'd make an awesome gladiator."

Sullivan affected the manner of a ring announcer. "All hail the mighty Follicles, behold the unshorn man-beast of fallen Detroit!"

"Leave Detroit out of this. What happened there was not my fault."

CHAPTER NINE

Sharon Platt sat and watched with her heart in her throat.

Across an open gymnasium, the brilliant scientist winced while a small blond girl just shy of her ninth birthday tried to play with a noisy knot of her peers. It should have been the most natural thing in the world. This same scene would play out on a million playgrounds across a million little towns all over the planet. Most of these interactions would follow a natural progression from tentative to testing and on to trust as the new applicant is slowly absorbed into the social dynamic. Sometimes, the applicant did not get that far. Social groups formed and dissolved in this manner every single day. All of this she could take without issue. The evolutionary biology driving the rituals, tests, milestones, and success rates of these interactions were well known to her. What she had not been prepared for was her own emotional investment in the outcome for one little blond girl trying to make friends.

There was nothing she could do to help, either. She was a powerless observer to this time-honored rite of passage, and things were not going well. Platt knew why, and this made the hurt even worse. The older woman next to her observed the same clumsy overtures from the child as Platt did. The corners of her mouth rose in a knowing smile and she gave Platt a gentle pat on the arm. "She'll work it out. Give it time."

"She's too different," Platt said. "She doesn't understand them. What they want from her, how to understand their needs..."

"But she is extremely intuitive. She is studying them right now. Learning. Once she figures out what they need from her she'll be able to give it to them."

"Do you think so? Will they ever be able to relate to her, Maris?"

"I'd be more concerned about whether or not she can relate to them," Maris said with a touch of warning. "Their problems will seem small and easily solved to her. The things they find important she may find trivial. Intuition isn't enough. She will need to develop empathy for them as well."

"Empathy starts to show up around age seven. She benchmarked normally through her eighth birthday. There's hope at least."

"I think there is more than just hope, Doctor Platt." Maris nodded toward the cluster of children, now engaged in a bizarre and unstructured version of dodgeball. The game seemed to revolve around the older and more athletic children tormenting their less developed playmates, and for reasons Platt did not understand, this had broadened the older woman's smile considerably. Seeing Platt's confusion, Maris winked toward the game and said, "She will get her chance to shine soon enough."

Several stark differences separated Emilie from her chimera brethren. The most prominent deviation lay in the fact that she had not been designed for combat or athletic endeavors. Sullivan and Vincent Coll were designed to be fighters and killers. They had been constructed with physical attributes appropriate for that purpose. Emilie had been the first real attempt at designing a tactical and organizational genius. The more egregious physical enhancements were systemic, so the child had been spared most agility and proprioception enhancements to preserve brain chemistry for more desirable traits. This had not prevented Doctor Platt from nudging the child's athletic potential well into the 'above average' range. Thus, her skeletal muscle, connective tissue, and bones were about as good as one could hope for without drastic alteration to the overall genotype.

Despite her small size, young Emilie found herself competitive with the older boys. Her ability to catch a hurled ball and return it to the sender with speed surprised them. The boys soon determined that the new little blond girl was a sub-optimal target and adjusted their play accordingly. Detecting their fear, the child gleefully turned the tables on her bullies, which in turn made her a hero to the smaller players.

Maris noted the upswing in Emilie's social prospects with an old woman's knowing chuckle. Platt shook her head in disbelief and horror. "Are all childhood rituals built around violence?"

"No, Doctor Platt. They are built around positioning. Each child having a known position in relation to its peers builds confidence and trust within the group. If you do not know where someone stands in relation to yourself and the others, then you do not know how to interact with them. To secure a position, Emilie needs to demonstrate that she is not a threat to the group and illustrate what value she brings. Right now, she is showing that she is a match for the bigger ones, and willing to protect the littles."

Emilie sent a pink rubber ball caroming off the head of an older boy, eliciting screams of laughter from all players except the target. Platt winced at the ugly scowl on the boy's face afterward. "So she is showing the others that her position is high with physical abilities and demonstrating value to the smaller children by protecting them?"

"More or less."

"That is pretty clinical, Maris. Even by my standards."

The old woman did not appear at all chagrined. "Childhood is merely practice for adulthood, Doctor. They are learning how to enter and move within social structures now while the requirements are easily met and the stakes are low."

Platt pursed her lips. "So right now, even though Emilie is demonstrating to the smaller kids that she has value, isn't she threatening the position of the bigger ones?"

Maris shrugged. "Probably not. It's just a game, after all. If she plays nice, wins and loses with grace, and displays empathy, they will probably not even notice the shift in the dynamic. How each individual reacts to her will have much to do with specific psychological factors."

"It's all a test?"

"More like an interview," Maris corrected. "But games make it easy. Where I see Emilie struggling is with normal everyday interactions. Children like to be dramatic. They feel things very strongly and act out. Emilie..."

"Emilie does not," Platt finished the thought. Then she added more quietly, "Because we changed her brain."

Maris agreed with an emphatic nod. "Our little Emilie not only does not become dramatic, she does not understand why others might. It's possible her enhanced intuition will cover that deficiency. We will have to guide her, though. The risk of her disassociating from peer interactions is high. She will need to learn to assert her position and defend it, even when her instinct will be to abandon interactions altogether."

"So she'll be as popular as I was, then?" Platt's reply was flat. "I disassociated pretty early, too."

"Don't be coy, Doctor Platt. I know for a fact you graduated high school at thirteen years old. I can't imagine you had anything in common with your classmates."

Platt looked back to the game. "I suppose that's fair. Emilie isn't showing signs of abnormal genius, so I guess there's hope."

"So humble," said Maris, eyes rolling so hard the irises disappeared. "How are the child's studies coming?"

"She's well ahead of her age group, if that's what you are asking. She would not struggle to get into any school she wanted to. It's the socialization that's lagging."

"I think we have that well in hand," Maris said. "Looks like the game is wrapping up. Shall we quit while we are ahead?"

"Good idea."

The women went to collect their charge, and the little blond girl pouted with age-appropriate intensity at being forced to leave the game. She said goodbye to the other kids and left holding Doctor Platt's hand.

"Did you have fun with the other kids?" Maris asked.

"Yeah," Emilie said. "They were nice."

"Did you make any new friends?"

The blond head tilted and her face scrunched with deep thought. "I don't know. The boys were kinda mean. Celia was nice to me, but I don't think she likes me yet."

Platt smiled at her. "Oh really?"

"She seemed more scared of me. Not like Max was scared, though."

Maris asked, "What was the difference?"

"Max thought I was going to hurt him or be mean. Celia is just kinda worried that I'm not normal."

Maris gave a sage nod, then pried more. "And those are different kinds of scared?"

"Yup."

When nothing else followed, Maris let it drop. "Well, I'm sure they'll all learn to love you soon enough."

"I hope not. Boys are dumb."

Maris and Platt both laughed at this. The scientist hugged the child with one arm. "That they are, kiddo. That they are."

The trio stopped to buy an ice cream from a mobile vendor as they left the gymnasium. Platt's memories of enjoying a cold treat on a hot day jangled against the current reality of sucking down frozen custard a thousand feet below the surface of the earth. There was no breeze, no bright sunshine, and the temperature in this part of the complex hovered near seventy all the time. It was as if ice cream tasted different than when consumed outside of the context of a warm summer day, and not for the better. Fortunately, Emilie did not notice or care. She dug into her cone with a kind of single-minded gusto only a child could muster.

They elected to walk back to the laboratory section. The Lenexa terminal was far from the bustle of Hubtown and the concourses were occupied by minimal pedestrian traffic. Platt could not see any, though she assumed that Maris had stocked their path with Railroad sympathizers to ensure they were not bothered. Letting Emilie out into the unprotected open areas was a risk, but unless they wanted to lock the child in a cell until her final breath, they were just going to have to deal with it.

Emilie waved to a man seated on a bench near a tram stop. Platt frowned and Maris chuckled.

"Who was that?" Platt asked, confusion apparent in her furrowed brow.

"One of Miss Maris's friends," Emilie answered while licking her ice cream.

Maris rumpled the girl's hair. "Well done, Emilie! How did you know?"

"He's not waiting for a tram ride. He's just sitting to sit. That means he's watching."

"How could you tell?" Platt was legitimately curious.

"People who are waiting want stuff to happen. He doesn't want anything to happen. He just wants to sit and watch."

Platt chewed her lip before replying. "So you can tell that he's not waiting?"

"Yup."

"How did you know he was Maris's friend?"

"Because she saw him too, and she didn't seem to mind that he wasn't waiting for the tram. Normally weird people make her nervous. But she wasn't nervous at all when she saw him."

Maris laughed out loud. "Doctor Platt, our Emilie is quite the little detective!"

"I like detective stories," the child said. "I want to be like Mister Sullivan when I grow up."

Platt's heart lurched and her stomach soured at the name. If Emilie noticed, she did not mention it.

"Really?" Maris said with a raised eyebrow.

"Yup. He's a good detective."

The older woman steered the girl toward the silver sliding doors leading to the lab section connector. A man in dirty gray coveralls limped by and nodded to the three women. Maris ignored him and said, "Well, let's hope you don't end up too much like Mister Sullivan. He has a lot of bad habits, you know."

"He swears too much."

"That's the least of it!" Platt blurted.

The laboratory section of the Lenexa terminal was not as large as other areas. This end of the KC complex had produced heavy equipment for the war effort, and much of the square footage had been allocated to production and assembly areas. The lack of facilities for personnel made Lenexa unattractive real estate to the people who had taken over the enormous underground metroplex, and for this Platt was grateful. It meant that they had a place to hide and some rudimentary equipment with which to continue her research.

"I have to get back to work," Platt said to Emilie. "Maris will bring you home. Later on we'll get some dinner and maybe watch a threedie, okay?"

"Okay," said the child. "But it's okay if we don't get to the movie. You'll probably be busy."

Platt frowned. "Why do you say that?"

"Because Mister Sullivan is back. He's probably in your office and he'll probably want to talk to you and Maris for a long time."

Platt's stomach lurched again. "How on earth would you know that?"

"The man watching the door was limping. He wasn't limping when we left. He must have tried to stop Mister Sullivan from going inside. People shouldn't try to tell Mister Sullivan what to do. He doesn't like it."

"Maybe he hurt himself?" Platt knew she was reaching but felt compelled to try. The years she spent manipulating Emilie's DNA to produce preternatural intelligence, recall, and intuition had not been wasted. Despite her advantage in years, in this sort of contest Doctor Platt was thoroughly outclassed. A situation that appeared to delight the youngster.

Emilie wore a cocky smile as she explained. "No. He was embarrassed and angry at someone. Plus he didn't run away or anything. If something was really wrong, he'd run away or warn Maris, right? Since he didn't, I think he got beat up for not doing what Mister Sullivan said. Mister Sullivan can be very mean to people who don't listen."

Maris tried to stifle her mirth and it escaped through her gritted teeth in a snorting chortle. "This child is going to be no end of surprises, isn't she?"

"Oh goody," was all Platt could manage. Her tone as dry as a desert wind. "I guess we need to go in and talk to him, huh? You want to drop of Emilie and meet me back here?"

"Can I go in?" Emilie asked. "I want to see Mister Sullivan too."

"Nobody here 'wants' to see Mister Sullivan, kiddo," quipped Platt. "But sure. Might as well."

Maris took Emilie by the hand and shook her head at Platt. "He's not that bad, Doctor. You are being unfair."

"None of you really get how bad he really is," said Platt. But nobody was listening.

CHAPTER TEN

Doctor Platt did not like John Sullivan.

This antipathy sat in ironic juxtaposition to the fact that she was probably the world's foremost expert on the man. The discovery of his creation had come when Platt was merely eleven years old, and the infamous chimera had been a source of unending academic fascination from that point forward. At the age of seventeen, Platt completed the first of her three PhD theses and Sullivan was its subject. A few years and two doctorates later, GEED had sought her input on his application for employment as a warden. She knew more about John L. Sullivan than he probably knew about himself. As a scientist, he was the ultimate subject.

As a person, Platt found him far less fascinating and much more terrifying. It was one thing to study laboratory records and progress reports. It was quite another to interact with a man bred entirely for violence at the genetic level. Worse, nobody else seemed to comprehend her aversion. They did not understand that there was so much more going on inside his genes than his unpleasant demeanor or his physical attributes. What had been done to Sullivan's DNA was a crime against nature. A crime further compounded by a childhood spent under the ungentle tutelage of a mobster. He was a genetically perfect fighter, raised by a criminal, and trained by the best instructors money could buy in every style of violence known to man. Worse than that, his brain had been fundamentally altered to prevent empathy from interfering with his decision making. His testosterone and acetylcholine levels kept him irritable and angry all the time, buffered only by a dopamine trigger shoehorned into his serotonin re-uptake feedback loop to prevent psychotic breaks. Sharon Platt was one of perhaps ten people on the planet who understood what it had taken to warp his personality that far without creating an uncontrollable killer, and even she was not sure if it had worked. She hated how cold and uncharitable she was being, but someone had to point out the danger and that job fell to her.

When her eyes fell on Sullivan, the familiar cold sweat began to form on the back of her neck. He was leaning against her desk, arms folded across his chest and his face locked into the familiar scowl. He was still shaving his head periodically. Right now, the sandy field of stubble had grown out to about a half-inch, and thus was due for another brutal cropping soon. His attempts to let his beard come in were not going well. His five o'clock shadow had progressed into a wiry two-day proto-beard but seemed unwilling to do much more than that. He looked scruffy and unkempt, and she supposed that was intentional. Until the various law-enforcement agencies updated their facial recognition database, the metamorphosis from the chiseled good looks in his GEED credentials remained sufficient to confuse the all-seeing eyes of the traffic grid. The broken nose helped, too. What had once been a flawless bridge now bore a noticeable kink courtesy of Vincent Coll.

Sullivan was not alone in her office. Platt's professional gaze recognized his companion's features for what they were; selectively optimized acromegaly. SOAPs were rare, and she could not stop herself from staring at the giant. For a moment, she forgot to be afraid of Sullivan while she took in the other man's enormity.

Maris lit up at the sight of Fagan and extended a hand. "Hello, Mister Suds." She used the pseudonym he had adopted for his first trip into the Complex. "I am glad to see you have recovered."

"I hear you had a lot to do with that, ma'am," said Fagan as he shook her hand.

"You are very strong. All I did was keep you stable. Not many people would have survived injuries like yours. How do you feel?"

Fagan smiled. "Good. I healed up well and then had ten weeks to rehab and get back in shape. One of my optimizations is testosterone, so the bone and muscle mass came back fast."

"Excellent. I can only assume that you are not here to make arrests then, Warden Fagan?"

"I've been read in on everything, ma'am. We are well beyond GEED, Genetic Equity, and my duty to the law." The shaggy head shook in disbelief. "I still don't get how it all got so far out of hand. But I figured if Sully was going to try to save the world, he was going to need a babysitter." Thick arms stretched out wide and his beard parted to reveal a cocky smirk. "I'm the only guy he listens to. I had no choice."

"It's because you're too loud to ignore," Sullivan said.

Emilie broke the spell as only a child could. She gasped and stared up at Fagan. The big man, seeing the small girl's unfiltered awe, beamed a warm grin her way from under his bushy beard. "And you must be Emilie," he said.

Emilie just gaped. At last she said in a hushed whisper, "Are you a real giant?"

"You betcha, kid," he replied. "But I don't eat people."

"It's about the only thing he doesn't eat," said Sullivan. "I hope you aren't missing any kittens down here."

Emilie only had eyes for the big warden. "This is the best day of my whole life! Auntie Sharon! It's a real *giant*."

"Well, sort of..." Platt began to explain. "He was born with acromegaly, and so some doctors—"

Maris interrupted. "For the love of all that's holy, don't ruin this, Doctor Platt."

"Best. Day. Ever." Emilie squealed with delight. "How tall are you?"

"Seven feet, six inches," Fagan answered. "A hair over five-hundred pounds, too." He waggled his eyebrows and held out his hands. "Wanna come up?"

Emilie ran and leaped into his arms, whereupon he hoisted the child all the way up to the ceiling. She giggled and laughed in a way that made Platt's heart lurch in her chest. This is how childhood was supposed to be, and Emilie got precious little of it. Guilt turned the inside of her mouth to ashes.

"Well," Sullivan grumbled. "Fagan, that's Emilie. Emilie, meet Fagan."

Neither person was listening to him, so Sullivan turned to the pair of women. "All right. Before I bring you guys up to speed on the wide world of bullshit outside, how are things down here?"

Maris answered, "SoA attacks are up. They smell something big afoot. We don't know how much they know, but they are definitely hitting harder and more often. Silk Road is quiet enough for now. Getting burned by Coll made them cagey. We have people watching them for the time being."

"Good," Sullivan grunted. "Keep it that way."

Maris raised an eyebrow at his tone. "I've been doing this since before you were born, John. You've been at it for all of three months. I'll thank you not to bark orders at me. Especially when those orders are something I'm already doing."

Sullivan winced. "Yeah. Sorry. You know what I mean, though."

"I do. But that doesn't mean I care to be disrespected by those benefiting from my organization and experience."

Sullivan nodded. "Message received, Maris. Sorry I'm such a dick."

Platt was not sure he sounded sorry, but with him it was hard to tell for sure. She brought the standoff to a close by changing the subject. "What's going on out there?"

"We have leads. Good ones. We're getting jerked around by Mickey Sullivan, but there's nothing to be done about that for now." He spent the next fifteen minutes bringing them all up to speed on his and Fagan's discoveries. Fagan and Emilie played happily in the background. When he had finished, the older woman's face had collapsed into an irritated map of deep frown lines.

"This is not good, John."

Sullivan nodded. "But it's not all that bad, either. I get to find out who is running the whole operation, and Mickey will keep everyone off of Emilie."

"You can't possibly trust him?"

"Of course not." Sullivan spat the words with a healthy serving of contempt for the idea. "But Mickey believes he has me cold, and as long as he thinks that, he'll give me what I want. He's not interested in Emilie's DNA right now…"

Platt opened her mouth to speak, but Sullivan cut her off with a wave of his hand. "I said 'right now.' He'll come for her when he's settled his current business. Make no mistake about it. She's worth too much. This is him pretending to give me what I want. As long as we keep that front up, he'll play along. He's patient as hell."

Platt did not share his confidence. "How can you be sure?"

"He spent almost twenty years in prison just to give himself an alibi and hide from his enemies." Sullivan curled a lip. "He'll sit tight on the secret of immortality for another few months, or years even."

"If you say so," Platt's irritation with his attitude overrode her fear for a moment. "Far be it from me to question the great John Sullivan."

The scruffy face turned to fix her with the kind of glare that had probably made professional killers void their bowels. She refused to be cowed by it, though her blood pressure chose that moment to soar to new heights. Platt decided this was coincidence and nothing more.

After several long seconds Sullivan spoke, grinding each word against clenched teeth. "Do I go into your lab and tell you how to ruin an innocent baby's life with a centrifuge and a scalpel, Doc? No. I wouldn't know how 'cause I'm just a dumb GiMP some smart fucker like you dreamed up when they wanted a pet monster. So I've learned to shut the hell up when matters turn to subjects I don't understand." He turned his whole body her way, letting his height and width fill her field of vision. "You know a lot of mob bosses, Doc? You ever run a drug ring or an extortion racket? Maybe one of those three PhDs of yours is in criminology?" He held a hand up to his ear as if listening for something very quiet. "No, huh?" His face broke into a big, fake, terrible smile. "Then maybe you should just go ahead and let the psycho GiMP criminal handle the gangsters and mobsters, okay? That sound fair to you, pumpkin?"

Maris hid her face behind a palm and said with a warning in her voice, "Ease up, John..."

Sullivan relaxed at the rebuke. The tension in his jaw and neck faded, and he retreated to lean back on the desk. "Sorry, Maris. It's been a long day." Then he looked to Platt. He locked eyes with her, daring her to say something stupid. "Sorry, Doc. But I guess it isn't really my fault I'm an asshole."

Platt shivered where she stood. His meaning was clear. A constant insatiable anger plagued Sullivan's entire existence because someone just like her had built it into his brain chemistry to please a client. Her moment of irritation with Sullivan now felt stupid and selfish. Her nature as a scientist prevented her from protecting her ego with a lie, and shame followed. She met his gaze and replied, "There's more than one asshole in here, it seems." Then more quietly, "And I don't have any excuse. I'm sorry. I was rude and out of line."

Sullivan nodded, and it seemed that was all the acknowledgment she was going to get.

"We all good?" Fagan asked. Emilie was perched on his shoulder, eyes wide and curious as she observed the growing conflict between Platt and Sullivan. "Everybody all done squabbling?"

"Mister Sullivan is still mad," Emilie said helpfully.

"Sully's always mad," Fagan said to the girl. "You get used to it."

"Anyway," Sullivan growled. "I have about three-hundred terabytes of intel on the chimera program in that bag." He pointed to the cache of memory cards still in its canvas bag atop the desk. "Most of it is way beyond my feeble understanding of genetics. A bunch more of it has to do with finance, and would you believe I'm no expert on that either?"

"We have people," Maris said with a smile.

"I figured," Sullivan replied. "But this is beyond sensitive. This data is worth more than any of our lives. If anybody untrustworthy finds out about it, we're all dead."

Maris bobbed her head from side to side. "Maybe I'll rerun all the background checks on my people before I parse out the analysis, then." She frowned. "Can't have another problem like Porter..."

"Obviously I'll get started on the lab reports and project files," said Platt, if only to change the subject. "There might be some clues as to locations and supporters in there. If there are, I'll find them."

"Good," Sullivan said. "Fagan and I are going to look into this Corpus Mundi outfit some more. Our last attempt ended up getting a guy murdered. In this business, that's a good sign."

"What business is murder a good sign in?" Emilie asked from atop her shaggy mount.

"It's complicated, kid," Sullivan said. "But when we get close to bad guys, they get scared. When they are scared, they like to cut out loose ends."

"What's a loose end?" the child asked.

Before Sullivan could answer, Maris interrupted. "That's enough of that for you, dear. Time to get some dinner."

"Awwwwww…"

Fagan helped Emilie clamber down from her seat on his shoulder. He rumpled her hair with a hand big enough to cover her whole head. "Be good, kid. Eat your vegetables and you'll get as big as me someday."

"That feels unlikely," Emilie said as Platt began to lead her out of the office.

"He's joking, kiddo," said Platt.

When they were gone, Maris turned to Sullivan. "You are too hard on her."

"She's earned it. If she had ever even once stopped to consider the consequences of what she was doing, a lot of people would still be alive and an eight-year-old kid wouldn't have to sleep in a bunker a thousand feet underground. All of this is her fault, either directly or indirectly. The sooner she gets over that and starts un-fucking her mistakes the better."

Maris did not argue that point. "I see. So your plan for that is to terrify and browbeat her every time she speaks?"

"Yes, because every time she speaks she's dead wrong. You and I have been fixing her fuck-ups since she got here. She hasn't managed to do a single thing right on her own but she still talks like she has all the goddamn answers. It's annoying. Worse, it's preventable. Nobody bothered to tell the wee baby genius that her intelligence came with responsibilities when they had the chance. Now her arrogance is getting people killed and ruining lives." He bared his teeth, snarling the rest. "I'm going to ride her for every mistake she makes because nowhere along the line did anybody teach that arrogant little wunderkind that her brains were dangerous. Not enough people have told her 'no' in her life. She was always the smartest person in the room and she knew it. Nobody can tell her shit because she's the genius, so she never gave a shit about what happened to everybody around her. Now that the universe has demonstrated exactly what it thinks of her cleverness, she's scared and wants you and me to fix it all for her."

"And you see it as your role to correct that?"

"Who better than me? I'm exactly what happens when people like her don't accept responsibility for their actions. I'm not cute and harmless like Emilie, either. I'm dangerous and she knows it. She knows better than any of you exactly how dangerous I am and what could happen if her colleagues decide to produce a few thousand of me. Or worse, a few thousand Vincent Colls."

"So it's not because you too were a juvenile prodigy?"

Sullivan looked like he wanted to spit. He did not. "At least with me, they made damn sure I understood that I was dangerous. What I can do? It's a responsibility, not a gift. I got my ass kicked fifty times a day just to make the lessons stick. The fucked up part is that I am nowhere near as dangerous as she is. Where were her ass-kickings?"

Maris seemed satisfied with his response. "You're using her fear of you to teach her a lesson, then? That's poetic, John."

Sullivan shrugged, not sure if Maris had tricked him into saying something best left unsaid. "In a way, she's just like a GMP, Maris. Intelligence like hers is something special, all right. But instead of being forced into government service, people threw money at her, told her she was a genius, and got her to do some really messed up shit in the name of science. Now there are consequences and she needs to get her head around it or that kid is doomed. If Platt had spent a little more time listening to other people and less time admiring her own IQ, we wouldn't be where we are right now. I don't see why I should coddle her ego while she figures that out."

Maris looked past Sullivan to Fagan. "What do you think, Mister Fagan? Is he being too hard on Doctor Platt or is it just tough love?"

"I think that Doctor Platt has a lot of growing up to do and very little time to do it. Sully's not wrong about how she got here, and he doesn't do 'love' of any stripe. Tough or otherwise." Fagan slapped his partner on the back, startling him and Maris both. "Mostly because people like our wayward Doc Platt went ahead and made sure he couldn't." Then he looked to Sullivan. "But you don't have to enjoy it so much, partner. Kind of being a dick there."

"Not my fault," Sullivan grunted back. "It's how I'm built."

CHAPTER ELEVEN

Margaret McLeod lived for new challenges.

She loved her job. She loved the lifestyle it afforded her. She loved the travel, the hunting, the spying and stealing, and more often than not she loved the killing. However, after her first few years in the field she could not help but notice that the murder part of her career had taken a turn for the boring. Industrial espionage was always a challenge, and she loved it. The shifting landscapes of various marketplaces and corporate structures meant no dearth of new and interesting problems to solve. Assassination, on the other hand, was fairly straightforward. She fulfilled her first lethal contracts with an almost perfunctory ease that was only masked by the novelty of it all. As the novelty wore off, the repetitious nature of recon, stalk, seduce, and kill began to feel stale. She killed dozens of people during those years, and she had very strong opinions about the archetypes she encountered. Men were the worst, she had decided early. Most males were entirely at the mercy of their hormones, and she had numerous unfair advantages when it came to those. As her skills increased and her targets became more and more influential, she dared to hope for greater stimulation in her hunts. It seemed logical that wealth and sophistication might temper the lustful blindness that turned men into helpless fools and make for more interesting kills. Reality went on to teach her that this was not the case. If anything, the more wealthy and powerful a man was, the easier it was to manipulate him. These men had no fear; they took no care in their indiscretions. They were not worried about the risks of illicit trysts because there never were any. They did not worry about danger, because their influence and money bought them all the protection they could want. All she had to do was appear vapid and pretty, and the great minds of industry and finance would dismiss her as just another not-so-bright gold digger or whore. Certainly no threat to one such as they. She found these targets contemptible and consider their elimination to be a service to women everywhere.

Politicians could be trickier, but not by much. Obsessive about image and optics, getting a governor or a senator into position for a clean kill took some extra work. Though she had to admit that, in the end, politicians were no more or less depraved than the average tycoon. Their lust for power and planet-sized egos left enormous blind spots for Margaret to exploit, and exploit she did.

Criminals she found to be much more interesting. Successful criminals tended to be suspicious to a fault. Gaining the trust of a mob boss or senior capo could be quite the challenge. Low and mid-level crooks were easy, but the high-level leaders surrounded themselves with a thick layer of paranoia that could take weeks or months to penetrate. They loved women, usually. However, most had regular girls from places thoroughly vetted. Often, a steady mistress was employed for years, simply because they could be trusted. The history books were filled with criminal masterminds who died at the hands of female assassins, and the modern crop of mob bosses had learned from those mistakes. Trying to reel in the heads of crime syndicates was a challenge that did not come her way often, and Margaret relished those jobs.

It was for this reason Margaret was excited for the next contract. It was all but a foregone conclusion that she would be tasked with bringing down Michael Sullivan. She suspected that the only reason his release had been arranged at all was to give her a clean shot at him. Under normal circumstances, killing a man in prison did not present much difficulty. One need only get a few ounces of whatever drug his fellow prisoners preferred into his cell block, and then have your mark shanked in his bed one dark night. This of course would not be possible in the case of Mickey Sullivan. Ever the paranoid one, the wily mobster had spared no expense buying off his whole facility. It completely reversed the normal dynamic and thwarted those who wanted him out of the picture. Instead of a lone mark trapped in a box filled with potential assassins, he became a powerful leader ensconced in a well-garrisoned fortress. The move was nothing short of brilliant, keeping him alive and in the game while his co-conspirators battled for supremacy on the outside. She wondered if her client understood how well Mickey had manipulated the situation. She supposed she was about to find out. Her eyes flicked to her phone next to her. Soon it would chime and she would have her next job.

Margaret sat in the living room of one of her many apartments, feet folded beneath her on a large leather couch. A glass of some ludicrously expensive Bordeaux stood on a nearby table, half-finished and filling the air with the complex tang of tannin, oak, fermented fruit, and ethanol. One of the great wonders of her condition lay in how much pleasure she found in her food and drink. The exquisite joy of a glass of wine was a full-body experience for Margaret. Her nose, her taste buds, her sense of touch, they all provided so much more of everything that made comestibles enjoyable than anyone else would ever understand. She could savor that wine without ever touching it. The very air itself carried all those delicious volatile organic compounds to her nose and throat with nary a twitch of her little finger. She did not merely smell the wine; she could taste it from here in all its glory. If she deigned to sip it, an entirely new sensory experience would follow the first. All the dissolved solids not carried by the vapors would mix and mingle across a tongue capable of discerning as many as a hundred separate compounds at once. She would know what side of the hill the grapes grew on, how much rain fell on the fields, how many times the barrel had been used prior to aging this bottle. Margaret did not understand how normal people lived their lives so blind and numb to all the sensations the world had to offer. She supposed she did not care, either.

The phone chimed.

Like the beat of hummingbird wings her hand flicked out to snatch it from the cushion. She thumbed "accept" and slipped a pair of clear AR lenses over her eyes. The panels came to life with caller information she already knew was fake. "Hold on," she said before anyone could speak. "I'm scrambling now." The glasses gave her updates while their phone connection endured several layers of encryption and spoofed signal data. When the process was complete her tone softened. "There we are. The line is secure. What can I do for you today, Mister Sharpe?"

"Hello, Ms. McLeod." The voice that came across her earpiece sounded like a normal male voice, though Margaret knew it had been distorted. She was not supposed to know this, of course. Whoever had done the job had both excellent equipment and talent. The work was so subtle nobody else would have suspected the deception. Margaret, of course, always suspected deception. Thus it came as no surprise when her lenses lit up with a display showing the waveform of the disembodied voice highlighted with the probable levels of alteration. The dance never changed, and she dismissed the ploy as mere professional discretion. The voice continued. "First, let me just say 'thank you' for your excellent work with the Hanson situation. That problem materialized rather quickly, and we appreciate you taking the job on such short notice."

Her fee had been exorbitant, so Margaret could afford to be gracious. "And I appreciate your prompt payment, Victor."

"Services rendered is payment tendered," the voice replied with a chuckle. "It's our unofficial motto."

"Words to live by, Victor." Then, as an afterthought, "especially in my profession."

"I imagine so! I don't think that anyone really wants to deal with your version of accounts payable!"

Sharpe's mirth seemed genuine to her, and the voice stress analysis from her lenses agreed. That was a good sign she was dealing with a live human and not a clever AI. Corporations loved to use AI 'bots for illicit conversations. Law enforcement was fond of them as well. The level of deniability provided by this technique was unparalleled. However AI still lacked creativity and nuance, so the truly important things still needed that human touch. Margaret refused to deal with an AI, and this rule had saved her life more than once.

Satisfied with her situation, Margaret got to business. "Who is the target this time?"

"Michael Sullivan."

There it was. The words had been spoken. The ultimate mark, the greatest target of her entire career, a man now doomed.

"That, Mister Sharpe, will not be an easy task. Nor will it be cheap."

"For a professional of your caliber?" Sharpe sounded incredulous. The negotiations had begun. "I'd think a woman like you would have no trouble approaching a mobster who just spent the last twenty years in prison."

Margaret's riposte came without hesitation. "A mobster who allowed himself to be incarcerated to insulate himself from people just like you, Mister Sharpe. A clever, paranoid, master strategist who was willing to go to prison because it suited his plans. I do not believe for one second he lacked for female company while inside, and I do not believe for one second he won't sense trouble the minute he lays eyes on me. This is no horny ex-con incapable of looking me in the eyes, Mister Sharpe. This is a man who has been out-thinking your group for most of three decades. This is a man whose plans and goals go much further than you realized. Let's not pretend I don't already know what this is about, okay? Mickey Sullivan has been playing you for a long time, and you are just now seeing the extent of it, aren't you?"

A long pause followed. The display of her lenses counted the breaths picked up by Sharpe's microphone. "And you know this how?"

Margaret laughed. "I didn't know anything, Mister Sharpe. I had a hunch and just let you confirm it. I don't know exactly what your issue with old Mickey is but it's not hard to see why you suddenly sprang him from prison, and why you had me service poor Harry Hanson on such short notice. You were happy to let him rot for twenty years, then something happened. Now you need him dead. He didn't do anything from prison, so it means you discovered something he was already doing. He tricked you. Played you. Now you need him gone."

What Margaret did not tell Sharpe was that all of these observations meant he was almost certainly a corporate man and not another mobster. The way he approached the issues, how he handled the burgeoning crisis all stank of committee-based decision making. They were reacting to Mickey Sullivan, not acting on their own ambitions. The decision to eliminate Sullivan was coming very late in the game. A mobster would have had Sullivan killed years ago. Or never allied with him in the first place. It was no secret that Mickey Sullivan was not a team player and that he did not share power. Sharpe's organization must have needed the Sullivan Mob's money and contacts very badly after the war, because making a deal with the devil himself would have been safer in the long run. She knew how charming Mickey could be, though. It was not hard to imagine Sullivan convincing whatever board of directors Sharpe reported to that he had everything they needed in a safe and affordable package. There were always enough weak links in any corporate boardroom to secure the votes one needed. Diluted leadership and aversion to risk were the most obvious failings of large corporations, and every part of her relationship with the mysterious Mister Sharpe had been fraught with signs of both. Obviously Mickey Sullivan had capitalized on this.

Sharpe's reply only cemented her impressions further. "I can't deny that our relationship with Michael Sullivan has run its course. I am impressed with your analysis, Ms. McLeod. Do you think you can do this job?"

"Of course I can, Mister Sharpe. My point was that this will take time and quite a bit of money. I can't just try to vamp him at a nightclub. I will need to get close to him without arousing suspicion. He will need to trust me. With his recently announced political ambitions, we also need to take care that no aspect of his demise can be traced back to us. It does offer us a few angles, though."

"You have a plan?"

"Naturally. But your people will have to render assistance."

"We are at your disposal. What do you intend to do?"

Margaret reached over and picked up her glass of Bordeaux. "Trying to get into Mickey's bed is a waste of time. He has all the whores he wants, and a mobster dying in bed with a woman is hardly subtle. It positively screams 'professional hit' and will have all manner of official inquiries turning over rocks best left unturned. I think there is a much better way to get Mickey done that will leave the kind of scapegoat no one would look twice at."

"And that would be?"

She sipped at her wine, a dramatic pause for effect. "His son."

CHAPTER TWELVE

Sullivan was covered in sweat.

His muscles burned and his breath blasted from his lungs in tortured gasps. The bones of his hands throbbed, dull pain lancing from his metacarpals and radiating up his forearms. With his head slumped he kneeled on the floor, shoulders rising and falling while he tried to catch a clean breath. Long before he was ready, a timer chimed three times. Sullivan rose.

He returned to the heavy bag with a snarl, and started throwing punches. Sixty minutes into his workout and it felt like fighting underwater. A jab, normally so fast the eye could barely follow it, lumbered out to thwack the worn synthetic hide of the bag. Right behind it a cross, delivered with a twist of the hips to give it power, crashed into the same spot. The bag jumped, making the chains snap and groan. Sullivan was still swinging. A left hook fired from down by the hip dented the side; an overhand right finished the combination with enough power to send the whole apparatus swinging. Sullivan slipped to the side to avoid the wobbling bag and pivoted to slam three alternating hooks at it. His anger grew when he saw the reduced power, his frustration surged when he detected his own flat feet. His instructor's voice screamed in his imagination.

"Don't like getting hit? Move your fucking feet!"

Sullivan bounced back on the balls of his feet and torqued his hips to deliver a furious Thai round kick. He imagined Coach Pianna's small brown face as he did so and the power surged through the bag, nearly folding it in half. He followed it with a left hook and an uppercut. This brought him close enough to seize the bag in a crushing clinch. Like a terrible piston, he drove his right knee up and into the bag over and over again, gasping and bellowing with each impact.

The timer chimed.

Sullivan stopped and simply sucked wind. This was not working. He was no more or less angry than when he began. Returning to a regular exercise regimen had been difficult after recovering from his fight with Vincent Coll, and the familiar post-workout lethargy no longer provided the comfort it once had. He did not need exercise to stay in shape. Being resistant to myostatin and bursting with testosterone guaranteed a flawless physique no matter what he did to maintain it. However, Sullivan had lost enough fights to know that settling for anything less than maximal fitness invited disaster. It was not enough for him to be physically gifted. He was born with superhuman physical potential, and his instructors made it clear that falling short of that goal was unacceptable. Sullivan shared their opinion on the matter. None of the hell of his existence made any difference if he failed to achieve his full potential. Part of him understood the self-destructive nature of this conceit, yet the grueling physical strain had always brought him comfort. The results spoke for themselves, as any of his dead enemies could attest to. The voice of Coach Stevens echoed in the corners of his memory, speaking with the gruff brevity that Sullivan had eventually adopted. *"Graveyards are full of good fighters who got killed by great fighters. There will always be someone stronger, faster, tougher than you, kid. Until there isn't. When the day comes that you are the baddest mother on the planet, then you can rest. Today ain't that day. Get up and do it again."*

The voice of his coach and the roar of blood rushing through his ears faded after just a few seconds. It was only after he had caught his breath that he heard the sound of tiny hands clapping. He turned to see Maris and Emilie at the door of his impromptu gymnasium. The little girl was clapping hard, a wide smile on her face. Maris stood with a knowing smile.

"Can I help you?" Sullivan said. He did not mean to sound as irritated as he did, but their timing was terrible.

"Emilie has a problem I think you might be uniquely suited to handle, John," Maris replied.

Sullivan switched his round timer off and walked toward them. He was wearing only workout shorts, though he seemed unaware of his own state of undress. His physique had never been something he was self-conscious about. "What the hell could I possibly help her with?"

Maris looked down at the girl, who now appeared very nervous. "Go on, Emilie," said Maris. "Tell him."

"There is this boy at the playground..."

Sullivan's face soured. "I don't think this is—"

"Oh, hush up and listen," Maris snapped.

"Sorry."

Emilie continued, her voice gaining strength. "He uh... he's being mean to me. He pushed me off the slide today, and yesterday he took my snack. I got really mad at him and I..." She paused and Sullivan scowled. It was unlike Emilie to struggle with speaking or expressing herself. She looked like she might cry. "I uh... I hit him. Then he hit me back and we got into a fight and..."

"Go on," Maris said. "He will understand."

"I got scared 'cause he was bigger and meaner. He was hurting me and I couldn't make him stop." Tears started to form in her big eyes. "I wanted him to stop but I couldn't make him. I..."

"I get it, kid."

Emilie looked up, confused.

"I said I get it." Sullivan looked to Maris, a decision made. "I hope you didn't bring her here for therapy, Maris. You know I can fix this, but you and the doc may not like how I do it."

Maris gave Sullivan a look of such steel Sullivan almost stepped back. "Half the world wants to own her, John. The other half wants her dead. It's time for her to learn to take care of herself."

Sullivan gave the woman a respectful tilt of his head. Then he looked down at Emilie. "Do you remember how it felt? When you couldn't make him stop hurting you?"

"Yes. I felt scared."

"Anything else? Think hard, Emilie. Use that big brain of yours."

"Angry. I was angry... I am angry."

"What do you want to do, kid?"

"I want to never feel that way again."

"Tell the truth, kid. This won't work if you don't tell the truth."

Emilie stared, fresh tears in her eyes and tiny hands trembling. "I want to hurt him."

"Good." Sullivan straightened. "You can't win a fight if you don't want to hurt the other guy."

Emilie nodded, all business. Sullivan looked at Maris. "She's going to need comfortable workout clothes, some protective gear, and a couple of kids her age or slightly older to work with. Pick kids her size or larger, boys and girls. You might as well get ones you think can use the skills."

"So easy, John?" Maris looked disappointed.

"What?"

"I thought you'd put up more resistance to the idea of training a child. I had a whole argument laid out. I was looking forward to scarring you with many scathing rebukes of your character."

Sullivan wiped sweat from his forehead. "I know you were. It's what you do. I've never won an argument with you yet. Every time I try you turn it into a therapy session and I'm not in the mood for that shit." He wiped his slick hands on the dirty gray shorts. "That's half the reason I didn't bother arguing."

"And the other half?"

"Keeping the kid safe will be a lot easier once she knows how to run, fight, and shoot. This is going to be her life for the next couple hundred years. She might as well get good at it."

"I'm going to learn to shoot?" Emilie sounded excited and scared at the same time.

"Of course," said Sullivan. "You're too small to take on a grown man unarmed. But we'll probably start with knives."

Some of the self-satisfied glee left the old woman's features. "Knives? Guns? I thought we were talking about some judo or something."

Sullivan, delighted to have retaken the high ground, gave Maris the kind of look she was very fond of giving him when he said something stupid. "She's eight years old and all of sixty-five goddamn pounds, Maris. How much Judo do you think it takes to overcome the laws of physics?"

Unlike Sullivan, Maris possessed an excellent sense of when she had lost a point. "Very well then, John. I see what you mean. I'll break that to Doctor Platt gently."

"Do that. For now, Emilie, come with me." He gestured to the dirty little room he had claimed for his workouts.

"What will I learn first?" Emilie asked.

"Your limits," replied Sullivan.

Maris watched the tiny child join Sullivan in his gym. She paused long enough to congratulate herself on the completeness of her victory. Emilie needed to learn to protect herself, that part had not been subterfuge. However, Sullivan needed something else. In here, Sullivan was going to get the chance to confront and correct all the things he hated about his own childhood. The old doctor did not bother to conceal her smug smile.

She left the pair to their training and went to find Doctor Platt. Doctor Platt did not see her plan in the same optimistic light. This too, Maris had expected. In some ways the old woman found Platt to be far more tiresome than Sullivan. It was past time for Maris to address that.

Platt's verbal explosion was as uninspired as it was predictable. "You did WHAT?"

Maris did not flinch. "The girl needs training, Doctor Platt. He's the best fighter in a very large radius. She will receive the kind of instruction wealthy folks would pay thousands of dollars for."

"He's insane, Maris! I know you don't believe me, but only I understand what they did to him!"

"Doctor Platt!" Maris used her command voice. "There is only one person in this room with the proper credentials to diagnose insanity in anyone. You are not that person. If you find that hard to remember, you can start calling me 'Doctor Cartwright' until it sticks." Platt looked like she wanted to say something. Maris did not give her the chance. "Furthermore, if you want to hear my professional opinion, I'll give you one. You are suffering from an acute case of the Dunning-Kruger effect, and you had better get over yourself."

"What the..."

"Your confidence exceeds your expertise, Doctor Platt. You do not know everything about everything, and it's high time people started telling you as much."

Now Platt was mad. "I earned three PhDs before my twenty-first birthday, Maris. I think my confidence is appropriate, especially when it comes to that..."

"Thing?" Maris correctly guessed what Platt had prevented herself from saying. Platt's eyes revealed the truth of it, though she said nothing.

The old woman's smile held no warmth. "Therein lies the problem. So you fancy yourself the expert on John Sullivan, do you?"

Platt's expression was a challenge.

Maris accepted. "The last piece of scientific data you have on him is most of a decade old, Doctor. You never even laid eyes on him until he saved your life three months ago. One hundred percent of your analysis is based upon things you read in reports. That is hardly what anyone would consider 'scientific rigor,' Doctor Platt." Maris folded her arms across her chest. "Despite your woefully outdated and minimal understanding of his psychology, you speak to him as if he was a dangerous criminal and get upset when he points out your arrogance. Well, he is wrong on many things, Doctor, but he is right about that much. You are arrogant." A crooked finger extended, punctuating the forthcoming accusation with a stern jab. "Your understanding of him was never as good as you thought it was. Your own notes admitted that you do not understand the psychological ramifications of his condition. You may comprehend the genome that he grew from, but you don't know a damn thing about the *man* who saved your ungrateful life. Do you know his favorite color? How about what he likes to eat? What does he dream about when he sleeps? What keeps him up at night? What makes him do any of the things he does?"

"None of that changes what's in his brain, Maris—"

"It doesn't?" Maris feigned surprise at this. "So I suppose the entire field of psychology is a sham, then? Shame. I was rather good at it."

"That's not what I meant..."

"But it is what you said."

"It's not what I said!"

"Enlighten me, then. Because you are making very little sense right now."

Platt ran her hands through her hair. She knew Maris was leading her, and that the old psychiatrist had a well-crafted point lying in ambush somewhere. Nevertheless Platt needed her to understand that Sullivan was not like other people. "It doesn't matter what his favorite color is. Not even to him. His brain does not make that kind of connection very well." She flapped her hands, fumbling for an explanation that would make sense to Maris. "He can't really form emotional bonds. He can barely uptake oxytocin under normal conditions, and under stress not at all. But Maris, he's always stressed! He will never feel for Emilie the way you and I can. The people who created him made sure that when the time to make decisions comes, he won't feel anything at all. Not fear, not love, not empathy or sympathy. Just a little anger."

"So why do you suppose he's decided to throw his whole life away protecting her, then?"

"It's not because he *feels* anything for her. He can't. He's probably just mad."

"And you know this because...?

Platt's brow furrowed. "Because I've seen all his files. It's how his brain works."

"Worked," Maris corrected her.

When it became obvious that Platt was not catching on, Maris switched gears. "What traits were you trying to enhance in Emilie's genotype, Doctor Platt?"

The question put Platt off balance. "Memory and neuroplasticity, but I don't see what that has to do with—"

"And what is neuroplasticity?"

"The brain's ability to adapt to stimulus over the course of..." Platt's voice trailed off.

"Do you suppose that John Sullivan might have any of this magical property in his brain? Or is he just a 'thing' that does not learn or grow?"

There was no point in arguing that Sullivan could not learn or grow, and Platt suspected she had lost the rhetorical ambush before she ever realized it had been sprung. Stubborn to her core, she was not ready to surrender just yet. "I'm sure he does, but—"

"But nothing. I'm going to tell you something I saw in him once. It was the moment I knew he was a lot more than a 'thing.'" Maris made sure Platt was paying attention. "I saw him while Warden Fagan was dying on the bed of that disgusting sleeping pod over in Rosedale. This 'thing' you don't believe can love or feel for others? I watched him agonize over the thought of losing his only friend. I am a real honest-to-goodness psychologist and psychiatrist, young lady. I know what I saw. Maybe his creators tried to breed that out of him, but humans are social animals. Over the years, John Sullivan learned to form a bond with that hairy SOAP." She forestalled Platt's response with a raised hand. "I concede that this ability is rudimentary at best. Warden Fagan was the easiest person for him to bond with because our Patrick can't really be bullied by anyone. Sullivan needed someone who did not fear him. Someone who would not be pushed away by his personality." Maris smiled now. "He *learned* how to form a bond this way."

Platt pursed her lips. "That is still a long way from having him teach Emilie to play with guns."

The smile left the old woman's face. "Your ignorance is showing again. You need to get much more observant. Stop assuming you already know the answer and start looking at the data like a scientist is supposed to."

That seemed to sting Platt somewhere personal. "What am I missing, then?"

"John Sullivan does not 'play' with guns. Or knives. Or anything lethal. While you keep your nose in old files, I'm out there observing and gathering data." She tapped a finger to the side of her head. "You know, like a scientist? I just watched him nearly kill himself on a punching bag just for the workout. He does it all the time. You'd know if you cared to study the man. But then you'd have to admit that you don't already know everything."

"Okay, okay," Platt threw her hands up. "I get it, I'm a bad scientist because I think I know everything. You win! Why does his workout matter?"

"John doesn't ever 'play' with violence, Doctor. Fighting is more than a skill to him. It's a culture. More importantly, Doctor Platt, it's a language. Conflict is where he communicates his thoughts and feelings. It's in your own files, woman! He only ever understood his combat instructors, remember? His strongest bond was with this Scott Stevens, the judo man, correct?"

Platt could not argue when her own words were being used against her. She glared her affirmative instead.

"Stevens figured out that poor, broken, nearly-psychotic boy's language and used it to teach him how to be a man and not a killer. We see it all the time in other things. It's why we have art therapy, music therapy, group therapy, things like that. Sullivan needs physical conflict to internalize and communicate what he cannot say out loud. My late husband was a boxer, Sharon. Trust me, fighters have a language all their own. Warden Fagan speaks that language too. Ask him yourself if you think I'm wrong."

Platt pondered this. Then she nodded. "And now Sullivan will teach this language to Emilie?"

Maris smiled again. "And they will communicate."

"And bond?" Platt asked.

"I hope so," said Maris. "They need each other."

CHAPTER THIRTEEN

Since their previous inquiries had resulted in the untimely demise of Harry Hanson, Sullivan and Fagan elected to go up the chain of command at Corpus Mundi to see if the order had come from inside the company. This led the pair to a regional VP named Saul Lewiston and a late-night operation in the heart of New York City's crumbling entertainment district. "This place used to be the crown jewel of American financial power," Fagan opined upon exiting the 'loop station. 7th Avenue stretched before them with an uninviting palette of gray and brown office buildings. "Not so sparkly these days, huh?"

Sullivan had shrugged in that uncaring way of his and replied, "Supply chain disruptions from the war drove regular folks away from the hyper-dense urban centers like New York and Los Angeles. Twenty-five million people go through a lot of toilet paper, you know. When the small folks can't afford to live nearby, the rich bastards can't get good help for cheap anymore. So they left, too."

Fagan eyed the dirty street. "A lot of the businesses hung around at least."

"Business is business. The city still has a lot of good infrastructure for that sort of thing. It'll bounce back."

Their destination was only a few blocks from the station, so the pair decided to walk.

"You figure they'll murder this guy, too?" Fagan asked after a few minutes of silent plodding.

"That's what we're here to find out," Sullivan replied. The toneless throbbing of music hit their ears as they turned down a side street crowded with bars and night clubs. Raucous crowds clogged the sidewalks; clumps of men and women deep into their cups lurched from brightly lit threshold to dark-windowed doorway with equal abandon and devoid of shame. The whole block seemed to pulse with an unearthly magenta glow and a pervasive sense of reckless revelry. Sullivan's nose crinkled. "I still wish we could have just shook him down at his office. I hate these places."

"You hate bars?" Fagan's incredulity could not be disguised. "You drink more than anybody I know."

"I hate these kinds of bars." Sullivan pointed to a digital billboard showcasing buxom women writhing around in lingerie.

"You hate strip clubs?" This seemed even less likely to Fagan. He had more than once been forced to drag Sullivan away from his amorous pursuits when they interfered with mission goals. The only thing Sullivan loved more than drinking was the company of indiscriminate women.

Sullivan stood by his claim. "Can't stand 'em," he said. "Nothing in there but fake smiles, fake tits, and fake interactions. Places like this are filled with dumbass norms either too stupid to know they're getting scammed, or too pathetic to care."

Fagan suggested a third alternative. "Maybe everybody already knows the score, man. Maybe it's just a quiet transaction between consenting adults where both people get what they want and go home satisfied."

"Nope. Just idiots and con artists."

"You are really invested in being disagreeable tonight."

Sullivan sniffed and took a bite of protein bar. "Aren't I always?"

"Tonight feels worse."

"You're only saying that because you don't like these places, either."

"I scare the girls. It makes me uncomfortable."

"Christ," Sullivan said with a sigh. "We are just not cut out for this clandestine shit, are we?"

"I do have a hard time blending in," Fagan said.

"Let's get this over with."

The pair left the cover of the clogged street to approach the illuminated facade of an ostentatious gentleman's club. It stood out from its peers on the neon promenade. The expensive trim, the creative use of light and sound, the enormous screens flashing lurid advertisements all conspired to tell the riffraff that this was no seedy dive. The entire design of the entrance had been constructed to dissuade normal people from attempting to get inside. Despite the otherwise inviting facade, a forest of brass handrails, one well-dressed and oversized doorman, plus an army of liveried valets made it very clear that this was the sort of place wherein only the most well-heeled of gentlemen should expect to enjoy the delights inside "Cabaret Nero." This presented a problem for the two men stalking across the street. Neither gave a convincing impression of wealth or class. Suits in their sizes had been procured, but the increasingly furrowed brow of the doorman as they approached told both that it would take more than a suit to get them inside.

"Good evening, guys," the doorman said when they were close. He made no move to open the door for them. "Can I help you?"

"Not unless you serve whiskey or give private dances," Sullivan fired back. "What's the cover?"

"Are you a member?" the doorman asked. He made a game attempt to look intimidating. He was as tall and wide as Sullivan, though in the presence of Fagan this turned out to be woefully inadequate. He did not appear afraid, and this was telling. Sullivan suspected he would find a firearm under the man's black jacket if he cared to look. Fagan might be physically imposing to the initiated; however, professionals knew that SOAPs and trolls were big, not bulletproof.

"We're considering joining," Fagan said with a friendly grin. "New in town and all that. Everyone says this place is the best."

"Oh, it is," said the doorman, matching Fagan's amicable tone. "But tonight its members only in there. Real sorry about that."

"How much to join?" Sullivan asked,

"Got to be invited." The doorman was still being polite. "But if you head over to Hostler's a few doors down the street, tell them Rhino sent you and they'll waive the cover."

"You Rhino?" Sullivan asked.

"Yeah. I didn't pick the nickname."

"How much to get you to open the door, Rhino?" Sullivan removed a digital currency vault from his pocket and tapped it against a palm. "We came to have a good time and we don't mind paying for it. We're good for whatever."

Rhino's eyes went to the vault and then back to Sullivan. "Man, any other night and we'd do business. I just can't make it happen for you guys tonight, though. Go to Hostler's. The girls there will let you get away with way more than the ones in here, anyway."

Sullivan looked closer at Rhino. Something caught his attention. The cords of sinew around the burly doorman's throat stood out from the column of his neck. His trapezius muscles rose like foothills from his back, connecting to shoulders every bit as wide as Sullivan's. Deltoids bulged under the jacket like swollen soccer balls, completing a picture quite familiar to him. Rhino noticed the scrutiny and squinted back. "What are you looking at, man?"

"Myostatin inhibition," Sullivan said, his voice cold and flat. "A whole lot of it."

Rhino paused, his face twitching nervously for a second before his composure returned. "What the fuck is it to you? You a warden or something?"

"No," Fagan said. "But I am." He flashed his GEED identification for the man's benefit. It was switched off to prevent tracking, though Rhino failed to notice that.

Both men waited and watched. Whenever a Genetically Modified Person found his or her self confronted by a GEED warden, a moment of indecision always followed. GMPs were barred from all private sector jobs, so the doorman found himself outside the law and about to pay for it. Sullivan did not know if Rhino was registered and just moonlighting as a doorman, or unregistered and hiding from GEED. If it was the former, the offense was minor and would result in a ticket and some community service. The latter meant arrest, incarceration, and then evaluation for government employment. The answer became obvious when Rhino neither ran nor attacked.

"Aw shit, man. I'm just making some extra money, okay? Don't pull my card, please! I just got out after doing five on a CoMA charge last year. They got me working in animal control, man. How am I supposed to get ahead in animal control?"

"Relax," Sullivan said. "Nobody is here looking for moonlighters, okay? Maybe if you let us in, we can put in a good word and get you moved from animal control, though. You look like you could handle a courthouse security job. Maybe something military?"

"Military would be cool. You really aren't gonna pull my card?"

"Bigger fish to fry tonight," Fagan said with a stern wink. "Can we count on your discretion?"

"Hell yes," Rhino said with no hesitation. "We're all cool with GEED in here."

"Let me see your card," Fagan said. "If we get done with no trouble in there, I'll recommend your number for reassignment to military."

Rhino lit up like a child. "No problem, boss. I'll call up concierge and tell them you are some weird government official and his bodyguard incognito. That should keep the hosts from harassing you inside. No one will look twice at a SOAP if they think he's on a government gig, right?"

"Nice touch," Sullivan said. "I like that."

"Don't let it go to your head," Fagan warned. "I ain't your damn bodyguard."

Rhino slapped the door panel with a keycard. "Go on in guys. Good luck. I'll be out here if you need me."

Fagan snorted as they passed inside. "He got real helpful at the end there, didn't he?"

"They put a guy with heavy myostatin inhibition in animal control," Sullivan said. He shook his head. "It's like Coll said. They want the GMPs pissed off."

He could say no more as a hostess greeted them in that moment. Both Sullivan and Fagan were saddled with excess testosterone, and only ironclad personal discipline kept either from gawking at the buffet of anatomical delights the tanned woman chose to display. Her body looked as if it had been sculpted from teak into a teenage boy's most lurid daydreams. The men were intelligent enough to note where good genetics left off and expensive plastic surgery picked up, yet in the moment both found themselves incapable of caring. Fagan spoke first, and he hoped the woman accepted the compliment as delivered.

"Lady, if you're the hostess, we are fucking screwed."

The hostess laughed. "Okay, tiny. That's a new one. Points for originality. Are you gentlemen interested in ladies, gentleman, or both this evening?"

Sullivan found his voice. "We are definitely interested in ladies."

"Follow me, then," said the hostess. She turned to lead them both through a dark hallway to a clear door limned in blue light. The door vibrated in its frame, thumping in time to music neither man could hear. "Through here is our famous Playboy Lounge. Please enjoy watching the performers with a drink from our world-class bar. If you decide you'd like more private accommodations or some special attention from one of our entertainers, just ring the hostess and she will make any arrangements you need." The hostess winked a big brown eye at the pair. "Have fun, boys."

"Yes, ma'am," Fagan said with an enthusiasm that was probably exaggerated for effect. Probably. They went inside and stopped a few steps beyond the door for a good old-fashioned gawk.

Fagan spoke first, and his voice dripped with wonder. "Dear. God."

Sullivan did not respond. He needed a moment himself. He recalled his fifteenth birthday, where he had received as a gift the services of a very expensive prostitute. His father's lieutenants had all pitched in for the travel and time of the most expensive professional in the country. The evening proved a formative experience for a teenage boy with the body of a professional athlete and testosterone levels several standard deviations above the mean. That little present both deeply altered and fundamentally warped his sexual identity well into his adulthood. From that day forward he had lived the life of an unrepentant Lothario. He enjoyed women of all shapes and sizes. He liked them younger, older, lean, or curvy. When the attentions of a woman were available, it took a lot of effort for Sullivan to find a reason not to indulge himself. Years of this debauchery meant the plastic charms and intricate fantasies of the adult entertainment industry were often lost on him. He had seen too much to buy into any of it. He figured that at this point in his life there was nothing a strip club, no matter how opulent and upscale it may be, could do to surprise him.

He was wrong.

In retrospect, Sullivan admitted that there were levels to everything in life, and he had perhaps not experienced this level of strip club before. The women were all beautiful. While one might expect such of a professional in this field, Sullivan knew the truth of that assumption to be a touch more nebulous. Normally an exotic dancer needed a certain quantity of make-up, lighting, and inebriation to keep the fantasy alive. Sullivan had woken up next to enough of them to know that what could be an intensely erotic performance in the dim blue illumination of the club often looked entirely different in the combined buzzkill of daylight and sobriety. It took only a cursory glance to see these women did not suffer from that reality, and Sullivan's appraisal ventured well past 'cursory.' Faces, bodies, hair, skin, all flawless. They looked like dolls, and Sullivan supposed that to be intentional. This wry thought helped him tear his eyes away from the dancers and look around the room. Two stages flanked an area with tables and chairs, and burgundy couches lined the walls. A few dark niches had been carved into the perimeter where women gyrated for the semi-private pleasure of glassy-eyed men at round tables. A long bar ran along the back wall, the shelves of liquor at its back rising far higher than the bartender had any prayer of reaching. A few sullen men sat there brooding into drinks while staring at the various sports games displayed on several large monitors. They made banal chat to the bartender, another impossibly attractive woman, while pretending to be too sophisticated to leer at the dancers.

"See our guy, Fagan?"

"What?"

"Focus, partner. Do you see our guy?"

"Oh. Yeah. He's getting a lap dance in that corner." Fagan jerked his chin to their right, and Sullivan let his eyes wander in that direction. As Fagan had indicated, the man they were looking for was seated at a table in one of the dark alcoves. A half-consumed drink sat alone on the table, ignored by the well-dressed occupant. This could be understood, for the woman twisting and grinding in his lap commanded the attention of both his eyes and his wandering hands. Sullivan had to admit it looked like he was having a very good time.

"Being a high-paid corporate scumbag must be nice," he mused aloud to Fagan.

"Do you want me to flash the badge like last time?" Fagan asked.

"I was thinking of just walking up, telling him who I am, and then giving him the old 'oblique intimidation' routine."

"So mobster shit, then?"

"I figure he'll either start spilling his guts or get aggressive. Depends on the kind of guy he is. Either way, all we'll have to do is stake him out and see what happens afterward." Sullivan sniffed. "I like the atmosphere here for mob shit. I figure a mob shakedown is more believable in this joint than GEED hunting him down at a titty bar."

"You spotted his people yet?"

Sullivan nodded. "Yup. Two guys at the bar drinking ginger ale. One more at the stage tipping way too much, another hanging out at a table staring at his phone."

"You missed the guy by the bathrooms."

"Shit. Good call."

Fagan signaled a passing hostess and ordered two beers. "I'll go blend in at a table where I can see everything. You go ahead and ruin his evening."

"It's like a calling or something," Sullivan said. "Ruining people's evenings just speaks to me. The goon by the bathroom is going to try to stop me from going in there. Can you buy me ten seconds to get past him?"

"He'll be indisposed," Fagan said. "Just wait until you see me move on him."

"Let's do this, then."

Fagan slipped off to a table. He picked the one closest to the bathrooms. When his beers arrived a moment later the big man chugged one down in a single pull, belched into his fist, and rose to walk toward the bathrooms. Sullivan smiled at the act. When Fagan got to the bathroom, he stumbled and bumped into the poorly concealed bodyguard. When Fagan jostled someone, just remaining upright took all of one's attention. Sullivan used the distraction of Fagan's effusive apologies to slip into the alcove where their prey was enjoying his session with the dancer.

Sullivan walked up behind the woman. He took a moment to admire the geometric perfection of her waist-to-hip ratio before tapping her on the shoulder. When she turned to scowl his way Sullivan discovered that her face matched her body with its shocking symmetry and striking beauty. He did not have time to stare, though he felt his skin flush when they made eye contact. That was new and uncomfortable.

"Take a break, honey," he barked. It was rude and condescending and her face snapped into a mask of indignant anger. For reasons he did not understand, he wanted to apologize right away. This was also uncomfortable and Sullivan began to wonder just what the hell was wrong with him tonight. To cover his confusion, he pulled out his coin vault and showed it to her. "A hundred bucks if you go to the bar and grab us a couple of drinks, okay?"

"That's better," she said with a smile that hit Sullivan's guts harder than a heavyweight contender. She held up her wrist where an electronic bracelet blinked in expectation. Sullivan tapped the vault to the wristband to transfer the money and she climbed off her customer. "I'll be right back, Saul."

Saul was looking at Sullivan the way small children looked at boiled vegetables. "Sure thing, baby. Make mine a Manhattan, would you?"

"Sure thing," she said as she stepped back into a shimmering green sleeve dress. Sullivan refused to stare at her body, but it was as if his eyes were not connected to his brain anymore. Some other organ directed his attention and she caught him doing it. With a chuckle like crystal wind chimes she moved off to the bar with a serpentine stride designed to hold attention. It worked.

When all parties were certain the woman was out of earshot, Saul gestured to a seat across from his. "Might as well sit. Who do I have the pleasure of speaking with?"

"John Sullivan."

"That sounds like a fake name to me. You care to tell me why the most gorgeous woman on the planet isn't naked and grinding on my crotch at the moment? Or do I hit my panic button and bring my security team in?"

"You mean the five amateurs too clueless to stop me from getting this close already?" Sullivan's snort of derision put a deep frown on the other man's face. "You just go ahead and ring your goons any time you want. But remember this, Saul..." Sullivan folded his hands on the table, incidentally encroaching on Saul's personal space. "If you do, I'm going to kill them all and break your legs for putting me through the hassle of doing it. You and I need to have a conversation. We can do it here over cocktails and surrounded by beautiful women, or I can drag you half-broken out of here and do this with you tied to a chair and your balls connected to a large battery." Sullivan leaned back and smiled like a hunting cat. "It doesn't have to get ugly if you don't want it to."

Saul tried to bluff, though it did not convince anyone. "Big talk for a man alone in a public place. Why should I believe that you are a match for my security at all?"

"Because it's not a fake name. I'm John L. Sullivan. In some circles, I'm pretty well known."

"Well, not in my circle obviously."

"I doubt that very much, but I'll play ball. Maybe my father's name will ring a bell then. It's Michael, but everyone calls him Mickey." Sullivan leaned forward when he saw the man's eyes grow a touch wider.

"So what does the somewhat famous son of Mickey Sullivan want with me?"

"Who is funding Corpus Mundi's chimera research?"

The muscles in Saul's cheek twitched. For an instant terror was writ plain across his features, but the counterfeit confidence of a salesman quickly reasserted control of his expression. His answer came with all the polish of a well-rehearsed performance.

"That is a serious accusation, Mister Sullivan. You are a GEED warden, yes? You should already know that chimera research is illegal outside of government contracts. Corpus Mundi has no such contracts."

Sullivan shook his head. "Come on, Saul. Don't do this dance with me. I'm not built for subtlety. You should know, your company built me."

Saul did not rise to the bait. "In any eventuality, Warden Sullivan, our investors value their secrecy very highly—"

"More than your life?" Sullivan interrupted.

Saul's recovery was smooth as glass. "More than Harry Hanson's, as you've no doubt already discovered."

"Did you order that hit?"

"What hit? I heard it was a heart attack."

The dancer returned with their drinks before John could lose his temper. Her presence had a calming influence on him, and the distraction of her shapely form cooled his rising irritation.

"Hey guys," she said with a smile that softened their faces and hardened other things. "Here are those drinks. Can I offer you guys a two-for, or maybe have another girl join us? I can get a special rate—"

She never got to finish her pitch. A tremendous crash from the main floor seized their attention, and the subsequent wall-shaking roar of an enraged Patrick Fagan told Sullivan that their cover was probably blown.

"Plan B it is," he said aloud. Then he lunged across the table and grabbed Saul by the throat.

CHAPTER FOURTEEN

The first sign of trouble came only a few sparse seconds after Sullivan had approached Saul Lewiston.

Fagan saw the dancer leave the alcove and go directly to the bar, and he had taken this as a good sign. Sullivan had a manner with women all his own, and when his mood turned amorous, his attempts at romance invariably went one of two ways. Either he got slapped hard, or he got laid. Fagan had never seen a third outcome, and he had watched that particular scene unfold often enough to consider it canon.

The first thing to go awry was the introduction of several more poorly disguised security guards. It was not clear to Fagan if Sullivan had spooked Saul, so he did not know if these newcomers worked for their mark or for someone else. The whole purpose of their foray into the club was to see if someone was taking out anyone who talked to them, so the possibility remained that these men belonged to the opposition. Fagan ground his teeth. If they were here to hit Saul, then whoever was funding Corpus Mundi had very good spies and very quick reaction time.

Indecision drove his teeth together even harder. He had no way to tell, and if he waited too long to move, Sullivan would be trapped in the alcove with little cover and no room to move. He watched the first group of guards, searching for signs of recognition. They appeared as put off by the new group as Fagan did, and the giant felt the first bead of ice-cold sweat roll down the back of his neck. The newcomers fanned out from the door to take positions around the main floor. Fagan scowled at the lack of subtlety. When five men entered the strip club as a group, they tended to sit down together. This was a social place. These men made no pretense toward blending in and sat alone at stools and tables that would give each clear fields of fire.

This was the second thing Fagan took note of. The new men were oriented for gunplay. He thought of his own department-issued 10mm pistol in the small of his back and wondered what was hidden beneath the smart black jackets of the new group. Fagan knew he was running out of time to make a decision. The original guards were making all the same judgments he was, and their own commitment to blending in evaporated like so much dry ice. The man by the bathrooms shifted over to get closer to the alcove, and the two men at the bar turned around in their stools to stare at the new group. The guard at the stage stood up and took a seat at a table right across from one of the newcomers. With no drink in hand he simply sat down and made conspicuous eye contact at his counterpart.

"Shit," Fagan mumbled to himself. There had to be sixty patrons in the room and at least a dozen dancers, and two squads of hired muscle were seconds away from shooting it out with each other. Fagan could not decide what to do, so he improvised.

With an expressive grunt he stood and walked over to the two men having the staredown. He stood between their tables, beer in hand and swung his head from side to side looking at both. When he was sure he had their attention he simply said, "Not in here, boys."

Both men looked up, bemused and irritated with the interruption.

"Move along, troll," said the newcomer. "This is above your pay grade."

"Oh, I think you're misreading this situation pretty badly, man," Fagan replied. "And don't call me 'troll' if you enjoy eating solid food. I'm gonna reach into my pocket to show you something. Don't worry, I'll go slow." With all the haste of a lethargic tortoise, the giant removed his GEED ID from his jacket and showed it to both men. "I'm on the clock, boys. As of this moment, you haven't done anything illegal. But you are about to, and that's not going to work for me."

One of the original guards curled a lip. "You're the big fucker who talked to Hanson?"

"I am."

He gestured toward the newcomer. "You figure who that guy is?"

"I suspect."

"So fucking arrest him."

"It doesn't work that way." Fagan kept his voice even, meeting the eyes of the newcomer with a level glare. "He hasn't done anything illegal yet. Right now, he's just another jerk in a titty bar." Part of Fagan hoped against desperate fear that the guard would get the hint. "Now, nothing would please me more than to have you idiots start shooting each other. But this place is filled with what the press likes to call 'hapless bystanders.'" Fagan shook his head. "That means I can't sit this one out and question the survivors."

The newcomer curled a lip. "Well, Warden, It looks like we got ourselves a little Mexican standoff, don't we?" His head tilted side to side, as if in deep thought. "Nobody wants the feds to crash our private little party, right?"

"Exactly," Fagan said.

"Problem is, troll, I heard that you and your partner aren't exactly on the reservation right at this moment. I hear you are all alone out here. No GEED support or nothing. Just two GiMPs out making trouble for their masters."

Fagan's heart skipped a beat. "You heard wrong."

"Did I?" The man seemed very confident. "I wonder."

The man's hand went for his belt line so fast his sleeve cracked like a whip. Fagan knew better than to try to out-draw him and simply kicked the table he was seated at. The hitman's weapon cleared the holster at the exact same moment the table collided with his chest. Man and gun spilled backward over the chair and crumpled to a heap on the floor. With a roar, Fagan was on the downed man and hauling his body skyward.

The main floor of Cabaret Nero dissolved into pure chaos. Nine men drew guns at once and quickly realized they had no clear targets and no clear shooting lanes. Positioning tactics became irrelevant as the battlefield transitioned from the orderly movements of drunks and dancers to the frenetic thrashing of close to a hundred panicked people.

Fagan degraded his captive's capabilities by sending his flailing body through a nearby tabletop. The cheap faux-wood cracked in a dozen places as the might of an enraged giant drove a two-hundred-pound man against the surface four times. Finally it shattered and left Fagan's improvised bludgeon in a sobbing heap among the detritus.

"Told you not to call me a troll," he grumbled as he drew his own pistol. "Bigot," he added then ran through the crowd to help Sullivan. Patrons and employees bounced off Fagan like ping-pong balls and he made the alcove in a few seconds.

Sullivan met him at the entrance. His left fist clutched Saul Lewiston by the throat, and the deep purple hue of his face told Fagan that the man had not elected to come quietly. Sullivan's other hand clutched his Hudson H10 in a white-knuckled grip. Fagan was sympathetic to Sullivan's aversion to guns, though he was glad to see another weapon on his side all the same. "Sitrep!" Sullivan snarled.

"Five bogeys, four tangos outside. Bogeys may engage the tangos if we leave them alone." He pointed to Saul. "If they see you strangling their principal, however..." Fagan shrugged. "Probably nine tangos then."

A voice from behind Sullivan called out. "I know a way out!"

Fagan looked and saw that the dancer was crouched behind Sullivan, using his bulk as a shield. She stood and pointed to the right of their alcove. "This way! Follow me!" She darted between the men and sped along the wall. Sullivan looked at Fagan, who shrugged back. "You wanna shoot it out in here?"

"Follow her!" Sullivan ordered. Fagan complied. Their path ran along the wall and beyond the bar. They ducked into the back of the house and Fagan realized she was leading them through the dressing rooms. He whispered a silent prayer of thanksgiving that no gunshots had rung out yet. He hoped nobody got hurt who had not earned it.

At the end of the dressing rooms an exit door stood clearly marked. The dancer was about to yank it open when Sullivan stopped her with a rough shove. He shouldered in front and cracked the door to peek through. Shots rang out and sparks flew from the door frame. Sullivan cursed and the woman screamed. Sullivan slammed the door shut with another expletive and hurled his prisoner away. Fagan found himself holding the sputtering Saul while Sullivan took Hudson in a two-handed grip, inhaled, and kicked the door open.

From Fagan's perspective, John Sullivan was not a large person. However, there was no denying he was big by any objective standard. This made it very easy for most people, Fagan included, to underestimate his speed. Fagan heard the rapid discharge of Sullivan's big pistol, and he knew the perfectly balanced sidearm in the steady hands of John Sullivan would be making quick work of the poor bastards in the alley. He also knew that Sullivan was prone to senseless risk-taking and often leaped into action devoid of a plan. He transferred Saul to his left hand and leaned out of the door, sweeping the alley with the gun in his right.

Sullivan had dropped two men already. His pistol spat orange flame as he sent burning lead downrange like a metronome. Two men disappeared around a corner while a grim-faced Sullivan stood behind an enormous green waste receptacle and ran his weapon dry. He dropped the empty magazine and slapped a fresh one in place in a quarter-second. The muzzle never even wavered and the pistol breathed fire once again. Sullivan moved and shot, charging down the alley behind his wall of hot lead. Fagan threw Saul against the dumpster where Sullivan had just hid and added his own covering fire to Sullivan's. Perhaps not the marksman his partner was, Fagan considered himself an adequate pistol shot. His rounds peppered the edge of the intersecting alley, sending the two men scurrying for deeper cover under a hail of bullet fragments and chipped mortar. Sullivan sprinted safely up to the corner and pressed his back against the cold masonry. He tossed a quick nod of thanks to Fagan and waited.

The pair had used this trick before. Fagan's suppressing fire had bought Sullivan maybe three seconds of free rein. Most enemies did not understand just how much ground Sullivan could cover in three seconds, leading to a false sense of confidence in long, narrow shooting lanes. More than once an enemy had found to their chagrin that a forty-yard killzone may as well have been forty inches for all the advantage it granted them. The two men in the alley proved to be no exception. The first stuck his arm around to return fire, assuming Sullivan was still in transit or behind any of the random dumpsters and junk providing cover. Sullivan reached out and grabbed the hand around the wrist and twisted it backward until it popped. He then dislocated the shooter's shoulder for good measure before dragging him out and breaking his jaw with a short chopping elbow.

Sullivan then disappeared around the corner for a few seconds. His return was heralded by a gurgled scream and the appearance of a flying man. Fagan understood that the man could not fly of his own volition, and as a gentleman of significant strength himself, he smiled in professional approval at the speed and altitude of the airborne gunman. Fagan could not extend that approval to the man's landing, however. He struck the wall at speed and slid down to bounce off the dirty curb. Sullivan re-emerged with a grim scowl and his last empty magazine in his hands.

"Clear!" he shouted back to Fagan.

"Move," Fagan said to Saul and the dancer. Both complied without complaint. While they caught up to Sullivan, Fagan turned and put his shoulder against the trash receptacle. Inhaling a huge breath, the giant threw his weight at the mountain of metal and drove his feet into the ground like twin pile drivers. With a tortured squeal, the two-ton hunk of grimy steel ground across the filthy concrete until it blocked the back door to the club. Fagan smiled at his handiwork before trotting up to join the rest of his group.

"Nice touch," Sullivan said. "You *are* back in shape."

"I know," Fagan agreed.

"Think they're watching the street?"

"Wouldn't you?"

"Shit." Sullivan looked down at his pistol. "I'm dry. Only brought two mags."

"Too bad those guys you just took out didn't have any ten-mike, huh?"

"Fuck you," Sullivan huffed, then began searching the corpses and quietly writhing bodies of his live victims. A minute later and he had topped off a magazine and slid it home with a click. Fagan had been searching the street while Sullivan re-loaded.

"Okay. The good news is that nobody wants a firefight where the grid can see it. Local MLEO is already going to be headed this way—"

"I can't get picked up by cops!" The dancer seemed more terrified by this than the gunmen.

Fagan smiled. "That's something we're all trying to avoid, miss."

"You got your own car, lady?" Sullivan barked.

"Yes?" Her answer was a small terrified squeak.

"Where?"

"Around the corner. Employee lot."

"Give me the key," he ordered. "You can run away now. Should be safe. They're not after you."

"Fuck you!" Now she sounded mad. "Everybody in there saw me help you! Besides," she jerked a thumb at Fagan. "Jumbo here won't fit in it anyway!"

After a moment of what appeared to be indecision, her facade of helplessness dissolved with the frustrated shake of her head. "Fuck it. Come on!" She yelled, "This way." She took off to the right, accessing the surface street at a fierce run. The men followed.

"The traffic grid," Sullivan called to her retreating back. "They're closing the street!"

True to his word, bollards were rising from the road, flashing blue and red to warn cars that the street was now off-limits. Sullivan knew that drones would be next, scanning and searching for suspicious persons not at all unlike their little group. Just past the bollards, the dancer turned to the right and raised her hand. It held some sort of device Sullivan did not recognize, but after a few seconds of frantic waving an automated taxi swung up to the curb.

"In!" she shouted.

Fagan threw Saul into the back of the passenger compartment and then shoved his own bulk in behind. Sullivan followed suit and then the dancer after that. The car pulled away when the door slid shut and the four escapees all took a collective breath. Crammed as they were into the back of the cab, Sullivan asked the question on everyone's mind.

"And how long before the traffic grid makes us and shuts this cab down?"

"Never," she said.

Her proximity filled Sullivan's nose with her scent, and it made his head swim. This irritated him, as his head never swam. Certainly not over women. He snorted a harsh breath to clear the offending scent, but it stuck like a thin film to the inside of his nostrils. Rapidly losing his patience, he gripped his pistol in a manner not entirely nonchalant and simply barked, "Talk."

The dancer met his scrunched brows with a look of pure disdain. She held the mysterious device out in her palm for Sullivan to inspect. "It's a bug-out switch." When this did not seem to register with the man she added, "It pulls a car and scrambles the occupant and location data for the ride. Right now the traffic grid can see the car, but whatever protocols it's operating under won't be applied to this car. So even though the block is on lockdown, the grid will let this car out and forget it was ever here. If the grid doesn't mark it, the drones won't either."

"Where does a stripper get something like that?" Sullivan asked.

"Where does anyone get something like that?"

Sullivan shook his head like a cat and snorted again. "Don't be coy, lady. I'm having a bad night."

"Maybe I'm not really a stripper. You morons ever think of that?"

Fagan groaned. "Oh what the hell is this, now? Who the hell are you, then?"

"My handle is Mata Hari, I'm an independent journalist, and you guys just blew my whole investigation."

"A raker?" said Sullivan. "Aw shit. That's all this nightmare needs."

CHAPTER FIFTEEN

"It wasn't a nightmare until you two boneheads showed up." She tried to lace her retort with irritation, and considering her aching head, this proved easy enough to do. "And don't call me a raker. I'm a goddamn journalist!"

With the SOAP crammed into one half of the passenger cabin, she found her body pressed between Lewiston and Sullivan on the seat across from the giant. Saul faded in and out of shock and consciousness with some frequency, and the giant sat poised to restrain him if the thin executive decided to try something stupid. An acute discomfort came with her proximity to Sullivan. Enough men had responded to her ample charms for her to be accustomed to the range of intensities she might expect. Even the secretions of the most susceptible males never really affected her own thinking. Sullivan, however, was giving her a headache. The quantity of androstedionone in his sweat exceeded anything she had ever experienced. As a by-product of sexual arousal, it served as a barometer for how well her own sexual weapons were functioning. In this case she wished she could switch them off because if her nose could be believed, Sullivan might pounce on her right there in the car.

I need to be very careful around him, she thought to herself. *If he makes testosterone at these levels, he might have impulse-control issues or psychotic tendencies.*

She supposed she could handle him in any case, but smart operatives stayed alive by being careful. She allowed a moment to reassure herself. *So far, so good, though.*

Her plan was working more or less as anticipated. The SOAP stood out as a wrinkle she had not anticipated. His excess human-growth-hormone levels and sheer mass were going to blunt her effect on him, especially if the acromegaly compromised his sinus cavity as it often did. He was still a man and she was still a beautiful woman, so she figured she would just manipulate him the old fashioned way if it came to that. Otherwise, they were on schedule and the men were buying her story wholesale.

Sullivan gestured with his pistol. "Lady, do you have any idea what your nosy ass is into, here? You think you got a nice juicy corporate scandal to sell to the rags or something?"

The journalist cover was one she had used in the past. Well-constructed and plausible, the identity served to get her past many of the gatekeepers she found in her career. "That guy is deep into illegal genetic research. I think he had an underling murdered over it. I was going to get him to spill it all."

"By showing him your tits?" Sullivan barked a harsh laugh. "This guy sees a hundred girls like you a month. If he isn't talking in his sleep to them, he won't sing for you, either." His face twitched, and then he added, "Even if your tits are nicer than most."

"Fucking hell, Sully," the SOAP groaned. The giant turned to Margaret. "Excuse him. He doesn't know how to talk to humans."

"Sorry," Sullivan mumbled. "I'm not myself tonight."

Margaret suppressed a satisfied smile. She already knew as much. "My plan was to get him back to a room, get him doing drugs with a stripper on video, and then blackmail him for more information. He's married. His wife would get half his wealth in a divorce, and that's the sort of thing that gives a girl like me a lot of leverage."

"That is a much better plan," said the SOAP.

"You think he'd incriminate himself?" Sullivan asked.

"No, but he'd throw someone else under the bus. A lead is a lead."

"Well, Miss Mata Hari," said the SOAP. "There's just a tiny little problem with your investigation."

"Yes?" She played along. She very much enjoyed this part. Assuming a role and playing it so well no one suspected had its own special thrill.

"Our mister Lewiston is part of our investigation, and it's all much bigger than a murder and some illegal research."

She deflected, playing the intrepid reporter trope for all it was worth. "I don't even know who you two are. You saved my ass in there, and you kept my lead alive, so thanks. But don't think you can put me off this case!"

"My name is Suds," said the SOAP. "And this—" he pointed to Sullivan "—is Sully. You don't get to know who we are because then people will try to kill you. We'd like to avoid that."

"Those don't sound like real names," she said.

"Neither does Mata Hari," Sullivan replied.

Only Margaret could appreciate the irony of this accusation. Her handlers at the academy called her that as far back as she could recall. It was the first name she remembered having and she liked how exotic it sounded. When she found out who the real Mata Hari had been, she decided she liked it even more.

The SOAP continued. "The point, Miss Hari, is that you are going to end up dead if you persist in this."

"Let me help," she countered. "I'm good at this, and I'm not eight feet tall or a walking pile of tactless muscle. Let me have my story, and I'll help you with whatever the hell your investigation is all about. We could team up."

The SOAP seemed poised to refuse, and Margaret prepared her rebuttal. It proved unnecessary, as Sullivan spoke first. "Not a terrible idea, partner."

She breathed an internal sigh of relief. The headache would be worth it if it kept Sullivan somewhat pliable.

Suds gave his partner a pointed look, then turned to Margaret. "Is there any point in warning you that this is very dangerous and that your survival is not guaranteed?"

"Not really," she said with a winning smile. Even a SOAP had to react to that.

"Your call, Sully," Fagan said. "I suppose we could use all the help we can get."

"Where's this thing taking us?" was Sullivan's cryptic reply.

"To my place," said Margaret. "Well, the place where I'm staying, anyway. It will be safe."

"Safe enough to interview our pal Lewiston?"

"Oh yes," she said with a smile. "This is not my first rodeo. I was going to let him snort coke off my ass, remember?" She winked and congratulated herself for the flush of heat she saw in Sullivan's neck.

The cab deposited them well outside of the downtown area. "Where the hell are we?" Sullivan asked upon exiting.

"White Plains," Margaret answered. "This section of the traffic grid has been down for a week. We're out of sight for now."

The men dragged Lewiston from the cab. He was awake and cognizant at this point, and his fear-widened eyes darted all around the dingy streets. Margaret saw his furtive movements and patted him lightly across the cheek. "Hey, Saul. Relax. Nobody here is after you, okay?" Her hand closed around his chin and held him in place. "But we all have a lot of questions for you. We are going to walk down the street to my place and have a chat. If you try to run, the freak with all the muscles is going to run you down and then the SOAP is going to stuff you into a pocket, all right?"

Lewiston jerked his chin away from her hand. "You are all dead, you know that?"

"Death comes for us all," said the woman. "But you first if you don't behave."

Sullivan dropped a hand on his shoulder from behind and spoke a single syllable. "Walk."

Lewiston walked.

He shuffled down the sidewalk with a sullen stoop to his shoulders and a dejected expression. Half the street lights were out, though he stared at each grid sensor with a fervent hope that died as each passed with no sign of alarm. In a few minutes Margaret lead them to a set of stairs that went below street level. At the bottom, she keyed a door code and let them all into a dim and musty apartment.

"Lights," she called out to the empty air. A warm glow emanated from strips in the ceiling and illuminated a sparse living area and tiny kitchen. "Locks," she added. The doors clicked audibly as bolts slid into place.

"Beer," Sullivan said, hope in his voice. Nothing happened. "Worth a shot," he mumbled.

"No butler systems in this neighborhood, muscles," said Margaret.

"Sully," Sullivan corrected. "Unless you want me to call you 'tits.'"

"I've been called worse," she replied. A sly curl turned the corner of her lip and she added, "Usually by better."

"God damn it, Sully," the giant rumbled. "Stop embarrassing me in front of the prisoner."

"Get him comfortable, boys," Margaret said to the pair and headed toward a door by the kitchen. "I'm getting out of this hideous dress." She swung it open to reveal a small bedroom. She turned to give them all a hard glare, and also a good look at her body while it was still barely covered by the flimsy garment. "No bullshit. We have an agreement, right?"

"We'll wait for you," Sullivan said.

I bet you will, Margaret thought to herself as she closed the door.

Inside the bedroom she paused to take a breath and clear her head. The magnitude of Sullivan's physiological response to her felt overwhelming. Yet, he was not behaving like a man smitten or in the throes of burning lust. She did not doubt the lust was there. He was sweating enough arousal by-products to set off a female gorilla. What she did not like to think about was her own sensitivity to the effects. The copulin in her sweat might be making him uncomfortable, but there was no way for her own systems to ignore the androstedionone in his. The awkward reality of she and Sullivan saturating each other with chemicals signaling fertility and sexual receptivity was that they were both hypersensitive to those same chemicals. Margaret now understood that her own heightened senses in concert with Sullivan's staggering testosterone levels made for a dangerous combination. She had not planned for this, and a bitter internal rebuke for her lack of foresight came unbidden.

This is dangerous. He is a borderline psychotic with obvious psychosexual issues we did not know about. Tread carefully.

The instructors at the academy had taught her that the offending biochemical reactions were easily dismissed if one remained cognitive. They caused urges at only the most basic levels of mammalian neurochemistry, with little tangible impact on the higher order brain functions. They could nudge a person toward attraction, but they did not manufacture one. However, with psychotics, a sexual obsession could turn violent without warning. She leaned back into her training and took comfort in that. She was a professional, and she could not deny that this sort of challenge was the best part of the job.

With a few deep breaths and an irritated toss of her hair, Margaret felt better. She had always known Sullivan would be dangerous prey. There would be no profit in whining about it now.

She grabbed a pair of black pants and a white tee shirt. Both were snug, though Margaret decided to eschew overt seduction in Sullivan's case. Something about his reactions did not feel right. He wanted her, yet he seemed adamant about pretending otherwise. This ran counter to her research. His proclivities with regard to amenable women were a known quantity and she had expected some kind of overture by now. It went beyond professionalism or goal-oriented tunnel vision. Furthermore, considering how strongly his body was reacting to her presence, he should be showing other signs of stress from the mere act of suppressing his desires. The normal signs of fumbling hands and loss of focus should be occurring on some level. Yet, other than some bad manners and a lingering eye, Sullivan appeared more annoyed with her than anything else. She decided to play this cool and subtle for the moment. The big guns could come out when she had a better handle on him.

With a quick examination of herself in the mirror, Margaret re-entered the living area. Lewiston cringed in an easy chair while Sullivan sat on a coffee table directly in front of him. Suds stood behind Sullivan with a look of cool amusement. All three looked up when they heard her open the door.

"Ready boys?" She asked it with a single arched eyebrow and her hands on her hips. Lewiston, despite his dire straits, ogled her proud chest and the graceful sweep of her hips. Suds nodded, his gaze appreciative yet neutral. Sullivan struggled to look her in the eye, though his face told her that he was determined to succeed. That was less than she was used to, but good enough for now.

Sullivan turned back to the terrified executive with noticeable effort. "I thought we might start with my original question, Saul."

The man looked back with blank eyes.

Sullivan prompted him. "Who is backing you guys these days? I know it's not Mickey. Who is picking up the tab for your little science projects?"

Lewiston tried to shrink further into the chair. "You know I don't know that."

"You know something."

"What do you want from me?"

Sullivan's eyes bored into his prey. "Account numbers. Names of players. Addresses. Anything that will convince me not to send you back to your masters in a very small container."

"It doesn't matter if you kill me. Hanson barely knew anything, and they had him killed just for letting GEED do an inspection."

Sullivan sniffed. "He was a weak link and they knew it. Something in his head was worth a hit. I'm guessing you know even more than he did. You talk and you get the chance to run. That's the deal."

Margaret had a character to maintain, so she added a mild tremor to her voice. "Wait, wait, wait. Nobody said anything about killing anybody!"

"You didn't ask," Sullivan replied without taking his eyes off the prisoner. "I'm not myself these days, and all the things that kept me straight are pretty much vapor it turns out." He gestured to Lewiston with his pistol. "This is a piece of shit who has been pumping out designer chimeras as part of a plan to supplant the Global Republic with a new corporate GMP ruling class." Finally, he looked to Margaret. "There's your story, Mata Hari."

Margaret let her eyes go wide, and the surprise was genuine. Sharpe had not mentioned a plan for global domination or armies of designer chimeras. It was not her place to ask such things or know such things, so she let it pass. "That does sound like the sort of scoop that can make a gal's career," she said after a brief pause.

"Either way," Sullivan continued. "I'll kill this piece of garbage right now and sleep like a baby tonight if it comes to it. If that's too much for your scruples, try to stop me. I'll understand."

"Or," Suds interjected, "Saul can just give us something to go on and we'll let him run. Then nobody has to die or worry about ethics or morals or stuff like that." Now the SOAP fixed his own gaze on Lewiston. It lacked the brooding malice of Sullivan's fierce glower, though it remained far from amiable. "I'm a pretty ethical guy myself, but I couldn't stop Sully from killing you if I tried. So I won't.

Do us all a favor and start talking, okay? This is stupid. Give yourself a fighting chance and help us out."

Sullivan raised the gun and pressed the barrel against Lewiston's head. "Or don't."

Lewiston's breath caught in his throat. The stink of his fear-sweat drowned out the smell of Sullivan's lust in Margaret's nose and she nearly coughed. There was no decision to be made, no bargain to be struck. Lewiston was going to sing and everybody knew it.

Finally the executive started to talk, and what he said made Margaret shiver.

"I can't tell you who they are. But I know where they are doing a lot of the research. We get product reports and testing protocols from all over, but one place always sends us testing packages with material we know is not sourced through legal means. We've had to run viability studies on genomes and packages that obviously came from wartime Pan-Asian research. Top secret stuff from wildly mutated stock."

"Like what," Sullivan asked, lowering the gun.

Lewiston slumped in the chair, resignation weighing him down like lead weights. "Berserkers, ogres, hybrids, shit like that. But mutated or manipulated, not the original genotypes. They've been having us test stability and viability in both chimeroid and non-chimeroid DNA."

"Shit," muttered the big SOAP.

Margaret felt forced to concur with his obvious horror. Then she noticed something else that sent a shiver of cold fear up her spine. Sullivan no longer smelled like a man fighting with powerful urges. The pervasive sea-salt tang of androstedionone tinging the taste of his sweat faded to nothing. Worse than that, she found she could not detect any sweat at all. It was like Sullivan's body had flipped a switch and stopped feeling anything. The tension in his shoulders and the set of his jaw spoke to anger and resolve, though neither came with any heat or intensity.

It appeared that Suds had noticed something too. "You with us, Sully?" The question was asked with more concern than fear, though the giant's own sweat reeked of acute apprehension.

Sullivan did not answer. The pistol in his hand snapped up to re-take its place against Lewiston's forehead. When he spoke, the sound that came from his mouth was neither loud nor angry. Nevertheless the single uttered syllable seemed to drain the color from the room and send the temperature plunging.

"Where?"

CHAPTER SIXTEEN

"It appears the bait has been well and truly taken, Mickey."
Malcom Hargrave contemplated his cigar as he said it. It was long and fat and dark brown. It smelled like autumn leaves and old leather. Hargrave approved of the heft and aroma, and with a motion well-rehearsed he clipped the end with a guillotine cutter and clamped it between his teeth to light it. After a few perfunctory puffs to get a good ember going, he looked up to his employer for a reaction.

Mickey sat in a huge leather chair behind an enormous desk. A bank of monitors stood to one side and the mobster tapped absently at a keyboard while perusing each through a pinched expression of absent interest. Sunlight flooded the spacious office through enormous windows behind the mobster. Beyond the windows, the rolling green of an expansive lawn stretched out for what looked like miles. Despite his insistence to the contrary, Hargrave knew that prison life had not been to Mickey's liking, and now he preferred to surround himself with natural light and plenty of open space.

"I told you they'd bite," Mickey said after a few seconds. "And it's about goddamn time. Prison may have been a safe place to hide, but holy shit I lost the ability to ride these idiots toward the finish line. I didn't think they'd be this far off track, but whaddya know? It looks like they've been up to a ton of weird shit since I went inside. No wonder they want me dead. I was the only thing keeping them on-task. It's like herding cats with these fuckers."

"John grabbed one of their product development executives from Cabaret Nero last night. You remember Saul Lewiston? He won't know anything, but it looks like the desired message is being sent. The board of directors will not sleep well knowing your son is out there sweeping up executives."

"Johnny's a good boy. After that shit with Coll, they got a real fear of him going on. It's a fear they needed, too." The mobster's tone swelled with fatherly pride. "Now they know that when you sic Johnny on something, you can bet your bottom dollar it's gonna get got."

"But is he reliable?"

"Isn't that what I just fucking said?"

Having worked for Mickey for many years, Hargrave recognized the warning in Mickey's tone. He held up a hand to placate his boss. "I mean, he's not doing this all that willingly. He might turn on us at any moment."

"He wants to save the kid. I'm giving him the chance to do it. I'm also feeding him a target to satisfy his need for justice or whatever. If you show Johnny an ass what needs kicking and a decent reason to go do it, that ass is as good as kicked. No question. He'll play ball for a while yet." Mickey looked up from the monitors and began to fumble around his desk. After a brief search he located a cigar of his own and set about getting it fired up. When he looked settled, Hargrave asked another question.

"Do you think John really has a sense of justice? Or is he just angry?" Hargrave remembered the old days. The days when John Sullivan was a child battling the demons of artificially enhanced anger and more strength than a grown man. People had been hurt, and the boy had never displayed anything approaching an appreciation for 'justice.'

"Oh, he does. It's always been a thing with him. He gets the maddest when he thinks something's unfair or somebody's getting over on someone. He likes things to be fair, because stuff that's fair is predictable. It helps keep him calm. When shit ain't fair, he gets agitated, and that's when he gets really mad."

Hargrave used his cigar as an excuse to take a moment to consider this. He had to admit that the analysis, though blunt and pedestrian, felt entirely accurate. Hargrave reminded himself in that moment that underneath the South Boston swagger and lowbrow vernacular, Mickey Sullivan possessed a criminal genius that defied all measurement. He did not know if Mickey acted the way he did to hide his intelligence, or if Mickey just did not care to elevate his appearance. It did not matter. Mickey was the boss for a reason. Hargrave exhaled his smoke and said, "I did not realize that, but it makes perfect sense. It must be very hard keeping a lid on his anger all the time, and having things be predictable and equitable is probably very calming. No wonder he went to GEED. It probably appealed to this sense of justice."

The mobster flicked ash from his stogie and pointed the glowing end at Hargrave. "We did that shit on purpose, Mal. What good is a sense of justice if it doesn't make you angry from time to time?" Mickey puffed. "Johnny's always a little bit mad. So am I. Shit gets done faster when folks are a touch pissed off."

"What I'm most worried about is all the injustices he probably holds you accountable for."

Mickey waved his hand to stop Hargrave's predictable lecture. "Yeah, yeah. Johnny thinks he got a raw deal from me. That's fine. Thing is, he doesn't know what a raw deal really looks like yet. But he will soon enough. When he sees what Corpus Mundi has been up to he's gonna get in a real bad mood. When he sees the whole picture, the real picture..." Mickey leaned back and took a long pull from his cigar. "Well, then that sense of justice will kick in good and hard. Mark my words, Mal. Johnny's gonna break that company like kindling, and I won't have to say a damn word. After that, he'll be on to the next juicy target I toss his way. Eventually, my enemies will be gone and there won't be any more targets left. It's why we had him made in the first place."

"No targets except you," Hargrave pointed out. "He won't stop just because your enemies are gone."

"By then, he'll have figured out that my way was right all along. Johnny wants justice, but he ain't no angel and he ain't stupid. When he sees what I'm building and why, he'll come around. Mostly because it's gonna appeal to his need for order and fairness."

"I hope so, Mickey, because even I'm a little scared of him. Everybody was calm and rational when they thought Coll would be enough to handle him. You were in prison so you missed a lot of the back and forth. The consensus was that John's mental issues were too severe to make him a match for Coll. Now, John has them all terrified. They'll kill him any way they can. He's not pliable enough for them."

"That's because they don't get him. They thought they could send a mad dog after a bona fide Sullivan fighting man?" Mickey snorted a harsh and unpleasant guffaw. "Coll never had a goddamn prayer. Now they know I was right and it scares them. Pliable? Fucking eggheads! You can't make a real fighter pliable. They ain't got the right wiring to be goddamn pliable! It takes commitment and drive to kick ass the way Johnny does. Johnny ain't never put his hands on a guy without already knowing how he needs it to end. He doesn't play with his food like Coll did because it's not a game to him. When Johnny gets it in his head to put somebody down, he puts everything else out of it. You don't try to control guys like that. You give them a purpose that aligns with your needs and you get the fuck out of the way." Mickey calmed himself with visible effort. "Pliable? Fuck that noise. Johnny ain't pliable. Never will be. Lions don't take orders from fucking hyenas, Mal. But he's sure as fuck point-able, though. He's dancing to my tune right now, ain't he? And all I had to do is let him think he was saving one lousy kid."

"So you really have no interest in the girl?"

"Of course I have an interest. I also have goals for the near future that won't benefit from the distraction of another multi-decade research project. She'll be around when I have the time and energy to go after her. Fuck, she's immortal. All she's got is time, right?"

Hargrave acknowledged that with a dip of his head. "Excellent point, Mickey."

"What's got me boiling right now is how quiet everybody's being. Corpus Mundi is acting real coy, when I know they got to have a hit out on me by now. They can't go to war, of course. I control GEED and that means I control the GiMPs. The others won't have that bit messed up by anyone. But man, my gut says they ought to be taking swings at me by now."

"Perhaps your political aspirations are putting them off? We've seeded the press with enough rumors about your possible run for a seat on the Genetic Equity oversight committee. If you were to die in a suspicious manner, the subsequent investigation would be quite thorough."

Mickey rolled his eyes. "You know how many ways there are to kill a guy like me that don't look suspicious?" Mickey held up the cigar. "I smoke old-fashioned tobacco stogies. I drink the better part of a liter of Yellow Spot most days. I like to fuck wild women of dubious moral character." He slapped his belly, not overlarge but far from trim. "And I eat whatever the fuck I want. If I had a heart attack tomorrow, nobody would fucking blink, Mal."

"We have your medical records from prison. Your heart is fine. Better than fine, really."

"I could choke on the olive from my martini."

"You don't drink martinis. If anyone finds you dead with an olive lodged in your throat, you can be sure people will point that out."

"The point, Mal, is that the kind of pro these dinks can get will make my demise look very un-suspicious. These ain't mobsters. Corporate crime has its own kind of professionals. We may use guys like Vincent Coll, but they still got Mata Hari, remember?"

"They won't use her. You already know everything there is to know about her. She'd never get close."

"We fucking built her to get close, Mal," Mickey sounded frustrated. "The bones of her face can be moved around, her hair can be whatever color she wants it to be with a buck and a half's worth of dye. She speaks nine languages, knows six different martial arts, and can bench 315. Do you know how many tools we had built into her body? She could walk in here butt-ass naked and kill us all before we knew it. Trust me Mal, if they send her after me, we're gonna have a bad time."

"Is that what you think they've done?"

"It's what I'd do. But you know what's really bugging me?"

Hargrave waited.

"She ain't here. It's been weeks. Where is she? Every day I'm out is another day I'm making moves on them. Corpus Mundi can't touch me openly. They know that. So it's going to be whoever the fuck picked up the tab when I pulled my cash." Mickey paused to frown at his cigar, now cold. He reached for his lighter. "I don't know. I suppose they might be using other assets. You ain't wrong that if anybody is going to spot Mata Hari, it's us. Normally I'd blame corporate decision-making bullshit for the delay, but I smell that new player's stink on this, and they don't seem like the type to get bogged down in board meetings."

"What do you want us to do?"

"For now, I gotta keep my dick out of weird women, that's for sure. Full scan on anybody who comes near me, Mal. The bones in her face will be a dead giveaway. There's shit in her hands and feet, too. It ain't metal so it's gotta be an x-ray or something. In public, I should be on a nice conspicuous camera feed at all times. Press, GEED, cops, whatever. They can still shoot me in the head from a half-mile away if they want to, but we know they can't take the heat of a public hit. The best defense is attention right now."

"We can do that," Hargrave said with a smile.

"I know you can, Mal." Mickey decided to change the subject. "Where's Johnny now?"

"Well, we know Saul Lewiston has disappeared, and I can't see Saul not cracking under the kind of pressure your son likes to put on. I thought for sure he'd get what he needed out of Hanson, but I guess the other team got Hanson first. Either way, Saul will only have one lead worth exploring. Which means there is a very high probability that John will be looking for Camp Zero."

"Good," Mickey said with an approving nod. "If he gets there, you can bet your ass what he finds is going to send him in exactly the direction we want him going."

Hargrave's face split into a grin suffused with professional awe. "You really do have him dancing, don't you?"

Mickey smiled back and pulled from his re-lit cigar. He sent blue-gray smoke toward the ceiling with a long breath and put both feet up on his desk. "Don't you ever fucking doubt it, Mal." Then, shaking his head slowly, he added. "Pliable my fat Irish ass."

CHAPTER SEVENTEEN

Sullivan and Fagan sent Saul Lewiston packing once the sun came up. The skinny executive looked a haggard mess. Hollow-eyed and rumpled, his departure from the mysterious Mata Hari's apartment was a sad and pathetic affair.

"Over-under on him being dead is twenty-four hours," mused Sullivan out loud.

Fagan nodded into the burgeoning dawn. "I'll take the under for a hundred. You see him on his phone? First thing he did was check his accounts. Moving money around so he can run. Rookie mistake."

"Yeah, but he's rich. Rich folks can cover distance fast. He'll get a ways before they catch up. I think he's got a real shot at forty-eight if he stays off the traffic grid and out of nice hotels."

Fagan shrugged. "We'll see, then."

Sullivan turned to head back inside. "You figure he'll call in a hit?"

"What's one more contract on you? Besides, he'll need the money to run. He won't bother."

At the bottom of the stairs the two men considered their other problem before going inside.

Fagan wiped his face with a thick hand. What are we going to do about this raker, Sully?"

The question made Sullivan uncomfortable. "I don't know. She's not letting go of this, and unless she's a total dingbat, she has probably figured out who I really am by now."

"You okay, Sully? You look flustered."

Sullivan tried to hide his discomfort with irritation. "I'm always flustered. Come on, man."

Fagan's answering snort told Sullivan he was not fooling his partner, and he supposed the giant had a point. Ever since meeting the woman, a fuzzy haze obscured his thoughts. Her presence confused him. Women were a pastime, a welcome distraction from his stormy disposition. Never did his pursuit and enjoyment of the fairer sex interfere with his focus. *Almost never,* he corrected himself. Something about Mata Hari was burrowing under his skin and he did not like it. His lust for the woman would have been nothing special except he could not shake it. For his whole life he wore aggression like armor, uncomfortable yet protective. Now the familiar heft of his anger turned soft and permeable. He felt exposed around her. Naked. The only thing that kept him from acting on the urges inside was how much their very existence irritated him. A fierce tug-of-war between anger and lust thus ensued, and the distraction maddened the man to his volatile core.

He stopped Fagan from opening the door, not wanting to say what came next where the woman could hear it.

"My head isn't right."

"I know. I can tell. You gonna be okay?"

"Am I ever?"

"Is it the woman?" Fagan's concern was clear. "I've never seen you flustered around a lady before."

"It can't be. I've been... changing lately. My brain is, I don't know... figuring shit out differently. Maris says it's growth, but I can't say I agree with that just yet."

"Maybe you're human after all. Girls that hot have been messing guys up for millennia. Maybe you're just hitting that special age..."

John Sullivan expressed his opinions in the same manner he did everything else in his life. Which meant his response to Fagan's idea was delivered entirely without tact.

"No fucking way."

A few hours later, this sentiment got repeated when the three considered their next move. Lewiston's revelation of the mysterious 'Camp Zero' left little doubt as to where they had to look next. Fagan's plan for getting inside, however, left much to be desired.

"No fucking way," Sullivan had reiterated through a mouthful of garlic bread.

He supposed that this was entirely too blunt to be helpful to anyone, so he amended himself. "We walk you in there, and they'll descend on you like piranhas." For emphasis he popped a meatball into his mouth a chewed it as if it had offered him personal offense.

Fagan, as was his way, deflected Sullivan's poor manners without acknowledging them. "Piranhas don't actually do that, you know—"

"—Yes I fucking know!" Sullivan barked back to his giant partner. "That's not the point. We can't just waltz a warden in there! Especially the extremely recognizable sasquatch-looking warden ex-partner of the guy who's all up their ass at the moment." He shook his head and curled a lip. "Even a total idiot would suspect you."

"They can suspect all they want, Sully. I'll have official paperwork from Captain Horowitz. They pull any shit and they're going to invite a GEED crackdown. Since your dear old pops owns GEED, that should force them to behave."

Mata Hari chose this moment to speak up. "So you are *that* John Sullivan? Figures."

Sullivan slapped Fagan with a withering glare, and the giant had the presence to look down at his food in shame.

The woman went on. "And they might behave..." She picked at her own chunk of bread. "Unless they don't care. This 'Camp Zero' place isn't even supposed to exist, right? It's a decommissioned military base. If there's some weird people using it to do super-illegal genetic experiments for Corpus Mundi, then the whole GEED problem may be something they're willing to risk. If Suds starts waving search warrants around places like that, it just might set them off. They've been offing their own for a lot less than that lately." After a pause she pointed to the bowl of meatballs in the middle of the table. "If I try to grab one of those, are you animals going to stab me with a fork?"

"I'll distract him," Fagan said with a wink. "You go for the grub while he's attacking me."

"There's another bowl coming," Sullivan told her. "Eat all you want."

"Look at big bad Sully being a gentleman," Fagan said, narrowing his eyes at Sullivan. "You sweet on the raker, partner?"

Sullivan considered this while reconsidering ever confiding in Fagan again. He decided it was nice to have someone arguing his side for once. "I'm never sweet, but she's not wrong on this, partner."

"Yeah, maybe 'sweet' isn't the right word for it," Fagan fired back, rolling his eyes.

"I'm still here, boys," Mata Hari said, snapping her fingers. "And don't get any ideas, muscles. I'd ruin you for other women." The two made eye contact across the table, and it held a heartbeat too long for anyone's comfort.

Fagan cleared his throat. "With regard to our little infiltration issue. Do either of you have a better idea?" He held out his hands in surrender. "As Miss Hari has just mentioned, this site is a literal fortress. Not even you could shoot your way in, Sully." He looked to the woman. "And I don't see your press credentials getting you any further than Sully's sparkling personality."

Sullivan had no answer for this. Storming the site was out of the question. He would never make it past the third security checkpoint. Fagan was also right about chances of infiltration. His physical appearance made blending in difficult, and it was no secret he lacked the imagination for effective roleplay. His jaw flexed in frustration.

Fagan smiled. "Yup. That's what I figured. I'm not interested in dying either. So let's make a plan, okay?" A forkful of pasta disappeared under his mustache and he chewed it with a thoughtful frown. "We need Horowitz in person."

Sullivan jerked his head up at the suggestion. "For what?"

"Administrative pressure." Fagan wiped his mouth with a napkin. "She shows up, all official-like, right? Waving a warrant, but at the same time not-so-subtly implying that she is on the take and it's all gonna be okay if they play along. That gets her in without spooking everybody. We can have our little raker tag along, but it'll be Horowitz they watch. She's the captain. She has the ear of the director, who they all know reports to Mickey Sullivan."

"It'll be too tense for them to jump," said Mata Hari. "You think they'll keep it quiet and polite just to avoid a row with the Sullivan mob?"

"I think that is very likely, yes. You can't murder a GEED captain without people noticing."

Sullivan broke in. "Yeah, but you're both missing the real point. Even if you two get inside, there is no way you are getting into any interesting areas."

"Why not?" Mata Hari asked. "Suds just said they'll believe this captain is on the take, right? Have her say she's there to make the search look official and take pressure off. They'll show her whatever. It'll all be part of the dog-and-pony show. You can call me 'raker' all you want, but when I want to find something, I know how to dig it up."

"I thought you were on my side."

"That was before Suds made his idea better."

Sullivan surrendered. "Fuck it. Call the captain then. But Suds and I are staying on overwatch. If shit looks sketchy, we're coming in after you the old-fashioned way."

"My hero," she crooned with batted eyelashes.

"I'm nobody's hero," Sullivan muttered through a mouthful of meatball. "You can ask Horowitz if you don't believe me."

"Who is this Horowitz to you guys?" she asked.

"The only woman to break Sully's heart," Fagan said, his face beaming.

"The only thing she ever broke was my balls," Sullivan fired back.

The woman called Mata Hari sank her teeth into a meatball, sending the shattered pieces back to her plate with a wet splat. She winked at Sullivan, "Same thing, I hear."

A heat rose up the back of Sullivan's neck, threatening to bring a humiliating flush to his cheeks. Thankfully, the sharp lance of irritation drove it back down where no one could find it. His eyes went cold and he watched the woman finish her meatball with a frosty detachment more akin to his normal manner.

The icy grip of truth clutched his heart like a vise. He needed to stay away from this woman. Whether she knew it or not, she was dangerous to him. Some parts of his brain loved what she was doing to him, though a great many others hated it. It was clear that a wiser John Sullivan would run far away from her, though he was equally certain that he was going to do the opposite.

He wondered if that was his fault or hers.

CHAPTER EIGHTEEN

Margaret shifted in the cracked synthetic leather seat of their official GEED transport. The last leg of their trip would take them from the sprawling post-war metropolis of Anchorage north to the depths of Denali. The last forty miles would be along the old State Route Three. Once a twenty-lane thoroughfare transporting tons of supplies and personnel to the Continental Air Defense Center, the highway now served only the occasional tourist bus or auto-mated supply hauler servicing the research and hunting stations that still peppered the frozen north.

The first few hours of the journey had been easy enough. A few hyperloop stops took them to the Anchorage Metro. They met the captain there and Margaret's hopes for an uneventful trip north evaporated within seconds of the doors closing.

Margaret did not like Elaine Horowitz, and the feeling was mutual.

Trapped in a ground transport together and separated from the driver's compartment, the women were forced to feel each other out with no prying eyes to bother them or provide a cooling presence. The first thing Margaret noticed was that the GEED captain was as hard as flint. She wrapped her tall and lean body in a black suit that hid her shape behind a solid wall of darkness. Her hair was dark and short, her shoes sensible. Every part of her screamed 'business first' to the rafters and beyond. She spoke with a flat acerbic bite to her words that brooked no arguments. This was a woman accustomed to command. It reminded Margaret of her instructors at the academy, souring her impressions further. She stared at Margaret for the first half of the ride in stony silence, an inscrutable expression on her face. Margaret tried to engage in small talk, leaning into her role of hard-nosed reporter on the hunt for the big story.

After ten minutes, it became clear the captain was not buying any of it.

"Mata Hari?" Horowitz spoke her handle as a question. "Really?"

"What about it?" She tried to make it a challenge.

"You know what happened to her, right? She ended up playing too many sides at once. She got betrayed by one side and executed for treason by the other." Horowitz squinted into Margaret's face. It felt like the captain was looking right through her disguise and into her soul. "I hope you aren't playing too many sides with Sullivan." A small, mean smile teased the corners of her mouth. "He's not like other boys."

"I'm not playing with anyone, Captain. I'm a journalist—"

"Sure you are," Horowitz dismissed the claim with a wave of her hand. "Whatever your angle, stay clear of him and what he's doing. For your sake."

"Worried I'll break his heart? Is this the scary big sister routine?" It was a cheap shot and a weak play, but Margaret needed an edge and wanted to see the woman react to the accusation.

"I'm worried you'll disappoint him and get yourself killed. I saw him look at you in Anchorage. I saw you look at him. Whatever you are up to, it's more dangerous than you realize." Horowitz twirled a finger in a circle while rolling her eyes. "Fine then. Maybe you are a journalist and maybe you're just another hot young thing mesmerized by his pecs and that awful broody charm he thinks is cute." The flinty stare returned and she dropped her hands to her lap. "But I'm not buying it. You're on a graft of some kind." Horowitz let her eyes wander over Margaret. It felt like standing in front of an infrared heater. "It doesn't matter, really."

"It doesn't? If I'm really a liar, why not tell him?"

"As long as it doesn't affect his work, I don't care what you are. My first guess is that you are a spy for his father. You fit the mold."

Margaret was not sure if the characterization bothered her or not. She shrugged her indifference. "Me, work for the mob? Hah! Why not make me an assassin, then?"

"You've had a dozen chances at him already. Have you slept with him yet?" Horowitz raised an eyebrow. "No. You haven't."

"Have you?"

The Captain laughed out loud. That was all the answer necessary and all the answer she gave. "No, Miss Mata Hari, you don't want him dead. You'd have tried it by now. No, you are after something else. Like I said, as long as it doesn't keep him from doing what he has to, it won't matter."

"That's not a very protective stance for the big sister routine, Captain. Not convincing at all."

"John doesn't need my protection. John Sullivan is a weapon un-to himself."

Now that was something Margaret could agree with. She smiled back at Horowitz. "That explains your attitude quite a bit. You probably got to swing that weapon around quite a bit, huh? You mad because someone took your favorite toy away?"

This shot landed. Horowitz lost control of her placid expression for just a moment, and something like guilt flashed before she could recover.

With the upper hand hers, Margaret cooled her temper. Her eyes traveled down the lapel of the boring black suit to rest on the pistol at the captain's hip. "Ever use that thing, Captain?" she asked. She allowed a touch of her own ferocity to reach her eyes. "Or do you just wait for the GiMPs to fight your battles for you?"

Horowitz must have recovered, because she actually smiled at this. "What? This old thing? Not today, anyway." She gave the weapon an affectionate pat, and her expression turned to steel without a so much as a twitch. "But it's early yet."

Margaret smiled right back. "Don't be in a rush, Captain." She pointed to the captain's right pants pocket. "As long as you have that little panic button, you can have the big strong men to pull you out of the fire any time you want. Is that how it usually goes?"

"If I have to push that button, little girl, I promise that you will be glad I did. You still think Sullivan is a game to be played, or a puzzle to be solved. That's why I'm not worried about your real motives. You are so far behind the curve you'll be lucky to survive when it all goes sideways on you." Horowitz stretched and crossed her legs. "If Fagan and Sullivan have to come crashing in to pull us out, you can bet your round little ass that things will be well out of your hands."

Margaret's calm returned. The woman was clearly trying to rattle her, and to her credit it almost worked. For an instant Margaret kicked herself for relying on her wiles for so much of her career. All the copulin in the universe would mean nothing to a woman like Horowitz. The captain would have been formidable under any circumstances and not having an unfair advantage had taken Margaret off her game. Once again seated within the calm of professional detachment, Margaret soothed her bruised ego. She could kill the captain whenever she needed to, if it came to that. It probably would. Horowitz reported to the director of GEED, who reported to Mickey Sullivan himself. There might be conflicts there best avoided.

The car lurched and interrupted the growing tension.

"Just went to manual drive," Horowitz said. "Always makes me nervous."

"With what we are about to get into, self-drive is what makes you nervous?"

"I can handle the flunkies at this Camp Zero place," said Horowitz. "It's the things I can't control that make me anxious."

"Like me?"

Horowitz acknowledged this with a tip of her head. "Among other things."

As Horowitz fell silent once again, Margaret affixed a bored look on her face and stared out the window. Inside, her thoughts were a churning soup of conflicting impressions. This job was far more dangerous than she had planned for. Getting Sullivan pointed at Mickey and mad enough to kill should have been easier than this, yet it was proving a far more complicated thing than she was accustomed to. Simple seduction she had already abandoned. Getting Sullivan into bed would not have been so hard had she wanted that. Now that the hook was set he would be an easier mark than most. However, the mere act of doing so offered no advantage. Lust usually clouded a man's mind to consequences, and nursing an attachment would give her influence over his decisions. But it did not appear that Sullivan could form the sort of attachments she needed him to, and a lifetime of elevated testosterone had inured him to the folly of lust. He thought of sex partners as disposable tools, like a back scratcher or dental floss. Items to be employed until satisfied and subsequently discarded. Because he was a fool, he did not realize the actual cause of his callous opinions towards physical intimacy. Margaret had studied the psychology of sex extensively, and the answer was plain as sunrise. His own cherished sense of self-loathing made him contemptuous of any woman willing to have sex with him. The behavior coincided with his proximity to psychopathy in a pattern well known to Margaret. It was a situation she had brushed up against more than once in her career.

She needed to switch tactics, and the infiltration of Camp Zero seemed like a gift-wrapped opportunity to try another approach. The introduction of Elaine Horowitz was a wrinkle she did not appreciate, but like all obstacles, the good captain could be overcome with the right plan.

A plan Margaret had already set in motion.

The gates to Camp Zero proved no obstacle at all. With a ream of GEED paperwork fully in order, the gate guard had no choice but to usher them to a reception lobby for security checks. A full-body scan was called for, but Horowitz had the credentials to refuse and Margaret's surreptitious calls to Victor Sharpe ensured that she too avoided the kind of scrutiny that might reveal the assorted tools hidden inside her body. A handheld scanner beeped annoyed protest at the presence of the captain's pistol, but otherwise nothing else set the little device off and they were led deeper inside the compound. In a well-furnished but otherwise boring office they met Doctor Brendan Calloway. A nervous and garrulous old man of some height and little hair, his obvious discomfort with the presence of a high-ranking GEED official filled Margaret's nose with the sour stink of abject terror. A man like him would never see daylight again if GEED found out what he was up to in the bowels of the abandoned military base, so this was to be expected. Margaret approved. The doctor was acting normal and that meant he suspected nothing.

Horowitz deftly put him at ease with several oblique references to GEED's unique relationship with Mickey Sullivan. Convinced that he was not about to be hauled off in chains, Calloway relaxed. Soon Horowitz had the man chatting about the work done at Camp Zero, and then convinced the administrator to show them around the laboratories. Margaret allowed for a small degree of silent approval at the captain's skillful manipulation of the man. Horowitz never broke a sweat, never flinched. Margaret began to wonder if the woman was even capable of getting flustered.

That changed when they reached the lower levels.

Margaret thought she was prepared for the types of things they might find. Genetic manipulation was the next great scientific frontier, and progress always came with a price. How high a price, she had never put much thought into. When the dark realities of the brave new world began to reveal themselves, even the grim operative found herself shaken.

The first signs of the captain's unshakable calm cracking came when the trio found themselves overlooking a large open room from an elevated viewing booth. A team of technicians manned several computer stations, and large screens scrolled with data couched in jargon Margaret did not understand. Horowitz gripped the sill with trembling fingers, though her voice stayed calm. If not for the subtle aroma of stress just barely wafting her way, Margaret might not have noticed her rising agitation. "And what are we looking at, Doctor?"

What Margaret saw below was two groups of what looked like Neanderthals engaged in a horrific war game of some kind. Naked except for vests in either red or blue, the things were fighting furiously over a raised platform in the center of the room. Several unmoving forms from both sides lay still on the floor while their brethren brawled with bare hands and bared teeth over nothing that Margaret could see.

Calloway stood with his white tablet computer in front of his eyes. "This lot is part of our refinement efforts on Pan-Asian swarm troops."

Horowitz nodded, brow furrowed. "Those were only superficially effective, though. I thought once we deployed unmanned area-denial systems swarm tactics lost their popularity."

"The concept of 'human-wave' style assaults with low-intelligence, high-durability assets was never truly abandoned by the Pan-Asian alliance, Captain. A single swarm trooper cost a fraction of what our drones did. Until we started killing them at a rate of twenty-to-one, the swarms were still a serious threat to our ground forces."

"So what is the purpose of this research, then?"

Calloway swiped across his tablet before answering. "Our investors are exploring the possibility of using improved versions to pursue search and destroy operations where target prejudice can be extremely high."

"And they need to be improved for this?"

Calloway nodded. "Well, yes. A normal swarm trooper is little more than a play at atavism. They actually turned the evolutionary clock backward to produce individuals with greater bone and muscle density, minimal intelligence, and rapid maturation intervals. The building blocks already exist within the human genome, so the product, while rudimentary, proved adequate. With just enough training not to shoot themselves, they would be pumped full of aggression-enhancers and dropped into a combat zone to run amok."

"I'm familiar," Horowitz said, her voice tight.

"For our purposes, we need a more intelligent product. That means less atavism and more manipulation. We can produce a very good swarm trooper, which is cheap and easy. We can produce a very good soldier, but that is difficult and costly. We still haven't figured out how to do both at the same time." He pointed to the brawling mob below. "You can see that this group still struggles with unit cohesion. They fight as individuals. We've tried to enhance their communications skills, but once their cortisol levels elevate, we lose the advantages. They revert to instinct."

Calloway's bland tone made Margaret's skin crawl. She could not say if the things below were human beings as she understood the term, but part of her knew that being pedantic about definitions did not change the facts.

"I see," said the captain. "Shall we move on?"

"Absolutely," Calloway said.

In the next lab, the smell of stress from Horowitz grew even stronger. Margaret began to feel a touch of anxiety herself. A giant man lay on a slab. He was restrained with manacles and leg irons that Margaret assumed could hold an elephant. She estimated him to be nearly ten feet tall with oversized hands and feet. He wore nothing but a paper gown which rose and fell with his slow breathing.

"Is that..." Margaret began, but her voice trailed off when she saw one huge eye open to look at her.

"I assume you are referring to an ogre-class GMP, Ms. Hari?" Calloway asked.

She merely nodded.

"In a way, yes."

The thing on the slab moved, startling everyone in the room. The overpowering stink of male sexual response clubbed Margaret's senses in unrelenting waves, so strong she could taste it. Calloway fired a sharp glare at a technician. "It should be sedated!"

"It is," said the terrified woman. "Something is agitating him!" Her pointed look to Margaret made it clear what she meant.

"Give it more, then!"

"Yes, sir," the woman blurted and scurried away to a work station.

Margaret cursed her inability to control her secretions. The ogre had not taken his eye off of her since she walked into the room, and a part of his paper garment was rising in a manner that had nothing to do with breathing. One of the devices attached to the thing beeped, and a glazed expression washed over its brutish features a few seconds later. Its head slumped back to the table where a single line of ropey drool leaked from one corner of its mouth.

"Now this one," Calloway said as if nothing had just happened, "is most promising. The introduction of gigantism on this scale had enormous ramifications on potential marketplace disruption. Specimens like this one," he pointed to the monster, "were less than ideal for combat purposes." The doctor looked up to parrot a common slogan left over from the great war. "There is no gene for bullet-proofing, after all. An ogre might be scary, but it's not terribly hard to kill one with a good rifle. But the enemy soon discovered that as logistics and labor assets, they are superb. This one has been optimized to run on fewer daily calories than anything previous, with no loss of mass or strength. He is currently at the upper limit of what a human skeleton can realistically maneuver within the constraints of the square-cube law." Childish pride rode with his every word. "It weighs more than three-hundred kilograms and can carry twice as much for several miles. It can operate at fifty percent total musculoskeletal capacity for six hours every day on a diet of only nine-thousand calories. Three of these can clear a landslide from a mountain road faster than any bulldozer for a fraction of the fuel cost." He looked back down at his tablet. "Currently, we are selecting for docility and pliability among the new models. The required elevation in various hormone levels leads to a tendency toward aggression and uh..." he glanced at Margaret. "Ah... shall we call it 'reproductive drive.' We are still dialing in the sweet spot for intelligence, too."

Margaret did not like to think about the implications of that last point. Neither did Horowitz, if her nose could be believed.

Calloway did not appear to care. "But you can pass it along to interested parties that things are going well. We might even be able to deploy prototypes within three years."

"I'm sure that news will be well received, Doctor. Is there anything else you want me to report on?"

"Absolutely, you simply must see what we are doing with the animals."

Horowitz let an eyebrow rise but declined to comment. Calloway brought them through another lab and down a long hallway. His incessant prattling about their various projects paused only once while he received a message on his tablet. Acknowledging the blinking icon with a frown and a swipe of his finger, he then ushered them into a small conference room and invited them to sit. "Please wait here, ladies, I just need to take care of one small issue then we can continue the tour."

After he left, the pair sat in uncomfortable silence. Margaret tried not to look at Horowitz while they waited. Her nose told her as much as she needed to know about the woman's state of mind and she found no fault in it. A terrible fear consumed the captain, and Margaret did not want her face to reveal just how much of that same fear gnawed at her own insides. Margaret's training and experience screamed at her to put aside the nausea and disgust scratching at the edges of her professional indifference.

I am Mata Hari. I do the jobs no one else can. I do not get to be squeamish.

Try as she might, the creeping horror of what she had already seen could not be swept aside. They had seen two of the secret areas below the surface, and she suspected she had only just begun to explore what Camp Zero had to show her. It could always get worse, and likely would. She hated herself for the weakness, but Margaret did not think she could take much more without showing signs of her own growing discomfort.

The sound of the door latch startled her, and her head snapped up to see who was entering the room. She half-expected Calloway to return, though finding someone else in the threshold surprised her less than it should have.

"Good afternoon, ladies," said a well-dressed blond man.

Margaret did not recognize the newcomer, but Horowitz must have. Her hand darted to her pocket, where Margaret saw her frantically thumb the panic button concealed in the lining of her pants.

CHAPTER NINETEEN

"How long have they been in there?"

Sullivan asked the question without thinking, and Fagan's reply conveyed the requisite irritation.

"Two minutes longer than the last time you asked me. Relax."

Sullivan could not relax. Their vantage point offered little in the way of visibility to the compound, and the extended radio silence from the women dragged across his nerves like an unskilled child sawing at violin strings with an un-rosined bow.

The ground was cold and damp, so much so that even through his cold weather gear he could feel the earth sucking the heat from his backside and chilling his bones. His eyes were glued to his AR binoculars, scanning the gray bunkers and guard houses of the re-purposed military base a half-mile away. He checked his own watch, unable to tolerate Fagan's non-answer.

"Seventy-one minutes. They were supposed to check in eleven minutes ago. Horowitz is all about procedure. She wouldn't miss a check-in."

"Unless she had to," Fagan said. "We don't jump until the second missed check-in." He shifted his own body to get some relief from the chill of the ground. "I'm not anxious to die today, partner. That's a whole base full of armed security."

"Not so many of them," Sullivan replied. "Maybe fifty guys at most, spread thin and manning internal checkpoints. This is corporate security, not military. They're set up to catch thieves and spies, not repel an assault."

"Only you could look at a force of fifty well-armed and en-trenched opponents in a defensible position and think the odds aren't too bad. Nobody is that good, partner. Not even you."

"I'm just saying it's doable. If we are smart."

"If we are smart, we will sit tight and let our two highly compe-tent assets do their jobs."

A persistent bleeping from their secure phones ended the debate. Both men made eye contact for an instant and then surged to their feet.

"I'm going high," Sullivan said as he affixed his earpiece.

"I'll go knock on the door," Fagan replied. "Don't ping her loca-tion until you are inside unless you want the whole place to know where you are."

Sullivan took off through the dense forest at a run while Fagan made his way to their waiting vehicle. A half-mile run through the woods might take Sullivan two minutes, a pace the quarter-ton war-den had no prayer of matching. Sullivan ignored the cold wet sting of branches and pine needles as they slapped him across the face. He kept his breathing low and regular, allowing the sudden spike in cor-tisol to trigger all the sympathetic reactions that would make him the fighting machine he needed to be. He no longer yearned for the re-lease of true anger or the intoxicating kiss of fear. He let his brain and body do what they had been built to do without conscious effort or desire, and within seconds he slid into the quiet, emotionless cold of pure purpose.

His heart rate never rose above ninety for the duration of his run. Bursting from the tree line on a low ridge running parallel to the exterior wall of Camp Zero, Sullivan slid down the muddy incline and sprinted for the fence. A low wall prevented vehicles from dri-ving through the chain-link barrier, and loops of razor wire glinted above to dissuade climbers. Sullivan made for the fence, hurdling the wall without losing speed. He pulled a small device from his pocket and thumbed it to life. When he reached the fence, he dragged the edge of what looked like a blunt knife along the metal weave in a wide semicircle. Sparks erupted and engulfed Sullivan in white motes and acrid smoke. Two more sweeps of his arm and a man-sized section of the fence fell away.

In the distance, from somewhere inside the huddled buildings, an alarm began to howl. Sullivan ignored it. "I'm inside the fence," he called into his team channel.

"Ten seconds out," Fagan's voice replied.

"I woke the neighbors."

"Don't you always?"

"Heading inside. Check in when you can."

Inside the compound, people were running back and forth to the tune of the alarm's insistent two-note wailing. Sullivan kept a wary eye out for security personnel as he ran for the largest building. Though not dressed like an armed assaulter, Sullivan's casual brown pants, rumpled gray shirt and dirty jacket marked him as a man out of place even if his physical dimensions did not. The scurrying masses parted before him like rats looking for dark corners. This suited Sullivan just fine, but it made it impossible to hide from security. He was yanking fruitlessly on a locked exterior door when the first uniformed guard careened around the corner to accost him.

"Stop right there!" the man shouted, one hand going for his holstered pistol.

Sullivan covered the intervening ten feet before the gun had cleared its holster. He put the guard down with a single right hand to the chin. Seeing an opportunity, Sullivan then grabbed the guard's keycard and identification badge. He wasted no time hoping the drooling man had any high-level access credentials, but keys were always helpful. Horowitz had made it clear that the real security professionals would be deep inside disguised as employees. The uniformed element of site security had no idea what was really going on underground. That reality and his criminally slow draw had saved the poor man's life. The keycard, however, did in fact unlock the exterior door. Sullivan disappeared into the laboratory building with only seconds to spare before more armed guards arrived.

Inside the lab, he found the hallway empty. With the whole site on lockdown, Sullivan surmised that most personnel were barricaded in the various offices and laboratories. What he did not know was how many secret plainclothes security professionals he would encounter in his search for Horowitz.

The lower levels would house the more sensitive research. The surface needed to be kept at least superficially legitimate if only to keep the site uninteresting to drone patrols and satellite passes. He decided to try not to kill anyone until he got below ground or encountered resistance that looked like a real threat. While the absolute innocence of anyone working here was probably a moving target, he found himself unwilling to add any more deaths to his ledger than completely necessary.

He sprinted down the halls, scanning signs and monitors for directions to the stairs. Locating them, he kicked his way through the locked door and leaped into a dark stairwell. Two flights down he detected the clang of a door opening and screeched to a halt. Two men ascended at a jog from below. He ducked back into the corner to wait and hoped they were not too much of a threat.

Sullivan's hand went to his pistol, but he resisted drawing it. When the first head appeared above the top stair, he put a single booted foot into the man's face. A carbine fell from limp fingers and the uniformed guard flew backward. Only the quick reflexes of his partner prevented a collision from sending both back down the stairs again. To his credit, the second man opened fire without hesitation. Sullivan had already moved, however, and the short burst sent copper-jacketed projectiles into the empty darkness where he had been hiding. Sullivan's boot flashed in the uneven light as his other foot whipped through the air. It took the man across the chin and sent him tumbling down to sprawl across the broken body of the first on the lower landing. Satisfied both had been rendered harmless, he pulled the firing circuit from their carbines and stomped the electronic widgets into fragments.

Assuming lower was better, Sullivan continued downward until he could go no deeper. From the bottom of the stairs, the landing opened out into a clean white hall. Sullivan swept the length and breadth of it with the muzzle of his Hudson before venturing forth. The alarm still howled and illuminated instructions meandered along the walls informing employees on what to do. Sullivan moved to the first door he found and swiped one of his stolen cards. The door panel switched from flashing red to glowing green and hissed open.

Inside, a half-dozen scientists and technicians stared back at him with terrified eyes.

"Where is the GEED woman?" His roared question tore squeaks from several of the squirming people. No one answered.

Sullivan raised his pistol and fired a round two inches to the left of a man's head. A monitor exploded into sparks and plastic shrapnel. Several people screamed and started sobbing.

"Where?" he shouted again.

Someone stammered a reply through trembling lips. "The pens! They were going to the pens!"

When Sullivan did not leave, the voice added, "Down the hall, take a right and go to the big green doors!"

Sullivan turned and left without a word. A small ember of righteous satisfaction burned beneath the permafrost of his emotional armor. Terrifying the scientists had not been strictly necessary. He could get a location on Horowitz via their encrypted team channel at any time, but these were willful participants in the horrible things going on in this place. Their terror was justified and he felt justified in causing it. The word that wafted through his head when he considered this was 'satisfying.'

Soon Sullivan discovered that "down the hall" meant nearly a quarter-mile of running before he found the right turn he needed. Two-hundred yards later and the doors were before him. He realized that the labs had to be connected via underground tunnel, because he could not fathom how he might still be under the main building.

The door had a screen flashing the same alarm instructions he saw all over, though a label beneath was marked "Zoological Containment." It yielded to one of the three keycards jangling around in his pocket and opened with a groan.

A wave of gunfire greeted him and Sullivan dove for the concealment of a reception kiosk. Three men in lab coats were peppering his position with sporadic bursts from several different models of handguns. Beneath the thick layer of his own neurochemical calm, Sullivan noted that he had found the secret security force. The controlled and methodical shooting from across the lobby supported this conclusion and left Sullivan scrambling to avoid shrapnel and ricochets. The desk offered little protection and he grimaced under a stinging hail of plastic debris. Sticking his head out would be fatal, but so would staying put. Taking a chance, Sullivan flipped the Hudson's selector to full-auto and let a long rip go directly through the flimsy cladding of the kiosk's front fascia. As suspected, the ten-millimeter bullets knifed through without difficulty. He could not see the enemy through the desk, though he knew which way to direct his fire to scatter the opposition. They dove for connecting hallways and the safety of thicker walls. This bought Sullivan time to improve his own cover.

From the kiosk he sprinted to an alcove formed by the intersection of the lobby wall and an adjacent hallway. This left one hall obscured, one with limited visibility, and one with clear sightlines. The clear one presented the best shooting lane, and the right shoulder and arm of a single enemy could be seen protruding from an alcove not unlike Sullivan's current position. When the guard peeked out with a single eye, it met Sullivan's matched expression at a distance of fifty feet.

The two men opened fire nearly in unison. Sullivan's Hudson roared with a five-round burst that drowned out the quieter attempt at a double-tap from his opponent. The guard missed cleanly, clearly rushed by the swarm of incoming projectiles. The fusillade from the larger pistol scored three deep gouges along the hall before walking the last two bullets across the guard's torso. He spun to the tile spewing two great gouts of arterial blood from his upper chest.

Sullivan did not watch him fall. He had already shifted to sweep the closest hall with the muzzle of his weapon. Another guard met this action with two shots that nearly blew Sullivan's arm off. With no more expression than a small frown, Sullivan served this man with a quick burst of his own that put two bullets through the offender's ribcage. The preternatural heightening of his senses warned Sullivan of movement to his right, and he dove without looking. Masonry and wallboard exploded over his head as the third shooter emerged from the hidden hall to aid his teammates. Sullivan landed in a prone position in the middle of the lobby. With no cover and no concealment, he remanded his fate to his training, genetic advantages, and the overwhelming firepower of his Hudson. He pressed his finger to the trigger and held it there. With the muscles of his shoulders and forearms locked against the rapid cycling of the bolt, Sullivan bored into the enemy. He forced the muzzle down and dared the recoil to raise it while round after round flew downrange. The pistol was well-made, with a gas-block system and counterweights to control muzzle flip. Still it tried to buck and leap as the burst went longer than both his training and the manufacturer thought prudent.

Sullivan lost sight of his target after the sixth shot. Muzzle flashes killed his vision, so he simply focused on keeping the front sight in line with the hall and putting rounds down range. When the bolt clicked shut on an empty chamber he charged. There was nothing stupid or suicidal in the charge. He knew the prolonged barrage would have either killed the man or sent him scurrying for cover. He had perhaps a full second to cover forty feet of lobby and hall before the target even recovered, let alone got a shot off. He burst into the hall like a comet, finding the man leaning against the wall with a mangled right arm pouring blood onto the tile. Another bullet had ripped through his guts, a third had pierced him high on his left thigh. The eyes were not dark, however. He lurched forward and tried to lift his gun, blood-covered and dangling from his ruined arm. Sullivan hit him like a freight hauler, felt the solid mass of hyper-dense musculature beneath the lab coat, and drove the GMP back into the wall with all his strength.

Even with the benefit of myostatin inhibition, the guard's wounds proved too severe for him to fight back with any real strength. His weak defenses crumbled before Sullivan's savage assault, and his resistance ended when a brutal throw drove his head into the floor with enough force to crack the skull. Sullivan did not care. He grabbed the man's keycard and kept moving.

He hurtled down the hall leading to the animal labs. As he ran, he called into the team channel. "You up and running, Fagan?"

"Had some trouble at the gate. Found my way to the main building but I've lost you in the tunnels."

"Look for the zoological containment area. That's where I'm headed."

"Did you ping? I didn't see a location."

"Got directions the old-fashioned way."

"Roger that. How's resistance?"

"Scattered groups of plainclothes pros on the lower levels. I downed at least one MINK, probably two."

"Great," Fagan said with a heavy sigh. "Map says I'm two levels above. You gonna wait for me?"

Sullivan considered that for a quarter-second. "No."

"Figures. I'm heading your way. Save some for me and don't get killed."

"Roger. Sullivan out."

The blinking monitors on the walls pointed Sullivan toward the Zoological pens and he ran. His senses sharpened with every second as his body continued to react to the rising levels of stress hormones in his blood. His limbic system grew quieter with each passing second, reducing fear and anger to pale shadows flickering across the wall of the dim room. The next patch of guards he took by surprise, having heard their barked instructions to each other from around a corner. Sullivan took two with a series of double-taps, missing only one member of the team. A single individual possessing obvious speed and agility enhancements managed to use his brethren for cover. He delivered a single shot in return before taking a ten-millimeter bullet to the face. Sullivan felt the hot pinprick of a bullet slicing into the meat of his upper arm and immediately dismissed the glancing hit as superficial. Past the knot of corpses he found a locked door that took three tries to breach.

Beyond that door, he paused. Even with his emotions blunted, what he saw stirred his guts with the sour burn of his rising gorge. The door had opened into a wide room. Cages were stacked in neat rows from floor to ceiling, and in each steel cube a horror stared back at John Sullivan. Human bodies twisted into strange shapes shifted from side to side while gnarled fingers clutched at the bars of their prisons. No two were identical, though most shared obvious signs of a common genetic heritage. Some had hair covering their naked bodies, others did not. Some were as large as Fagan, many were smaller than an average man. To a one, they were rangy and muscular. Their smell was a physical thing. Body odor and human waste mixed with cleaning chemicals and a powerful medicinal aroma. It stank like someone had crammed a hospital room into a barn, and then poured sewage on the floor. Heavy breathing and the clanking of metal on metal set a background noise only broken by the occasional tortured howl or guttural vocalization of frustration. A few tugged at metal collars or armbands, scratching at the red irritated skin marking their electronic manacles.

One aspect became clear as Sullivan looked at the dozens of creatures trapped inside this menagerie. From beneath the brows of each, their eyes sparkled with the glint of intelligence and sentience. A powerful urge to retch came over Sullivan. His own creators had gone to great lengths to make him the master of his emotions, and even at the height of his powers those eyes pulled something from the depths of his lizard brain and dragged it kicking and screaming through the black iron sphere of detachment protecting his brain. He did not know if it was anger. He could not say if he would even recognize true fury if he felt it. But his blood ran hot and cold at the same time, and the inside of his throat felt like he had tried to swallow battery acid.

A voice, calm and confident, shattered the shocked paralysis holding Sullivan in place. It boomed from hidden speakers and echoed through the cavernous warehouse like the call of some petulant god.

"Good afternoon, Mister Sullivan. My name is Doctor Calloway. I cannot begin to express how delighted I am to see you here! The opportunity to work with so fascinating a specimen as yourself is a rare thing indeed. Now, we have your Captain Horowitz, of course. You know that already. I suppose the next step is for you to come rescue her. Naturally, we cannot waste this opportunity to gather data by having you run roughshod over our security forces. Your performance so far demonstrates that there is no new information to be had there." The speakers clicked while the doctor paused. "But what we haven't seen is how some of our more promising prototypes stack up against a chimera of your obvious quality."

Sullivan did not think it possible, yet his mind sank to new depths of glacial antipathy. The sheer depravity of what he now understood was coming drove his cortisol levels to heights he had never known. He reloaded his Hudson without conscious thought and dropped his jacket to the floor."

He assumed the man in the speakers could hear him, so he looked up to the shadowed ceiling and forced strange words through lips pressed into a tight, thin line. "Don't make me do this." He had never asked for mercy or quarter before. "If you do this, I will find you and kill you."

The answer to his threat came in the form of a series of loud clicking sounds. The warehouse fell into streaks of competing shadows as most of the overhead lights blinked out. The shadows did not stay dark for long. Like rising stars at twilight, fifty collars and armbands lit up with red indicator lights, and the dim gleam of intelligence fled from the eyes of the caged creatures. A horrible racket of snarling and howling erupted. Steel enclosures rattled in protest as muscular bodies tore at the doors and slammed against the bars.

Then, with a squeal like a hundred enraged harpies, all the cages opened at once.

Laughter boomed from the ether. "Good luck, Mister Sullivan."

CHAPTER TWENTY

S ullivan could not feel anything at first.

This was normal. Doctor Platt had once told him that under stress, his right supramarginal gyrus 'over-represented' in his decision making. Most people paraphrased that to mean he became an emotionless machine when pushed too hard. The horror and stress he experienced during the opening seconds of the creatures' assault drowned beneath the cooling warmth of dopamine and the cold precision of acetylcholine. His pistol spat hot lead in glowing ropes without him even thinking about it.

Turning off the lights changed nothing. His night vision was excellent and the emergency lights were more than bright enough to serve his needs. Two hairy humanoids went down immediately with multiple solid hits to their torsos. A third fell to a gut shot rushed by a headlong charge from a fourth. Sullivan took advantage of the close quarters to dispatch that one with a single round to the face. He worked his pistol like a metronome, swinging the muzzle in precise arcs to place bullets into bodies with a precision only endless hours at the range could hone.

Then something changed. The red lights on their collars illuminated bestial faces under the weak emergency light in vermilion masks. The contrast of red and black highlighted the features as the rest of the body remained wreathed in the comforting obscurity of shadow. Sullivan could mark his progress by how many crimson faces lay on the deck with unblinking eyes, and something about that visual forced a single needle of doubt through his neurochemical armor. Another went down, shot through the chest and howling. For an instant, Sullivan saw its eyes open wide, marking the moment when it realized that death was imminent and all the fear and pain of its existence had been for nothing. The thing did not even know who it was fighting, *why* it was dying. Worse, it did not know why it had ever lived. Sullivan felt his respiration speed up, and the familiar cold trickle on the back of his neck grew warm and clammy.

He killed another. This time, he tried not to look at the face, electing to shoot it in the center of the chest. His eyes betrayed him, darted upward at the last second, and he again witnessed the light of life leave the eyes of the poor creature. For the first time in his life, Sullivan's hands began to shake. His cold detachment was melting, giving way to something fiery and uncontrollable. He wondered if this was true rage, or if he was about to have the psychotic break everyone was so afraid of. What he knew was that he was losing the control he needed to get through this.

His next shot missed. A shrieking gorilla of a thing distracted him and rushed his trigger pull. The round went low, throwing sparks from the floor, and the hairy anthropoid was upon him in an instant. Sullivan's strength beggared the abilities of virtually any unmodified human and most of the modified ones. It meant nothing. The creature took his blows without so much as a grunt of pain and battered Sullivan like an abusive father with a small child. A swat from a big right hand sent Sullivan sprawling to the floor. Lights danced across his eyes, obscuring his vision and allowing the misshapen horror to leap astride his body. With Sullivan's arms trapped under its legs, a giant fist ascended and the beast howled in triumph. Before the killing blow could descend, Sullivan twisted his Hudson against its inner thigh and squeezed the trigger. The bullet tore through the thing's groin and exited in a geyser of blood from the left hip. It screamed in pain and anger and more than a little fear. The red light from its collar painted the expression in gruesome crimson brushstrokes. For one long second the face stood against the darkness beyond like an impressionist's rendering of death's final triumph. Then all light left those eyes and the beast slumped to the side to bleed to death.

Sullivan felt pity.

The experience rocked him to his core. A million questions sprang to life in his mind, though did not have time to deal with any of them. More creatures were upon him. Dead-eyed and lost, he fired his gun on reflex and he killed things out of habit. The sense of dread and shame eroding his calm gathered strength with every pull of the trigger. Every slap of the backstrap against his palm was a recrimination. Every flip of the muzzle an accusation. Every corpse lying on the cold metal floor wearing a red-limned death mask was monument to his own failure and he hated it all so damn much he could puke.

The final monster he dispatched at point-blank range, gripping its throat in one hand while emptying the Hudson into its guts. With his nose two inches from his victim's, Sullivan closed his eyes to block out the sight of one more innocent creature slaughtered by his hand. When he had run out of things to murder, and murder was the word that stuck in his head, Sullivan collapsed to his knees and retched. It took a full minute for his bout of nausea to pass, and the eerie silence of the now empty warehouse asserted itself once the roar of blood in his ears subsided. Like water melting off an icicle, the calm that had been his companion his whole life began to cut through his mental haze in tiny frigid drips. He took stock of himself. Disheveled and on his knees, Sullivan realized he was soaked in blood. His ruined shirt was drenched up past his elbows and his pants liberally spattered with sticky red liquid. He looked wretched. In that moment of quiet, Sullivan understood that he hated himself, and that was new. He hated that the only solution he could think of was to kill. He hated how good he was at killing, because it meant they had to die and he had to live with the shame of making that happen.

Most of all, he hated that killing them was probably the right thing to do. He pulled a collar from a dead humanoid. As he suspected, several reservoirs of what he assumed to be aggression-enhancing chemicals lined the inside. Everyone from the last great war knew what those collars were for, and their existence here only confirmed his worst fears. He imagined this Calloway bastard with a coffee in one hand, throwing a switch from some safe place, and watching fifty helpless sentient beings turn into blood-thirsty monsters. Another thought wormed its way forward, cementing the need to kill this Calloway bastard even further into his agenda. The scientist had to have known Sullivan would win this fight. Fifty psychotic swarm troopers with low intelligence could be devastating with armor and weapons. Sending them naked against a genetically modified fighter with a fully automatic firearm amounted to little more than target practice. Calloway had killed them all just to collect the data on their performance.

Calloway killed them.

The thought burned like a beacon, casting welcome light in the direction of someone else to blame. Sullivan had pulled the trigger, but this doctor, this place, had caused their deaths. Sullivan needed this to be true, so he clung to it like a drowning man clings to driftwood.

Calloway's voice returned. "Well, Mister Sullivan, that was most impressive! To be honest our swarm troopers are still very much a work in progress. Shall we move on to something else?"

"Calloway!" Sullivan bellowed to the ceiling. "Stop this! You're murdering them for no reason!"

"Oh, Mister Sullivan, I think 'murder' is a very strong word. One doesn't 'murder' laboratory specimens. And data is always a good reason."

"They are people, Calloway..." Sullivan knew he was wasting his breath, so he let it drop. "Fuck it." He started for the other side of the warehouse and a door with a glowing exit sign. He turned his bare forearm to his face, and pressed the screen of his wristwatch. The word "ping" lit up in block letters and flashed for several seconds. Then an arrow and the number '126' filled the display.

"Hey, Calloway?"

"Yes?"

"Tell the captain I'm one hundred and twenty-six yards away and closing. As for you? You've got a little more than one football field's worth of space to stop me. Every one of your projects I have to put down is another minute I'm going to keep you alive before I kill you. You're at fifty minutes as of now. Keep that in mind as you flip your damn switches."

"I think that is a very ambitious threat for a man in your position, Mister Sullivan." Calloway's voice still sounded confident, though Sullivan thought perhaps a touch of uncertainty might have colored his reply. "Bravo on your hidden tracking device, though."

Sullivan stood and ripped his blood-crusted shirt from his back, leaving his undershirt on. He checked the Hudson for damage then slid his last magazine into the grip.

Thirty rounds and a little more than a hundred yards, he thought to himself. *Keep your head right and go rescue the captain. Kill if you have to, run if you can. Either way, this is on them, not you.*

He exhaled a long breath. He forced the tension out of his back and shoulders. He searched for the calm that made him so good at what he did. He set his jaw against fear and accepted his circumstances. Though it made him sick, he allowed his brain to do what it was designed to do without resistance. He had done this all before, yet this time something went wrong. Something else wriggled around his brain, disrupting the usual patterns and preventing him from settling into the cold darkness of perfect focus. He resisted the urge to chase it. Years of chasing his anger and fear had taught him that chasing was useless. This thing would get him killed if he tried to fight it, so he surrendered. He forced himself to *allow* it. To let whatever it was find its own place in the twisted emotional lattice of his mind. Whatever it was altered the baseline, changed what he was accustomed to. When he had the time, he might talk to Maris about it. For now, he let it be. It calmed, and so did he.

And then he ran.

He wanted to cover the distance as fast as possible. He hoped against fear he might avoid lengthy battles with whatever fresh horrors Calloway had waiting for him. Speed would be his tool, not violence. At first, it worked. He burst through the exit door into a hallway lined with monitors and offices. He streaked across the white tile at breakneck speed and paused to check his watch for the correct direction only once. Once oriented, he set to kicking down a locked access door he hoped would lead to Horowitz. It took too long to bash through the door, and Sullivan heard the first footsteps of pursuit just as he slipped through the opening.

He whirled and raised the Hudson, but paused at what he saw in the illuminated sight reticle. A man in a gray coverall sprinted his way. He was unarmed, which Sullivan found to be strange. Then the man leaped and Sullivan understood. Like a grasshopper the gray-clad GMP knifed toward Sullivan. The speed of the leap took him by surprise and both went down with the attacker on top. The man was strong, perhaps not as strong as Sullivan but far stronger than he looked. He fought without skill. Eschewing defense he struck over and over with hands and feet both. Sometimes punching, sometimes scratching and gouging, he snarled and huffed like a wild animal. Sullivan saw eyes with dilated pupils surrounded by a halo of swollen blood vessels. A bestial rage burned from behind those eyes. They were the eyes of a psychopath.

Not wanting to kill the thing, Sullivan closed his legs around the man's waist and clubbed at his head with the butt of his pistol. It opened a long cut over the eye which the wiry man ignored. Sullivan dropped the pistol and sat up. Levering the man to the side with his hips, Sullivan assumed a mounted position astride the man. Four quick punches ruined his opponent's face, but the thing did not stop fighting. *He can't feel pain,* Sullivan realized. No longer willing to waste time bashing at the thing, Sullivan trapped one of its arms against the side of its neck in a vicious figure-four grip. When he squeezed, blood stopped flowing to the brain and no quantity of pain resistance could prevent the trip to unconsciousness.

Rolling off, Sullivan's hand quested for his dropped weapon, only to find it being kicked away by a bare foot. The foot was attached to a thick, hairy shin that immediately rose to connect with Sullivan's face. Sullivan flew sprawling into a wall and the follow-up assault left him no time to recover. The newcomer was heavy with hyper-dense muscles and thick limbs. Naked except for a pair of small shorts and the same metal collar he had seen in the warehouse, this foe wrapped Sullivan in a crushing bear hug and lifted him from the floor. The thing squeezed and Sullivan felt his ribs groan under the pressure. He loosened that horrible grasp with a brutal head butt that smashed the pug nose flat, then forced his own arms up to slip out of the hold. He drove a left fist to the thing's flank, right above the liver. Normally such a blow would drop any man, but his wrist folded and his knuckles screamed in protest when they collided with what felt like a bag of rocks. Sullivan ducked a clubbing right hand and chose a softer target for his next strike. A rising knee found the monster's groin. Sullivan did not wait for a response, but followed it with a right fist to the thing's protruding Adam's apple.

Like the previous fight, this opponent lacked any training, and despite its great strength the thing was helpless before Sullivan's superior skill. Coughing and gagging, it fell. Sullivan did not get time to congratulate himself. Investing a quarter second to scoop up his pistol, he ran. He barely made it twenty more yards down the hall before two more things fell on him. One set of arms wrapped around his legs from behind and he went down hard. Another pair grabbed at his neck and he felt the crushing weight of something large and muscular land on his back. Sullivan kicked and rolled to his back, toppling the shaggy-headed humanoid reaching for his throat. Fire lanced up his thigh, and he looked down to see a smaller version gnawing on the meat of his thigh like a rat. He swung the Hudson like a club, bashing the biter across the temple and dislodging it with a yelp. His hand snapped back to his right and he fired to the side without looking. He knew the other would be on him by now, and a cry of pain confirmed this. Sullivan was too cagey to check his handiwork. Firmly in the clutches of his modified brain chemistry, he was moving and shooting unencumbered by things like indecision, fear paralysis, or confusion. The unfamiliar emotion now playing in that matrix did not seem to be making him less effective, though it brought with it a strange discomfort he could not shake.

Hating himself, he snapped the pistol back in line as he stood and squeezed off a single round. It took the skinny one high on the chest and killed it instantly. It was the best Sullivan could offer the poor thing. There was no point in pretending he was going to get through this without killing a lot of Calloway's creatures. Checking his watch, he followed the arrows to a side hall and a large double door. His brow wrinkled at the lock panel. It blinked a cheerful green that set Sullivan's lips in a thin line. It should be locked. He was mere yards from Horowitz's signal. He glanced over his shoulder and listened, and his suspicions grew. There were no more things pursuing him, either. Sullivan exhaled, only partially aware of the exasperated growl that emerged from deep in his chest.

Calloway wanted him to go through that door. Sullivan had to go through it. He had been funneled here and that was not a good thing.

"Son of a bitch," he said under his breath. He checked the Hudson again, ground his teeth, and punched the door panel with an irritated fist.

The door hissed open and Sullivan fired at the first hostile he saw. He needn't have bothered. The thing behind the door shrugged off the direct hits and put a fist the size of a melon directly into Sullivan's chest. As he flew backward, Sullivan clung to consciousness with only middling success. Through the growing cloud of static in his mind, he lamented, *Aw, shit. They have an ogre.*

CHAPTER TWENTY-ONE

S ullivan awoke to the sound of a roar that made his eyeballs vibrate in their sockets.

He found himself against a wall more than thirty feet from the source of his brief flight. He rose quickly, and then wobbled when his senses caught up with his reflexes. The pain in his chest, distant and numbed by his stress response, pulsed in waves with every breath. If it hurt this much now, Sullivan knew that when the endorphins wore off he was going to be in agony. Until then, survival would be his primary goal. Sullivan had never even seen an ogre-class GMP before. Based on what he had read about them, he could not shake the nagging observation that either this one was larger than average, or they just looked a lot bigger up close. Either way, he wasted no time pretending that winning a straight fight with this thing was possible. He raised his pistol in one shaky hand and thumbed the selector to full auto. Aiming would be irrelevant. He hoped for hits to soft areas, because the bone density of something like that would prevent good penetration.

But it's not bulletproof.

The Hudson spewed a prolonged burst of ten-millimeter caseless directly into the advancing monster. Too close to miss, too wide to dodge, the thing took twenty-eight bullets to the torso with nary a flinch. By the time the bolt closed on an empty chamber it was upon Sullivan and no less motivated to kill him. Sullivan dove away from the clutching fingers with only inches to spare and staggered back down the hall.

He needed to stall. It was obvious his bullets had missed anything vital, and that was a disappointment. On the other hand, almost thirty holes in the torso could not be ignored by any creature. His old shooting coach had never respected Sullivan's physical gifts much, and his mantra of "anything that bleeds, dies" came to Sullivan's thoughts as he lurched away from the nightmare chasing him. Sullivan took solace in just how much bleeding the thing was doing and directed his efforts to staying alive long enough for blood loss to weaken the ogre. Not knowing what drugs it was on meant not knowing how long that might take. Outrunning a wounded eight-hundred pound giant should have been easy, except Sullivan's own injuries were slowing him down. Breathing was hard. He did not think any ribs were broken, though damage to his internal organs remained a distinct possibility. He was still bleeding from his own minor gunshot wound, and something was very wrong with the bite to his leg. A strange tingling radiated from the injury that set alarms off in Sullivan's mind.

He made for an office door, hoping for a defensible position. He fumbled with the latch and something like a small car crashed into his back. He was airborne again, cartwheeling across the tile to thwack into another wall. An explosive grunt of pain and frustration burst from his tortured lungs, and he dove again to avoid a crushing stomp from an enormous hairy foot. Sullivan scrambled now, wheezing and clawing at the floor to get distance before it got a hold of him again. His hand settled on something weighty and solid and he hurled it at the ogre's face. One of the ubiquitous monitors lining the hall flew through the air and exploded against the craggy brow. The monster shook its head and snorted. Then it charged again.

"Oh, for crying out loud..." Sullivan ran.

He retreated back the way he came, sliding through the doorway on wobbly legs. He reminded himself that it was just a matter of time before blood loss slowed it down. This thought kept him focused and moving until his foot struck the body of one of his previous victims and he fell. A spike of agony lanced from his knee before his forward motion spent itself and Sullivan's subsequent roar of pain and exasperation rivaled the ogre's. A desperate lurch turned Sullivan to his back in time to see the sole of an enormous foot descending to end his life. He summoned all his strength for a clumsy roll out of the way, but too many of his muscles were not responding. All that was left to do was brace himself for the pain, and twist to take the brutal impact on his back and not his head.

The impact never came.

The foot, and its attached leg, hovered quivering overhead. Both the ogre and its victim paused, perplexed by the bizarre turn of events. Still protecting his head, Sullivan could not see exactly what had saved him. However, he could think of only one thing that might stop an enraged ogre from stomping him into a puddle of greasy meat and red goo. A rasping guttural grunt of exertion confirmed his theory immediately.

Sullivan guessed that the ogre might weigh seven or eight-hundred pounds, though he did not know for sure. In the gym, with a barbell and a good warm-up, Sullivan could lift seven hundred pounds from the floor a couple of times in a row. He did not know for sure how many. What he did know for sure and without any doubt, was that seven-hundred pounds on the bar would be considered a light warm-up weight for Patrick Fagan. He turned his head to look up. Fagan stood astride Sullivan's prone body, the ogre's whole leg wrapped in his arms and his face locked in a tight-lipped frown of irritation. His own wide back flexed so hard his jacket split down the middle and with a bestial war cry the giant warden hoisted that foot like a Highlander flipping a caber. The ogre toppled backward with a thud that shook the floor. Fagan followed it down and sent a flurry of punches to its face. The flat nose exploded into a bloody nodule of weeping mush. The great slab jaw cracked, sending yellow teeth flying. The ogre reached up to claw at Fagan's face and the big man broke two of its fingers by yanking them backward until they popped.

The ogre howled. Rage mixed with pain, fear with despair. The thing tried to sit up with Fagan still standing over it. Two more punches slowed the ascent but the monster's desperation proved too much. Fagan was shoved back, only to drive forward once more. He caught the thing while it was still rising with a low tackle. Powerful legs pistoned against the floor and the ogre flailed backward until both titans slammed into the far wall hard enough to send monitors cascading to the deck in a hail of sparks and debris. The ogre clubbed at Fagan's back, driving the lesser giant to his knees. The huff of exhaled air from Fagan was more irritated than hurt, and he took advantage of his lower position to snag a foot and yank the ogre's leg out from beneath it.

The monster went down again. This time Fagan kept the foot and twisted the ankle until a wet pop could be heard over the beast's howls. It kicked with its good leg, clipping Fagan in the shoulder hard enough to tear a bark of pain and anger from him. Fagan responded with a stomp to the ogre's groin and then he threw the captured leg to the side. Dropping a knee onto the ogre's chest, he rained punches down once more.

Sullivan dragged himself upright. The urge to do something loomed large, though he could not figure out how to help. In truth, it was hard to say if Fagan even needed any help. It became obvious that at last the ogre was slowing. Blood loss, injuries, and shock took their toll in increments. If Fagan noticed his foe weakening, he gave no indication. Sullivan understood. Neither man knew exactly what drugs had been pumped into the dying monster, and neither knew exactly how badly its body and brain had been twisted by genetic manipulation. At any moment it might explode into new heights of aggression and violence. Sullivan pitied the thing, but when one had an ogre on the ropes, the wise combatant did not let up.

Sullivan dragged himself toward the thrashing fighters. Through the dense fog of his altered mental state, his body throbbed with the promise of horrible pain later. For now he merely ached, and his limbs felt far heavier than they should. When he moved close enough to see the ogre's face clearly his stomach lurched and he croaked, "Fagan! Enough! He's done!"

Fagan stopped mid-punch, his arm bloodied to the elbow and poised to drive another pile driver fist home into the ruined face of what was now a pitiful mass of writhing flesh. The great chest heaved like a bellows and Sullivan caught the look of fear and horror on his partner's face. He often forgot that physical combat was emotionally stressful for most people. He could not experience the overwhelming intensity of fear or anger or even pain when he fought, so it was easy for him to disregard all the ways those things traumatized regular people. In this moment, he saw the toll this fight had taken on his friend's mental state. Fagan's hands trembled when he lowered them and his legs wobbled as he stepped away from the ogre's broken body. His face morphed from beet red to ghostly pale in a matter of seconds. He tried to posture, to show strength in front of Sullivan. Fagan forced a smile, though even through the thick beard the curl of the lip looked more awkward than cocky.

"Saved the best one for me, huh runt?"

For some reason, Fagan's attempted machismo bothered Sullivan. Fagan wanted his respect and was hiding his emotions to keep from losing it. That felt cheap. Stupid. He had just fought an ogre to save Sullivan's life, and he was worried about looking weak?

Sullivan did not know what to say to the man who had just saved his life, and he did not have the time to come up with anything. There was a task to complete that he dreaded. "Give me your pistol," he said.

Fagan's eyes met his. Then he handed over his GEED-issue Beretta without a word. Sullivan put the muzzle against the ogre's temple and whispered. "Sorry, big man. I hope it's better for you on the other side." Then he pulled the trigger.

"It was the right thing to do," Fagan said when a hollow-eyed Sullivan handed the weapon back. "He was dead already, and this—" he gestured to the carnage of the laboratory "—was no kind of life."

"If it was the right thing to do, then why do I feel like shit?"

"The right thing often does."

"People wonder why I drink so much." Sullivan met Fagan's eyes with his. "Thanks for the save, by the way." His eyes shifted away, unable to cope with the awkwardness. "I, uh, I don't know that anyone else would slug it out with a fucking ogre to save my unlikable ass, man. That's some serious shit, partner. I won't forget it."

Despite the tragic lack of eloquence, his words had the intended effect of releasing some of the tension in Fagan's face. Sullivan wondered if the precision of the words was less important than the intent. Emotions were strange.

Fagan waved a hand. "My pleasure. Let's go get Horowitz."

"Roger that." Sullivan cast about with his eyes until he found his Hudson under a pile of monitors. He checked his watch. "She's through there. Let's go."

The door to what appeared to be an open lobby stood before the pair. "What do you suppose is waiting for us beyond that stupid beige door?" Fagan asked without humor. "Berserkers? Hybrid werewolves? Please let it not be more ogres." He shook his head. "Fuck, who knows what they've been doing here." His eyes darted to Sullivan. "You up for a fight?"

"Always," Sullivan said. "But you can do the heavy lifting for a bit." He waggled his pistol. "I'm dry and a little worn out." The lie came easily. His leg was going numb, he could not expand his lungs enough to get a decent breath of air, his knee struggled to accept his weight, and his arm throbbed where he had been shot. Sullivan possessed enough self-awareness to acknowledge his position. If a brutal fight awaited them beyond that door, then it would be Fagan who had to win it. It was the sort of conclusion that made Sullivan's skin crawl, but it would be all he could do just to stay alive.

CHAPTER TWENTY-TWO

M argaret's blood went cold.

Calloway had been coldly dismissed by the blond man, leaving the two women alone with the newcomer. His identity did not remain a secret for long. Horowitz addressed the man, her words edged with razor-sharp steel.

"Director. This is a surprise."

Pale eyebrows rose and a vulpine smile broke across his face. "As surprising as finding out one of your trusted captains is a traitor?"

"That is a strange choice of words, Director. I'd think 'traitor' might fit you better, considering your position."

"If you have no imagination, sure. Why not?" The director leaned back in his chair. "I'm not here to debate the philosophical shortcomings of the Genetic Equity Act—"

"How about the shortcomings of a high-ranking government official working for a mobster?"

This wilted the predator's grin. "Michael Sullivan is a free man, Elaine. You should have known better."

Margaret strained with every fiber of her being to control her irritation. This was not the plan. She was supposed to implicate Mickey Sullivan in the deranged experiments going on here. Sharpe had provided her with a huge cache of fake intelligence that would pull the pressure away from his group and dump the blame squarely on Mickey Sullivan. There was even an entire fake scheme to assassinate some child thrown in to really get his back up. The presence of what she assumed was the director of GEED made everything more difficult. He was on Mickey's payroll, she reminded herself. This could all still go back to Mickey. Still, she hated it when her clients improvised. Plans existed for a reason.

Then the director said something that shattered the calm she had only just reassembled.

"Mickey is out for a reason, Elaine. If you had just stayed the hell out of this you'd be all done with him sooner than later."

Horowitz proved faster on the uptake than Margaret. "You're double-crossing Mickey Sullivan?" A derisive snort followed. "Good luck with that, Tom. Been nice knowing you."

"No, Elaine. You are. And I get to tell him all about it. I'm loyal as hell." A theatrical wink followed the obvious lie.

Margaret needed answers, fast. "Who the hell are you working for?" She tried to sound like a scared reporter and not a seasoned operative fishing for situational awareness.

The director switched his gaze to Margaret. "Ah, yes. Mata Hari came as well. How's that article coming?"

Margaret did not like the smug tone of his voice. She let her character slip just a little. "I was almost done writing it when you showed up. If I have to start over, I'll make sure you get mentioned. Prominently." She hoped the threat was not too oblique. It was hard to tell how much this man knew and she still did not understand his role in the game. If Sharpe was changing the play on her, he was going to get a very blunt earful about it later.

The sound of an alarm ended the repartee. The director looked down to a screen set into the table and frowned. He looked back up to Horowitz. "I knew you couldn't resist bringing him here." He punched an icon on the screen with a thin forefinger. "Calloway?"

The doctor's voice came from a speaker in the table. "Yes?"

"The subject has arrived. Do as much testing as you like, but don't let him get out of here alive, do you hear me?"

"Of course. Calloway out."

Margaret's heart began to beat faster. If Sharpe wanted Sullivan dead, she could have done that already. It made no sense.

Sharpe doesn't want John Sullivan dead. So what the hell is going on?

She wracked her brain for a plausible narrative that explained the collapsing situation. She could not find one. She switched gears and began worrying about her own prospects. She needed to get out of here. If Sullivan and Fagan were walking into a trap, she wanted to be far from the resulting carnage.

"So what's your plan, Tom?" Horowitz asked. "You're going to kill John Sullivan?"

"Whether he lives or dies is up to him and Calloway. You see, the doctor is very excited to see how his little crop of wonders up here stacks up against the famous John L. Sullivan. The people who have recently secured my services want very much to send a message to Mickey about his attitude. When I heard you were coming up here to sniff around, I saw the chance to make myself very helpful."

The answer hit Margaret like a thunderclap, sending her senses reeling.

He's not working for Sharpe. There's a third player in the game.

Her, Sharpe, Sullivan. They had been set up. Somebody had led them all here for a purpose and the trap was now sprung. This whole operation was about to implode and she could not stop it. Now she had a decision to make and she did not like it. Margaret considered her options without letting her expression change. She could kill the director and make her escape. That would blow her cover and sink her whole plan for getting John to kill Mickey. She could kill Horowitz and the Director both and try to make it look like part of the trap had gone wrong. She dismissed this as complicated and messy. She could wait and hope Fagan and Sullivan got to them. It sounded like the director remained unaware of Fagan's presence, and that gave her some hope that the idea might work. She hated to re-ly on others, though. That sort of planning invited disappointment. She made a choice and prayed it was the right one.

"Did your employer think of everything?"

The director frowned. "I kind of think so. Why? Is this where you tell me something I've missed?"

"Just a question, really. If your employer is so smart, and you're so gosh-darn loyal and helpful, why did they want you alone in a room with me?"

The director did not reply, though his frown deepened. Margaret smiled. "You don't know, do you?"

"Know what?"

Margaret went from seated in a comfortable chair to sliding across the table in an eighth of a second. Her right hand snapped forward to strike like a spear into the side of the director's neck.

"Gah!" he blurted as he fell back against the wall. His hand clasped the wound and his eyes blazed with fear and anger. Blood seeped from beneath his fingers. "What the—?"

Margaret sat on the table and held her hand up so he could see the thin red smear of blood on her middle fingernail. "You're dead, Director. She closed her fist to leave the middle finger up in a rude gesture. "This little piggy has poison. It'll take about five minutes to kill you. Less if you run around and elevate your heart rate. She folded the middle finger down and raised her pinkie. "This little piggy has the antidote. If you tell me who you are working for, I'll give it to you. If you're fast, the damage to your nerves may not be permanent."

The director's fierce and indignant scowl melted into a mask of fear. Margaret smiled sweetly. "Lips tingling? Feeling numb at the toes yet?"

"You bitch..."

Margaret said nothing. She knew what came next.

The director whipped his coat back and grabbed at a holstered pistol. As he raised it Margaret reached out and plucked it from his hand. She flicked him across the nose with a finger and tutted like a disproving mother. "You might as well talk. If your masters sent you here to try to hold me, then they sent you here to die. On purpose." She leaned in to whisper in his ear. "I'm not like other girls." The smell of his sweat told her that even with death looming, her charms still had an effect.

"Better say something, Tom," Horowitz piped up. "I don't get the impression this is a joke to her."

"It's a little funny," Margaret said. She dropped the pistol to the floor. "But I'm getting bored." Margaret whispered silent thanks for the captain's quick uptake. The woman would have a lot of questions for her if they got out of here alive, and she was not ready with a good story just yet.

"I work..." a coughing spasm overwhelmed him for a moment. "It's a bunch of politicians. They found out about Corpus Mundi and the Sullivan mob..." More coughing. "They want the GiMPs for themselves..."

"Names!" Margaret snapped.

"Keating! It's run by Rep Keating! He's got a whole group of them on board!" The director gasped. His eyes went to Margaret's right hand. "Give me the antidote! I'll tell you whatever you want!"

"There is no antidote, asshole. You were dead the minute you walked in here." Margaret kicked him in the throat. The gagging man fell to the floor in a gurgling heap and Margaret turned to Horowitz. "Yes. You have questions. Later, okay?"

The captain nodded. Other than narrowed eyes and a permanent scowl, she seemed otherwise unperturbed by what had just occurred. She stepped over to the director's twitching body and rolled it roughly with her foot. She retrieved her pistol from under the dying man and checked the magazine. Satisfied, she looked up to Margaret. "We need to find Sullivan and Fagan."

The distant sounds of gunfire reached their ears. "I think they're close," Margaret said with a wry shake of the head.

The pair left the conference room and moved toward the commotion. With only a single weapon and a single magazine, they could not afford to be reckless, so they managed only slow progress. The end of the hall opened into a wide lobby. Horowitz swept the space with her muzzle before venturing forth. Margaret smelled the trouble before she saw it.

"Look out!"

Her warning came too late. A muscular man wearing only gray shorts sprang from a doorway to tackle the captain. The woman went down hard under the thing. Margaret flew into the fray, hooking the snarling humanoid around the neck and tearing it away from the captain. Its strength was incredible, and it took all of Margaret's own considerable power to drag it free. Inhuman sounds spilled from its mouth, and fingers like steel pincers clawed at the forearm clamped across its throat. Margaret stomped the back of its knee to stagger it and cranked her chokehold tighter. Horowitz rose on unsteady legs and Margaret shouted, "Fucking shoot this thing!" The pistol barked twice and Margaret felt the man jerk with each hit. It fought for another five seconds before the strength left its body and it slumped.

The captain swayed in place. She looked pale to Margaret. "How did you know the bullets wouldn't pass through and hit you?" Horowitz asked.

Margaret pointed to the pistol. "That little thing get through this?" she nudged the corpse with her toe. "Never. Too much muscle. You all right?"

"Bastard bit me," the captain said. "Hurts like hell."

Margaret examined the wound on the captain's neck. It looked like an animal bite. The thing had sawed its teeth back and forth while chewing, and while not on a major blood vessel, the cuts were deep. Worse, the edges were already turning an angry red. Something about it made Margaret very uncomfortable. "Let's keep moving—"

She never got to finish her thought. The sounds of a horrific fight erupted beyond one of the doors on the far side of the lobby. A huge crash followed by a long burst of full-auto gunfire painted the picture of a pitched battle to her experienced ears, and she changed her mind. "New plan. We hunker down here until it quiets down. We're not equipped for whatever the hell that is."

"Sounds good," Horowitz said. Margaret turned to see the captain leaning against the wall. Her teeth were visible just beyond slightly parted lips, clenched together in a rictus of pain. "I think that fucker poisoned me."

Margaret agreed. The bite mark now stood out against her neck, red and angry. The lump seemed to be stealing the color from everywhere else, leaving her face ghost white.

"Sit," Margaret ordered.

Horowitz complied. Margaret grabbed the gun and tucked it into her belt. She tried to get a better look at the wound and hissed when she saw blue-black blotches forming under the surrounding skin.

"Bad?" Horowitz asked.

"Looks like some sort of venom. Hemotoxic. Like a snake's."

"So bad, then."

"It can't be that bad, you're still alive."

Horowitz could only cough in response.

Margaret did not know what to do. The reaction looked aggressive, and this raised a conflict. If Horowitz died, her cover would be safe. She could pin the death on Mickey Sullivan and virtually guarantee the desired response from John. However, in light of the new information they had just acquired, Margaret thought this might be a touch myopic. The whole business with Sharpe and Corpus Mundi had felt like the usual corporate conflict that kept her busy and well-paid at first. Seeing the grotesque experiments conducted here at Camp Zero, and learning that a senior Representative of the Global Republic was involved drove tendrils of doubt through the dense shielding of her professional code of indifference. Doubt was the sort of thing people in her line of work were supposed to avoid. Something told Margaret that this case was special.

Certain she would regret the decision, Margaret began to try to clean the injury on the captain's neck.

"It's not moving as fast as it could be, so just hang in there, captain."

"If they... work with venom..." Horowitz struggled to get the words out. "Probably... bite kit..."

Margaret nodded. "Got it. Hang tight."

She scanned the lobby with all her senses, trying very hard to not hear the crashing and roaring of the insane war going on just beyond their hiding place. The aroma of isopropanol brought her to a first aid kit hanging next to a door. She ran over and ripped it open. She found nothing that looked like antivenin, but she grabbed a few empty syringes and antimicrobial dressings. When she got back to the captain, her eyes were barely open.

"This is probably going to hurt," Margaret said. Then she plunged the end of a syringe into a puncture and began sucking blood and venom away from the wound. "This will slow the reaction down," she said as she worked. She could not be sure if this was true, but her limited medical training seemed to indicate the possibility.

She was still sucking fluid from the bite when the door to the lobby burst open. Margaret spun, dropping the syringe and scooping up the pistol in one smooth movement. She settled the front sight on the first figure to enter the lobby and nearly shot Patrick Fagan in the face. In his unrecognizable state of bloody disarray, Fagan looked like the sort of thing Doctor Calloway might come up with.

Blood-soaked, limping, and bleeding from a dozen places, Sullivan followed. Margaret lowered her gun and called, "Over here!"

The two men approached, Margaret forestalled their questions with instructions. "The captain's been poisoned by one of these freaks. She needs a hospital now!"

Without a pause, Fagan grabbed the woman and put her over his shoulder. "Quickest way out?"

Sullivan checked his watch. "We are forty feet underground, near the west end of the compound. We need to go up."

"I saw stairs back this way," Margaret said. "Come on!"

They moved as a group back toward the conference room. Just beyond it, a clearly marked stairwell took them up to the ground level. "Looks like they cleared the place," Fagan said when they encountered no people.

"Calloway released all his projects down there," Sullivan said. "Everyone is either evacuated or dead." Something in Sullivan's voice made Margaret shiver. His sweat smelled of uric acid and cortisol, with no trace of anything else. No fear or aggression byproducts whatsoever marred the aroma, like an athlete after a relaxing yet strenuous workout.

With helpful monitors flashing the evacuation route for personnel in every hallway, they found the exit without incident. Eerie quiet greeted them once they got outside, and Fagan spoke first.

"Where the hell is everybody? Where is security?"

"Shit," Sullivan spat. "We gotta run. They're burning the place. Head for the fence!"

They ran. Sullivan's deduction proved prophetic, as the group cleared the fence line with only a few seconds to spare. With a sound like a tornado, fire engulfed all the buildings at once. Windows shattered and doors blew open to spew white flames in enormous gouts. The offensive tang of chemical smoke hit Margaret's nostrils like poison gas and she gagged. Even at a hundred feet away, the wave of heat following the initial explosions forced her eyes closed.

"Shit!" Fagan bellowed.

Margaret thought of all the living things that were probably still inside that compound, most locked in cages. She thought of them dying in smoke and fire, scared and confused. Their deaths were unclean, and she felt dirty for her part in them. Sullivan must have been thinking the same things, because his words echoed her thoughts. "Fucking bastards. They're going to get away with it, aren't they?" The morose set of his chin stayed with him as he turned back from the conflagration and began to drag himself toward the woods. "Let's get Horowitz to the hospital."

"John," Fagan said quietly. "It's too late."

Margaret looked to the big man and found him cradling Horowitz. The body was still, and Margaret could neither smell nor hear the breath leaving her lungs.

Sullivan stopped walking. He turned to the two remaining members of the group. Margaret saw his body sag as if something heavy and cold had just been placed on his shoulders. His face aged a decade before her eyes, and he wiped at it with the palm of one bloody hand. It left a streak of scarlet down one cheek. He did not appear to notice.

"Okay," he said after a long pause. His mouth worked as if it had something more to say, though the only words to come out were, "We need to get out of here."

When he turned away Margaret stifled a shudder. She thought about saying something, then decided against it. The creeping darkness of his hollow tone told her it was best to leave him alone.

CHAPTER TWENTY-THREE

Unlike his son, Mickey Sullivan had not spent years under the stern tutelage of a sports medicine PhD and former judo Olympian. Mickey had not enjoyed the careful and measured discipline of some of the best coaches in the world, nor had he been guided through his bad moods and habits by the firm hand of a champion fighter who could twist even strong men into whimpering pretzels. So even though his anger was not born of extensive neurochemical alteration, Mickey's ability to contain his temper fell well short of his son's. He paced a track into the carpet of his office, a cold cigar clamped between teeth locked together in an unshakable grimace.

"What the fuck happened out there!"

Malcolm Hargrave, being accustomed to the occasional outburst from his employer, answered with a dryness born of long years' suffering. "Keating turned on us. Looks like a third chunk of our group is now split off."

"He took GEED with him," Mickey pointed out.

"Yes, he did," agreed Hargrave. "But there is a victory there. One of his captains, the Horowitz woman, was working against us all along. We have all the security feeds from Camp Zero, and we know she is now dead."

"That Johnny's old captain?"

"It was."

"He's gonna be good and pissed then. Shit. He's not so easy to predict when he's good and pissed. Fuck!"

"We don't know what he knows, Mickey," said Hargrave. "He might blame you, or he might blame Corpus Mundi." He decided to calm Mickey down with a technique that always worked. "The security feeds show Calloway loosing the last round of prototypes on him. Almost fifty swarm troopers."

Mickey stopped pacing. "Berserkers?"

"No. The new models. The non-psychotics with neural implants."

"How'd he do?" Fatherly pride was insidious.

"Oh, John killed them all. Calloway is a brilliant scientist but he knows absolutely nothing about fighting. John had Coll's old Hudson with him."

"The dumbass sicced fifty insane GiMP soldiers on a chimera with a machine gun?"

"With predictable results." Then Hargrave amended himself. "It was still a close call. Calloway eventually deployed some of the more advanced models with non-human DNA, too. When that didn't work, he sent an ogre prototype to finish him."

"Johnny dropped an ogre? Holy shit!" Mickey's face brightened. "You'd think those assholes at Corpus Mundi would get the hint by now. Johnny is top dog because of the training and life *I* gave him." He made a rude gesture at no one in particular and mumbled, "Talk about leading a horse to water..."

Hargrave nodded, pleased with himself for heading off one of Mickey's legendary tantrums. "So the good news is that a traitor is dead, an enemy has revealed itself, and Camp Zero is well and truly destroyed. Billions in research projects had to be scrubbed. Whoever it is supporting Corpus Mundi out there just took an enormous financial and strategic hit."

"So did we," Mickey said.

"There's another thing..."

"Spit it out, Mal."

"Mata Hari was there."

Mickey paused to consider this. "And just what the fuck is she doing breaking into Camp Zero with Johnny?"

"An excellent question."

"If she wanted him dead, she's had her chance, right? Johnny's good at a lot of shit but staying away from easy women ain't one of them. It can't be that."

"I imagine it's not. Maybe she's trying to bring in the girl? She'll need to be in John's good graces for a chance at that, I suppose."

Sullivan waved the idea away. "She did Hanson, and that was a Corpus Mundi facility that just got trashed. So she ain't working for Corpus Mundi. Was she part of Keating's thing?"

"It looked an awful lot like she was in as much danger as any of them."

"Not Keating, not Corpus Mundi. Gotta be the mystery partner, then." Mickey resumed his pacing. "I can work with this. Send Johnny a message through the Silk Road. Clue him in about Mata Hari and who we think she's working for. Then I want a full-court press on Keating. I own as many Representatives as anyone. Every bill he sponsors I want blocked. Every committee he's on I want bogged down in bullshit. I want hecklers at every public appearance. Let's throw some scandals his way, too. I need his position fucking degraded, Mal. When we are done with this prick, he'll have less political pull than a freshman rep out of Micronesia."

"That should not be difficult. Keating is hardly a saint. What about GEED?"

"Where's the director now?"

"Under the rubble of Camp Zero."

Mickey rubbed his forehead. "Damn. The rakers are real quiet on that. You'd think we'd have heard something on the news by now."

"I suspect a plausible story is being formulated. Give it six more hours and I'm sure the InfoNet will be buzzing with whatever cover story Corpus Mundi cooks up to cover the catastrophe."

"Bet you a grand they blame SoA."

"Not taking that bet, Mickey," Hargrave said with a chuckle. "Terrorists make for very useful idiots."

"This is gonna be a shitstorm. GEED is gonna go on the warpath. Who's taking over?"

"Deputy Director Chopra."

Mickey scowled. "Do we own this guy?"

"Woman, actually. And no. We maneuvered her into the role because she was of unimpeachable character. It deflected accusations of corruption, if you recall."

"Fuck. Yeah. I remember now." Mickey pulled the cigar from his mouth and stared at it like he just realized it was there. He stomped to his desk to find a lighter. "Okay. Here's the plan. We gotta fabricate a scandal for this Chopra chick and either push her out or bring her in. In the meantime, increase the activity among all the activist groups we got at GEED work facilities. I want the GiMPs good and riled up about GEED corruption. This transition is going to be fucking ugly, you hear me? I want it ugly. When Johnny comes looking for trouble, I want him to find it and I want it to lead right back to these bastards running Corpus Mundi. They want to use SoA? Fine. We can play that game too. Let's get some SoA attacks going too. We can—"

A soft chime interrupted Mickey's orders. He threw his hands up in frustration. "God damn it, Millie! I told you I was fucking busy!"

A woman's voice came from an unseen speaker, dry and unimpressed. "GEED is doing a live press release, boss. I thought you'd want to know."

"Fuck!" Mickey ran his fingers through his hair. "InfoNet!" He called to the air. "Put News First on the big screen!"

The curtains to his office slid closed and most of one wall lit up with a crowded room in what Mickey and Hargrave knew to be the GEED headquarters press room. The flawless face of Bonnie St.

Claire took up much of the scene, and she was mid-sentence when they tuned in. "—death of GEED director Tom Hastings in what is believed to have been a terrorist attack on a genetic research facility in Alaska. The chairman of the Genetic Equity Oversight Committee, Representative Oscar Keating of the US First District has announced that Deputy Director Priyanka Chopra will be assuming the role of GEED Director. We are expecting an official statement from Keating and the new Director any moment now." Her head cocked as if listening to something only she could hear. "Yes. Keating is entering the room at this time."

The picture moved away from the reporter and floated above the crowded press room. A tall man, silver-haired and blue-eyed, stepped up to a podium emblazoned with the GEED insignia and the motto "Aequalitatem Omnium." He placed his hands on the top and leaned into the floating drones with a perfect expression of professional sadness. "Good afternoon everybody. I'm going to get right to it. As you all know, a terrible incident at an illegal genetic research facility in Alaska has resulted in the death of Director Tom Hastings. We have very little information on exactly what happened, but we believe at this time elements of the Sons of Adam organization took advantage of his presence there to strike a blow against the Genetic Equity Enforcement Department. One of our most effective and decorated senior GEED captains, Elaine Horowitz, was also killed in the attack. This incident has severely damaged an ongoing GEED investigation and worse, robbed our great society of two of its best servants. At this time, Deputy Director Priyanka Chopra will be promoted to Director, and she will be spearheading a robust and invasive investigation into this incident. Let's be clear. The Global Republic, the United States of America, and this department will not and cannot tolerate this type of brazen lawlessness. Action will be swift and decisive. As Chairman of the Oversight Committee, I have authorized a broad increase in GEED latitude with a concurrent increase in resources.

An emergency session of the Global Security Council has been assembled, and a quorum has already approved initiatives that Director Chopra will explain herself momentarily." Those sincere politician's eyes swept the room, giving the crowd a chance to digest what he had just said and letting the tension build. "The forces arrayed against our democracy and the law that protects it have declared war on the good people of the world. They are going to regret it." The room fell deathly silent, just as the man intended. "I will now step back and let Director Chopra explain in greater detail our new initiatives."

"Son of a bitch..." Mickey whispered and shook his head. He kept his eyes on the screen and said no more.

A few reporters shouted questions to Keating as he stepped back. He ignored them politely and the group fell silent once again when a stern woman in a smart brown suit stepped up to the podium.

"Good afternoon. As Representative Keating has said, I am Director Chopra. I worked closely with both Tom Hastings and Elaine Horowitz for many years, and their deaths weigh heavily on me at this time. They were the best of us all, and we are poorer for their loss." She paused to clear her throat. "Ahem. With the approval of The Genetic Equity Oversight Committee, GEED resources will be stepping up all enforcement activity, with a special emphasis on those illicit marketplaces financing illegal research. Primarily, GEED will be moving to cut off these resources through the elimination of secondary economic structures left over from the Great War. Those bad actors who are utilizing cryptcoin, the underground market known as the Silk Road, and hiding in the various Military Production Complexes will be targeted extensively. For too long have these areas given refuge to those who refuse to obey the laws of our Republic. Organizations like the Sons of Adam and The Railroad, though opposed philosophically, continue to operate under the exact same cover. Until now we have had neither the will nor the resources to engage either in their entrenched positions. Positions both physical and economic. Our failure in this regard has led to this day and this horrible incident. Effective immediately, access to any zone with physical connection to any former production complex will be strictly monitored and controlled. The people living inside any such place are hereby put on notice." She leaned in, pointing a finger out at the reporters. "Leave them and rejoin society. Your days are numbered." She straightened. "That is the end of my prepared remarks. I will not be taking any questions at this time."

The room exploded in shouts and waving hands. Keating and Chopra walked away from the podium and left without addressing any of the hurled inquiries.

"InfoNet!" Mickey barked. "Kill it!"

The curtains reopened and the screen wall went blank. Mickey looked to Hargrave. "That rat bastard just declared war on all of us."

Hargrave nodded slowly. "What can he be thinking?"

"He wants us all out. Dead. Gone. He's jumping everybody's timeline and bringing the fight out into the open."

"He's the government," Hargrave said. "That's a fight only they can win."

"And using Chopra..." Mickey smacked his palm with a closed fist. "That's just fucking smart. She's clean as the driven snow. The press will love her." The mobster stamped his cigar out in an ashtray. "But is he overstepping? He's going to pick a fight with the complexes, right? Does even the Republic have the resources to do it?"

"Military? Yes. Political?" Hargrave winced. "Maybe?"

"It ain't gonna be an attack on the complexes. That's just stupid. It's gonna be something more subtle. They can't do shit about cryptcoin, but that's them taking a swipe at Corpus Mundi. The Silk Road? That's a deliberate shot at me. I don't own it but he knows I make a fucking mint off the damn thing. Why the fuck does Keating care about SoA or the Railroad, though?"

"He doesn't. Chopra does."

"Right," Mickey said. "She's a true believer, and that gives Keating lots of cover and a scapegoat when things go wrong." Mickey wagged a finger at Hargrave as comprehension dawned across his features. "And it's damn sure gonna go wrong."

Hargrave caught on. "Because they can't do anything about cryptcoin and any fight with the complexes is going to be a disaster, win or lose."

"This is his play for that little girl, isn't it? Attack the Silk Road? Pressure on the Railroad? Restricting access to the complexes?" Mickey's finger wagged harder, becoming a blur of excited movement. "Clever son of a bitch! He's locking them down so she can't be moved! I bet whenever GEED makes their move on the complexes, win or lose, Keating will be the one who ends up with that annoying little kid. Oh fuck me, this bastard is good," Mickey said. "I like his style."

"Enough to let him live?"

"Of course not, Mal."

Hargrave raised an eyebrow. "So what do we do?"

"I don't know. But get ready for war. Get on degrading Keating's political position like I said before, that's still key. Leverage anybody inside GEED still loyal to us. I want to know when Chopra is moving on the complexes. Tighten up our Silk Road assets, too. We gotta find out what he's moving and what's already been moved. Christ, who knows what the bastard's been smuggling in there? We probably can't stop Keating from starting his shit, but we can at least keep him from surprising us. He's making a mistake though."

"And that is?"

"He thinks I give a shit about the kid. I kind of do, but not enough to go to war over her."

Hargrave smiled. "But we are going to war."

"Fucker wants a war? We'll give him one." Mickey rubbed his palms together. "Just not the war he's looking for."

CHAPTER TWENTY-FOUR

"**Y**ou know this is not your fault, John."

Maris handed Sullivan a cup of coffee. Seated in her apartment deep in the KC Complex, Sullivan looked out of place and uncomfortable on her threadbare couch.

"Then why do I feel like shit?"

"Because you could not prevent it, I'd wager." Maris sat herself down on an old stuffed chair. "You like to control your environment, to dictate the action. This time you could not." Maris sat down across from him on an old stuffed chair. "Was she a close friend?"

"Most of my career I hated her and thought she hated me."

"What changed?"

"I found out she was using me to protect the department from mob reprisals. She would send me on missions knowing I'd see things I shouldn't or otherwise ruin things for Mickey and his cohorts, and then she'd blame my lack of discipline for the problems that got caused for his operations. Nobody realized she was setting me up to make things hard for them, so nobody suspected she wasn't playing ball."

"You sound in awe of her."

"It was fucking brilliant, Maris. Nobody has ever gotten one over on Mickey Sullivan, and she played him like a fiddle for years. When the devil made her an offer she couldn't refuse, she tricked the bastard into shooting himself in the foot." He stopped talking for a moment, staring at his reflection in the black mirror of his coffee. "And I acted like an asshole to her. I should have been paying attention. I could have helped her—"

"Would you have helped her? I mean, if she had asked?"

Sullivan thought about that. "I don't know, okay? I thought I had a pretty good thing going, and I thought that GEED was going to be my thing forever." He shook his head. "It wasn't even that long ago. Three months? Feels like a goddamn lifetime. I didn't know who I was then, and I sure as hell don't know who I am now."

"Who do you want to be?"

Sullivan looked up, his brow furrowed. "Come on, Maris. Are we really doing this therapy thing right now?"

Maris smiled and mimicked his tone. "Come on, John. We both know that's exactly why you came here."

She had him there, and he acknowledged it by answering the question. "I guess I kind of want to be her. Or like her, anyway. I've never met anyone who had their shit together like she did. It was like she was made of steel, you know?" He pursed his lips and exhaled through his nose. "All the years she was up my ass, all the crap she put me through, she was just trying to help me and stop a criminal. She didn't care if I liked her or not, she only cared about getting over on the bad guys. She sacrificed everything, and she never acted like a martyr or a hero." He finally sipped from the coffee. "I guess I respected that. So many people out there bitch and moan about bad stuff. She never said a word. She just did the work."

"I must admit, John, it's strange to hear you admire altruism so much. Doctor Platt would have us believe you are incapable of it, yourself."

"Maybe that's why I admire it." He sipped. "Or maybe I just hate to see assholes win. Either way, Horowitz was ten times as effective as I was in stopping assholes. And that's some bullshit, too. I'm supposed to be the one with all the advantages."

"Are you sad because she is gone? Or just angry?"

"Both. I can feel sadness." He pointed a finger at his own head. "That's not something they took away from me."

"But it's not something you are used to, either?"

"Good guess."

"I never guess." Maris sipped her own coffee with a satisfied smirk. "What does sadness feel like to you?"

Sullivan frowned at the bizarre question. Maris explained, "Sadness manifests differently for everyone. I'm asking you to describe it."

"Something's missing." The answer came so easily Sullivan surprised himself. "Something is gone. Something big. It feels like I've lost an important part of the world." He stopped there, pondering his own words. Then quietly, "Something I should have been more careful with. Now it's gone forever and I can't help but want it back." He let his eyes fall to the thin maroon carpet. "For most of my life I couldn't have relationships. Platt's right about that. I've always had a hard time making connections. But now..."

"Something is different?"

Sullivan waved a frustrated hand toward his head. "It's not like it used to be. There are... things... happening. The thought of these bastards getting their hands on Emilie was the first time I noticed it. It made me sick. Angry. Fagan getting hurt, I wanted to puke then, too. And at Camp Zero..."

"Yes?"

"What they were doing there, Maris. It's inhuman. And when I say it's inhuman, that ought to mean something. I'm mean, I'm angry, I'm a right proper bastard. I get all that. But these people?" he shook his head as if the memories could be dislodged by physical force. "It's not malicious or even evil. It's..." he searched for the right word. "It's apathy. Pure disregard."

"Why does that bother you?"

Sullivan was ashamed by his response. "Because I get it. Apathy? Amorality? It's wired into my very DNA. I'm not capable of feeling things very strongly, so I know exactly why and how people like Calloway can be the way they are."

"And you do not like it."

"Yeah," Sullivan said. "It's all new and unpleasant and I don't like it. I understand them, and it makes me hate myself, because I am them."

"That is a ridiculous statement," Maris said into her own coffee cup. "You came from them, but you are not like them. You would not be sitting here if you were. What you are is afraid."

Sullivan let that one slide. "Maybe I am afraid. I'm not sure I'd recognize fear if I was, though."

"That's very honest of you, John. Not all fear is bad. Fear encourages change."

"Unless you fear change."

"Honestly," Maris chuckled. "More so, then. Now tell me, John. When did you last feel something wrong with your emotions? Pick a moment that stands out."

He answered without hesitation. "In Camp Zero. When Calloway released those swarm troop prototypes. Normally when I'm in combat, everything but technique and situational stuff flatlines. If I let it happen and don't go chasing things like anger, I can go completely dark and get this incredible focus. I'm faster, stronger, my senses sharpen, my technique and strategy improve. Stuff like that. It's what I'm supposed to do, right?"

"Right."

"This time, something didn't flatline. Part of me couldn't relax during the fight. It sort of jumped around in my head the whole time while I was trying to get to the captain. Something about what they made me do..."

"What did they make you do?"

Sullivan took a deep breath. "The specimens... Calloway activated their collars for maximum aggression, but I saw them before he did. I saw their faces, Maris. They weren't monsters or psychotic until he hit that god damn button." He paused, then said, "And I killed them all. Like rabid animals I put them down. They were people, Maris. Poor, helpless, innocent people bred to be experiments. Calloway kept them like lab rats, drugged them up so they couldn't think or defend themselves. Made them live like animals..." His jaw ached from gritting his teeth. "And then he cut them loose on fucking Super-GiMP." He opened his left hand to look at the fingers. "I know what they made me to be, Maris. So did Calloway. The bastard did it anyway. I had a goddamn machine pistol in my hand and he threw half-naked, drugged-up, untrained people at *me*." The layer of contempt on that last word nearly choked him. "I don't mind the violence or the killing, Maris. That's no secret. But this time..."

Maris nodded, her eyes brimming with compassion. "This time was different?"

"It was like killing myself, or Fagan, or Emilie. And it was a slaughter, not a fight."

Maris simply nodded and waited.

"And then the ogre. That was the first real attempt to kill me, I think. Calloway was just fucking around up to that point. Collecting data for his experiments. Fifty dead innocents so he could take notes for his masters." He stopped again, not sure how to explain to Maris everything he was thinking and feeling. "And the ogre—" he thumped his palm with a fist. "Do you know what it takes to make an ogre? What they have to do to a baby to get it to grow like that? They tortured a child, Maris. Blunted its intelligence, stretched its bones, pumped it full of chemicals, fed it from tubes..."

"Sounds something like your own childhood, John."

"Yeah, I figured that out, too. Is that what I am to them?" Sullivan asked. "When they conceived of me all those years ago, is this what they saw? Just another biological fighting machine? The only difference between me and that ogre was that Mickey Sullivan wouldn't let them put one of those collars on me."

"Does that bother you?"

"What?"

"That Mickey made your life different from theirs?"

"I think it does," Sullivan said. "I'm glad that he saved me from that horror, but seeing those poor bastards?" He shook his head without looking up. "Makes me hate myself. Shit, Maris, I lived in a mansion. I had servants. I had the best teachers in the world. I ate food prepared by a personal chef. Worse, I was a shitty spoiled brat about it. I could have just as easily been in one of those cages with a collar around my stupid neck. I have Mickey Sullivan to thank for that. It makes me sick." His voice shook with frustration. "And how do I atone for being such a rotten punk?" He pantomimed shooting with his thumb and forefinger. "By putting bullets through the whole lot of them. Just like the remorseless monster they wanted me to be. I went in there to save Horowitz, instead I just killed everybody. That's what Calloway wanted to see, and that's just what I showed him."

"Does it really matter what he saw?" Maris asked by way of reply. "These are not your masters anymore. Not Corpus Mundi, and not Mickey Sullivan. You get to decide what you are, not them."

"And I decided to do what I do. The only thing I'm good at."

"I don't think they gave you a choice this time."

Sullivan stared at his hands as if they were dangerous animals. "Maybe? I'm not stupid, so I get you. There was never anything else for me to do in there. It was kill or die from the start. But holy shit do I hate that my choices always seem to boil down to that."

"You are a fighter, John. You have the intelligence and capability to do any number of things, but you choose this life. If I offered you a job fixing equipment here in the complex, would you take it?"

"No," Sullivan said, sullen.

"Exactly. The price for freedom of choice is responsibility for those choices."

Sullivan refused to meet her eyes. "What does that make me then?"

"A fighter. I already said that. I told you once before, the world needs fighters. The world needs John Sullivans to do the things that others can't."

"You forgot to mention the part where the line between fighter and monster is fuzzy as hell, Maris."

She shrugged. "You weren't ready to hear it then."

Sullivan allowed that this was probably true. "It's hard not to wonder what people see when they look at me. And I guess the real question is, why do I care all of a sudden? I never cared before." Finally he looked up, and all traces of his grim ill humor were gone. "I'm *feeling* things Maris. Things I don't think I'm supposed to feel. I was a shit employee to Horowitz, a shit friend to Fagan, and I'm sure as hell a shit person overall. None of that ever bothered me before, but it's fucking eating me alive right now."

"Well John, as your doctor I'd have to say you seem to have picked up an acute case of conscience."

Sullivan's answering scowl invited Maris to elaborate.

"Whatever mechanism they used to separate your ego from your actions is failing. Probably because you have formed connections that supersede your individual needs and desires. Where before your behavior was entirely self-serving, now you are forced to consider how your actions affect these other connections. Connections like Emilie and Fagan and Horowitz, as well as your emotional invest-ment in protecting Emilie and stopping the forces conspiring against the republic. All of these goals and relationships require considera-tion of things outside your own ego."

Sullivan gave her a crooked nod, unable to deny the logic of her assessment. Maris winked back at him and continued. "Your whole life your desire for success was about ego. You won fights because you were the best and you needed the world to know it. It made you feel good to succeed." She began to list things, tapping a finger to mark each one. "You don't care about the women you sleep with, because the act of getting them into the sack is what makes you happy. You were the best GEED warden ever because you liked to hold your superiority over your co-workers and your captain. You kill yourself in the gym because it's not enough for you to have genetic advantages, you want to be exceptional even among your peers. Platt assures me that even if you never stepped foot in the weight room you would still be twice as strong as most men your size." She scoffed. "You like being the biggest and strongest and fastest, don't you? Tell me, does it bother you that Fagan is stronger than you?"

It did and she knew it. "When you say it like that I kind of sound like an asshole," Sullivan mumbled.

"You are an asshole, John. That's not the point. What I'm trying to explain is that this emotional framework, the feedback mechanism that informs your decision making, is shifting. It's less about you and more about others."

"So I'm nice now?"

Maris snorted, nearly blowing coffee out her nose. "Dear god, no. You're just afraid."

"This," Sullivan said with a deeply furrowed brow. "This I gotta hear."

"Before, you craved success because it's how you defined yourself. What's happened, in my opinion, is that the driving force has shifted beyond the need for dominance and evolved into the fear of failure. Here's the fun bit, John. I think you are scared because people you are attached to need you to succeed, and you don't like what you must do to achieve that success."

John thought about this for several seconds, chewing his lip. "I won't say you're wrong, Maris."

"Smart boy."

"But the big hole in your theory is that I'm not supposed to do any of that."

Maris dismissed his deflection with a wave of one hand. "Brains are wonderful things, John. Even yours. They grow. They adapt. Yours is no different. Sure, your creators went to great lengths to limit your ability to form the kind of relationships that might make you harder to control or reluctant to engage in the behaviors they found desirable, but they didn't destroy that capacity completely. How could they? We're social animals. Much of our brain is dedicated to exactly that sort of thing. It has simply taken you a long time to develop emotional thresholds most other people achieve before their tenth birthday." She smiled into the battered face of a very confused man. "Congratulations, John, you are learning to give a shit."

"Just in time for Horowitz to die."

Maris let her smile wilt a bit. "Everybody dies, John. I'm going to assume no one has told you this, so I'll tell you what I tell all the other emotional ten-year-olds I deal with. Grieving is part of life. So grieve for her. It's not strange or unhealthy or weakness. Be sad. Feel guilty for not saving her. Blame yourself and weep for all the opportunities you missed with her. Then, when you are done, get on with your life."

Sullivan looked aghast. "Get on with my life? That's your advice? God damn you are a shit psychiatrist."

"Well, for a remorseless engine of violence, you're kind of underperforming, yourself."

"So what the hell am I supposed to do with all this? I feel like I'm losing control."

"You never had control, John. You had distance. Being distant meant you never had to exercise control."

Sullivan let the frustration come through in his voice. "Is 'not giving a direct answer' a course they make you take in psychiatry school? I came to you for help. Advice or whatever. Something I can use to keep from losing my mind out there. I am not the kind of guy you want losing control, Maris."

"So Platt likes to warn me. But you won't lose control."

"You sound very confident."

"I've read all Doctor Platt's notes, John. Somebody went to great lengths to ensure that when the time came, you would have enough self-discipline to face your demons."

Sullivan knew who she meant. "I wish he was here now."

"Don't be such a baby. You don't need him. He's already taught you what you need to do."

Sullivan could not deny the truth of that. Only through the careful exploration of his anger with his old combat instructor had the young Sullivan ever learned to live with his psychological damage. "Yeah, I suppose you're right about that." He looked at his watch and stood up, exhaling a cleansing breath as he rose. "And now it's time to go pass that knowledge on to Emilie." He paused before turning to leave and said, "Thank you, Maris."

She arched a brow. "That had to be painful to say."

"I still think you're a terrible shrink, but you're all I have."

"You're welcome, John."

Doctor Platt met him at the door. Out of breath and looking distraught, she nearly crashed into Sullivan when she stormed across the threshold. He grabbed her by the shoulders to prevent a collision and asked. "What the hell is wrong with you?"

Her eyes were wide with fear. "I found something in those stolen files. You need to see this right now!"

CHAPTER TWENTY-FIVE

Margaret McLeod punched in Sharpe's code with her heart in her throat. She waited while the various communications networks completed their dance of dueling encryptions, drumming her fingers against a tabletop. She had rented a private sleeping pod in a dingy satellite section of Hubtown for the sole purpose of making this call in private, and her nose wrinkled at all the lurid stories the competing aromas in the air told her about previous occupants.

Sharpe did not even bother with a greeting. The modulated voice simply said, "It wasn't us."

"What the fuck happened, Sharpe?"

"The director of GEED, who we know was on the Sullivan payroll, flipped to someone else. We don't know who, but they knew we were going in."

Margaret knew all of this already. Something told her to play this cagey, and she listened to it. "Whoever it is, they seem to know all the players really well, Victor. They knew Horowitz was a double agent, they knew Sullivan would be there, they knew what was going on at Camp Zero. The only reason I'm alive is because they either didn't know who I really was, or they wanted me to kill the director."

"You killed the director of GEED?"

"My options were limited."

Sharpe chose not to argue this. "I understand. How does our situation look? Is it salvageable?"

"I can still convince John that Mickey was behind Camp Zero, but he's never going to buy that the ambush was his father. Mickey has put too much effort into getting John to do his dirty work for him. It's just not going to make sense in John's head. The death of his captain seems to have gotten under his skin. It will probably get him riled up enough if I spin it right."

"I would think that the younger Sullivan would be well in your hands by now."

Margaret considered how to answer this. There was no way she was going to reveal to Sharpe just how problematic their competing biochemistry was turning out to be. "Seduction is not always the best strategy, Victor. Sullivan is a borderline psychotic. I need to be very careful about psychosexual ideation with him. If I have to kill him before he does the job, then we are right back to square one."

This seemed to satisfy her client. "I suppose you make a good point. What is your plan, now?"

"I don't know, Victor. I called you to see what you knew before I made my adjustments."

"I'll share everything I have, you know that."

Margaret harbored serious doubts about his sincerity. "Did you know what they were doing at Camp Zero?" she stared at the voice analysis, unsure if she wanted him to lie or not.

"Did what you saw there bother you?"

"That's a 'yes' then."

"Well, of course I knew, Margaret. I'm paying for it, after all. Is it going to be a problem?"

Margaret wondered if Victor Sharpe had a voice analyzer working on her. "Not for the moment. The job is to kill Mickey Sullivan, and I will get that done. How I feel about your little shop of horrors can be addressed later."

"I'd expect nothing less from a professional like yourself."

"Our options are to accelerate our timetable and get John to go after Mickey, or to pump the brakes and figure out the new player before proceeding." Margaret could not say why she declined to mention the Representative Keating lead, but she had learned to trust her instincts. Her instincts told her that Sharpe was not telling all, and a wise operative looked to her own safety first. Whatever Sharpe was keeping to himself might be bad news for her.

"Obviously," Sharpe said. "My preference is to accelerate."

"Obviously," said Margaret. "But it's my ass out in the breeze." She sighed. "I'll give John the fake intel tonight. See how he takes it. If it looks like he's primed to act, then I'll push him toward Mickey."

"It's your operation, Margaret. I trust you to do what's appropriate."

"I'll follow up after. To let you know what is going on."

"Excellent. Sharpe out."

Margaret cut the connection and exhaled for several long seconds. She discovered an uncomfortable sensation in her head, a sense of doubt and foreboding that could not be squelched by force of will. Sharpe was holding something back, and a lie by omission was still a lie. Her own discoveries painted a picture far more complex than Sharpe had led her to believe. If a high-ranking global representative was trying to kill them all, and her client was financing genetic research so heinous it was still considered an international war crime, then she needed to have that information before taking a job. For the first time in her career, Margaret wondered if she had bitten off more than she could chew. The thrill of taking on a challenging target all but evaporated, and now the prospect of completing the objective filled her with more doubt than elation. She needed answers, and nobody was telling her the truth.

Sullivan expected her to report in later that afternoon on what she had discovered while in the camp. After assembling her forged materials and compiling a plausible narrative, she went to Sullivan's quarters and rang the chime. The door slid open with a hiss and a squeal, and the grim visage of John Sullivan met her with a scowl etched deeper than the usual.

"What?" he said by way of greeting. "Is it that time already?"

"Yes." She matched his tone. "And we need to talk."

Sullivan's cheek twitched. "Fine."

He stepped aside to let her in. He was shirtless and did not seem to care that the long scar down his side was clearly visible. It had been closed by a competent professional, she noted. The line was no more jagged or pinched than absolutely necessary. She wondered what the story was, but decided not to ask. His newer injuries were healing rapidly, leaving only ugly purple blotches and the odd angry streak of healing flesh to mar his physique. As a professional seductress, she could not help but make note of his excessive musculature and lean frame. He looked as if he could lift a car and run a marathon with equal facility, and she supposed there was probably some truth in that. He had been handsome, once. If he let his hair grow to a decent length and paid to have the kink in his nose fixed, there might be a good-looking man underneath all that blood and scruff. He had just showered, and her nose told her that he was fond of cedar-scented soaps. Cheap ones. All in all, she could see why women tumbled for him. If he could figure out how to be less of an offensive brute, she would have probably handled that part of the job already. She supposed a roll with him might be fun. Margaret enjoyed sex as much and probably more than most women. It might even help with the mission.

She let her own frown soften and shed her jacket with a non-chalant shrug before sitting down at the small table he used for his meals. She had not dressed for a vamp, but even a plain white T-shirt looked like expensive lingerie on her frame. The whole charade had the desired effect, and her nose told her that Sullivan was responding the way all men did when she cranked up the heat. As it had before, the strength of his response triggered her own. She stifled the tingling with a stern reminder about the danger he represented. It helped a little.

"So what are we talking about?" Sullivan's voice wanted to be gruff. His attempt to hide his sudden discomfort amused her.

"I pulled a lot of data out of Camp Zero while they were walking us around. I was able to clone some of the databases when I got close enough. I've been digging for references to Keating or whoever is providing funding to Corpus Mundi."

Sullivan walked to his refrigerator. Margaret suspected he just wanted to get away from her and the mounting pressure in his pants. He put his back to her and opened the door. After a few seconds of rummaging he emerged with an armload of food. He plunked the trove down on the table and grunted. "You hungry?" It sounded to Margaret like he offered out of habit.

Margaret looked at the pile. It had fruit, cold meat, something that looked like pasta, and far too much cheese to be healthy. "No thanks," she said with a wince. "I'd rather not die of dysentery."

"I need to eat a lot," he said by way of answer. "Or I shrink."

"Can't have that," Margaret said. She pointed to the sealed containers. "Have at it, big boy."

Sullivan began to eat. During a brief break in his chewing he gestured to the woman "So what have you found?"

"You won't like it."

"I never like anything. Spit it out."

Margaret smiled. She could hear the effort Sullivan was putting into being rude. Her presence distracted him, maybe even calmed his anger. He did not like it and Margaret seized the advantage. "Most of the records implicate your father. He's been pushing this research from behind bars for years now."

Sullivan kept eating. He betrayed no emotion while he pondered this. At last, he took a long drink of some thick white beverage that smelled to Margaret like chalk dust. "I mean, we kind of knew that, right? Any idea who picked up the tab when he stopped paying?"

"Nothing solid." Margaret needed him to focus on the father connection. She leaned over the table, her chest straining against her shirt, and willed John to breathe in the copulin coming out of her pores. "I think your father is playing both sides, John. I saw what they were doing in there. It's horrible. Mickey Sullivan is going to release an army of those genetically modified monsters on the planet, and he's been building that army for two decades. One of those things killed Horowitz." She leaned in more, oozing sincerity and sex appeal, powering her earnest good-girl fantasy with as much pure charm as she could muster. "We have to stop him!"

Sullivan kept eating. He took a long time to respond. When he did, his voice was calm.

"Ah. So that's the angle."

Margaret did not understand. "Huh?"

"Your angle," Sullivan said, wiping his mouth on a napkin. "Two things wrong with your story, Mata Hari. One, Mickey Sullivan has always been a manipulator. He's a puppet master. He likes his power subtle and absolute. He gets what he wants by convincing other people they want to give it to him. He almost never uses brute force. When he does, it's quick and decisive. If your intel says he's building an army of GMP swarm troopers, then your intel is bad. It's not his style and Mickey Sullivan is all about style."

"Bad?" Margaret almost stuttered. She was sure he was ripe for a push. He was pumping out arousal hormones like a college football team at a strip club. "How could it be? I pulled it from their own vaults."

"Second thing. Before she died, Horowitz sent me a message. I didn't find it until we got back here and Doctor Platt showed me something weird. Do you know what it said?"

Margaret's breath caught in her throat. "No. Obviously I don't."

"It said, 'Who is Mata Hari?'"

Margaret relaxed. Horowitz had not given too much away. "She never trusted me. She made that clear as day." The reporter cover story was airtight, complete with published articles and a rich life history. It would hold up.

Sullivan was still talking. "So we went ahead and started trying to answer that very question. The whole reporter thing?" He waved a hand. "That looked legit, all right. Nice work. I didn't think much about it until I ran into Doctor Platt this morning. Like I said, she found something really weird, but also really interesting. I had to know for sure..." He gestured with his fork. "So I came up with my own little scientific experiment which we will get to in a minute."

Margaret said nothing. She needed time to figure out a story, and the more he talked the more context she got. The better the context, the more convincing the resulting lie would be.

Sullivan sighed in the face of her stubborn silence and asked a strange question. "Do you know who Vincent Coll was?"

"You mean the mob cleaner? He's kind of legendary. He's the guy they called when the crooks needed a mess handled without witnesses. I don't get what you're—"

"No. The original."

"There's an original?"

"Yes. He was a hitman for the Irish mobs of the early twentieth century. They called him 'Mad Dog' Coll. The guy you're thinking of is named after him. Except it's not a name. It's a model."

"I don't follow—"

"Same with me. The original John Sullivan was a bare-knuckle boxer. Possibly the greatest that ever lived. Big, strong, drank too much." He let his posture relax as he settled into his narrative. "When they made me, that's what they called my model. The 'John Sullivan' configuration."

Margaret's discomfort grew. Sullivan spoke in cryptic non-sequiturs, with his reactions running counter to her expectations. His sexual desire remained palpable yet his body language conveyed strict composure. Underneath the stink of his desire for her, she began to detect the anger he never seemed to be able to shake. He chewed his food without looking at her. After swallowing, he raised his eyes. They were blank. Hollow. Angry.

"They built us in labs, Coll and me. Assembling us from hundreds of genetic lots that had desirable traits. Coll was a killer, I was a fighter. Different models for different roles. Products to sell to the world's new masters once the Republic either failed or got subverted. Coll was first, I came second. Two more prototypes followed."

"And Mickey did this?"

"Among others, yes. The plan was to produce enough designer chimeras to manage the problems that arose with the shift to a new world order. This way, whole armies would not be needed. It was subtle, decisive, and let's be real, here, it was elegant. That's the Mickey Sullivan way."

"Just what are you getting at, John?"

Sullivan kept eating. "Do you know who Mata Hari was? The first one?"

Margaret blinked. "Yes. It's why I picked it for my pseudonym."

"Did you?"

"What?"

"Pick it." Sullivan pointed his fork at her. "Or did someone else call you that first?"

Margaret swallowed. The teachers at the academy called her that for as long as she could remember. She assumed it was an affectation or a code word.

Sullivan saw her face and nodded. "You grow up with a mom and dad, Margaret? Or maybe you were raised at a facility somewhere? Coll was. I suppose that makes me the lucky one."

"Just what the hell are you—"

Sullivan jabbed the fork at her face. Margaret slipped to the side and fired back with a spear hand strike. Sullivan caught her hand in his and held it in a grip of iron. "Well, look at that. Mighty fast for a reporter, aren't ya?"

Margaret growled from behind bared teeth. Her left hand darted forward, her middle finger poised to slash him in the eye with a diamond-hard fingernail. He leaned back to let the swipe pass. Margaret was accustomed to being stronger than the men she faced, but she knew Sullivan was practically a different species. She twisted in his grip and slashed at the arm holding her. He released her to avoid having his veins opened and she leaped back.

"What the fuck are you doing?" She refused to drop the act, not while there was a chance to salvage this.

Sullivan stood, his face darkness itself. The wounds he took at Camp Zero added to an already gruesome sight. "My experiment. So far, results are as expected."

Margaret crouched, ready to defend herself.

Sullivan put both hands on the table and leaned forward. "You don't know, do you?"

"Know... what...?"

"Christ, woman. What do you think it cost to give you all your little tricks? How much cash for a Mata Hari? Who paid for the moving bones, the poison fingers, the fucking pheromones in your sweat?" He slid the table to the side, upsetting his pile of food and clearing the path between them. "You don't even know what you are, and you're out here messing around with my hormones? I couldn't get you out of my head, I thought I was going crazy. I *dreamed* about you. Do you know what that kind of voodoo does to a guy like me?"

The way he said that made Margaret very nervous. This was a man on the edge, struggling with his own brain chemistry. His overwhelming arousal stopped feeling like a good sign as she began to understand how dangerous the situation had become. She tried to remember exactly where the door was and prepared herself to make a break for it.

She refused to fear. If Sullivan knew about her secret weapons, then he also knew he could not fight her the way he wanted to. Two of her nails were hard and sharp enough to cut light metals. Three of her ten fingers were loaded with toxins that ranged in potency from 'rapid death' to 'drunken stupor.' She could even discharge a powerful electric shock from her palm, though that one hurt like hell when she used it. Not even he was fast enough to put her down before she stuck him with something nasty. He knew it, and she knew it. An uneasy standoff followed.

It did not look like Sullivan wanted to fight as much as he wanted to make a point. "You are as fast as me. You think that's normal? You're strong, too. What line did you get? Did they tell you that you were a MINK? Or do you at least know you are a chimera?"

"What the hell are you talking about?" It sounded silly to her own ears. She was every inch a GMP, and her documentation very clearly listed her various enhancements as a MINK with a GMOD score of three across all metrics. She said as much, which made Sullivan laugh.

"GMOD of three? Lady, my neuromotor score is a seven and you matched me without even trying. That's custom work."

Doubt thrashed like an angry snake in Margaret's mind. "I'm not a chimera!"

"Yes, you are," Sullivan said. "Doctor Platt has been going through all the records from Mickey's operation. She's annoying as hell but she's the best genetic engineer in the world. First of all, let me give you the real bad news. There were four designer chimeras in the original program." He held up a finger for each as he listed them. "Vincent Coll. John L. Sullivan. Audie Murphy..." He stopped to make sure he had Margaret's full attention. "... and Mata Hari. That lady's plotted your genotype down to the last peptide. We know lots of things about you that you are probably going to find real interesting."

Margaret scrutinized his face and body language, looking for a lie. She saw nothing. Still, she was not ready to believe him. "This is wrong. I don't know what Mickey has going on, but there is no way—"

"Don't be stupid. It doesn't suit you. Platt has all the files and you can see for yourself if you want. You were born in the same lab I was. You were raised to be a spy. You are an urban operative designed to get in anywhere, manipulate powerful people, steal things and find things. And occasionally kill people in ways that do not attract attention." His eyes were crystal blue pits of ice. "You're just like me, *Margaret*."

Her heart pounded against her sternum like a bass drum. He knew her name. That meant he knew everything.

Sullivan twisted the knife even more. "And you are working for the same people who want you dead."

CHAPTER TWENTY-SIX

Sullivan stared down at Margaret.

He steeled himself for an attack, hoping she would not. Her weaponized body presented a threat to him with no easy solutions.

"Somebody tried to kill you in there, Margaret. I'd bet my ass it wasn't Mickey, either. Was it your own people? Or was it somebody else?" He held his hands out to his sides. "I can't say. Only you can. But this is the second time I've heard that more than one party is competing to bring down the Republic."

Margaret's chin wavered. "Let's say I believe you—"

"—Oh, you believe me."

"Shut the fuck up. Let's say I believe you. If you know all this, why aren't you killing me?"

"One, I'm not sure I can. Not without a gun and mine is in the other room. I did that on purpose so I wouldn't get tempted just to shoot you in your pretty face. Two, Maris insisted that you get the opportunity to choose for yourself what you were going to do after you had the information. She's a real hero like that."

"Can you prove it?"

Sullivan sniffed. "That you are one of Corpus Mundi's four horsemen? Absolutely. We have all the data you could want. You might not understand most of it, but the parts you do will be all kinds of convincing."

"Then what?"

"Then you choose."

"Choose what?"

"Who you want to be." When she did not appear convinced, he added. "Don't pout. Vincent Coll was the one who broke the news to me. You're getting lucky. I didn't like it either, for what it's worth. When I got all whiny like you're about to, this is the line I got from Maris. Up until now, you haven't had enough information to really decide who and what you are. That makes shit easy because you don't have to take the blame for when you do something awful. It's not your fault, right? But not anymore. Now you know everything. You know exactly where you came from, exactly what's been done to you, and you even have a real good idea about who did it and why. Now if you decide to go right back to being the Mata Hari they want you to be, then you are making that choice with all the facts and taking full responsibility for the consequences. She made it sound very liberating, I think it's a huge pain in the ass, myself."

"It sounds very stupid to me."

"That's our Maris." Sullivan tried to watch her eyes, but his head struggled to stay ahead of his hormones and his gaze insisted on roving. He bit the inside of his cheek, hoping pain would keep him focused.

Margaret caught his struggle. Now that he was aware of what caused it, the effect seemed to bother her. "I can't turn it off, you know."

"Turn what off?"

"The pheromones. I'm not trying to do it. It's just part of me. Like your bad attitude."

"It's a very desirable trait in a spy. That it's dangerous or inconvenient doesn't mean shit to them. I'm in control, so you don't need to worry."

"It's not just you I'm worried about."

Sullivan's mouth twitched at the corner. "Careful. I am not the guy to play these games with."

"These games are all I know. What I was made for, apparently. I'm as susceptible as anyone else, and it drives me crazy sometimes. You sweat sex hormones like a high-school kid on steroids."

"Maris would tell you that I *am* a high school kid on steroids."

"Well it's giving me a god damn headache."

Sullivan laughed, though the sound was hard and mean. "You do not want to know what goes on in my head when you are around. Be glad a headache is all I'm giving you."

"If this is you flirting, you're terrible at it."

"If you're trying to seduce me, you're just as bad."

Margaret blew a long gust of air from her lungs and rubbed her eyes. She was either deeply conflicted or an excellent actress. Sullivan assumed some of both. She dropped her hands and blurted, "What the hell am I supposed to do with all this? Where do I go from here? Can I keep doing the things I've always done? Do I want to? Does it matter where I came from? I don't feel like I'm choosing anything, John. It feels like all my choices have been made for me."

"That's exactly what I said," Sullivan replied. "I was wrong. It takes time to figure that out, though. There's only one choice you need to make right now, either way."

She looked up at him. He knew his face was not kind, his expression still twisted by his own mental demons. A strange urge to be helpful tugged at the back of his mind. Sympathy was a curse he did not think he would ever get used to. He put it aside. This was not the time for sentiment, and he was ill-equipped for that either way.

"What choice is that?" she asked.

"Are you going to try to stop me?"

"Stopping you was never the mission." She deflected out of reflex, and Sullivan shook his head.

Now he let his anger come forward. "What was the mission, then?" This time she hesitated and Sullivan could almost see her trying to spin a believable lie. Whether she needed to trick him or just did not want to answer, he could not say. He hoped it was professional pride keeping her from revealing her goals. That he could understand. Though at this point in the game he had no time for it. He dismissed whatever fanciful story she might be building in her head with a wave of his hand. "Don't get confused. I'm not here to help you. Call Maris if you want to talk about your feelings. I need to know what job you are on, plain and simple. Right now I don't know if you are the enemy or not. Make me guess and I might have to go for that gun I mentioned."

"Threats? Spare me." If the woman feared him, she did not show it. "The job was to kill Mickey Sullivan. I have to be circumspect because he has employed me before. He knows who I am and what I can do. I'd never get close to him."

"But I can."

"Exactly."

"So you were going to throw a little ass at me, convince me that Mickey was up to that unsavory shit at Camp Zero, and then send me off to clobber the old man?"

"That's about right."

"What's your plan now?"

"I'm going to hunt down the man who hired me and find out who he really is. Then I'm probably going to kill him."

"Emilie?" Sullivan called out over his shoulder.

"She's telling the truth," a small voice called back from his bedroom.

"What the hell?" said Margaret.

"Margaret, meet Emilie. The mysterious fifth horseman and the world's first immortal chimera."

Emilie stepped out of Sullivan's bedroom and gave Sullivan a recriminating frown. "I'm not immortal. I just won't get old."

"Emilie," Sullivan said to Margaret, "is why all the bastards trying to take over the world right now are having trouble getting along."

"I heard rumors," Margaret said. "But there are always rumors."

Sullivan ignored her. "Corpus Mundi is all a-flutter over her magical telomeres, but one of Emilie's other little tweaks is an abundance of mirror neurons and enough extra recall to use them. When you feel uncomfortable, she can see your feelings in your body language and hear them in your voice. It's damned creepy if you ask me. That kid knows what got under your skin even if you don't. When you decide to turn left rather than right, she knows why you picked one over the other."

"She can tell when someone is lying!"

Emilie corrected her. "I can tell if something a person said makes them scared or angry or guilty, stuff like that."

Margaret fixed the child with a calculating stare. "What if the liar is a very good actress?"

"You aren't that good." Emilie said it in that special way children have of being totally offensive without realizing it. "And Mister Sully makes you squirm funny."

"I make everyone squirm funny," Sullivan said.

Emilie wrinkled her nose. "She squirms different. It's weird. Auntie Sharon says I'll understand when I'm older. But I understand now. She wants to—"

"We get it, Emilie!" Margaret blurted. "I'm convinced."

"So does he—"

This time, it was Sullivan who interrupted the child. "Thank you, Emilie. You can go now. Get your calisthenics done before bed, or there will be extra work tomorrow."

"But my arms hurt!"

"They're supposed to. Go."

After the girl left Margaret said, "You had a child in there the whole time? What if we tried to kill each other?"

"She had instructions to bring me the gun in that case. Or use it on you if it looked like I was losing."

"She's just a kid!"

"So was I, once. Nobody lost any sleep over it."

Margaret grabbed her head with both hands. "I need a drink."

Sullivan nodded toward the chair she had abandoned. "Sit. I have beer."

"No wine?"

"Do I look like a wine drinker?"

"I suppose you don't."

"Beer it is, then." No body language expert himself, Sullivan thought she might be relaxing. Her expression lost some of the fierce concentration and her movements became smooth again. She was settling back into her persona, her face becoming cool and businesslike. He hoped that meant the fighting was over. Feeling his own stress levels fall, he grabbed a pair of cans from his fridge and tossed one to Margaret. "So now I know you aren't lying to me about your plans. That's good. If you were pulling anything, Emilie would have caught it."

"That is a very convenient little girl."

"The whole world wants her dead or in a lab. I've decided to not let that happen." He took a very long pull from his can. "That's not exactly convenient. But the good news is that I can let you go. If you want to hunt this son of a bitch down, I wish you only success. Kill him once for me."

"There's something you should know," Margaret said. "The Director of GEED was there. He flipped on Mickey to some other side. He gave up Representative Keating before he died. I'm not sure what it means, but I think the implications are obvious."

"You killed him?"

Her head bobbed a curt affirmative.

Sullivan smiled in that way of his, conveying neither warmth nor happiness. "Couldn't have happened to a nicer asshole. But what does a high-ranking Republic official have going on with Camp Zero?"

"I take it you weren't the brainy horseman. I think the Republic has its own faction. They'd almost have to, right?"

Sullivan took the insult in stride. "It follows. Once the news about Emilie broke, the whole damn group fractured. Mickey wants to stay with the original plan, Corpus Mundi wants to pursue Emilie's mutation. Whoever is footing their bill wants us horsemen dead, and I'll eat my shoe if that isn't the same asshole who hired you. Keating might be playing his own game, but that ambush is a pretty clear indicator that he'd be happy to see us out of the picture, too. No matter how well-made we are, Emilie will always be the holy fucking grail."

Margaret sipped her own beer. "Thank god you don't like IPAs," she remarked. "The acid is brutal on my nose. And you are right about Keating and Corpus Mundi. Their new financier is the one who hired me to kill Hanson and Mickey. I can't believe he wants me dead, too." She huffed. "But why not? I know too much about him already. I suppose once these horsemen are all gone I'll merely be the last loose end."

"You did Hanson? Should have figured that out myself." Sullivan drained his beer. "You handing out names while being so generous with your intel?"

"Victor Sharpe. It's fake. He uses multi-level encryption and a voice modulator in his calls. He also uses a third-party security proxy, which he thinks I don't know about."

"Source of the money you get?"

"These are not amateurs, John."

"Right. Okay. Let's talk business, then."

Margaret tilted her head. "Do, let's."

"You got a ghost to hunt, I got a GiMP messiah to protect. How do we help each other?"

"What do you offer?"

"Muscle, cover, witty repartee."

"Two out of three ain't bad, John. Go on."

"The Complex is way bigger than you realize. Between the Silk Road companies and the Railroad, you can get whatever and wherever you want without tipping off the grid. Even things like bulk contraband. It's insane what goes through here. There's a whole underground economy between the Complexes and the real world upstairs. That's your cover. When the time comes to hit something, you got me for muscle." He affected an exaggerated businessman's manner. "I trust my credentials are satisfactory?"

"They'll do," she said. "And what does all this splendor cost me?"

"Fagan and I suck at spy work. We got Hanson killed and we turned that strip club into a war zone. You, on the other hand, might just be the best covert operative in the world. I think you know what I want." He leaned forward, a growl entering his words. "You find that financier, and you feed him directly to me. You leave nothing out, you play it straight the whole time. Anything you find out about Keating comes my way first. I don't care if you want to kill this Sharpe asshole or even Mickey, but you don't drop anyone until we get all the information I need out of them. That's the deal."

"Those terms are not so onerous, John. Why so generous all of a sudden? You were ready to kill me ten minutes ago."

Sullivan leaned back. "I'm learning from old Mickey, I guess. I ask you for a small favor, and then I offer a big one in return. Makes it hard for you to say no."

"It does. But I always look a gift horse in the mouth. What's the catch?"

"Besides the obvious one?"

Margaret looked confused. "Not so obvious to me..."

"If you fuck with me, I will find you and kill you, obviously. This is no cushy corporate gig, lady. We're into mobster shit now."

"I guess that really should have been obvious."

"Guess you ain't the brainy horseman either, huh?"

"Fuck you. Throw in some of that witty repartee for free and we have a deal."

"Done," Sullivan said. "Now go find Victor Sharpe."

"With pleasure."

CHAPTER TWENTY-SEVEN

Margaret supposed that it was not Sharpe's fault she found him out with so little trouble.

She was a trusted asset, a known quantity. He paid well and he paid on time. The man had little to no reason to think she would ever come after him. Why would she? Her situation was as much a surprise to herself as anyone. Digging into a client's business went against the grain; however, in this case, the exception felt justified.

For once, the lack of challenge failed to irritate her. With her head now full of terrifying new information, the last thing she needed was a protracted mission. She needed answers, so she started with the money.

All of her clients paid her through a network of electronic clearing houses that verified, held, and transferred her payments across multiple levels of anonymity. Most of these clearing houses existed only in the electronic ether of a vast network of automated banking servers. The currency was cryptcoin, and thus untraceable, with the transaction records buried under endless strata of unrelated data. Margaret fostered no illusions about her ability to run down any given transaction to its originator. In short order she determined that any such attempt would be wasted effort.

Next, she went after her old targets. She pulled the records on anyone Sharpe had employed her to track, steal from, blackmail, or kill. It was here she noticed that until the Hanson job, most of these operations focused on rising Global Republic politicians and their campaign donors. By itself, this did not reveal any great secrets. Then she looked into the telecommunications records. Margaret employed a lot of high-level signal security herself, and something about Sharpe's calls proved quite familiar. There were only so many underworld signal security consultants to check on, and only one good enough for Victor Sharpe.

That was how she found herself inside a gaudy Manhattan nightclub, nursing a terrible cocktail and watching a pathetic little man spend far too much money trying to buy the popularity he could never achieve on his own. The target was holding court in the VIP section protected by two bodyguards. Through the clear walls of the private lounge, she watched several women that Margaret had already pegged as professionals drape themselves across his lap. They rubbed and tugged at their host as he poured thousand-dollar champagne down their throats and put all manner of intoxicating chemicals up their noses. Like so many men with more money than sense, he dressed like someone who watched way too many netcasts on the latest fashion trends and spent all his money taking their advice. From the bottoms of his ludicrous shoes to the top of his hideous hat, Armin Kinzei looked every inch the spectacular jerk Margaret already knew him to be. At the academy, Margaret had endured endless lessons on the difference between 'fashion' and 'style.' Lessons Kinzei had quite clearly been spared.

She found herself conflicted on just how to proceed. Just a few days prior, this would not have been an issue. Some exposed cleavage, a little vapid banter, and the brush of her hand across a thigh would have gotten her everything she needed. Something about that bothered her now. Knowing she was not merely trained and augmented for her career, but *built* from the ground up to manipulate men made the whole process feel dirty. She did not want to reward her creators for their deception by being the thing they wanted her to be. Her shame at being so completely manipulated tainted everything she thought she understood about herself.

These reflections were useless and counter-productive, so she abandoned her thoughts and started for the clear polycarbonate partition of the VIP room. The VIP lounge was the logical place to do this, and she had chosen it for a reason. With a full suite of privacy settings active, she would be free to work on the target as long as she wanted to once the room was clear. Getting inside did not present her with much of a challenge, either. Her ticket past the gargoyles was a black dress both short in length and deep at the neckline. Her hair had been dyed jet black as well, and all her adjustable curves were dialed to their most provocative proportions. The look was tawdry and she set her walk to match it. Crystal blue eyes sparkled with sultry promise when they met the leering gaze of Kinzei's bodyguards and she flashed perfect white teeth in a big smile.

"Hi, boys!" she greeted the hulking goons. "What's a girl got to do to get invited inside?"

One guard let his eyes slide up and down her body, and for the first time in her life Margaret felt uncomfortable with the attention. "Oh, I think you probably know. I'm sure Mister Kinzei could be convinced to let you in," he said. "You down to party?"

"Always," she purred right back.

The guard knocked on the panel to get Kinzei's attention. The little man looked up from nuzzling the half-exposed breasts of one of the women already inside. When his eyes reached Margaret, his goofy smile expanded to a full-on idiot's grin. The bodyguard keyed the door and gestured for Margaret to pass. "Have a good time," he said. "And if things don't work out, find me after."

"Sure thing," Margaret said. She passed the guard with a wiggle and stepped into the VIP lounge.

The only thing that kept the stink of sex hormones from choking her was the overwhelming aroma of opioid vapor. The haze stung her eyes and clung to the inside of her nose with acrid tenacity. Margaret had never been particularly susceptible to drugs, and knowing that this was a design feature and not an accident of birth angered her. The two young women already in the room stared daggers at the newcomer, but scamming rich morons was a lot like improv comedy. It was bad form to contradict the other players. Conflict might spoil the mood and thus end the game early. They assessed her with angry eyes and then returned to groping Kinzei while consuming his drugs.

"Well, hello my pretty pretty pretty thing," Kinzei said to Margaret. His voice came just a touch too high to sound normal. He spoke fast, with a spastic hyperactivity Margaret knew well. An array of ampules and delivery devices littered the table in front of the lounging man, confirming her suspicions and adding a wrinkle to the plan. Sunglasses hid his eyes, though Margaret did not need to see them to guess Kinzei's condition. She could smell the byproducts in his sweat when she stepped over to the couch, see his fingers twitch when he poured her a drink. The man was high enough to head butt a satellite and this made her job much more difficult.

First, she dealt with the other women. Over the course of the next hour, Margaret managed to dose each with a mild soporific from one of her nails. It took a while to get them all the way out, as the quantity of stimulants in their blood blunted the effect. Margaret increased the dosage as necessary, and rendered oblivious by their own state of advanced inebriation, neither bimbo was the wiser. Soon both were snoring on the couch while Margaret writhed in the lap of a very self-impressed Armin Kinzei.

"These other bitches can't hang, baby," he slurred up at Margaret. "But you can party all night, can't you?" He reached around to grab her buttocks, a firm round mound in each clammy hand. "Kinzei is all about that party, baby!"

Next, Margaret removed the bodyguards from the equation. "Damn right, baby," she cooed. "You and me both!" She reached back to a remote control on the table and dialed the clear partitions opaque, then she locked the door. Last, she set the interior noise canceling to its maximum setting. "Time for some privacy, honey," she explained.

"I like the sound of that!" Kinzei said. He slipped his hands beneath her dress and pulled the hemline up to her waist. "It's about to get hot in here!"

She let Kinzei's hands wander while she ensured the lounge was secure. He had freed her breasts from the front of her dress and was fumbling at his own pants by the time her professional attention to detail was satisfied. Kinzei, oblivious to the impending death of his amorous ambitions, tugged at his crotch with hands made clumsy by intoxication. Margaret reached down as if to help and the man leaned back with a look of glazed satisfaction. When Margaret found her grip, Kinzei's eyes went wide with delight. This melted into confusion when the subsequent ministrations did not give the impression of a woman with sex on her mind. He tried to sit up. Margaret pressed him back into the couch with her free hand and squeezed Kinzei in a manner communicating in no uncertain terms that the fun portion of his evening had ended. His confusion blossomed into fear, expanding the scope of his dread as the pain in his testicles penetrated the fog of alcohol and amphetamines like a dentist's drill.

"The party is just starting, Armin," Margaret whispered into his ear. "Scream if you want to. Nobody is going to hear you."

"Wha—" was the best he could manage.

Margaret hoped he was not too high to be useful. "Armin, are you with me?"

When he did not answer right away, she gave him a rough squeeze. Kinzei yelped. "What the fuck are you doing?"

"I'm asking questions, Armin. Give me answers and you get to keep your tiny little balls."

"What do you want you crazy—argh!"

Margaret hissed through her teeth. "Careful, Armin. I need you to tell me who one of your clients is and where I can find him. That's all. Give me what I want and you can live the rest of your life as a biological male."

"What the hell are you... what client?"

"Victor Sharpe."

Some of the haze in Kinzei's eyes evaporated. His body stiffened and his breathing went shallow. "Oh, no. Oh, no, no, no. You're *her*, aren't you?"

Margaret felt the corners of her eyes narrow. "Her?"

"Mata Hari! Don't kill me! I'll do anything you want!"

"Give. Me. Sharpe."

"Sharpe is a ghost, okay? I scramble his signal, but his signal comes scrambled already, you get me?" Kinzei was babbling. "I can un-scramble my scramble, but I have nothing to do with his scramble! I just cross the wires, you know?"

"Not helpful," Margaret said. She dragged one of her nails along the wrinkled skin of Kinzei's scrotum. He howled and bled with equal vigor. "Do better."

"I got all his calls!" Kinzei screamed. "To everyone! I record them! You can have them all! Please!" The tears flowed freely from his bloodshot eyes. "Please," he sobbed again. "I know..." Kinzei hesitated, and Margaret squeezed. "...I can tell you where he makes his calls from! Okay? I can tell you!"

Margaret considered this. "That will do." She fished her phone from her clutch without releasing Kinzei. "First, put all the calls on here."

"You gotta let go of me," he whined. "I can't work with my balls in a vise."

"Figure it out."

Kinzei figured it out. After retrieving his own handheld, a flood of data began to stream from his device to hers.

Margaret checked the data and said, "Good. Now where does he call from?"

"He rents a raker's hotel. Uses a really well-built fake identity. Took me a year and a half to crack it. It's up in White Plains."

"Perfect. You've been very helpful Armin. For that, you get to keep your balls. But if I get the notion you're trying to burn me..." She did not have to complete the threat. Kinzei's utter defeat lay etched into the lines of his face.

"He's going to kill us both now," he said.

"Who? Sharpe?" Margaret laughed. She took her hand from Kinzei's crotch and gripped him by the chin. "What's my name, little man?"

"M-Mata Hari?"

"That's right. And Mister Sharpe is about to find out why double-crossing me is a very bad idea."

"You don't get it," Kinzei moaned. "You can't kill him. He's not real. Sharpe is a construct. A composite identity used by..."

Kinzei stopped, as if reconsidering the wisdom of saying more. A single nail drew a line of blood from Kinzei's cheek down to his carotid artery. Kinzei hissed and tensed. "It's PAR! He's a PAR guy! They're tricking Corpus Mundi into doing their dirty work, okay!"

"What dirty work?"

"They're after some kid in the KC Complex. Worth more than money to them. They're gonna hit the Complex and let Corpus Mundi take the blame for it!" His lips quivered and his pupils expanded and contracted as drugs and terror competed with each other for control. "It's all in the calls! I swear!"

"How will the Pan-Asian Remnant get Corpus Mundi to take the fall for a GEED raid on the KC Complex?"

"GEED ain't doing shit. It's the GiMPS! They're gonna use the GiMPs!"

Margaret thought of the things she had seen at Camp Zero and her blood ran cold.

"How?"

"They've been smuggling them in through something called the Silk Road. It's going to look like all the GiMPs hiding inside staged a takeover..."

"And that will be the excuse GEED needs to raid," Margaret finished. "It's going to be a massacre."

CHAPTER TWENTY-EIGHT

A courier from one of the many gangs running the KC Complex brought the encrypted file to Sullivan while he was eating lunch with Fagan. The diner they had chosen was two rings out from Hubtown, quiet, and filled with people who knew how to mind their own business. The main concourses of each ring, huge by design to give the impression of fresh air and open space, fell well short of capturing the freedom of being above ground. Looking out a diner window in the KC Complex held all the wonder of staring through a clear panel into a large open stadium. People and vehicles moved along lighted tracks, each staying in their appointed lanes. The boring electric vehicles looked to Sullivan like hairless herd animals, blindly following the illuminated and holographic signage telling each where to go and when to stop and wait. Commuter tram access doors spewed people into the concourse or swallowed them like gaping black mouths as those coming came and those going went. Lights were plentiful, yet despite the lack of shadows the space still never managed to shake the appearance of dimness. All in all, the KC Complex approximated topside life, and poorly at best. Sullivan thought it felt more like a parody than an homage.

The implications of Keating's press conference covered the population like a heavy blanket. No one knew what the dire threat from GEED would mean, but with more than ten thousand fugitive GMPs among the million-plus residents, implications alone were enough to fill everyone with a sense of dread.

The portly messenger shuffled up to their table and plopped a single data stick down. If he saw Sullivan's hand resting on the butt of his pistol, the courier gave no indication. "You've got mail," he said. Then left without another word.

Fagan looked at Sullivan. "Wonder what that could be? Word from Margaret?"

"Maybe," Sullivan said. "Only one way to find out." He picked up the thin plastic stick and pulled his phone from a pocket. He tapped the screen with the stick and frowned. "Requires plug-in authentication. Shit. Must be serious." He plugged the data stick into his phone and waited for the encryption to acknowledge a physical connection. When the two devices were satisfied with the handshake, the screen began to fill with text.

"Don't leave me in suspense, partner," Fagan said through a mouthful of tacos.

"It's Mickey. He has intel that Keating is using GEED to make a grab at Emilie. He's warning us. Says the GEED lockdown is to keep us from moving the girl. He expects a raid or something will follow."

"You sound unsure about that."

"I always have to wonder what Mickey's real game is when he does anything. Nothing is the way you think it is with him."

Fagan had the easy answer. "He needs you to keep working your case. If Emilie gets snatched, then his side of the bargain is null. He has no currency then."

"I suppose you're probably right," Sullivan said. "But still..."

"I hear ya." Fagan wiped his mouth. "Anything else?"

"Yeah. It looks like Corpus Mundi's mystery backer has been sneaking assets in here for the last few months. A bunch of big cargo containers, plenty of people, some weird tech."

Another taco disappeared into Fagan's mouth. "Any idea what it's for?"

"Nope. Mickey says they tried to hide the shipments as pharmaceuticals. Apparently he's been watching the Silk Road extra close since the press conference. With the GEED lockdown messing up access, everybody has been scrambling to move stuff in and out. The bribe rates have quadrupled, and that's how he caught this."

Fagan bobbed his head as he chewed. "I suppose we are going to hunt these assets down?"

"I suppose we are. Finish eating. I know where to start."

The final taco on Fagan's plate met its fate as had its brethren. The giant stood, still chewing, and gestured for Sullivan to follow. "I'm done," he said. "Let's go."

Twenty minutes later, the pair stood outside the Rosedale tram station. A veritable army of men and women in orange vests milled about. They directed passengers, took bribes, handled baggage, and ran games of chance along the walkways and kiosks dotting the station. Sullivan scanned them in search of a familiar face.

"Skip!" he called when he finally saw it. A young man looked up from the dice game he was running. When his eyes found Sullivan's, his face collapsed into a mask of chagrin. "Oh no," he said out loud. "Not you two!"

Sullivan and Fagan threaded their way across the platform. "Hey, Skip," Fagan said affably. "How ya been?"

"Not dead," the young man replied. "Mostly 'cause I avoid you guys."

"Remember that time you tried to shake us down?" Fagan asked. "You remember that, right Sully?"

"Good times," Sullivan agreed.

"Just tell me what you want so I can do it and be rid of you guys, okay?"

Sullivan's smile never touched his eyes. "Somebody who doesn't like me very much is sneaking people in here through Rosedale."

"Nobody likes you very much," Skip pointed out. "I don't."

"You could always end up liking me less," Sullivan said. "I'm serious, Skip. I need to find these people. The Road Crew runs access in and out of Rosedale. That means you can find them."

Skip sighed. "Fine. Whaddya got?"

Sullivan showed him the message.

"Okay, Sully. The equipment is probably stashed in one of the inner rings by now. Those are big containers, so the smart money says you'll find them in the warehouse district just west of Hubtown." He scribbled a note onto Sullivan's phone screen. "Go see this guy, tell him I sent you, and remind him that I get a cut of whatever he charges you for the information. He's gonna pretend he don't know shit, but if you charm him in that special way of yours, he'll talk. As for all these goons? I think I know where two of your guys are right off the bat. They came in maybe two weeks ago, and fuck me if I didn't have them pegged for trouble right off the bat."

"What do you mean?"

"They were muscle, plain and simple. Big MINK types. We get plenty of that through here, but they were super fucking squared-away, you know?"

"Military?"

"I thought so. I offered them credit for a cut of whatever action they got into, but they turned me down. I figured they were sitting on a shit ton of cryptcoin like you were when you came through, so I gave him fair warning about the exchange rate. Get this. He had credits, man. This guy had obviously never been here before, but his vault was swole with our local currency? Fuck that. I knew something was up."

Sullivan wiped his face with a hand. "And you said nothing?"

"Somebody wants to hire muscle for some gig here?" Skip sniffed and shrugged. "None of my fucking business."

"Recognize any of these others?"

"It's all fake names and shit, right?" he shook his head. "I only know these two cause they like to hang out in the Mercantile. Except they ain't really hanging out, if you catch my drift."

"They're waiting?" Fagan asked.

"Hell yes. They're on some kind of hit or something."

"Scouting," Sullivan said. "They are doing recon. Take us to them, Skip."

Skip looked up at the two men and said nothing.

"Two-hundred credits to point them out to us," Sullivan said. "And a hundred more for everyone on this list you find and show us after that."

"Now we're talking," Skip said with a grin. "Follow me, boys."

Skip took Sullivan and Fagan out of the station and across the Exchange to the Mercantile. Remembering their last trip through Rosedale's commercial district, Sullivan asked, "Any hard feelings still out there with the Pale Horses?"

"You're in the green," Skip said without turning. "Nobody takes business personal here. The Horses won't hassle you unless you hassle them."

"Glad to hear it," Fagan muttered.

Once inside the bustling zone, the noise and activity increased tenfold. Skip shouted to be heard over the dull roar caused by all the people, vendors, and advertisements competing for attention at once. "This goddamn GEED lockdown has the markets all fucked up. The value of credits versus 'coin changes every fucking hour. There's enough food production in-house to survive a siege, but luxury goods and non-essentials cost a mint now." He steered the two men toward the center of the cavernous trade zone, pushing through walkways thick with people. Near the edge of a wide, open square, Skip pulled them up short and gestured to a cafe. Two men sat on stools looking out into the crowd. Each had a drink, but neither looked to have touched theirs in a long time.

"There's your boys. Every day at this time they sit here and watch. After a couple of hours, they leave and go back to the Dorms."

Sullivan squinted through the haze of narcotic vapor, smoke, and steam. The men were large. His size or even bigger, sporting brutal crew cuts and thousand-yard stares. They dressed in dungarees and tee shirts, with loose jackets covering holstered guns.

"Belts," Sullivan said to Fagan.

Fagan nodded. "Yup."

"What?" Skip asked.

"Regular crooks don't usually wear a proper gun belt, Skip. Guns are heavy. They drag at the pants and flop around if you don't have a real sturdy belt and a good holster. Those guys have real nice belts."

"So you figure they probably have nice holsters, too?"

"And probably nice guns," Fagan finished the thought.

"Pros," Sullivan said.

"We going to take them here?"

"Let's go shake the tree, first," Sullivan said. "I'd like to see how they react to us."

"Oh, this is going to be good," Skip said. "Let me get clear so nobody associates me with the shit show you two are about to start."

Sullivan declined to acknowledge Skip and began to stalk toward the cafe. Pedestrians and patrons bounced from his chest with every step, most muttering dire imprecations but otherwise restraining themselves from foolish action. Sullivan let the two men see him coming. With Fagan in tow there would be no hiding it, anyway. An abrupt change in posture told Sullivan when his prey noticed him and the cool prickle of a cortisol response began to creep across the skin of his neck.

The two men rose when Sullivan and Fagan were still twenty feet away. Sullivan braced for whatever came next and kept walking. The taller man, blond and blue-eyed, glanced over to his partner who was shorter, wider, and dark-haired. Something transpired between them that Sullivan could not make out, and both men began to walk away from the cafe.

"Oh, don't run..." Fagan lamented.

"They're gonna run," Sullivan said, quickening his pace.

The two men made an attempt to lose their pursuers in the crowd, but Fagan's prodigious height made escape impossible. After twenty yards of fruitless twists and turns between stalls and store-fronts, all pretense of subtlety disappeared and the pair bolted. Sullivan took off like a cheetah in pursuit, leaving Fagan behind to exclaim, "Fucking MINKs," as he struggled to match the new pace. He soon fell far behind.

The density of the crowds kept any of them from reaching a full sprint, though the obvious hyperkinesia of the fleeing men had the duo knifing through the clumps of people and vaulting over obstacles like jackrabbits. Sullivan had never been enamored of gymnastics or acrobatics, and his mediocre abilities in that arena prevented him from overtaking the escaping operatives. He substituted sheer athleticism for skill and kept them in sight. Fagan would be well behind him, he knew. Once clear of the Mercantile if the men chose to turn and fight Sullivan would have to take them on alone. Normally, he might welcome the exercise, but the men he chased moved in a manner that had the more strategic areas of his brain wincing. They exhibited capabilities well beyond the normal sort of thing he saw as a warden or even Mickey's best-paid street muscle. These were military-grade GMPs, which would be bad enough, but the things he witnessed at Camp Zero filled his mind with a swarm of much more uncomfortable possibilities.

Without better options, he kept chasing. Their flight moved them further from the Mercantile's main entrance and deeper toward the back. Despite its enormous size, the repurposed construction floor was not infinite in size. Sullivan ran, convinced the men had a destination in mind that was not merely the bare metal wall of the giant section of Rosedale.

Moving away from the center also moved them into areas dirtier and less well-appointed. Sullivan watched the blond man leap a food cart, place a hand on the roof of a passing vehicle, and vault over its roof in a graceful arc to alight on his feet just beyond. His partner duplicated the feat, and this left Sullivan to navigate the slow-moving obstacle his own way. He ran at the meandering delivery truck, planting one foot on the front bumper and leaping like a hurdler over the roof. He landed on the far side just in time to see the two men disappear between two rusted metal shacks. The edge of the hangar was just beyond, meaning either a hidden escape hatch or a trap awaited him.

He entered the alley in a low crouch. No guns met his approach and he was greeted by the clang of a small man-door slamming shut. Wasting no time, Sullivan dove for the round metal hatch and ripped at the latch. He wrenched with all his strength to no avail. It had been locked from the other side.

"God damn it!" he shouted to no one in particular. He looked around for someone who knew where the door led, but found the alley dark and quiet. "Fuck!" he spat.

"At least you are easy to find," an exhausted Fagan said between great heaving breaths. The giant rounded the corner drenched in sweat and gasping like an asthmatic.

"They got away," Sullivan said, pointing to the hatch. "They had an escape route set up."

"Pros," wheezed Fagan. "Figures." He approached the door and examined the long handle of the latch. "Still," he sighed. Meaty hands wrapped around the metal. Fagan bent his knees and sat his hips under his spine. With a shrug of enormous shoulders and a bellow like an enraged bull, he lifted. Legs straightened, trapezius muscles stretched, and metal screamed like a wounded animal. With a sound like a gunshot, something on the other side of the door snapped. The handle jerked in a long arc and the hatch leaped in its frame. Fagan shook his hands and said, "Ow." Red-faced, he turned to Sullivan with a toothy smile. "Door's unlocked."

"You are really convenient to have around, you know that?"

"You should see me open a jar of pickles," the giant huffed. "Let's go."

Sullivan moved through the door first, though he waited for Fagan to stuff himself through the opening before moving on. The tunnel beyond was barely large enough for Fagan to stand in. Two thin strips of green emergency lighting ran along the floor, offering enough light to see by but not much else. Sullivan, with his excellent low-light vision, elected to lead. It was not hard to figure out that the passage was a smuggler's tunnel. Even a society run by the lawless had its own kind of criminals. The two men picked their way along for three or four minutes before the shaft opened into a larger room. Sullivan swept the space with eyes and ears both and found it empty. The light was no better inside, and it took a moment for Sullivan to recognize where they were.

"We're in a maintenance walkway, next to one of the tram tunnels," he told Fagan. He pointed to a rough-cut opening in one of the walls. Beyond it, the sound of tram cars whooshing along filtered into the room on a breeze that stank of hydraulic fluid and mold. "They must sneak stuff off of cars to smuggle into the Mercantile. Probably to avoid paying the Pale Horses their cut."

"Sneaky bastards," Fagan said. He gave the door a scowl. "You go first. I'm going to need a minute to get through that little thing."

Sullivan slipped into the tram tunnel. Dropping to a metal catwalk, he crouched and listened for signs of his quarry while Fagan struggled through the narrow aperture. Six separate maglev lines crackled below his feet. From the catwalk, they could see the cars whiz by below. Fagan grunted his frustration. "Fuckers could be anywhere."

"I figure they'll be moving away from the Mercantile, so we can assume they went this way," Sullivan said, his finger pointing to their left. "Let's go."

They moved along the elevated catwalk for about a hundred yards, at which point it widened into a square platform with ladders extending down to the maglev rails and three other service tunnels. "Now which way?"

Sullivan never got to answer. Several explosions collapsed the columns holding their perch over the intersection, sending three tons of metal and the two men plummeting into the river of speeding tram cars below.

CHAPTER TWENTY-NINE

T he platform plunged straight down.

For an instant the two men were weightless, giving each time to comprehend their plight before gravity asserted itself. The sixteen-foot drop did not frighten Sullivan nearly as much as the horrible tram collisions that were going to happen once the platform struck the maglev rails.

He nurtured no illusions about his ability to prevent the coming fall, though a burning desire to steer clear of the impending carnage drove him to desperate acts of physical prowess. He reached out a hand and snagged Fagan by the jacket. His other hand grabbed a piece of rail that did not fall with the rest of the platform. When Fagan's falling mass snapped his arm straight Sullivan roared with pain and effort. He pulled, knowing full well his grip would not hold. Fagan's jacket ripped, Sullivan's arms stretched, but both held for the split second it took to swing both away from the crackling rails and toward the marginal safety of the maintenance walkway to one side. When Sullivan's fingers tore free of the railing, they left bloody streaks across the gray metal. The fall was brief and the landing brutal, though Sullivan was moving even before his nervous system began to scream at him about potential injuries. The neurochemical door to his pain receptors had slammed closed as soon as the blast went off, so he was unlikely to hear it, anyway.

Fagan took the impact poorly. Without Sullivan's reflexes, the giant's cognizance of the situation remained several heartbeats behind the action. Sullivan threw himself on top of Fagan and rolled both as close to the wall as he could scramble. Sullivan heard the first tram try to stop. The shriek of emergency brakes warned him that impact was imminent and he covered his head with his arms. From underneath his fingers Sullivan saw a dull brown cargo tram strike the collapsed platform at almost forty miles per hour. The crash sent the tram car careening from its rail to tumble end over end, shedding body panels and spilling cargo for fifty yards before lodging itself between the maintenance walkway and another rail. Alarms howled, and the answering shouts of emergency brakes echoed through the dark tunnel like a flight of banshees bewailing a death in the family. Another car crashed into something, Sullivan could not tell what. He kept his head down and covered while a stinging wind of heat and shrapnel blew across their poor cover. A dozen shards of metal cut Sullivan through his clothes and he hissed a reptilian expletive at his own helplessness.

After a few seconds passed without an explosion, Sullivan risked looking up. The tunnel pulsed with the surging red light of alarm panels stippled with the orange and yellow of small fires burning. All movement had ceased, the automated systems ensuring no more cars entered the tunnel. Satisfied, he looked back to Fagan, who moaned softly and pressed at the floor with his hands.

"You okay?" Sullivan asked.

Fagan sat up. "I'll live." He looked pale, his breathing quick and shallow. "I guess we're even now."

The sound of booted feet on concrete broke through the background noise of the alarms. Sullivan stood. "If we don't get moving the score won't matter."

They rose together, and Sullivan led his partner along the maintenance walkway back toward the mercantile. Access doors to this section of tram proved few and far between. "We need a way out of here!" Sullivan whispered as both men trotted away from the wreckage. "We had to pick the section with automated everything?"

"Smugglers," Fagan said between breaths, "like privacy."

The sound of boots behind them grew louder. Sullivan pulled the Hudson from under his shredded jacket and turned. "You fighting fit?"

Fagan palmed his Beretta and nodded. "Would love some cover, though."

"Rails are shut down. Let's drop into the tracks and get behind that thing..." He pointed to a stopped cargo car. "Maybe we can surprise them."

Fagan's answer was to jump from the walkway down into the tracks. Sullivan followed, and both found their way to the stalled car. Each posted up at the back, Fagan on the left and Sullivan on the right, to await their pursuers. A slight curve in the tracks obscured their line of sight past thirty yards. At that range their pistols would be at a disadvantage if the enemy came well-equipped. Sullivan slowed his breathing and sought the perfect serenity of his stress mechanisms. His marksmanship would need to be flawless, his calm perfect. All the ways things might go wrong danced at the periphery of his thoughts, only to die there when the icy fog of preternatural focus washed everything but the reticle of his holographic gunsight away.

The first thing to round that corner did not look human. Through the light amplification of his sight, the reason for this became apparent. It stood head-to-toe in black armor and advanced with a carbine in high-ready position. Hard plates overlapped each other across all the larger surfaces, hinges reinforced at the joints, the head encased in a full-face helmet and AR visor. Had he been capable of feeling dismay in the moment, Sullivan might have uttered an expletive. Most of what made Sullivan the man people knew him to be was gone, though. He saw targets, aligned his sights, and commanded the pad of his forefinger to press with precisely one-point-eight pounds of force.

The Hudson bucked in his hand, though the gas block ate most of the recoil and the counterweight directed the rest straight back into his palm. The muzzle flipped less than an inch and Sullivan touched off a second round before the flash of the first had time to fade.

The first bullet struck the armored thing's carbine in the magazine, shattering it and spinning the whole weapon out of his hands. The second traveled under the chin to impact right where the clavicles came together. Either the man had armor enough to prevent penetration there, or he did not. Sullivan could not say just yet. He got his answer when the thing staggered back into the wall, hands grasping at its own throat. No blood flowed from under the helmet, but the gurgling of a man with a crushed trachea could not be mistaken even at this distance.

"Throat is weak," Sullivan called to Fagan. "But still armored."

"Show off," the big man replied.

The sound of boot heels on concrete stopped. Sullivan could hear the noises of composite plates rubbing against each other through the darkness, and he imagined a squad assembling behind the cover of the bend. "They're stacking up," he said to Fagan. "Grenade next. I got it."

Exactly as predicted, a small object arced in their direction. Fagan would not be able to see it in the poor light, but Sullivan picked it out and sent it back toward the bend with a single well-placed bullet. "Now I'm showing off," he said to Fagan just before the grenade went off.

The blast shook the tunnel and lit every crevice like lighting. "Cover me!" Sullivan shouted and charged.

Just like at the strip club, Fagan loosed a volley of bullets at the bend in the tunnel. He did not worry about scoring hits, merely buying time for Sullivan to close the distance. At a full sprint, Sullivan counted the shots as he ran. Fagan had twenty in his magazine, and

Sullivan wanted to ensure that at least half that remained when he engaged whatever lay beyond the corner.

He made the distance with time to spare. Five men in identical black armor met him. Their own grenade left them disoriented, and Sullivan pressed that advantage by putting four rounds into the first one he saw. From his position between the maglev rails, he fired upward at the men standing in the walkway. This gave him a perfect angle for putting rounds under their helmets. The first target dropped like a stone, and Sullivan put another down with a shot that went through the armpit. A black pauldron prevented the bullet from exiting the top of his shoulder, though a river of arterial blood from the wound told Sullivan that their armor did not extend to the armpits in any way. The three remaining men dropped back against the wall, putting the edge of the platform between themselves and Sullivan's gun. Sullivan ducked down and pressed his body against the cold concrete and scurried further down the track. After ten feet he placed a hand on the edge of the platform and vaulted up. Landing prone he rolled to put the enemy in his sights and saw the gaping muzzle of a carbine loom large in his view. A spike of fear lanced through the dead calm of his combat trance. These men moved far too quickly for regular soldiers or operatives. It felt like he was shooting it out with five armored versions of himself.

He twisted just as the first bullet left the carbine's barrel, rolling like a tumbleweed to his right and pumping his own trigger like a madman. Neither man scored hits, but the wall of the tunnel brought Sullivan to a halt before his opponent ran out of ammo. Sullivan's return fire sent the armored man backward, and this spoiled his shots enough for Sullivan to retreat himself. A final spray of bullets from the black-armored men tore a grunt of pain from between his teeth when a single round punched through the meat of Sullivan's thigh. Scuttling backward like a crab, he fired as he fled. Each gunshot punctuated by a resounding mental curse at his own lack of forethought. He never considered the potential GMOD scores of the enemy fighters before charging, and now he was pinned down and leaking from a hole in his leg.

The three surviving enemies did not pursue. A fresh eruption of gunfire tore their attention from Sullivan and put them into frenzied motion. Sullivan swore again, this time out loud. Fagan was a certifiable monster in any fight, but he was not fast enough nor a skilled enough shooter to survive a gunfight with whatever these men were. His stress response precluded the wound in his leg from encumbering him with too much pain, and the bullet had neither severed an artery nor broken the bone. Blood loss remained an issue, but he had a few minutes of fight still in him before the hole in his leg would require attention. He rose with a guttural snarl and charged back into the fray.

Sullivan kept the wall to his right and leaped muzzle-first into the knot of armored men. One had lagged behind to watch their back while the remaining two had moved to engage Fagan. Sullivan shot it out with the rearguard at less than ten feet. Deep within the frosty cocoon of his enhanced stress response, Sullivan picked his shots like a chef selecting produce for the night's entrée. Every choice deliberate, his judgment flawless. He harbored no expectations of penetration, rather he focused on inflicting trauma and degrading fighting ability. His first bullet threw a shower of sparks as it ripped across the receiver of the armored man's carbine. A single round escaped the barrel before the weapon got reduced to useless metal, and the wayward bullet took a chunk of Sullivan's left ear with it as it hurtled into the darkness of the tram tunnel.

Sullivan's next bullet struck the mirrored black visor. A perfect spider-web crack extended from the point of impact and drove the man's head back. Sullivan never stopped moving. By the third shot he was four feet away, and this one went directly into the exposed throat. The man was probably dead or dying at this point, but Sullivan took no chances. He grabbed the falling foe and jammed the Hudson under his chin to deliver a killing shot that pulped the man's head inside the helmet.

He did not wait for the man to fall. He kept moving. As he rounded the corner, he saw Fagan pinning one with careful bursts from his Beretta. The other man had crossed the tracks and moved to flank Fagan from the opposite wall. Using Fagan's own tram car cover to hide the maneuver left the giant unaware he was being stalked. Bracing the Hudson in a two-handed grip, Sullivan took his shots at more than fifteen yards. He did not care if he scored lethal hits and simply put bullets into the man where he could. This had the intended effect of thwarting the maneuver and forcing the now flailing enemy to find cover and return fire. It dropped back into the darkness where the wall and the walkway met, and Sullivan leaped down from the platform to further obscure the shooting angle. His leg nearly buckled on the landing and Sullivan narrowly avoided falling across a hissing maglev rail. A short stagger step arrested the fall and prevented a catastrophe, and he turned the stumble into forward motion at a speed he knew to be reckless. He charged across the rails, greeting every view of the black helmet with a two-round burst from the Hudson. His magazine held only three rounds by the time he made the other side, and he vaulted onto the walkway with all the grace of a wounded water buffalo.

The man crouched in the corner failed to react with the speed he had displayed earlier. The man failed to react to Sullivan's appearance at all. Urgent hands tugged and pulled at the helmet, and Sullivan soon understood why. Cracks obscured every inch of the faceplate and deep divots pockmarked the angled surface in several places where Sullivan's bullets had peppered it. Losing augmented reality assistance and nursing a concussion had changed the game to Sullivan's benefit, and he exploited the shift in fortunes without mercy. A booted foot sent the carbine to the walkway floor and a left hand like a vise closed over the armored throat. Sullivan hurled the man from the platform like a bouncer removing a rowdy drunk. A loud crackling sound and the stench of ozone filled the air when the armor interacted with the powerful magnetic and electric fields around the rail he landed across. Safety circuits killed the power within a second or two, but the damage was done. The aroma of cooked flesh followed and Sullivan moved on.

He located the final shooter, catching the man advancing on Fagan behind the safety of suppressing fire. Sullivan realized the giant was out of ammo and waiting, so he decided to give his partner the space he needed to make a move. He sent his last three rounds into the enemy as a distraction, and the single second it took him to reload was all the time Fagan needed to close the distance.

Watching Fagan grapple with the ogre had been impressive. Watching Fagan mangle a normal-sized person was horrifying. Fagan ripped the carbine away like an angry father snatching a toy from a child. To his credit, the black-clad man fired two punches into Fagan's mid-section without hesitation. Fagan failed to acknowledge these, preferring to spend the time securing a handhold on his victim. Once the giant got a good grip on the armor plates, the fight ceased to be a contest and devolved into a brutal one-sided pummeling. Fagan did not bother to strike the man. Sullivan knew the armor to be thick, and there would be no profit in ruining one's knuckles against it. Fagan seemed to agree, because he chose to drive the man against the tram car instead. The sound drew a wince from Sullivan. Fagan was not holding back. His right hand moved to the helmet while his left seized the chest plate where it met the ribs. Over and over Fagan drove the back of the helmet against the side of the tram car. Armored hands clawed at Fagan's face, black-booted feet kicked against his thighs. Nothing worked. With each strike, the side of the tram car buckled more and the enemy's resistance grew weaker. After seven or eight bone-crushing impacts, Fagan switched tactics and spun his prey head-first into the concrete of the maintenance walkway. The resulting crunch sounded less like the cracking of composite armor plates and more like the muffled snapping of bones. The man went limp in Fagan's hands, and the giant dropped the body like so much unwanted trash. It landed in a twisted heap. Sullivan poked the corpse with a toe just to be sure.

"Something ain't right about these assholes," Sullivan said.

"Yup," Fagan said between breaths. "That armor isn't civilian. High-end composites, fully AR capable helmets? This is somebody's private army."

"GMOD scores feel high to you?"

Fagan picked up his empty pistol. "Did seem mighty fast, didn't they?" He pointed to Sullivan's bleeding leg. "Got a piece of you?"

"Shit." Sullivan tore the sleeve from his ruined jacket. He tied it around the hole in his thigh and cinched it tight. "Almost forgot."

"We need to move, Sully," Fagan said while Sullivan finished dressing his wounds. "There's no way in hell I'm going to believe there's only five of these shits down here."

"What do you bet every name on that fucking list is one of these jacked-up shooters?"

"That's what I'm saying, man."

Sullivan turned thoughtful. "This is it, isn't it?"

"What?"

"Keating's plan." He waved a finger at Fagan. "Corpus Mundi has been stashing shooters down here for who knows how long, right? They could have hundreds of operators in strategic positions right now. Just waiting for the 'go' signal to turn this place into a war zone."

"But why?"

"To grab Emilie, obviously. Once they have her location and me out of the picture, their goons could close in and grab her. Railroad fighters are good, but..." He jerked a thumb back toward the dead men in expensive armor. "Not *that* kind of good. It would have been a nasty fight, but the CM troops would win it."

"Make it look like an internal power struggle or a GMP uprising..." Fagan added, finally sorting it out on his own.

"Bingo," Sullivan said. "If I had died at Camp Zero, I bet they'd have started already. But I didn't die, and then there's Keating to factor in. He betrayed them up there, and he knows what Corpus Mundi is up to."

"And he wants the girl for himself. And he still needs to beat Corpus Mundi to her."

"Exactly," Sullivan said. "So he puts GEED forces right at our fucking doorstep and he waits for CM to make their move." He shook his head at the sheer genius of it. "What do you think GEED is going to do if a few hundred GiMPs start a shooting war down here?" Sullivan holstered his pistol and started to walk toward the closest exit. An impatient bounce lent an air of urgency to his movements. "They sure as hell aren't going to sit back and let the Rosedale Riots happen all over again."

"Oh shit." Fagan's face went ghost white. "This is the excuse they've always wanted." He took off in Sullivan's wake.

"Yup. Once Corpus Mundi starts their operation, GEED is going to have all the justification they'll ever need to charge in, guns blazing. Then the real fun will start."

Fagan's long strides brought him abreast of Sullivan in short order. He looked down at his partner's face, saw a detached fury etched in granite across his features. His own voice was pitched to match. "It's going to be a massacre. For everyone."

"Unless we stop it."

"You have a plan?"

Sullivan nodded. "No riot, no raid, right? We just need to find these Corporate operatives and put them down. Without an army on the inside to light the fuse, GEED will be stuck holding their dicks outside the gates waiting for an excuse that will never come."

Fagan wiped his forehead with a meaty palm. "One tiny problem with your plan, partner. We may have just tipped off Corpus Mundi that we are onto them."

"It crossed my mind."

"So they may be inclined to start the fun very soon, now that the veil has been lifted, so to speak."

"I came to that conclusion myself, yes." Sullivan increased his stride to a jog. "Probably want to pick up that pace, Fagan."

CHAPTER THIRTY

Sullivan wanted to sprint, but his wounded thigh and the need to keep Fagan close prevented him from moving at top speed.

He grabbed his phone as he ran. Jamming an earpiece in while thumbing the screen to get the code for Maris, he never missed a step. "Maris," he shouted when he heard her pick up. "Grab Emilie and the doc and get to the holdout!"

"What's going on, John?"

"I think I just stumbled onto Keating's plan. There are Corpus Mundi operatives all over the Complex, and I think they want to start the Rosedale Riots all over again!"

"Oh no," Maris gasped. "GEED is already at the gates—"

"I know! Get under cover! Fagan and I will try to shut them down before it gets rolling!"

"I'll tell the Railroad assets to be aware and to put down any disturbances they find. How much time do we have?"

"Fuck if I know, Maris. I don't think it was supposed to jump off today but I just kicked a goddamn hornet's nest down under the Mercantile."

"Oh dear. What did you do?"

"What do I always do? I dove into some shit without looking first. Fagan and I just dropped a squad of high-dollar GMP combat troops, and I doubt their bosses are going to be pleased about it, okay?" He bit off an expletive and decided to eject from this part of the conversation. "I'll find you at the holdout. Whatever you do, don't try to move around or get out. It's what they want. It's all a play for Emilie!"

"I understand. We'll be there in ten minutes."

The two men burst from the tram tunnel at the first ground-level exit. They slowed once they entered an interstitial concourse that separated the Rosedale section from the G-ring facilities. Little more than a series of vehicle and foot paths for distributing materials and personnel between the main rings, the gray and brown tunnel sat mostly unoccupied. A few dozen people moved along the walkways and the occasional vehicle hummed past with safety lights ablaze.

"Where are we going, partner?" Fagan asked when he caught up.

"We are going to see what was in those smuggled shipments besides shooters," Sullivan said. "If it's valuable tech or materiel, they'll be guarding it. With any luck, we can hurt them enough in the next two hours to convince Corpus Mundi to abandon their plan."

"Lead on."

The two men raced to the nearest transit station and paid for a car to cover the distance to the warehouse district Skip had indicated. The cargo flatbed dropped them off thirty minutes later outside a grease-stained office standing guard next to a set of cargo doors large enough to drive a tank through. Sullivan stepped into the office like he owned it and found himself at the end of a long line of people queued up before a single window. A few heads turned to mark the man with the wounded thigh and bleeding ear before turning to stare at the backs of the people ahead of them. Sullivan moved to step around the line and a brawny man a full head taller than he was stopped him with a rough shove. "Back of the line, pal," the sneering man ordered in a deep laconic rumble.

The arm blocking his path was big and meaty. The forearm wrapped in thick cords of muscle connected to biceps and triceps even larger than Sullivan's. The man's chest was wide, his back strained the seams of his grimy work shirt. Sullivan caught the glint of beady black eyes beneath a heavy brow, saw the slab of jaw work with irritation and he understood. The word 'troll' crossed his mind, but he knew that Fagan did not like it when people used it, so he kept silent in the face of the massive acromegalic.

Sullivan had spent his whole life learning to manage the smoldering anger that infected his every waking moment. Most of the time, he did what he felt was an excellent job of stifling the six or seven thousand deeply antisocial urges he experienced in a typical day. He could not lose his temper like normal people, but this did not mean he was incapable of great cruelty and misanthropy when situations pushed his self-control beyond his desire to maintain it. It had been a long day, there was still much to do, and he did not have the time for common courtesy. Furthermore, he *wanted* to hurt someone, and this troll had just volunteered for duty.

Without warning, he struck the man in the Adam's apple with his fist. The tiny eyes grew wide with pain and surprise, and Sullivan grabbed the hand on his chest. Seizing a forefinger and thumb in each fist, he bent both backward until his antagonist dropped to his knees. The offender tried to roar in pain, but only choking sobs escaped his damaged airway. Sullivan closed his mouth with a knee to the chin that sent teeth and blood flying into the crowd of people trying desperately to back away from the brawl.

Sullivan released his victim, who promptly flopped onto the carpet. For the briefest moment, it looked like the big man might return to hostilities. The idea died as soon as Fagan stepped in and offered the heaving man a hand up. Sullivan supposed it was not often the idiot found himself on the losing end of a fight or looking up at someone even bigger than himself. He slapped Fagan's hand aside and lurched upright. Fagan held his gaze for a moment and smiled. "Sorry for the trouble. We're in a terrible hurry."

Most of the people in the office were now scurrying for the door. Being trapped in an office while a half-ton's worth of hairy giants bashed it out constituted a losing proposition for anyone with normal bone density. While the two giants stared each other down, the room emptied faster than a broken whiskey bottle.

"What the fuck is going on out there!" a voice shouted from beyond the window.

Sullivan left Fagan to handle the troll problem and stepped to the window. "You Thompson?"

"Who the fuck wants to know?" Thompson's face was flushed and round. He was completely bald with gray eyebrows and a pinched, angry expression. Sullivan disliked him instantly, and this antipathy influenced his subsequent actions to a large extent.

Wearing a look of bland irritation, Sullivan put his fist straight through the polycarbonate window and grabbed Thompson by the lapel of his grease-stained jacket. With a huff and a sharp pull, Sullivan yanked Thompson forward until his face pressed against what remained of the clear panel. Sullivan graced the man's squished features with a humorless grin. "I do."

The reply was sadly predictable. "Ow! Ow! Ow!"

Thompson's squeals grated on Sullivan's nerves, so he pulled harder. The panel popped and fresh cracks raced across the transparent plane like white lightning. "I. Have. Questions," he said.

"A thousand credits if you fuck this asshole up, Dipper!"

"Dipper?" Sullivan turned to look at the giant still glaring at Fagan. "Dipper, huh? Wow. Tough break on the nickname. I wouldn't take the money, Dipper," he said. "It ain't worth it."

"Oh, let him try," Fagan replied without taking his eyes off the other giant. "I haven't fought anyone in my weight class in a long time."

Indecision played across Dipper's face. Seconds passed with no response, and Fagan became impatient. "Fuck it," he said, and punched the other man as hard as he could.

Sullivan flinched. The sound of Fagan's fist hitting Dipper's jaw reminded him of the time his old judo coach had thrown him so hard his shoulder dislocated. The combination of dull thud, loud pop, and wet crunch was not the sort of noise that boded well for a man's health. Dipper staggered one step, looked up with lolling eyes at Fagan, then collapsed like a felled ox at Fagan's feet.

"Well, that was anticlimactic," Fagan quipped.

Sullivan snorted approval and heaved Thompson forward. A sharp crack split the air and the window buckled into large chunks around Thompson's face. Sullivan dragged him across the sill and the rest of the partition tore free of its frame when the airborne man sailed through the wreckage to land face first in front of Sullivan.

"I have questions," Sullivan repeated for a third time. "I will pay you for the answers, minus a fee for the hassle you just put me through and Skip's cut. Might as well take the money, because you are going to talk, anyway."

Thompson became very cooperative after that.

He lead Fagan and Sullivan into a cavernous storage facility. After an eight-minute ride at breakneck speed in a rickety transport, they disembarked in front of a long row of storage racks. These extended to the ceiling thirty feet overhead and stretched on for what appeared to be a quarter-mile. Fagan whistled.

"This is all from that one smuggler?"

"The client," Thompson said through gritted teeth, "is no more a smuggler than anyone else running cargo through here." Sullivan answered only with a glower, and Thompson heaved a sigh. "Yes. This is all of it. It's a shipping service out of what used to be Tajikistan. Kind of a no-man's-land these days, what with the Remnant running most of that territory, so regulatory oversight is pretty easy to sidestep out that way."

Fagan's face creased into a deep frown. "Tajikistan? That's a long way from Kansas City."

"Let's take a look," Sullivan said.

Thompson blanched ghost white. "I can't be no part of that!"

Sullivan, still bleeding and still in a surly mood, grabbed Thompson by the neck. "Listen, shithead. I know you know a lot more about this than you are telling us. I'm out of time and patience. We are trying to save your ass and the asses of everyone in here, okay? You take us to the containers that have the most security and you get them the fuck open or I am going to drink beer from your hollowed-out skull tonight." Sullivan gave the little man a savage shake. "Are we communicating?"

"Discretion is critical! You'll put me out of business!" he whined.

Sullivan lifted Thompson from the floor and slammed him against the nearest rack of crates. "You're going to be out of business in twenty-four hours anyway, asshole! You and everyone else! You're all going to die or get arrested!"

Conflict flashed across Thompson's face as he considered the demonic strength of the hand on his neck and the iron in Sullivan's words. "Okay! All right! Fuck!"

Sullivan released him. Thompson stalked off down the row, muttering expletives with each step. He stopped about a third of the way down and pointed to a large cargo container. The brown metal box sat on the lowest rack. Sullivan guessed it to be twenty-five feet long and ten feet in both height and width.

"There are ten of these, and the client made sure that I knew to stay way the fuck away from them. They are locked, coded, and scrambled so nobody can get into them. They monitor the controls, so as soon as you fuck with them they're gonna know."

"Oh, we're going to fuck with them, all right." Sullivan said.

"The die does seem to be cast at this point," Fagan agreed.

"Open it," Sullivan barked to Thompson.

"I can't," Thompson said. "I don't have any of the—"

"Finish that lie and I'll break your jaw." Sullivan was having none of it. "Get it open. Now."

Thompson gave up. He shuffled over to a blinking control panel and pulled a tablet from his pocket. Placing the device within a few inches of the lock, he swiped through screens and activated some program Sullivan did not recognize. Lights blinked across the lock panel. First a rapid flashing red message scrolled across the screen, then a slower more pleasant green one. A loud click pierced the air and made Thompson flinch.

The crate split along the long face, halfway between the top and bottom. The soft whine of electric motors announced the elevation of the top half as it rose to reveal the contents within. Stacked two high and ten across, twenty cylindrical sarcophagi tilted forward with a mechanical groan. Through a clear panel faces in repose could be seen, expressions slack with the oblivion of peaceful sleep. Sullivan recognized some of the more prominent features and his stomach lurched with memories of Camp Zero. Fagan whispered a quiet and terrified, "Holy shit."

"What the fuck are those?" Thompson wondered aloud.

"Monsters," Fagan replied.

"People," Sullivan amended. "Poor, twisted, doomed people."

"You say there are ten of these?" Fagan asked.

"Yeah," Thompson said. His aversion to helping them had not survived the sight of twenty unconscious people locked in a shipping crate. "Plus other crates. Smaller ones. No idea what's in them."

"Two hundred," Fagan groaned. "Two hundred of these guys just waiting for the signal to go."

A loud and insistent beeping interrupted them. Lights inside each coffin burst to life, and a series of hisses and clicks chattered like angry squirrels. Sullivan moved closer to look inside the nearest cylinder, peering at the bestial face beyond the clear viewing window.

The thing inside stared back with wide, feral eyes.

Drifting in from all around them, the sound of beeping and clicking washed over the men. The wailing of electric motors came like the sobs of a hundred banshees. It swelled to a crescendo of white noise, driving Sullivan's cortisol levels back up and locking him into the cold dark cell of quiet homicidal fury.

"Get everyone out of here, Thompson," he said with frost on his tongue. "And lock the door behind you."

CHAPTER THIRTY-ONE

Thompson needed no further encouragement. He took off at a dead sprint for the exit.

"Go with him, Fagan," Sullivan said, drawing his pistol. "No one can be allowed to get in or out of here. I'll clear the room as best I can."

"If you think I'm leaving you to fight two-hundred psycho GiMPs by yourself, you are an idiot. And an asshole."

"If I can hold the line here, we can stop this before it spreads. They're not distributed, they're still waking up. We have a chance!" Sullivan tore his jacket off and dropped it. "Get to the exit. You're not fast enough to check this place before they start moving around."

The noise of containers opening echoed from all sides.

Fagan shrugged out of his jacket and drew his own gun. "You are going to die."

"If I have to."

Sullivan moved toward the container and Fagan grabbed him by the shoulder. "Listen to me, John! I think it's great that you've figured out how to give a shit about something bigger than yourself. I've known you had that in you from the start, and Horowitz did too. But you're taking it too far! *We* will do this. Together. Or *we* will die trying."

Something in Fagan's tone pierced the frigid emotional shield that protected Sullivan from strong feelings. It hurt, and he could not define the pain right away. When he tried, what came out was, "I don't want you to die, okay?"

"I don't want you to die, either. So instead of locking you in here, I am going to go to the exit and hold that fucker until you get there. We will lock the door when you get out. You are my friend, you obtuse jerk. You don't get to leave me behind while you die in glorious battle, okay?"

Sullivan had always known this, but hearing it was strange. It did not make him feel better, either. The empty hole left by Horowitz still weighed heavy on his mind, feeding his growing self-loathing a steady diet of guilt and recriminations. If Fagan died, he imagined the tragedy would be much worse. His hands shook, and a strange tightness in his throat choked his reply into a croak. "I don't know how to do this," he said. "I feel... wrong."

"It's supposed to feel wrong," Fagan said and clapped him on the shoulder. "What we have to do here is awful. I'm scared we are going to die. I'm scared that we won't be able to do enough *before* we die. I'm scared that if we do enough and live that I'm going to be sick forever over what it took." Fagan straightened and squared his shoulders. "But we are going to fucking try, runt. And win or lose, live or die, no one will be able to say we didn't run toward the fire. Together, little brother. If death is what it's going to take to save a million lives down here, then I want to die fighting the good fight with my friend at my side. Call me hokey if you want to."

Sullivan did not think it was hokey. He did not know what to think. The thought that finally burst to life in his brain confused him. *I don't deserve a friend like Fagan,* Sullivan thought. Then, realizing he may be dead in mere minutes, he decided not to leave that thought unspoken. "I don't deserve you, man," he said. The words were uncomfortable and tasted strange in his mouth. "But I'm really glad you never gave up on me. Go. Hold that door. I'll be right behind you."

Fagan took off at his best speed. Sullivan turned and sprinted down the row. The opening containers beckoned like yawning mouths as they began to disgorge their contents. Flashing lights and hissing seals urged Sullivan to even greater speeds. Without the time to check the progress of the awakening, Sullivan was left to guess at how much time he might have. He assumed it would be a few minutes before the first of Corpus Mundi's shock troopers became mobile enough to be a threat, though he could not be assured of anything. He turned the corner at the end of his row and looked down the adjacent one. He found it empty and moved on. At the fourth he found a single man in a stock-picker driving along with his nose glued to the screen. Sullivan screamed a warning and waved his pistol. What the poor warehouse worker thought of the gun-toting psycho, Sullivan could not say. The man drove his rig down the aisle at its top speed while gibbering into his communicator.

Sullivan ran on. He covered what felt like miles at a blistering pace. He explained nothing, simply shouting and terrifying everyone he saw into panicked flight. He encountered dozens of workers in his headlong flight and he spared none of them any explanations. As long as they fled he was satisfied. There was no time. His perceptions were so warped by the deluge of neurotransmitters competing for dominance in his brain, Sullivan could not discern the difference between minutes or seconds. He drove forward without stopping until he found the far wall of the titanic storage bay. Then he turned to his right and ran down the last lane to find his way out. Sullivan felt his jaw cramping from the effort of clenching his teeth. He hated not knowing where the enemy was or what they were doing. He was certain they should have been on him by now. At every corner and intersection he expected to be swarmed by a horde of psychotic GMP monsters. The shadows of each container, or the metal jungle of the next line of storage racks, any hidden place might hold his doom at the hands of genetically-engineered killers. Yet nothing came for him, and this only made the apprehension worse.

When he turned the corner at the end of the last row, fixing his
eyes on the long run toward the main entrance, he knew he was running out of luck and into danger. He begged an indifferent universe
for just a little bit of the consideration it never seemed to give him.
He asked for a clear path to the door; he hoped against fear that Fagan had not been overrun trying to save his miserable life.

He made it most of the way there before the first of the enemy
was upon him. Four men burst from one of the aisles and Sullivan
blinked at the bizarre sight of them. While they shared many of the
external features of the things he fought at Camp Zero, these wore
tight gray skin suits and lacked the empty ferocity of their naked
brethren. Shock almost managed to penetrate his stress response
when Sullivan realized they were armed, as well. Each clutched a
short black rifle in high-ready position. Worst of all, they moved
with quick and controlled maneuvers, taking care to cover each other
and sweep the lanes as they went.

These are soldiers! The thought rattled around his brain for a fraction of a second, battering his hopes for survival with a new tactical
challenge.

Only Sullivan's breakneck speed, enhanced reflexes, and total
lack of fear saved him in that instant. The small fire team never saw
him coming and he used the split-second advantage to pepper them
with fire from his Hudson. He made no hits and the knot of men
fanned out like robots and retreated back into the cover of the aisle.
He passed the entrance of the wide lane at a full sprint. A spattering
of return fire marked his passing, though his fortunes held and he
took no hits himself. Luck was an unreliable ally at best, and Sullivan
harbored no illusions about his chances. His sixty rounds of 10mm
caseless and genetic gifts would not have been sufficient to take down
two hundred unarmed berserkers. Whatever model of GMP he had
just woken up was obviously much more sophisticated and better

equipped. His only options were to run or die, and John Sullivan could run like few other men could.

Another team of enemies tried to ambush him when he was a mere hundred yards from the main entrance. Sullivan leaned into his pistol and dumped what remained of his magazine into them at a full run. Like the other group, these troops dropped back to cover. Sullivan noticed something strange about their movements as he charged into the gap. They had not leaped for cover or hit the deck with any sense of urgency. They never even flinched. Each moved as if the hail of incoming bullets were a mere inconvenience and not a dire threat to continued existence. Sullivan knew for certain that at least one had taken a hit high on the chest, though. The struck man did not so much as glance at the wound before securing a covered firing position.

What these observations meant Sullivan did not have the time to ponder. He lowered his head and found new reserves of speed despite a wounded leg and flagging energy. Part of him understood that pushing his body like this was exactly the sort of activity he was made for, yet this knowledge did nothing to make the ordeal any more pleasant. Bullets whipped past his head as he ran. A dull impact nearly spun him from his feet and though he could feel no pain, he knew a bullet had just lodged in the meat of his back.

He ran faster.

Fagan's worried face came into view and the staccato cracks of his pistol told Sullivan that the big man saw the trouble, too. Fagan did not bother with careful aiming. He worked the trigger fast, sending his bullets past Sullivan with no other purpose but to keep the shooters from getting a clean shot off. It must have been enough, because Sullivan slid into the entrance without taking any more hits. Fagan grabbed him from the deck and tossed him back into the safety of the concourse. A hairy fist slapped the control panel, bringing the big bay doors together with a loud electric whine and a thunderous clang.

Over the sound of his own blood in his ears, Sullivan head Fagan's gruff order to Thompson. "Seal it! NOW!" Then rough hands hauled Sullivan to his feet and the giant's hirsute visage filled his view. "You all right, Sully? Are you hit?"

"Back," Sullivan managed to growl. "How bad?"

Fagan spun Sullivan around to examine the wound. "You're lucky you've got all that muscle. Angle is shallow, doesn't look deep. Let me plug it." Fagan ripped a first-aid kit from a nearby wall and went to work on Sullivan's back.

Fagan's first aid techniques left much to be desired. "Subsonic," Sullivan said through gritted teeth. "They have suppressed weapons shooting subsonic ammo."

"They wanted to run silent," Fagan said.

"Not like—argh! Fuck!"

"Sorry," Fagan mumbled.

"Not like Camp Zero," Sullivan finished through an enormous wince. "Not prototypes. These are front-line units, fully developed and ready for deployment."

"Well, they're all trapped in there now. Thompson says that the doors can't be opened from the inside."

Sullivan shook his head in violent disagreement. "All their gear is in there with them! How long before they blast or cut their way out?"

"Fuck," Fagan replied.

"These have got to be the shock troops," Sullivan said. "The other operatives will be coming for them." Sullivan waved a hand impatiently. "Those sleeper cells that Skip showed us. They're going to have to come and bust them out. We got two hundred pumped-up shooters trapped inside, and another hundred or so heading this way to retrieve them." Sullivan flexed his arms to test the wound in his back. Without much of a pain response, it was hard to tell how badly he was injured. "This isn't over."

"I'm low on ammo, and we're all alone, partner."

Sullivan tried to stretch his back some more, testing his range of motion with a frown. "Call Maris. We need railroad people down here now. Fighters. Shooters. Guns and ammo, too."

"On it," Fagan said and started to fiddle with his phone. A terrible sense of helplessness washed over him. It was all coming at him too fast. People were about to die, and he could not stop it from happening. The enemy was both behind him and in front, inside the walls and without. The cold, tactical core of his being told him what he needed to do, and he hated it. The logical solution was to run. To grab Emilie and get away from this unwinnable fiasco as quickly as possible. All the enemy's assets were here. Being somewhere else made a lot of strategic sense. It also meant abandoning the Complex and everyone in it to the mercy of those same enemies.

Nothing could stop what happened next. The unforgiving reality of that fact loomed over every tortured scenario Sullivan tried to imagine. Keating needed his riot in order to have his invasion. Corpus Mundi would not lose a second's sleep over killing everyone down here for a chance at Emilie, and they were already committed to action. Even if he somehow got away, the KC Complex would still be destroyed. Hundreds, possibly thousands of people were about to die because he failed them all. The noise in his head grew too loud for him to think. Sullivan longed for a moment's calm just to unravel all the weirdness rattling around in his brain, to make a decision, build a plan, to do *anything* besides growl in impotent frustration. It was time he did not have, so he shoved all clamor back down and slammed the lid closed on his new feelings.

"You okay?" Fagan asked.

"Yeah," Sullivan lied.

"Maris is sending everyone she can spare. Says she's got some real shooters in the mix. Ex-military types. We need a plan, partner."

Sullivan took in an enormous breath. He let it out slow, dragging the exhalation out for as long as he could. When he finished, he found his mind much quieter.

"They are going to kill a lot of people if we don't stop them."

Fagan's face scrunched at the non-sequitur. "Huh?"

Sullivan went on. "I don't think I want to be the guy who let that happen, you know? I think I'd rather die fighting than run anymore." The corner of his mouth twitched, whether in a smile or a frown even Sullivan could not say. "I think today might be a very good day to die, Fagan. As good as any other, I suppose."

"It certainly ain't a bad one," Fagan said.

"And better company than I have any right to expect. I'd tell you to leave me to this fight and save yourself but..."

Fagan shook his head in a solemn negative. "Wouldn't have this any other way, partner."

Sullivan smiled, and it was neither small, mean, sarcastic, or angry. "This is it, then." He pointed to the intersection of the concourse and the wide access to the warehouse. "Right here."

"What about it?"

"Win or die, this is where we make our stand."

CHAPTER THIRTY-TWO

"Thompson!" Sullivan yelled.

The bald man scuttled over, pale and red-eyed. "What?"

"Which gangs run this district?"

"The Trogs, the Dead Reckoners, and the Raw Dogs."

"They want to keep it?"

Thompson did not answer. The question made little sense to his fevered brain.

Sullivan went on, "If they do, they need to send every shooter they got to this intersection. There's going to be a big fight, and if we lose, GEED will be tearing through the complex like bears through a beehive in about six hours."

A large dark-skinned man stepped out from the gathering crowd. He fixed Sullivan with a single angry eye. "What the fuck have you brought down on us, GiMP?"

"Easy, Chewie," Thompson said. "There is some fucked up bullshit going on, but I don't think this guy is doing it"

"Chewie?" Sullivan said with a raised eyebrow.

"Dead Reckoners," the gangster said. "We have the security shift here this quarter. You know you're shot, right?"

"Twice," Sullivan replied. "It happens all the time. That's not important. What's important is that this GEED lockdown is part of a plan to attack the Complex. We just locked a bunch of GiMP killers in that warehouse so they couldn't start a riot."

"Why would they start a riot?"

"So GEED will have an excuse to storm the place."

"Fuckers," Chewie said. "So what now? You got a plan, or you just looking to get my people killed?"

"Those fuckers have friends on their way to bust them out. We have to stop them long enough to flood that warehouse with gas or something."

"You want me to put my boys against government bred GiMP hitters?" Chewie did not sound like a man in love with that idea.

"There's no gene for bullet-proofing," Fagan said, a single finger pointing to the gun at Chewie's hip.

"Tell that to this fucker," Chewie said pointing back at Sullivan.

"Sully's special," Fagan replied. "The Railroad is sending people too. GMP shooters with training. Everybody has to work together or we will all go down, Chewie."

"Or don't help at all," Sullivan spat. "Walk away and be the bitch who couldn't be bothered to defend his own turf. We don't have time for a rousing speech or an inspirational call to arms. Get your people here and in position or not. It's goddamn Saint Crispin's day down here and I have shit to do."

Sullivan turned and stormed away. Fagan looked at Chewie. "Sully's got a bad attitude but he's right. Are you in or not?"

"Fuck it," Chewie said with a lopsided smile. "I like that fucker's style, man. Can't let a fancy GiMP like that make me look like a bitch, right?" Chewie grabbed a communicator from his pocket and started barking orders into it. "Saddle up boys, I need every swinging dick down at the storage bay. Boots and suits, crew. We got GiMP hitters looking to fuck us all up."

Several competing voices crackled back, Chewie silenced them all. "This shit is priority one, fuckers. Call the Trogs and Raw Dogs too. Calling in all the favors today."

Within five minutes, more than seventy armed gangsters materialized at the bay doors. They were a scruffy, unprofessional mess. Rival gang members squabbled, mid-level captains argued over who was in charge, and nobody knew what was going on. Sullivan set to putting things in order right away. He had no military or practical leadership experience, but he had grown up a mobster's son, and thus he knew how to motivate this type of riffraff.

"Listen up, you limp-dick sons of bitches!" he yelled over the din.

"Speak for yourself!" a female gangster called back with a rude gesture. Laughter rippled across the crowd.

"In a few minutes, a bunch of armored-up GiMP motherfuckers are going to show up and try to shoot their way into that warehouse! If they do, it will release two-hundred bad-ass super-GiMP killers." This would not motivate any of them, but it set the tone for what came next. "These bastards think they can walk into your turf, drop off their gear, and then fuck up whatever they want. They think you are a bunch of dirty subterranean bumpkins who are going to fall apart at the first sign of a real fight." A murmur began to build. "There are a million people down in this Complex, and these mother fuckers sent less than three hundred shooters to take you all on. That's what they think of you. That's how much respect you get from the Hegemony. I don't know about you guys, but that feels downright insulting." Respect was the only currency that mattered to gangs, and Sullivan played that for all it was worth. "I hear rumors," he said with a big fake smile. "That the Dead Reckoners think they are the baddest motherfuckers in the warehouse district." He let that settle across the group for a second. "My boy Mister Thompson here says it's the Trogs you don't want to fuck with." More murmurings. "Ain't nobody even mentioned the Raw Dogs," he looked out at them all, incredulous. "How the fuck does nobody even mention the Raw Dogs?" Some laughter and a few shouts came back. Sullivan had them where he wanted them now. "I want to know which gang is the baddest there is. I need the baddest motherfuckers in the KC Complex right now, because it's time to fuck some shit up and send a message. We are going to tell the whole world and the hegemony that runs it that messing with us is a very bad idea."

The group roared as one, waving rifles and pistols in the air.

"Nice," Fagan mumbled to Sullivan.

"Mobster shit," Sullivan whispered back. Then he started ordering people into defensible positions. He had Thompson seal every entrance to the main storage bay and close off the ventilation as well. There would be enough fresh air in the giant room for days, but not indefinitely. He also sent the man in search of an aerosolized anesthetic, hoping to pump enough gas into the warehouse to render the occupants harmless. For some reason, Sullivan did not want to simply kill them. His memories of Camp Zero still plagued his newly-acquired conscience, and he resolved himself to at least attempt a solution that did not end with more blood on his hands than absolutely necessary.

The first signs of action came less than thirty minutes after his initial escape from the storage bay. A long chatter of full-auto gunfire interrupted his preparations and sent his ragtag group of defenders scurrying for cover. He had placed scouts at all the possible routes leading to their choke point. The lack of warning meant that these scouts had failed miserably. Sullivan supposed he should have expected as much. The gunfire increased in volume, interspersed with the shouts and screaming of men and women in various stages of combat. Sullivan ran to the main intersection, shouting orders and encouragement to the gangsters he passed. If there was to be any chance of victory, he needed to be at the front of the action.

"Where's the Railroad?" he yelled to Fagan as he ran by.

Fagan leaped up to join him. "Fifteen minutes out."

What Sullivan saw when he got to the fighting cast doubts as to whether or not they could hold for even that long. Bursts of concentrated fire from two different hallways crossed the concourse with merciless accuracy. Disciplined shooting and quality weapons chipped away at his vanguard, and with every second that passed more gangsters dropped. Like the inexperienced thugs they were, the defenders behind improvised fighting positions stuck their heads out way too far when shooting back. The precise marksmanship of the black-armored enemy dropped overzealous amateurs like wheat before the scythe. At least fortune smiled upon him in one small way. The enemy relied too much on their armor and did not take enough care with cover or positioning. Sullivan's Hudson roared to life, walking a line of hits up an exposed body until a single round found the crease between helmet and neck. The struck man went down in a shower of blood and the assault dimmed in intensity while the new threat was located and assessed. Sullivan sprinted to a stack of crates where two now-deceased men had been shooting into a hall. He grabbed a rifle from one headless corpse and began working the gap with short bursts. Fully ensconced in his cocoon of neuro-chemical calm, Sullivan placed bullets with care, wounding or killing any black humanoid shape unlucky enough to find its way into his crosshairs. The remaining opposition backpedaled to the deeper cover of the curving alley and hunkered down. The act of suppressing one lane of attack soon exposed Sullivan to fire from the others. Ricochets and near misses forced his head down, and he could only hope he had blunted the initial charge enough to make the others more cautious.

The growing cacophony behind him told Sullivan that the gangsters were renewing their efforts to flood the attack lanes with bullets. Without the skill to make lethal hits through the armor with any consistency, the mob applied volume where precision was unavailable. He hoped it was working because other than the three men just dispatched by Sullivan himself, it did not look like any kills could be attributed to their side.

Fagan gave voice to Sullivan's thoughts. "This is a fucking nightmare." The giant had grabbed the other rifle and was adding his own fusillade to the general destruction.

"If we let them have the concourse, we'll be trapped in front of the storage bay doors. If they have anything heavier than carbines, we'll be fucked."

"We're fucked now!" Fagan said between bursts. "They're dropping us three to one!"

"We just need ten more minutes!" Sullivan growled. "We can crush them between the Railroad teams and us if we just hold the line here!"

"I'm all ears," Fagan shouted.

"I'm going to get behind them," Sullivan said. "Can you shoot around me without hitting me?"

"If you run in a straight line, yes." Fagan's voice took on an edge of fear. "You got two bullets in you already, partner. Can you run fast enough?"

"Sure. I'm like a gazelle or something."

Fagan did not appreciate the comedic timing, and his scowl brooked no arguments. "I'm going to put my fire to the right side. You stick to the left. Once you make the tunnel, post up and I'll join you." He turned to look over his shoulder. "Chewie!" He roared, loud enough to be heard over the din. "Get me four more shooters for this spot! Sully's tired of sitting around and wants to take a walk!"

The gang leader looked up from behind a crate. He raised a fist, then he and three others ran up to Fagan and Sullivan's position behind the indiscriminate blasting of their rifles. Sullivan shook his head in disbelief at their brazen courage in the face of woeful incompetence. "Suds and I are going to take the tunnel across from us." He pointed to the tunnel to their left. "Your job is to make sure no one from that other tunnel shoots us while we do it. Got it?"

Chewie's head bobbed, teeth clenched. The fighting position across the other tunnel was down to two defenders, and he pointed this out. "Give me a sec," he said. Then he directed three of his men to reinforce that position. "I'll stay at this one," he said. "When you move, I'm gonna run up the middle and see if I can't catch them in a crossfire."

"There's no cover in the middle," Fagan said.

"Yeah, but there'll be enough shooting that if I make the far wall, I can sidle up to the entrance and hopefully catch a few coming out."

"Your funeral," Sullivan said. "But they're coming back so we're out of time!"

The men he had pushed back were advancing down the tunnel once again. Stacked up behind a riot shield in a single file, the line of black-clad killers looked like a hideous gun-toting millipede inching their direction. "Do it!" Sullivan shouted.

Fagan posted up and let a long volley fly. Sparks erupted from the riot shield and the encroaching line of men dropped to a knee behind the cover. Fagan stayed with the attack while Sullivan sprinted across the sixty feet of open space between them. He stayed to the left as instructed, each step reminding him that he had a bullet wound in his thigh and each pump of his arms reiterating there was another one in his back. It was not so much that the wounds hurt; Sullivan was well beyond pain at this point. Yet the muscles in the injured areas refused to perform at the levels he needed them to. By sheer force of will and the grace of Fagan's covering fire he made the tunnel without getting shot a third time. Once clear of the concourse, Fagan stopped shooting and Sullivan leaped. Feet-first he crashed into the riot shield with his full weight and at top speed. The man with the shield lurched back, upsetting the tight formation behind him and sending most of them to the deck. Sullivan lashed out with his booted feet and sprayed the writhing black mass with his pistol. Any second, one of the men would draw a bead on him and put a bullet through his chest, and Sullivan wanted to do as much damage as possible before that happened.

The narrow confines of the corridor, the chaos of the struggle, and the general fog of war lent Sullivan an advantage that he exploited for several long seconds. He stomped on errant limbs, he fired point-blank into exposed flaws in their armor, he hewed and bashed his way down the line until the sounds of gunshots that were not his warned him that he had used up all his luck. Sullivan dove to one side, not caring what was there. The desire to avoid another bullet hole kept him scrambling as more shots came. He rolled to his back with the Hudson clutched in a two-handed grip. A strange flush of heat filled his chest when in the illuminated reticle he saw Fagan and Chewie laying into the enemy with a furor equal to his own. In a moment of clarity it occurred to Sullivan that the need for luck was inversely proportional to the quantity of friends one brought with them to the fight. This pleased him in a distant, tactically aware manner. With the ghost of a smile behind his pursed lips, Sullivan began to pick targets out of the chaos.

Then he started shooting.

CHAPTER THIRTY-THREE

The shootout in the tunnel dissembled into a brawl.
Fagan abandoned his empty rifle to break bodies with his bare hands, and Sullivan resorted to the same when his Hudson finally ran dry. The black-clad men were genetically enhanced to various degrees, making for slow going against tough opponents. In the end, it merely prolonged the outcome. Chewie did what he could, fighting savagely until he met his death at the muzzle of a pistol. Fagan avenged him a second later by nearly tearing the helmeted head from the shooter's body with both hands. Fagan and Sullivan fought on with a brutal desperation that overwhelmed the squad. Both ignored all pretense toward defense and attacked like rabid animals. Their relentless onslaught reduced a dozen armored killers to a twisted pile of broken bodies in the span of thirty seconds. When the tunnel went quiet, Sullivan paused to catch his breath in a series of deep heaving gasps. Fagan did likewise. Then, without a word, they collected their weapons, scavenged more ammunition from their slain enemies, and pressed on.

Time dragged. Sullivan stretched his senses out, hoping to hear signs of approaching reinforcements from the Railroad. His limbs felt heavy, a sure sign that his injuries and work output were exceeding even his ability to operate at high intensity. His assorted hurts seeped blood in manageable amounts, though the steady loss of fluid through his bullet wounds drained his resources in a relentless trickle. A fierce warmth across his body told Sullivan he had depleted all the glycogen stored in his muscles, and now his calorie debt had his body digging deep for energy stores that were few and far between.

Still, he felt little pain and fear was no more than a shimmering mirage waving from beyond a distant emotional horizon. He had more fight in him, Sullivan knew, though exactly how much more was a question that gnawed at his confidence.

In a moment of uncharacteristic clarity, he realized that it must be worse for Fagan. The giant's mass came with no special enhancements for endurance and lugging five-hundred pounds around at top speed had to be a brutal ordeal. He looked over, and sure enough the signs of profound exhaustion marred the look of grim determination etched into the shaggy face. "Hold this tunnel, partner," he said. "We worked too hard to take it to lose it now. I'm going to try to get behind the other group." Sullivan forced swagger into his voice. If Fagan realized how drained he was, the giant would insist on coming along.

"Roger that," Fagan said. "Railroad help should be close by now. I'll call in a sitrep to Maris."

"Good idea," Sullivan said. "Stay alive, partner."

"You too," Fagan replied. He grabbed a dead foe in each hand and began to stack the armored bodies into a macabre bulwark.

Sullivan exited the back of the tunnel with caution. It became clear that the assaulters had staged in the loading docks off the cargo lines and then split up to hit the concourse from two angles at once. If the gangs had not assembled their fighting positions so quickly, the two-pronged attack would have overrun the concourse in a matter of seconds. Considering how little time they had to plan, the enemy had moved with impressive speed and precision. This cemented Sullivan's previous conclusion that he was dealing with a professional fighting unit. The stupid luck of it all was that he and Fagan had forced them to react, and that random happenstance may have ended up their saving grace. That they had blundered into that advantage irked Sullivan. Luck was an unreliable ally on a good day, and a disastrous enemy most others.

He followed the sounds of muffled gunfire to the entrance of the tunnel he assumed the second prong employed for their assault. With numerous identical doors to choose from, and the echoes of combat bouncing from a labyrinth of metal walls, there was no way to be certain. He started down the tunnel at a trot, keeping his pistol in high-ready and squinting through the light-enhancing reticle of its sight. The gunshots grew louder, and Sullivan took this to be a good sign. All too soon his sight lit up with the shape of an armored man hunched over a rifle. There were at least twenty-five of them, Sullivan estimated. All looking away from him and pouring carnage down the hall and across the concourse. Chewie's men were holding still, though Sullivan saw no dead or wounded enemies. The armor was too thick, the skill of the shooters too overwhelming. The enemy knew as much and were content to whittle the defenders down to nothing from the safety of the tunnel. The tactic was cool, measured, and going to be perfectly effective. If it were not his people dying to defend a cargo bay, he might have respected the enemy commander's choice.

As it stood, with Sullivan exhausted and bleeding, the intelligence of the enemy just pissed him off. He did not hesitate. He drew a bead on the closest man and examined the armor. Finding a crease between plates where the left thigh joined the hip, he touched off a single round with a feral scowl. The man went down with a shriek and two more turned to return fire. Their speed and cohesion staggered even Sullivan, who threw himself to the deck and began to work the trigger of his pistol. These men were good. Highly modified, well-trained, tough, brave, ruthless. Sullivan imagined they were brutally efficient killers and very expensive to hire. But he was John L. Sullivan and his mojo was pure black magic. Outnumbered, outgunned, and pinned down, the inevitability of death flitted across his consciousness like a butterfly passing a meadow. He ignored it because he had no time for butterflies. There were people who needed killing in front of him and people who needed protection all around him. Sullivan had never been so calm in his life. He had grown accustomed to the surreal sense of focus combat caused, but this was different. He was going to die, and that felt right. As long as he held on till reinforcements arrived, he did not care.

The Hudson danced in his hands. Bullets traced orange streaks down the tunnel to shatter faceplates and send armor pieces spinning off into the darkness. He rolled as he fired, hurling his body into bizarre contortions to thwart return fire. The enemy was trapped. They could pull back into the tunnel to engage Sullivan, and thus relieve the defenders of their burden, or they could escape Sullivan into the concourse. Whereupon they would take their chances with the massed fire of close to a hundred heavily armed gangsters. Until they managed to kill him, Sullivan had the bastards right where he wanted them. Life was good, and it was a good day to die.

Then the enemy commander did something strange. Sullivan saw a big man in black armor shout orders to the dregs of his rearguard, who immediately dropped back away from Sullivan's barrage. Sullivan could not make out exactly what the rest of the squad was doing, but the large man moved to the rearguard position and began to engage Sullivan on his own. Realization hit Sullivan like a hammer to the guts.

He's going to take me on by himself?

This did not make a lot of sense to Sullivan. As a group, the squad was going to beat him eventually. There was no way around that fact. Against any one man, however, Sullivan was too much. He illustrated this by picking a spot just under the helmet and sending a round downrange.

The bullet screamed off into the distance after just grazing the side of the helmet. Sullivan fired again, and again he missed. Something turned Sullivan's blood to ice water.

The bastard was dodging Sullivan's shots.

It seemed an asinine thing. An impossible thing. Sullivan worked the trigger harder, and each bullet spalled away after shattering against thick layers of composite. Subtle twists of the head and minor shifts of the torso took Sullivan's targeted areas out of danger each time the Hudson barked, and the man kept advancing as if he could keep this up all day. The commander did not give Sullivan a chance to process what he was seeing. When he had put some distance between himself and his men, the big armored man fired back. Sullivan, in his own display of superhuman reflex, dove out of the way. A rope of bullets traced a line of impacts across Sullivan's position, missing by mere inches.

Sullivan's response was a three-round burst targeting the faceplate. With some luck a solid hit might damage the AR capabilities and hurt his ability to control the actions of his squad. Two of his bullets drew ugly lines from the side of the helmet; the third managed to scratch a long furrow into the mirrored black facet of the commander's faceplate. This spun the head to the side and bought Sullivan a quarter second to think. His next rounds all went into the man's rifle. This must have surprised the enemy, because all three struck the weapon cleanly. The commander dropped it instantly and transitioned to his sidearm with a smooth draw that spoke of many hours' practice. Sullivan backpedaled wildly to avoid getting shot. He understood that he was getting pushed back. This was a deliberate strategy to take the pressure off the rest of his squad. It was working.

Sullivan fired to suppress. He did not bother with attempts for clean hits to weak spots any more. He put the Hudson on full auto and hosed the advancing soldier while retreating. The black armor shrugged of his hits and the approaching specter's stride never faltered except to shield his weak points with subtle shifts in posture. This exchange got Sullivan back to the loading dock in one piece and the safety of better cover. He dropped behind a cargo crane and hunkered down. Here, Sullivan reloaded and waited for the enemy to try to breach the dock.

Of course, the enemy did not try to breach the dock. The enemy was too smart. The enemy's goal was to hold Sullivan while his people continued to slaughter the storage bay defenders. Sullivan spat a silent curse when he saw the man post up at the alcove before the dock entrance and methodically pepper his position with the occasional bullet. The nonchalant misses insulted Sullivan. There was no real attempt to hit him, just a reminder that any attempt to move from cover would get him killed. Sullivan's only real advantage was his pistol. The Hudson was larger and more powerful than whatever the enemy commander was using, and he had a fresh magazine of thirty rounds seated. Sullivan made his decision.

He dove out into the open behind the cover of a long full-auto blast from his pistol. He held the trigger down and kept the muzzle flat as he sprinted for the alcove. There was nothing for the armored man to do but cover the flaws in his carapace and endure the barrage. Smoke, metal fragments, and sparks filled the entrance with an obscuring haze of destruction that hid the headlong flight of a bleeding John Sullivan. Just as the Hudson went silent Sullivan tackled the man in the armor. He stripped the pistol away with a practiced twist of the wrist and drove a forearm under the chin. A knee encased in hard black composite rose to strike Sullivan in the side, but the angle was poor and only scored a glancing hit. Sullivan drove the man into the wall of the tunnel, twisted his torso and threw the clattering black body over his own hip to the floor. The man landed flat, spun to his back and wrapped Sullivan into a closed guard between his legs. Sullivan drove the legs open and jammed his knee through to pass. He wanted to punch down, but the armored body left no targets for his bare knuckles to hit. The enemy shoved Sullivan away with a foot. The force of it came as a surprise, nearly sending Sullivan back into the wall. The man was on his feet in a flash, and Sullivan met him in the middle of the tunnel with another tackle. Punching a man in hard plate had no value, so Sullivan relied upon his years of grappling training. The armor offered numerous handholds and places to grip, so when it came to throws he found himself spoiled for choice. The enemy commander went down again, this time to a sneaky foot sweep that put Sullivan on top. His hands went for the throat, the desire to choke the man driving his fingers deep under the helmet. His opponent was no helpless goon, however. He spun, tangling the attacking arm with his legs in an arm bar that Sullivan almost did not see coming.

Sullivan dropped his weight down, braced his elbow, and pulled free. This time when the commander tried to rise, Sullivan booted him in the face with all the strength he could summon. An electric tingle of feedback from his shin told Sullivan that he was going to regret doing so, but the crunch of the faceplate shattering was so satisfying he did not care. The commander staggered back, clutching at his face. Sullivan followed with another kick, this time a stomp to the chest that sent the commander fifteen feet backward. Snarling like an animal, the man rolled to his feet and charged. Sullivan saw a youthful face cut in a dozen places by jagged pieces of his helmet and fierce blue eyes narrow with focused rage.

He came on like a thunderbolt, sending gauntleted fists out like black cannonballs. John did not often fight anyone faster than himself. The last time anyone had pushed him this hard in a fight was Vincent Coll, and disturbing similarities between the two encounters began to niggle at his mind. He slipped the first punch and blocked the second. He was a split second behind the third and a heavy fist collided with his shoulder. It spun him to the right and exposed him to a follow-up hook that took him flush on the chin. The combination of massive strength and armored gloves set off a fireworks display behind his eyes and for a moment Sullivan could not figure out which direction the floor lay in. The answer followed quickly when he crashed to the unforgiving metal decking with the taste of blood filling his mouth. He rolled, not caring which direction. All he wanted was to not be in one place long enough for the commander to hit him again. On instinct he lashed out as he rose, driving his own fist into the reinforced midriff of the commander to absolutely no effect whatsoever. The commander swung again, and Sullivan's training saved him when he bobbed out of range. Sullivan came forward without thinking. His head was too fuzzy to construct advanced strategies. He fought with instinct and the muscle memory of thousands of hours' training at the hands of champions. He slipped inside another lighting jab and struck out for the exposed face with his own straight left. The commander was too fast and whipped his head back to make it miss. Sullivan surged forward, catching the commander with a double-leg takedown while he backpedaled. He lifted the enemy high, took three running steps and leaped to drive his body into the floor with speed, momentum, and the combined mass of both men. Sullivan felt sharp impacts against the muscles of his back. Refusing to go down without a fight, the commander pummeled at Sullivan all the way to the floor, stopping only when the impact drove all the air from his lungs with a loud grunt. Sullivan quickly moved to a mounted position, shoved the enemy's chin off to the side, and drove downward against the exposed neck with his forearm. He snuck his other arm around the head to cinch the wheel choke into an inescapable tourniquet. Then something went wrong.

His arms lost their strength and his vision began to swim. The harder he squeezed, the more lights began to dance across his eyes. He felt like he was falling asleep and he did not understand why. He refused to let go. He locked eyes on the enemy as he cut off the flow of blood to his brain, determined to finish the job before he passed out. He turned his head to lean in further, and only then he saw the knife on the ground two feet from the commander's right hand.

The commander had not been punching his back at all. He was stabbing it.

Only when Sullivan searched for the sensations did he experience them. The sharp sting of puncture wounds, the hot sticky flow of blood, the ever-increasing lethargy sapping his will and strength. The commander's plan was perfect. John Sullivan was the best bare-knuckle fighter in the world. Only a fool would try to fight him hand-to-hand without an edge.

In this case, a literal edge.

He tricked Sullivan into a fistfight, keeping the blade hidden until the perfect opportunity presented itself. When Sullivan committed, the commander struck. Now all that remained was to see which one of them died first. The gray fog on the edges of his eyes grew darker and pinched his field of view down to a pinprick. He held on. The commander's hands pulled at Sullivan's forearm, peeling and tugging. The man's face had gone bright red, but his eyes never left Sullivan's. And Sullivan recognized himself in the exchange. An unspoken agreement passed in that protracted moment. Neither man would give up until the other was dead. No quarter asked and none given. This was a contest of equals, the last embrace of two warriors. To offer any less would be disrespectful.

They were brothers, after all. They owed each other that much.

CHAPTER THIRTY-FOUR

Margaret flew through the bowels of the KC Complex on feet of clay.

The horrific nature of the trap set by Sharpe and the reckless indifference of Keating sat poised to kill hundreds or even thousands of innocent people. While never moralistic, neither was she callous. What was about to happen sickened her, and Margaret wanted her conscience clear of the whole sordid affair.

Sharpe's shipment of GMPs had been easy to find, and the data from Kinzei had everything she needed to shut down all two hundred units. Margaret could end this nightmare before it got out of hand if given the chance. She just needed to get to them before Sullivan sprung the trap. This is where her plan fell apart.

The sounds of fighting reached her sensitive ears when she was still a half-mile from the storage bay. She wasted no time imagining the thunder of guns could be anything other than Sullivan's ham-fisted handling of a delicate situation and increased her speed. Sullivan did not know what he was dealing with, he did not know that the fourth horseman was here in the complex. An entire platoon of elite, high-end GMP mercenaries hid among them, led by a chimera designed to be the perfect soldier. The most frightening fighting force Margaret could imagine hid among the populace, just waiting for the signal to move. It did not matter how touch that big buffoon thought he was; Sullivan would be surrounded and killed in short order if she did not get to him first. She might have called him, except she could not trust her phone or Sullivan's. Kinzei had ensured that much. What the little worm had been able to pilfer from the various devices shocked and horrified Margaret. Kinzei was still alive only because she might need that type of information later. Though this decision sent a hot flash of irritation across her thoughts. She desperately wanted to kill Kinzei.

More pressing concerns ruled her choices, so she ran.

The halls turned to gray blurs as she approached her top speed. The velocity was suitably ludicrous, yet the joy this once gave her dimmed to a mere shadow of its former intensity. Her whole life she had assumed her gifts were comparable to the advantages others got when tinkered with in vitro. She was faster, stronger, and generally better than her peers at the academy, yet it had never occurred to her that this was anything other than hard work and a bit of genetic happenstance. The jagged little pill stuck in her throat. Margaret was not exceptional, she was a product. She did not excel, she was merely 'up to spec.' Her chimera status cheapened her victories and tinged her memories with a sour aftertaste. It made her angry. The knowledge weighed on her more than it probably should have, yet she could not help herself.

She slowed down when the din of battle grew too loud to ignore. Her path brought her along a wide concourse that curved slightly ahead of her. The sounds of fighting came from around that corner, and sprinting into the middle of a firefight did not strike her as a sound strategy. She looked to either side and saw a tunnel to her left. Markings along the arched opening indicated that shipping docks could be found in that direction. She assumed that all the local docks would eventually access the storage bay, so she ran down the first tunnel in an attempt to circumvent the fighting. The battle being waged nearby stayed with her as she moved down the dim corridor. She wondered just how many people were engaged and whether or not the GMPs were involved.

She paused at the end of her tunnel, peering out into the loading docks before entering. Just as she was about to step into the open area beyond, a wholly bedraggled John Sullivan lurched into view from another tunnel fifty yards away. His big pistol spat fire and noise as he staggered backward. Then he dove behind a big machine to reload. Somebody was shooting back, holding Sullivan in place, Margaret realized. Part of her wanted to help him, but another reminded her that John Sullivan was not her friend and not her client. Wanting to prevent a massacre was not the same as wanting to help a brooding psychopath in his ill-advised battle against the whole planet.

Her indecision was interrupted by a furious charge from Sullivan, who dove forward with his gun humming like a sewing machine. She did not know what the hell he thought he was doing, but Margaret decided to let him handle it his own way. She slipped from the tunnel when Sullivan disappeared from view. Picking her way across unseen the docks took some care. She moved from cover to cover like a commando. She kept her head down and her body low. She employed speed where there were no shadows and she crossed most of the intervening distance without incident. Knowing full well it was a bad idea, when her path took her past the tunnel Sullivan had charged down seconds before, she stole a look.

Sullivan looked terrible. His clothes clung to his body with a glue of clotting blood, and he was missing half an ear. Somehow he had disarmed a huge man in head-to-toe black armor and the two bashed at each other like two characters in a video game. She had seen Sullivan fight enough to know something was wrong. His usual smooth command of the action was not there, He fought flat-footed and his normally terrifying speed looked far more manageable from her vantage point. In a straight fight Sullivan should eat most any opponent for lunch, yet now he struggled. The man in the armor looked faster, stronger even.

Margaret found herself transfixed by the combat. She knew she should move on, but something made her stay. Something about the man in the armor sent waves of apprehension through her body and it took her far too long to figure it out. She made her move too late to help. The armored man drew the knife from a thigh sheath when Sullivan grabbed him around the legs. Margaret's eyes widened and her feet moved of their own accord. Sullivan never saw the blade. The black-clad hand pumped up and down one, two, three, four times before Sullivan brought him down with enough force to shake the floor.

Margaret was sprinting now. Time dilated to a crawl. The wounds in Sullivan's back blossomed with crimson petals before her eyes and she ran faster. There was too much blood. Too many holes wept rivers of warm red death down his back. Why was he still fighting? How was he still fighting? Did he not realize what had happened? Sullivan did not appear to care that he was dying, so intent was he upon crushing the man's neck with a bread-cutter choke. His forearms and triceps bulged with terrifying strength while his eyes bored into the purpling face of his foe. Sullivan had to know. It was impossible that he did not understand.

He was dying, and still he refused to stop fighting. What kind of person did that?

Margaret had no idea how long it took her to cover the distance, but Sullivan had dropped to a slump by the time she reached the fighters. His arms still crushed at the armored man's throat, even as his blank eyes rolled back in his head. She shoved Sullivan to the side and grabbed the semiconscious man beneath him by his bare face. Pressing her palm down as hard as she could, Margaret triggered a powerful electric discharge. Current flowed from beneath her palm and into the face, burning her skin and tearing a gasp of pain from between her clenched teeth. Her victim spasmed with a strength that upended the woman and sent her skidding to the wall. To her horror, the man rolled to his belly and pushed himself upright, a low growl rumbling from his chest. Margaret gaped. The shock should have been fatal, yet the man rose in defiance of logic and her will.

Desperate, Margaret drew her pistol and took aim at the face. The man in the armor threw an arm across just in time to deflect her first shot. Lurching like a marionette, he turned and fled back down the tunnel toward the loading docks. His posture looked twisted, and he leaned and wobbled. A single hand dragged along the tunnel wall for support as his steps took him further away. Margaret hoped this meant he would not be back and emptied her magazine into his back just to keep him running. When she was sure no counterattack was forthcoming, she turned to Sullivan.

The big man lay on his stomach, blood collecting in black pools along the crevices of his back. He breathed still, though each shallow inhalation barely moved his chest. Margaret's training kicked in an and without conscious thought she began to plug the deep punctures in his back with strips of cloth from his shirt. When she felt confident that the worst of the bleeding had been stopped, she checked him for other injuries. Someone had patched a shallow bullet wound across his upper back, and another on his thigh. Bruises covered his body, telling the story of a long fight at close quarters.

A small gasp from Sullivan interrupted her examination. His breathing became labored, and a quiet cough revealed foamy pink discharge collecting at the corners of his mouth.

"Shit," she hissed. With no idea as to the extent of his internal injuries, Margaret had done all she could for him. She did not have to stay by his side and watch him die. The urge to leave him and flee surged across her thoughts, though for reasons even she did not quite understand, she let it pass.

Whether she liked it or not, Margaret had questions about a great many things and Sullivan was the path to the answers she needed. She dug in her pocket for a phone. Consequences be damned, he needed real medical help and fast. The only code she had was Fagan's, and soon she heard the giant's voice in her earpiece.

"Not a good time, Mata Hari."

"Sullivan is hurt," she replied. "He needs medical now! I'll drop a location pin to this code. Find us!"

Fagan's arrival less than two minutes later meant he had not been far away. The huge man lumbered in from the dock side of the tunnel with a rifle in each hand. He dropped them when he got to Sullivan's side and scooped his partner up like a child. Turning to Margaret, he said, "Railroad reinforcements are taking on a whole group of GMP mercenaries—"

Margaret interrupted him. "I know who they are, and I know what they are after."

"We'll catch up later," Fagan said and started trotting down the hall. "Most of the fighting is at the concourse, but we've got numbers on them so it's turning our way." He looked down at the pale face of the man in his arms. "Fucker saved all of them by distracting the team in this tunnel. Bought us time we wouldn't have had otherwise." He increased his speed. "Dumbass." He looked over his shoulder to Margaret. "Call Maris. Tell her we are heading her way with wounded."

CHAPTER THIRTY-FIVE

T he body on the bed showed no signs of life.

Machines hissed and whirred, indicating their various functions with the occasional beep or flashing indicator light. The room was dark, the local time being set to three in the morning. Sharon Platt chose this time to visit because she knew no one else would be in the room.

John Sullivan always looked enormous to her. She knew that this was more than just his physical size. She was the only person who understood the enormity of what he was, and what his creation represented. It made him more than just a big man, more than a designer product. It frightened her and it shamed her.

She approached the bed. Her tentative steps betraying all the horrible things swirling around inside her head. He looked dead to her eyes, though she knew he was merely in a very deep sleep. His punctured lung, concussion, fractured jaw, deep lacerations, and extensive blood loss would have killed anyone else outright. John Sullivan did not die so easily, but neither was he immortal nor invulnerable. Platt had almost allowed herself to believe he was, and the abrupt correction his current state had applied to this conceit was what brought her to his hospital room in the middle of the night.

"I don't know how to talk to you," she said to his unconscious body. "You scare me, and I guess that's not fair to you. But you do. Everybody thinks being a genius is this great gift, but sometimes it sucks, okay? I can't help but see the processes, the purpose in your design when I look at you. You're a weapon, John." She paused, shaking her head. "That's not right. That's part of it, but there's more. You make me hate myself, okay? Every time I see the monster you are supposed to be, I have to see the monster I am, too. I know what you say about me, and it only makes me mad because you're not wrong." She gripped the bed rail for support. "I have ruined Emilie's life. I destroyed a little girl, John. I told people you were dangerous, but it's me who did the most harm in the end. Maybe you hurt people, maybe you are mean. But I made a magic baby from thin air and stardust and I sold it to the highest bidder. Who's dangerous now, right?"

Platt inhaled, catching herself before she started crying. "Unless the whole world changes overnight that baby is going to be stolen or tortured or killed. All because I wanted to be the smartest one in the room. What kind of horrible person does that? Who does that to a child?" Tears turned her eyesight into blurs of light and shadow. "So I ran away. I thought I was being a hero, but all I know how to do is run and cry and beg stronger people for help. I treated you like shit, when all you have done is try to do the work I'm too weak and selfish to do myself. I'm a piece of shit, and I'm not the smartest person in the room. I..."

A sob choked off her next thought, and Platt needed several seconds to find her voice again. "I'm so sorry, John. I'm sorry that people like me destroyed a magic baby like you. I'm sorry that I'm so weak. I'm sorry that I can't even let you rest in peace." She sniffed. "Because I need you, okay? I need you to live, and to fight, and to do all the things you are good at. You have to, because what Emilie needs is for someone to change the world into somewhere she can grow up and be the amazing person I know she can be. I can't do that. I can't save Emilie and I can't save you, John. Goddammit, I am the problem." Another fat tear traced a line across the curve of her cheek before falling unnoticed to the tiled floor. "You can be the solution. Please be the solution. You can save Emilie, I know you can. So please, please, please, don't die. Wake up, call me a horrible bitch, hate me forever if you want to. Lord knows I hate myself enough for the both of us. But go out and fix the world. Do it out of spite, if you want. But I can't let this awful place have Emilie. Not the way they want her."

Platt did not expect an answer from the darkness or the man on the bed. She did not deserve one.

"I don't hate you." The words were a thin, reedy whisper. Filled with pain, each syllable had to be forced out. Sullivan's eyes fluttered without opening. "But you are a bitch."

Platt gasped. Horror, humiliation, and shame competed for control of her expression with no clear winner. "Oh my god, I'm so sorry! I thought you were asleep!"

"Was asleep. Then somebody started blubbering next to the goddamn bed."

"I'll go—" Platt turned away.

"Don't."

When she looked back Sullivan had managed to open his eyes and his voice had gathered some strength. "I'm going to level with you, Doc. You *are* the problem. But that doesn't mean you can't be the solution, too." He shifted, and a wince darted across his features. "I've already decided I'm going to do this thing. I'm going to rip the hearts out of every bastard who thinks they get to own Emilie or rule the world or whatever. I don't really know why, but I'm mad and sick of playing someone else's game. But then what? New assholes are going to step up to the plate as quickly as I put them down." A cough wracked his body and the wince returned. "My father wanted me for 'urban pacification,' right? Gotta make the transition smooth if you want it to stick. He understands people, what they become when they get scared." The disgust in Sullivan's voice broke through the weakness. "And he built me and the others to deal with that. But that can't be our way, Doc. If we do it his way, there's no point. So you don't get to throw your little bedside pity party and wash your hands of the dirty work. GiMPs and norms won't want to get along. Somebody has to speak on the science of it, to guide the transitions or it's all going to end up in blood. I can do blood, but that's not what Emilie needs." He exhaled. "We all have a role to play. Maris can lead, I can fight. You, Doc," he raised a limp finger in her direction. "You are going to have to draw up the blueprints for cooperation, or the fighting will never end." The finger fell as if the act of raising it had taken all the vigor he had to spare.

"I don't know if I can—"

"You don't get a fucking choice, lady. Welcome to my world. If you want Emilie's world to be different, then you better stop bitching and get to work on a fucking plan."

Platt's face flushed hot. "I don't know what to do!"

"Nobody does. But aren't you the genius? Do some genius shit." Sullivan sounded very tired. "I'll do mobster shit. Fagan will do cop shit. Maris will do..." his eyes rolled. "Whatever shit Maris does. Between us, we'll figure it all out, or we won't."

"But what happens if we don't?" Platt heard the desperate plea of a child in her voice and hated it.

Sullivan's reply did not help. "A whole bunch of people will die and the survivors will live under a fascist hegemony of rich GMPs and the corporations that made them. Life ain't a fairy tale, Doc. We win or we die."

Platt decided to change the subject before fear and despair set her to crying again. "Was it him? In the tunnel, I mean."

Sullivan nodded, eyes closed. "Had to be. It was like fighting a souped-up version of Coll. Never felt anything like it."

"He's the worst one." Platt immediately regretted her choice of words. "I mean, tactically. Everything they learned from you, Coll, and Mata Hari went into Murphy. His physical abilities, all the tech implants..." She shuddered. "He's got a lot going on."

"He was just a kid, though. And something is wrong with his head. Like me, but different. He's smart, too. Suckered me good, the little prick."

"I'll find a way to beat him," Platt said, suddenly confident.

"Good," Sullivan grunted. "Because my plan left a whole lot to be desired."

"I'm going to let you rest, okay?" Platt turned to leave again. This time she paused at the door and looked back at the man on the bed. "I really am sorry. For everything."

"Sorry don't fix shit, Doc. But thanks all the same."

A smile stretched Platt's face in wry juxtaposition to her red and puffy eyes. "Don't ever change, John. Even if you are an asshole."

After Platt had left Sullivan let out a long breath. To the empty air he asked, "How long you been in here?"

"All night," Margaret said from the shadows. "How did you know I was here?"

"I got a boner, and Platt doesn't do shit for me."

"Crass," Margaret said. She stepped away from the dark corner where she had been hiding. The light from the hall cast her body in competing streaks of color and shadow. She looked good.

"I'm seventy percent dead, Margaret. Give me a pass."

"Bullshit. We're cut from the same cloth, you and me. You'll live."

"Doesn't mean it doesn't hurt or that I can't die."

"Stop being such a baby. Where's the gratitude for saving your life?"

"I had him. I could have killed him in that tunnel if you hadn't interfered."

"Killing yourself in the process. Bold plan."

"It was all I had at the time." He tried to gesture to his degraded state, but it hurt too much. "What with all the bleeding and shit."

"Did you mean what you said to Platt? Are you really going after Keating and Sharpe?"

Sullivan summoned the strength to nod. "Yeah. Don't see much of a choice. We drew a line today. We made a stand and there's no way these assholes are going to leave it at that. We stopped an invasion but started a war. They're going to come harder next time. And the next. Emilie is too valuable, and all their plans are in motion now. Like I said, it's win or die."

"It's all going to fall apart, isn't it?"

"Huh?"

"The Republic, the corporations, all of it." She sighed, a decision made in her mind. "John, I found something out about Sharpe. It's not good news, though."

"Spill," Sullivan's voice took an edge like chipped flint.

"He's not real. It's a just a synthetic mouthpiece for the Pan-Asian Remnant, and this is all part of their plan." She ticked off the elements on her fingers as she spoke. "They've isolated Mickey Sullivan, fractured the Republic by cutting Keating loose, and they've been funding Corpus Mundi since Mickey cut them off."

Sullivan tried to raise his head. "So the fracture in the cabal was deliberate? The Remnant *wants* everyone to start fighting each other?"

"They are taking the republic apart from within, and they are playing the corporations, the government, and the mob like fiddles."

"Fuck," Sullivan growled at the ceiling. "At least we have Emilie," he added. "Her presence is a big old monkey wrench, isn't it?"

"Looks that way," Margaret said with a nod. "She's too valuable to walk away from."

"I got to get out of this bed—"

"You need to heal up," Margaret said. "Because I have no idea how you intend to stop any of this, but I'm pretty sure bleeding to death is not a solid plan."

"And where do you stand?"

"Who the hell knows?" Margaret let a smile play at the corners of her mouth. "I just found out I'm not who, or even what, I thought I was. I want answers, John. Right now you seem to be the one with the best chance of getting them for me."

Sullivan answered only with a stern look.

"Aaaand I don't relish the thought of living in a world where GiMPs and norms kill and enslave each other, okay?" She waggled a finger at Sullivan. "But don't get it wrong. I'm not joining any suicide missions over you or that kid."

"Fair enough."

"So you got a plan, hero?"

"More of an idea, really."

"I have to hear this."

"First, I'm going to build me an army."

"An army?"

Sullivan settled his head back onto his pillow and closed his eyes once more. "Can't go to war without an army, Margaret. Good night." Soft snores followed a few seconds later. Margaret slipped from the room equal parts bemused and amused. For good or ill, the next few months of her life were going to be very interesting. She decided to treat them as an adventure and not a terrifying descent into madness. A positive outlook always made things better.

As the sun prepared to rise over the KC Complex and the budding plans of a wounded fighter, an altogether different scene unfolded in a sprawling mansion overlooking Nantucket Sound. Mickey Sullivan sat at his breakfast table considering the same problems as his son. Hargrave pulled up a chair across from his employer, blocking Mickey's view of the lush gardens just outside his solarium.

"A message just arrived, Mickey."

"What the fuck does that mean?" Still in his bathrobe, Mickey Sullivan chewed his omelet with a scowl. "Who the fuck sends messages? Just call or e-mail that shit."

"Your son, apparently."

Mickey extended his hand. "Give that shit to me, Mal." He took the small plastic data card from Hargrave's hand and brought his phone out of one of his voluminous robe's equally voluminous pockets. "Huh," he said. "Heavy encryption." He inserted the card into his phone and waited. Three seconds later, he started to read.

It took several minutes to take it all in. When he was done, he placed his phone on the table next to his plate.

"Johnny stopped the riot in the Complex from happening."

"That's excellent news."

"He also found out who's funding Corpus Mundi."

When he did not immediately continue, Hargrave prompted, "and?"

"Some prick named Sharpe, he's a front for the fucking Chinese."

"Oh. Shit." Hargrave could think of nothing else to say.

Mickey dropped his phone to continue eating. "Corpus Mundi threw Audie Murphy at him down there."

"Did John kill him?"

"No. He and Johnny almost killed each other, I guess. The message says nobody walked away from the fight under their own power, you get me?" Mickey's tone turned low and dark. "Murphy is fucking loaded with tech, Mal, but he's just a fucking kid. He couldn't have been ready for that shit."

"So why send him, then?"

"Same as with Coll and Mata Hari. Sharpe is trying to eliminate them all without getting caught by Corpus Mundi. Using me and Johnny as a scapegoat for losing the assets. Probably Keating, too." He went back to eating. "At least that means they aren't ready to burn everybody yet. They still want something out of Corpus Mundi."

"More prototypes and that girl," Hargrave said. "No point in securing a mutant chimera if you don't have the resources to exploit one."

"Good call, Mal. They need the research labs and other shit. Good. We can work that."

"What about John? He has fulfilled his obligation to you. Will you honor your end?"

"For now, sure. We made that boy a monster, no profit in pissing him off. The girl is immortal, she'll be around when we are ready for her." Mickey pushed his plate away. "But there's more. Johnny knows way too fucking much about all of this. Hell, he knows more than we do at this point. I don't like it. He's talking some scary shit."

"How scary?"

"Civil war scary, Mal. The Chinese are spoiling for a rematch, and they have been stacking the deck behind our backs for thirty fucking years. They ain't gonna come with ten million screaming berserkers this time, either." He struck a palm with his fist. "God damn it, I hate when I get blindsided! This Sharpe fucker played me for a fool, Mal. That's gotta get addressed the old-fashioned way."

"What are you thinking?"

"Get Mata Hari on the line. I got a job for her."

EPILOGUE

Doctor Calloway chewed his lower lip.

"I can fix the face, but there will still be some minor scarring. His osteoplastic polymers resisted too much of the current. It probably saved his life, but the skin is ruined."

The reply came from the speaker in Calloway's earpiece. "It doesn't really matter. As long as he is not so hideous as to be off-putting, it will be fine. It will probably add to his market appeal, to be honest. Soldiers are supposed to have scars."

Calloway nodded without looking up from the unconscious man on the slab. "He was not ready, Sharpe."

"I think he did rather well, considering all factors."

"He wasn't ready for Sullivan, I mean. He's superior in every measurable facet, sure..."

"But?"

"But he needs more training and development. Everything we know about Sullivan has proved to us that the insufferable mobster was right about a great many things. The real secret to peak performance has as much to do with the unmeasurable characteristics as anything else. Training, mental development, emotional maturity. All things that we are still figuring out with subsequent models."

"I think you are overreacting, Doctor. He performed as well as we all dared hope. The telemetry shows our Murphy giving Sullivan multiple stab wounds. Sullivan might even be dead right now. Your concerns would appear quite premature in that light."

"Do you really believe that he's dead?"

"It's a possibility."

Calloway snorted. "So you don't believe it." He went back to examining the sleeping man. "Sullivan was built to Mickey's specifications. He has too much muscle, too much bone density, too much trauma resistance built in. As long as he did not lie in that tunnel for too long, he'll be back. And Sharpe," Calloway paused to pinch the bridge of his nose between a thumb and forefinger. "He is going to be very, very angry."

"I thought he could not get very angry?"

"He can't have a psychotic break, Sharpe. He can and does get angry. We made sure of that. Plus..."

"Out with it, Doctor."

"At Camp Zero, his behavior was strange. Out of specification. He demonstrated emotional range under stress that he's not supposed to have. This is not the John Sullivan we grew in the lab anymore. He's more dangerous, if anything." Calloway's frown deepened. "It's an anomaly, and I don't like anomalies."

"Sullivan is an anomaly we will be eliminating soon enough, Doctor. Keating does not realize he is playing right into my hands. Even without a full-scale riot at the KC Complex, political will is swinging our way. Enough rumors will leak about what happened to get the special interest groups buzzing in all the right ears. Soon, the Complex will not be safe, and Sullivan will have to try to move the girl. He will be exposed and vulnerable. Just be patient, Doctor."

Calloway rested his hands on the slab and shook his head. "That girl's DNA is the most important thing ever discovered, Sharpe. Don't let your plans for the Republic cloud your vision. Remember, politicians come and go but immortality is forever."

"Oh, I know, Doctor. But the girl is driving our enemies to recklessness, and that has created many new opportunities for our group. There is no reason we can't have immortality *and* political power at the same time."

"So long as our reach does not exceed our grasp, Sharpe." Calloway despaired of reaching Sharpe's sense of caution. "I'm going to button Murphy up and get him back in action. We have to be more careful. Losing Camp Zero and five platoons of shock troopers has our ranks a touch thin. Murphy will have to do much of the heavy lifting going forward. Let's try to be more judicious."

"Let me know when he is ready. And don't worry. You have reinforcements coming soon."

Don't miss out!

Visit the website below and you can sign up to receive emails whenever Andrew Vaillencourt publishes a new book. There's no charge and no obligation.

https://books2read.com/r/B-A-UMPE-DBQCB

BOOKS 2 READ

Connecting independent readers to independent writers.

Also by Andrew Vaillencourt

Hegemony
Sullivan's Run
Sullivan's Stand

The Fixer
Ordnance
Hell Follows
Hammers and Nails
Aphrodite's Tears
Dead Man Dreaming
Head Space
Escalante

Standalone
Thor's Day

Watch for more at www.AndrewVaillencourt.com.

About the Author

Andrew Vaillencourt would like you to believe he is a writer. But that is probably not the best place to start. He *is* a former MMA competitor, bouncer, gym teacher, exotic dancer wrangler, and engineer.

He wrote his first novel, 'Ordnance,' on a dare from his father and has no intention of stopping now. Drawing on far too many bad influences including comic books, action movies, pulp sci-fi and his own upbringing as one of twelve children, Andrew is committed to filling the heads of readers with hard-boiled action and vivid worlds in which to set it. His work pulls characters and voices born from his time throwing drunks out of a KC biker bar, fighting in the Midwest amateur MMA circuit, or teaching kindergarteners how to do a proper push-up.

He currently lives in Connecticut with his lovely wife, three decent children, and a very lazy ball python named Max.

Read more at www.AndrewVaillencourt.com.

Made in the USA
Monee, IL
31 August 2020